Wild Rose

Wild Rose

PAULINE DONALDSON

Library of Congress Control Number: 2010916362

ISBN:	Hardcover	978-1-4568-0919-5
	Softcover	978-1-4568-0918-8
	Ebook	978-1-4568-0920-1

This book was printed in the United States of America.

To order additional copies of this book, contact:
Xlibris Corporation
0-800-644-6988
www.Xlibrispublishing.co.uk
Orders@Xlibrispublishing.co.uk
301115

Chapter One

The wind had changed direction and was now bringing a fine mist of cold, wetting drizzle across the open hillside. The grass and rocks underfoot were slippery as Alice made her solitary way home.

Yesterday had been soft and warm and winter seemed to have gone—but that had been Mother Nature in teasing mood. Many folk had been at the market and Alice had sold all her hanks of wool. Now she was coming home with a new pot for the fire and a new pair of boots. Both these precious purchases were tied safely into the bundle in the small, two-wheeled handcart that had been her most expensive purchase at the end of last year.

She only made the long trip to market three or four times a year, and this trip had been delayed. There had been much trouble along the routes through the hills because of the fighting between the Lancastrians and the Yorkists. A woman, or a man for that matter, travelling alone was an easy target for the dispersing soldiers, no matter on which side their loyalties lay. It was only three weeks since the terrible battle at Towton, and the armies and the hangers-on were still dispersing. A few of the latter were still roaming around the hills and dales preying on unwary travellers. Alice had heard how ferocious the battle had been as she had listened to conversations in the market yesterday. Thousands had been slaughtered and the snow had been red with blood.

Alice had waited as long as possible before making the journey but eventually she could wait no longer to sell the wool she had gathered and spun. It was almost half-a-day's walk to the market town, so she had been away from her home for almost two full days, but ahead she could see the solitary oak tree which marked the place where she must leave the main route through this part of the dales. Even the main track was not level. It now dropped down sharply before rising again towards the oak.

Just as Alice reached the bottom of the dip, she thought she heard a faint cry. The rain was still blurring her vision but the wind was quieter here. She stood still, straining her ears and had just decided it must have been a bird—a curlew perhaps—when the sound came again. It came from her right. Cautiously she made her way past a rocky outcrop and peered round. A woman lay on the grass and a very young child was sitting by her in great distress. It was the child's cries she had heard.

Alice watched for a couple of minutes. No movement came from the woman; not even a hand moved to touch the child as it hit her body and face, crying "Mama, Mama". Alice moved into the little hollow and walked towards the woman. As she got close it was clear that the woman was dead, or at least very close to death.

At the sight of Alice, the child stopped wailing but clung to the woman's body, looking at Alice with frightened eyes, red and swollen from crying.

"Hush child, I will not hurt you. Let me look at your Mama to see if I can help her."

The child whimpered but did not move. Alice touched the woman's face—it was wet with the rain, cold and still. She could see no flicker of movement from the chest and could detect no pulse in her wrist. The lips were faintly blue. Then she noticed a wound under the woman's hair, where her wimple had slipped to one side. Either someone had hit her or she had fallen and hit her head on one of the many rocks. Whichever had been the case, she was now beyond help. The child, however, was not.

What to do? Alice looked carefully around for signs of anyone else, or signs as to why a woman and child would be alone in this deserted spot. The clothes the woman was wearing were good quality and were travelling clothes, but there was no sign of her bags.

Telling the child, "I will return in a moment", Alice walked back to the main track. She had seen no recent wheelmarks as she had approached this spot but now, as she looked around, she saw hoofprints and narrow wheel tracks coming from the opposite direction. From the mass of hoofprints in one small area, it appeared that a horse had been startled. The wheel marks stopped, but a closer look showed clear sets of hoofprints going away from the spot, back the way the cart had come. Sure enough, over to her right, Alice saw the shafts of a very light, open cart—much too light for this rough land—sticking out of a patch of gorse. Alice walked across to it and could see two travelling bags which had been opened and their contents strewn around the cart. It would appear that the woman and child had been the victims of highway robbery and that the robber had taken the horse and perhaps some valuables too.

Alice returned to the child, who was now quiet, sucking a dirty thumb but still clinging to the woman's body.

"Come to me, child", Alice said calmly. The child did not move.

"Mama cannot help you any more. You will have to come with me."

By now, Alice had decided the child was perhaps two years old. It certainly could not be left here. The weather was still cold at night and in wet clothes the child too would be dead by morning. She had no idea how long it had already been sitting here.

Talking quietly and soothingly, Alice approached the child and bent to pick it up. It screamed and clung to the body. Fortunately, Alice was strong and she lifted the kicking, screaming child into her arms, and turned to address the body of the woman.

"I don't know who you were, but I will see your child is cared for. God forgive me, I can do no more for you. May you rest in heaven." Then, head down, carrying the distraught child in one arm and towing her handcart with the other, she continued on her journey home.

After a few minutes the child stopped kicking and screaming and subsided into occasional, deep, shuddering sobs. Then the eyelids drooped over the swollen eyes and sleep came. The child was heavy now and Alice had to take great care on the final part of the steep, narrow track leading down to her home, but at last they arrived. The child hardly stirred as Alice laid it down on a sheepskin. Then taking off her own wet cape, she stretched to ease her aching back and shoulders and, for the first time considered the problem that she had just taken on.

Alice lived alone in a stone cot in a hidden corner of the dale. She had little experience of children and was not equipped to cope with a child, but at least for now the child needed immediate aid. She must remove its wet clothes, clean and dry its little body and make it warm and comfortable. She gathered kindling and, using her tinderbox, lit a fire in the hearth at one corner of the room. Luckily she had a good supply of dry wood and in minutes the fire was burning. She filled her old iron cauldron with water and set it to warm.

Instinct told her to speak quietly to the sleeping child as she began to remove its wet and dirty clothing. The child was a girl. She roused and the little body started to shiver, hopefully Alice thought, with cold rather than fear.

"I am Alice. I am taking off your wet clothes so you can be warm and comfortable. Lie still little one."

The child lay there, watching her as she poured some of the warmed water into a bowl. Alice took a rag and gently wiped her clean from her head downwards. The fair hair, which had been covered by a cap, was reasonably clean and Alice would comb it later. Gradually the shivering eased and the child lay on the sheepskin, naked in the firelight and the fading light coming through the open doorway. Thankfully the rain had passed and rays from the setting sun shone on the wet rocks.

Alice was hungry and the child must be too. She had bought some oatmeal biscuits at the market. Perhaps the child could eat one if it was softened with some warm water. She mashed the biscuit to what she hoped would be a suitable thickness, then a flash of inspiration made her add a few drops of honey. She picked up the child, wrapped her in a warm shawl and, sitting her on her knee, offered her a spoonful of the mixture. The little mouth remained firmly shut, while the blue eyes filled with tears.

"Oh, you poor little one. I know you want your Mama, but Mama can't be with you. Please eat something. What is your name?"

Still no reply. Only tears slowly trickling down those baby cheeks. One tear reached the corner of the baby's mouth and a pink little tongue popped out to lick it away.

Alice dipped her finger in the bowl, scooping up a small amount of honey and placed it at the corner of the child's mouth. Again the tongue popped out and licked it. It continued licking.

"Is that nice?" Alice asked. She then spooned a little of the softened biscuit with some honey on and offered it again. This time the mouth opened and in a matter of minutes the bowl was empty. She then spooned a few drops of water into the child, who leaned her head against Alice and drifted off to sleep.

Once she was sure the child was sleeping soundly, Alice put her back on the sheepskin with the shawl over her and cut some bread and cheese for herself. As she ate, she watched the child and saw how lovely she was now that her face and limbs were clean and relaxed.

The daylight had gone but the firelight flickered on the heap of soiled clothing that Alice had removed from the child. It must be washed now if the child was not to be naked all day tomorrow. Alice went out to the side of the cot where she had a wooden tub in which she did her washing. The moon was rising and gave her enough light for the job. She added the now hot water from the cauldron to some cold from her bucket and started to wash the items of clothing one by one.

She washed the dress first, then picked up the petticoat. It seemed strangely heavy for such a small garment and as she started to wash it, her fingers encountered two or three hard areas in the hem. She finished washing and took the garments inside to dry by the hearth, then, lighting a precious candle, she took a knife to the stitches in the hem of the petticoat and carefully unpicked them. The first item to drop out was a thin, gold chain. On the chain was a small medallion with some pattern etched on it; next came a gold coin and finally, a buckle containing pretty stones in red and green.

Alice stared at the treasure she had found, as treasure it must be for someone to have made the effort to stitch it into the petticoat. So, the dead woman must have expected her journey to be dangerous. Who was she? Whose child was this sleeping so peacefully now on Alice's bed?

Alice put the precious items in the bottom of the chest which held her few clothes. Tomorrow she must find a safer place to conceal them. Carefully moving the child over, Alice lay on the bed beside her and tried to sleep.

Chapter Two

How had Alice herself come to be living alone in such a solitary place? Few women had any kind of freedom let alone the independence that Alice had achieved.

She didn't know her exact age but was fairly sure she was either twenty-three or twenty-four years old. She had been about nineteen when her mother had died. She had no idea who her father was. She had asked her mother several times, but all she would say was that he had been a good man and had been dead for many years.

Her mother, Agnes, had been cook at the manor of Arkenthorpe and they had lived there in a small room off the kitchen. Generally it had been a happy household. The master, Squire Thorpe, was distantly related, through his wife, to the Nevilles, who were among the most important families in England. They had three daughters and two sons. Alice had been almost the same age as the youngest son, Edmund, and in spite of the difference in their stations in life, they had been friends. When Edmund was having lessons from his tutor, he would often ask if Alice could come too and, as both his mother and his tutor knew that he worked better if she was there, frequently she had been in the room during his lessons. In this way she had learned simple reading and writing and had acquired basic arithmetic and even a few words of French.

Outside the house, of course, they were not together. There Alice's friends had been the gardener's children, Maud and John. Maud was four years older than John, and John about two years older than Alice. There had been twins born between Maud and John but they had both died within hours of birth. When Maud was twelve she became the assistant to the seamstress at Arkenthorpe, which left John and Alice to keep each other company. Alice had always been strong and loved nothing better than racing around the local hills and valleys with John. They had always helped John's father to harvest the fruit and pull the vegetables but, all too soon, John was working with his father in the garden and his short childhood was over. Not long after that, Mrs. Thorpe had taken Alice on as a housemaid.

The wider world had not seemed very relevant to the folk of the Dales, although they knew that there had been permanent war with France and local men were sometimes ordered to the King's army. Some men, of course, had never returned, but in the year of our Lord 1453 the news spread that the war with France had ended.

The ordinary people had just had time to sigh with relief and start planning for a future with the menfolk staying at home, when for reasons best known to themselves, the English formed into groups of nobles either supporting the Lancastrian claim to the throne of England or supporting the Yorkist claim. The folk of the Dales were geographically on land belonging to senior members of the warring factions. Loyalties among the local magnates were divided, thus dividing the "official" loyalties of the local people. People ceased to be able to trust each other and it wasn't long before local men were once more ordered to fight for the side of their particular lord. This time English were fighting English. Bloody battles took place only a few miles away and hundreds of lives were lost.

Squire Thorpe was too old to go into battle himself but his estate was expected to provide men for the Yorkist cause and his eldest son, Harald, went at the head of his men, accompanied by his younger brother, Edmund.

At Arkenthorpe, meanwhile, two things happened in quick succession which were to change Alice's life dramatically. First, the Squire was suddenly taken ill and died within a month. His sons had returned from the fighting and were at his bedside for his last few days.

After the Squire's funeral, Mrs. Thorpe decided to go to stay at their eldest daughter's house for a few months. The daughter had made an excellent marriage and was living comfortably in Lincolnshire. Soon after his mother's departure, Harald gave orders that the manor should be improved and cleaned. He said that, as there would be fewer people to feed, Agnes should help with the cleaning in the mornings and return to her kitchen for the evening meal preparation. The household would eat cold luncheons which could be prepared in advance.

Alice had not known Harald well, but it soon became clear that he did not have the amiable nature of his parents or Edmund, and he wished to prove that he was a force to be reckoned with. He was not yet married so it was expected that his one unmarried sister, Ellen, would run the household for him. Nominally she did but it seemed that she had to take her orders and do things as and when he wanted them done. She had little authority of her own.

The improvements included the creation of a solar for Harald and the family, separate from the main hall. Solars were becoming fashionable and he wanted to be up there with the best families. With the end of these changes in sight, the second major event occurred. Ellen called Agnes to her and told her that Harald wished her to remove a stone bust from the window embrasure on the staircase and take it into the garden for a thorough clean before putting it back. Agnes protested that she was not strong enough to lift such a valuable item and carry it safely down the stairs and she asked Miss Ellen to send one of the outdoor men to help her.

A man came from the stables and after that no-one seemed quite sure of what happened. The man was holding a ladder for Agnes. As she reached out to lift the bust, Harald appeared at the foot of the stairs and yelled at the man for being in the house in his filthy boots. The man turned to face his angry new master and the ladder slipped. Agnes fell forward against the stone wall and slid to the floor clutching the heavy bust. Whether the fall on to the stone floor killed her, or whether it was the bust hitting her chest that stopped her heart could not be decided. Ellen heard the dreadful noise and rushed across the hall. Harald was loudly raging about carelessness and punishment when his formerly timid sister flew at him, white with shock and anger, telling him to "be quiet—poor Agnes is dead!"

More staff were called and Agnes was laid on a bench in the hall, while Ellen went to find Alice. It was declared a tragic accident brought about by the clumsiness of the stableman, and two days later Agnes was buried after a short service at the village church. Alice returned to the house only to be told by Harald that she had better assume her mother's duties as cook immediately. She went to the kitchen and began to prepare the meal but she was in a daze and could not give her mind to her tasks. She was rescued by Miss Ellen coming into the kitchen and taking over. She sent Alice to her room to lie down, saying "If you can manage breakfast in the morning, Alice, Squire Harald will be leaving for Bradford immediately afterwards. He will be away for at least four days and you and I can work out a plan."

Next morning after breakfast, Alice had just carried a bowl of scraps outside for the farm hand to feed to the pigs when Harald came out of the stable yard, riding his beautiful chestnut horse for the journey to Bradford. She paused to give him a slight curtsey as manners demanded. He laughed and said, "You're a fine looking woman, Alice. Too fine for a cook. I must find a replacement. I can think of better services you can provide." He spurred his horse and cantered out of the yard.

Alice coloured furiously as she realised what he was suggesting. She vowed there and then that **that** was one service she had no intention of giving him. She would leave Arkenthorpe before he could force himself upon her.

When Alice was called by Miss Ellen to discuss how best to re-organise household duties, Alice quietly said, "I'm sorry Miss Ellen, but I will be leaving your service. I cannot stay after all that has happened."

The older woman looked at her with compassion. "I understand. I really do understand, but where can you go?"

"I have somewhere in mind", Alice replied. "I will stay for a day or two more, but I will disappear quietly. I do not want to put you in the position of having to lie to the Squire, so I will not tell you when or where I am going. I will leave a message on the kitchen table saying that I have gone."

"I will be sorry to lose you, Alice. You have been one of our household for so long. You must take whatever you can carry from your own room that will be of use to you and, of course, anything that was your mother's is yours to take too. Oh, and be sure to take food for your journey."

"Thank you". Alice smiled, "I am sorry not to be able to say good-bye to Master Edmund. He was always kind to me."

"He will be very sorry when he finds you have gone."

Over the next three days, Alice organised her departure carefully. She knew exactly where she was going, at first anyway. With careful planning she could get the bare essentials from the kitchen and her room without having to carry them all together. There was a small corrie only a short distance from the edge of the copse bordering Arkenthorpe's garden. Here she could secrete the more difficult to carry items a few at a time. She rose early each morning—it was March and dawn was breaking earlier. First she took an old iron cauldron with its chains. It was too small for general household needs and had not been used for several years. Three clay pots of different sizes, two small wooden platters and a drinking vessel, two knives and two spoons—all old but serviceable and not likely to be needed by the household. The old tinderbox soon joined the items in the corrie, along with a sickle from the barn. She found her mother's winter cloak and wrapped her other clothes in it, tying the bundle generously with strong hemp-cord.

Alice managed to make one trip each day, usually soon after first light when she was least likely to be observed, and by Friday evening almost everything she would need to survive was hidden in the corrie. By good fortune, the weather had been frosty and cold rather than wet.

Saturday was the day Squire Harald was expected home. Alice's plan was to ensure that he saw her going about her duties so that Miss Ellen could not be accused of letting her go in the Squire's absence. Her own clothes were still in their usual place and to a superficial glance, her room was normal. She would need her straw mattress and blanket, so immediately on rising at day-break on Saturday, she removed the mattress. To her amazement, she found two whole silver pennies and four farthings beneath the mattress. Quickly she concealed them in the bodice of her dress. She could only think that Miss Ellen had secretly put them there. Added to the few small coins of her own that she possessed already, her immediate future looked much more secure. Now, she rolled the mattress inside the blanket from her bed and again used a good length of hemp-cord to tie the bundle. That bundle was her last delivery to the corrie before her escape.

On Friday she had been to the old schoolroom and found the slate she used to use when practising her writing. There was a slate pencil too, and carefully she wrote out the message, "I HAVE GONE. ALICE". She had carried the board down to the kitchen and hidden it behind the chopping block.

She prepared and served breakfast. When the table had been cleared and the scullery girl was washing up, she told the girl, "I have mislaid something in my room, so I am going to go through and tidy things until I find it."

The girl, who was not very bright, just nodded and smiled, saying, "I'm always losing things Miss." Alice went and packed her remaining clothes into a bundle with yet more string.

The morning seemed to drag. She was beginning to think that Harald would not be home before it was too late for her to leave that day and that would cause her a number of problems, not least of which would be to get her mattress back in place. One bright spot occurred when the local candle-maker brought a box of new candles for the house. Several candles needed to be replaced so Alice removed the old ones. Some of these candle ends would give a better light than the rushlights she had managed to secrete so far. She tied them in an old rag and stuffed them into the bundle of clothes. She had just completed this task when she heard horses hooves in the yard and Squire Harald had returned.

The midday meal was served only slightly later than usual and she ensured that she ate heartily herself when she ate with the other staff. As the kitchen maid started the pot cleaning, Alice said "Make sure everything is as clean as you can get it, and stack things tidily. I think the Squire will probably be visiting our kitchen later today. Don't give him a reason to be angry with you."

The girl looked terrified and began to scrub furiously at the cooking dishes. Alice retired to her room, drew the curtain across the doorway and had a final look round. A brief pang of sadness, mixed with fear and excitement ran through her. She mustn't falter now! She wrapped her outdoor cape around her, pulled up the hood and, seizing her one remaining bundle, slipped quietly through the kitchen, lifted the slate with her message on to the bench, went out into the yard. Without looking back, she headed down the garden to the copse and the corrie.

Alice knew that she had only a few hours of daylight left to find her intended refuge. Fortunately the weather was still cold and dry with only a slight breeze. During childhood explorations she and John the gardener's son had discovered a partly ruined stone cot in a tiny, sheltered valley and, even more exciting at the time, a small cave with its entrance a few feet up from the valley floor. It could not be more than a half-hour's walk from the corrie, so she would be able to make the three or four trips necessary to convey all her goods. However, today only one trip would be possible so she must select carefully the things she would need most urgently. She could not risk her bundle of clothes getting wet, nor her mattress and blanket. The candles were with her clothes but if she was to light even one, the tinderbox was essential. Adding only a little bread and cheese, she was ready. Feeling like a pack-horse, she cautiously ventured out of the corrie and struck out across the undulating countryside hoping desperately that after six years or more, she would remember the small landmarks that would guide her to the well-hidden sanctuary.

Skipping happily along with a friend, when a child, had been very different from her solitary challenge now. Her burdens were bulky and awkward and though her stride might be longer it was also slower. Her memory held good though, and she only hesitated once over which way to go. The route was well away from frequented tracks and she encountered no-one at all. The sun was about to sink below the line of hills to the west, when she saw the strange, large rock which marked her way in to the hidden valley. Its shape resembled the head of one of the fantastic beasts on a carving at the church, and it was this that had attracted John and herself to go to the rock and so discover the valley beyond.

Now, she moved carefully around the rock and looked down into the valley. Evening shadows were creeping across it, but it was almost exactly as she remembered it. She stood for a minute, watching and listening, but the only movement was from a group of three rabbits and some blackbirds calling in alarm at her approach. The other sound was from the beck that, dropping into the valley from a small waterfall on the rocks at one end, ran along its rocky bed before disappearing into reeds at the other end.

The derelict stone hut was a bitter disappointment. The entrance was choked with madly tangled plants and a bare rose briar straggled all over what was left of the rough thatch roof. If she was to have shelter tonight she had to go into the cave.

Where was the entrance?

Of course, it had to be immediately below her. Carefully she picked her way down to the valley floor, put down her burdens and stretched. She looked upward and there, almost at eye level, under the overhang of rocks, she saw it. Daylight was fading fast. She pulled one of the larger candle ends from her bundle, got out the tinderbox and, quickly gathering together a small pile of kindling material, she struck sparks into it until, with gentle blowing, it glowed and a tiny flame appeared, sufficient to light the candle. With her candle lit, she clambered up the rock and peered into the cave.

It was dry and the floor, for as far as the candlelight reached, seemed smooth and quite clean. It would be better than the cot for tonight. She wedged the candle into a crevice and collected her bundles, bringing everything into the cave. The entrance was about four feet wide, but Alice had no idea how far it extended into the hill—childhood explorations had not included candles. The daylight was almost gone and it would be several hours before the new crescent moon appeared. There was no more to be done except try to sleep.

Returning to the valley floor, she found a corner in which to relieve herself, then went to the beck to wash the dust of her journey from her hands and face. She cupped her clean hands and drank from the cold, clear water. Back in the cave, by the light of the candle, she carefully untied the mattress and blanket, removed her shoes and, still wrapped in her travelling cloak, ate a small piece of bread and cheese before curling up on the mattress to rest.

She lay there, candle still lit, watching and listening. At first she was startled by each sound she heard; the eerie cry of a vixen was much more blood-chilling here than when heard from the safety of the manor. She heard the calls of several owls and saw one fly silently past, ghostly white. Gradually, in spite of her nervousness, the efforts of the day crept over her and she felt sleepy. Plucking up her courage, she blew out the candle, said a prayer and closed her eyes.

Chapter Three

The child slept through the night. Occasionally she whimpered and made baby sounds but then was quiet again. Alice drifted on the edge of sleep but, before dawn, was wide awake. Surely someone would come searching for the child soon; if not, life was going to be utterly changed.

In the three or so years that had elapsed since she left Arkenthorpe, Alice had transformed the cot and the cave into a surprisingly comfortable home. Originally she had not envisaged staying for more than a few weeks, but with the coming of the spring weather she had realised that living here would be better than going to find lodging, and having had a taste of independence, she had no intention of going back into any household as a servant.

The first weeks had been spent re-claiming the cot from the smothering plants while living in the cave. Three trips back to the corrie had been needed to move her possessions. The beck was a true gift from God—the water was purer than any she would get in town. It was constantly available for washing, cooking and drinking. She had cleaned out the corner of the cot which had obviously been used as a hearth sometime in the past, and restored it. She had also created her own privy in a sheltered, rocky corner only yards from the hut. Every few days she would chop some reeds or bracken and throw them into the hole, keeping it free from the usual offensive odours.

She had not wished to go back to the village at Arkenthorpe, so one fine morning she had set out to find another one, with half her supply of coins in her bodice. By leaving her valley going east she soon found herself close to a main track. She sat for a while and when she had seen three small groups of people all going in one direction, she had decided that, so early in the day, they must be going to a town or village. She joined the track and followed in their wake. If other people had not kept joining the track, she would have thought she had made a mistake. The sun had climbed high before she caught sight of the town, but the effort was worthwhile. She found herself in the small town of Skipton on market day. She had bought flour and yeast, suet, two pigeons and a skin of ale, and started the return journey with two farthings left.

Occasionally, she had slipped back through the copse to the end of the garden at Arkenthorpe and pulled one or two turnips and leeks, then later in the summer had brought a few pods of peas and beans. She had kept some pods and dried them so that in the second year she had been able to grow her own. The soil in most of the valley was only a thin layer over underlying rock, but in one small area there was enough depth to cultivate and she made a long, thin vegetable patch.

The hardest part of her new life, other than having no-one to talk to, had been learning to catch fish from the stream and to snare a rabbit or a stock dove to supplement the tiny amounts of store cupboard foods she could afford to buy on her occasional trips to market. Soon, however, she had worked out methods, but rarely took more than one rabbit and one bird each week. She was fairly sure that the little valley did not belong to anyone, but she did worry that, if it did, she might be guilty of poaching. Rabbits especially were valued and severe punishments were given to anyone caught poaching. The rabbits in this valley must have escaped from some magnate's land and settled here to breed. She saved and cleaned all the feathers from the birds and the skins from the rabbits. By the second winter she had a thin feather coverlet for her bed and a rabbit skin coverlet too.

As she ventured on to the higher slopes of the surrounding hills, she found bilberries in the warmer weather, and in other places elderberries, nuts and rosehips. It was not a luxurious life but it sufficed. She got thinner but not weaker. She had been taller and plumper than her mother but, with her now thinner figure, she found she could fit into her mother's clothing. Mostly the garments were a bit too short, but there was no-one to see her here and she saved her own clothes for going to the town.

One thing that worried her for many months was how she could replenish her dwindling pot of money. She would have liked to have sold some rabbit skins at market, but worried about being accused of poaching. Eventually, another possibility occurred to her. Sheep roamed everywhere and although they and their fleeces belonged to someone else, pieces of their wool were always getting snagged on gorse and briars. Alice began to gather these scraps of wool and clean them. Also, at the end of winter, she would find an occasional sheep that had been trapped by drifting snow and frozen to death. As Alice overcame her revulsion, she stripped the fleece from these unfortunate animals to add to her store. What she needed then was the means to spin her finds into woollen thread.

She remembered that there had been a small spinning-wheel in a corner near the schoolroom at Arkenthorpe Manor. She did not remember anyone every using it. On her last trip to market she had heard that fighting was starting again, which meant that it was possible Squire Harald would have taken troops to join battle somewhere, so she might be able to speak with Miss Ellen. It was worth taking a chance.

Fortune was with her and as she approached the old manor house, Miss Ellen was in the herb garden. Shading her eyes against the sun, she suddenly recognised Alice and came forward to greet her warmly.

"Oh Alice, it is good to see you; and you look well."

They had exchanged questions and Alice learned of the fuss caused by her departure. When Squire Harald found her message on the slate, he had been very angry. He sent everyone out to look for her and was furious when she wasn't found before dark. However, the next morning he had washed his hands of her and sent Ellen to the village to find a new cook.

Yes, he was away fighting at the moment. News was that Richard of York was going to London to claim the throne of England and it was likely that more battles would ensue.

Alice asked about Edmund and was relieved to hear that he had been to Arkenthorpe a few months earlier. He had immediately missed Alice, and when he was told of the circumstances of Agnes's death and Alice's sudden departure soon afterwards, he had been very angry and upset, especially when he discovered that no-one knew where she had gone. In his case, however, Miss Ellen assured Alice, Edmund's anger was at the way she and her mother had been treated, not the fact that Alice had left. On hearing this, Alice wondered if Squire Harald had actually told Edmund what he had said to Alice; however, she decided not to ask Miss Ellen.

"You were right not to tell me where you were going," Miss Ellen added. "Harald would have found a way of forcing me to tell him. As it was, even he could see I was telling the truth.

"Mrs. Thorpe only came back for a few months. She is now living permanently with my sister in Lincolnshire, so until Harald marries, I manage the household. Will you come and eat with me, Alice? You will be most welcome."

"No thank you, Miss. It would not be right for me to be seen by the other staff to eat with you. But I have come to ask something of you."

"Of course. What is it?"

"Is the old spinning wheel still unused?"

"The spinning wheel? Oh, yes. I had forgotten about that. I am sure it is still near the schoolroom where Edmund had his lessons."

"I wonder if I might buy it, Miss Ellen? I would only be able to pay you a little money now, but would pay the rest when I have used it to earn more."

"The wheel has not been used since my grandmother's time. I will willingly give it to you, Alice."

"Oh no, that would not be right. You were generous to me when I left, letting me take things and hiding the coins under my mattress."

"Very well. I'll tell you what we will do. You will not give me any money now, but when you have sold some wool, you can pay me then. Now, come with me and we will get it, though you might find it difficult to carry far."

Alice found it strange going into the Manor House again. The changes to the inside that Squire Harald had ordered were now all complete and they certainly were improvements. The two women moved through the house without meeting anyone else, and pulled the wheel out of its corner. It seemed to be complete. There was a distaff and no parts appeared damaged.

"Do you know how to use it, Alice?

"I am not certain but I think I can discover how."

"I can't help you, I fear. I have never tried to spin, but it looks as if the spiders have been using it! We must remove their webs. Can you carry it into the yard, Alice? I will bring something to clean it with."

Alice picked up the wheel. It was heavier than she had expected, but she could carry it. She reached the yard and set it down. Then, leaning against the mounting block, she looked around her. She could hear at least one horse in the stables; some geese were sitting near the small pond where a couple of ducks were swimming. The late September sun was warm and the atmosphere sleepy.

A girl appeared, walking towards her carrying a leather bucket. Alice did not recognise her—a child from the village probably, who had recently come to work at the Manor. The girl smiled shyly and, taking a wet rag from the bucket, began to clean the spinning wheel. Alice was about to ask her who she was when Miss Ellen re-appeared and, addressing the girl said, "Dorcas, I will be away for a short time, helping my friend to carry this wheel. Please tell Cook and say that I will be back before sunset."

As the girl returned to the house, Miss Ellen turned to Alice. "I would appreciate your company for a little longer, Alice. Since Mrs. Thorpe left, I have no-one here whom I can talk to and, with this war, we rarely leave for a visit to family or friends. I will come part of the way and help you to carry the wheel. I have some victuals here and we can find a place to sit and eat. Don't worry, I will not try to find out where you are living, although I do not think Harald would try to bring you back again now."

Alice led the way down through the copse and into the hidden corrie beyond. There the women sat to eat.

"I have not been here for many years," said Ellen. "It is a restful place."

"This is where I stored the things I was to take with me in the days before I left Arkenthorpe."

"How are you living?" asked Ellen. "You are clearly not in another household, and I do not think you have a husband."

"No," Alice laughed, "I haven't a husband nor likely to have one. I am living alone but I am quite comfortable. I have shelter and I care for myself and no other person, but I wish to start spinning wool to earn a little money."

"I may soon have to be as independent as you, Alice. The last time Harald came home, he said that he would be approaching a wool merchant in Bradford to make a marriage contract for his eldest daughter. If they marry I cannot see that there will still be a place for me here."

"I do not think he would turn you out, Miss; and what about Master Edmund? He will need his home and someone to look after him!

"Oh, I am sure I **could** stay but I would not be mistress any longer. As for Edmund, I know he has his heart set on a girl he met when he visited my younger sister and her husband near Penrith. He is hoping that Harald will let him build a house on some land a few miles from here, which was given to our father as a reward for some service to Richard Neville. Perhaps I would be more welcome and more comfortable there."

When they had finished eating, Miss Ellen walked with Alice for a while but then they parted, with Alice promising to visit again in the Spring.

On her next trip to Skipton, Alice had visited a small workshop where four women sat spinning woollen thread for a cloth maker. She watched them at work for some time before the cloth maker came to ask what she was doing. She explained that she lived too far away to come to town often, but she was hoping to spin thread at home in order to earn money. The man obviously did not see her as a threat to his own business and allowed her to watch and learn. He also said that if the thread she produced was good enough, he might be prepared to buy it.

In the Winter, Alice moved into the cave, which strangely did not get as cold as the cot, and there she worked at the spinning, gradually getting better at it. However, her stock of gathered bits of fleece was of poor quality, so the wool she produced was too. When eventually she did take some to town to sell, she knew it would not be acceptable to the cloth maker, but she sold it to a few women looking to weave cloth for their own use. In the Spring she had been able to visit Arkenthorpe and make a small payment on the wheel.

The child stirred, then woke with a start.

"Cissy needs po-po. Cissy needs po-po." She climbed down to the floor.

Alice got out of bed and, wrapping the shawl again around the naked child, carried her quickly out to the privy. It was obvious that the child would fall in if left to support herself, so Alice held her, thinking about how she could modify the privy to make it safe. The child gazed at Alice's face looking puzzled, but she did not cry.

Back in the cot, Alice dressed the child in her clothes, which were now clean and dry, if very wrinkled. She talked to her as she did so.

"So, you are called Cissy, are you? My name is Alice. Can you say Alice'?"

The child smiled just a little bit and, standing up, began to walk cautiously about looking at her strange surroundings. As Alice stirred the ashes in the hearth to start preparing some frumenty, Cissy pointed to the glowing embers, "Fiiya!"

"Yes," said Alice. This is a fire and fire is very hot."

"Ot," said the child.

While Alice prepared their breakfast and as they ate it, the child began to talk her baby talk, until suddenly saying, "Kaffy; Mama; Kaffy, Mama", she started to cry and ran out of the doorway. Alice watched her for a few minutes as she toddled around outside, probably looking for her mother and for "Kaffy", whoever she was. Alice guessed at a nursemaid or perhaps an older sister. Eventually the child sat down on the ground crying.

Alice sat down beside her, and speaking gently, said, "Your Mama is dead, little one. I know you don't understand, but she cannot look after Cissy now. I don't know where "Kaffy" is. Alice will look after Cissy until "Kaffy", or perhaps Papa comes to find you. Come to Alice and let me dry your tears."

For a few minutes, Cissy sat quietly sucking her thumb, sometimes looking at Alice and at other times just looking around. Suddenly she removed her thumb, pointed and asked, "Wos zat?"

"That's a rabbit. Look, there's another one."

"Nuvver wun. Wabbit. Nuvver wun wabbit. Oh, wabbit gone!"

"Never mind," said Alice, smiling, "the rabbits will come back again. I think we will go for a walk now."

Alice had already decided to go back to the wreckage of the cart to see if anyone had been to it, and to see if some more clothing for the child could be found. For a little while, where the ground was easy, she allowed Cissy to walk, but she had put the shawl in the bottom of her handcart so that, most of the way, Cissy could ride in it. The child seemed to enjoy riding, even when the ground was very bumpy. As she neared the oak tree by the main track, Alice proceeded very cautiously, hoping Cissy would stay quiet. She did, and was in fact falling asleep when Alice carefully settled the handcart on level ground with stones under its wheels to stop it rolling if the child moved.

There seemed to be no-one except themselves about. The place where the woman's body had laid was only a few steps away, so Alice made herself have another look. Yes, the body was just as it had been yesterday, except for the changes made by wind and rain. Swiftly, Alice left and made her way to the abandoned cart in the gorse bushes. She felt like a thief, but knew she wasn't. She would only take what was needed for the child.

The travelling bags had been emptied out and their contents scattered, but it only took a few minutes to collect some of them—two dresses, a few undergarments, nightgowns and a warm wrap—and put them into one of the bags. Some items were firmly attached to the gorse and, after making two of her fingers bleed, Alice abandoned her attempts to salvage them. She did, however, find a rag doll and a small, bone hair comb which she also put in the bag. She could have taken some of the woman's clothing for herself, but decided that would be sinful—she would then be a thief, so, content that what she had taken would help her to care for Cissy, she returned to the still sleeping child.

On several more days, when the weather was fine, Alice returned to the scene of the attack, but there was no indication that anyone had been to look for the woman and child. Of course, she did not take Cissy anywhere near the decaying remains of her mother, and it was only occasionally that the child said "Mama?" in a hesitant way. She was soon calling "Ahyice", and as Alice had predicted on that first evening, the pattern of her own life had totally changed.

It was good to have the company of another human being, even a child, but it was much more difficult to leave the cave and the stone cot to go to the town to sell her wool and buy supplies. Weeks went by then, early one glorious morning, with the dale scented and sparkling with early Summer flowers, Alice set off with Cissy, to make a visit to Arkenthorpe, which was much nearer than the town. This time, however, she made her way to the village not to the Manor House.

She had heard from Miss Ellen that her childhood friend, Maud the gardener's daughter, was married to Thomas the wheelwright. Once in the village it did not take long to find Maud's home. Maud did not immediately recognise Alice, while Alice was shocked by how old Maud now looked, but soon their initial shyness passed. Maud had three children, and was expecting another. She was surprised to see the pretty child with Alice and assumed that Alice was her mother, but Alice explained that she had found the child alone on the moors soon after the big battle at Towton, and that no-one had yet come looking for her.

"Don't you have a child of your own?" Maud asked. "Do you have a husband?"

"No, I have no husband and no child of my own. I was living alone until I found Cissy."

"Why have you not come back to the village where you have friends?"

"I had to leave after my mother died," said Alice, "because Squire Harald suggested that I might serve him better as his mistress instead of his cook."

"You mean, he wanted you for his bed !?" Maud was horrified.

"He did not say those words, but what he said, and the way he looked at me, made it clear. I could not stay and take the chance."

"So that is why you told no-one where you were going—in case Squire came after you."

"Yes, but I understand he is married now."

"Yes, his wife is now carrying his second child. The first was a girl, which didn't please him too well."

"What about Miss Ellen?"

"She has left Arkenthorpe too. Master Edmund married and has a house to the North-West. He has taken Miss Ellen to live there. Old Squire Thorpe's wife is dead now, so everything has changed."

"Are you still a needle-woman, Maud?"

"Yes, I do work when I can, but my husband, Thomas, makes a good living. What I make gives us a few extra pence to save in case of bad times. What do you do to live, Alice?"

"I have learned to spin and I sell my woollen thread at Skipton market. Cissy's arrival, though, has made it hard for me to go there now, so I came to Arkenthorpe today to try to sell some here, and to buy a few things for my store cupboard. I thought you might know if anyone would want to buy some wool. It is not, as you will see, high quality. It can only be used for rough cloth."

"If you only expect a small price, you could try the Widow Litton. She weaves cloth for farm workers and lead miners. She lives near the mill, where you can buy grain or flour."

"Yes, I remember her; but she was not a widow then.

"Maud, may I leave Cissy with you while I conduct my business? She and your boy there seem to be making friends. Cissy has not seen another child since I found her. It will not take me long to get what I need, as long as Widow Litton is able to buy the wool."

Alice was successful. The price she got from Widow Litton was better than she had expected and she was able to buy flour, cheese, salt and dried beans, and a piece of sheepskin from which she would try to make new shoes for Cissy, whose feet were getting too big for the baby shoes that had come with her.

When Alice returned to collect Cissy, the child started to cry, saying "Alice gone. Alice gone away." Maud, however, reassured Alice that Cissy had played happily most of the time she had been away, and the tears soon dried. They set off to return home but before they left the village, Alice was able to purchase the treat of a drink of goats' milk for Cissy.

The trips to Arkenthorpe village became a feature of life. They would go at least once in two months. Other little adventures increased as Cissy grew. Her legs became longer and stronger and she needed to ride less frequently in the handcart. The cart wheels had become worn from its more frequent use on the rough ground, but Maud's Thomas made replacements and he also improved its balance, for which Alice was very grateful.

Now Alice and the child would collect heather for its many uses, but Alice especially dried the flowers. When boiling water was added to some dried flowers, a pleasant drink could be made. Alice stored some and sold some. Other local leaves could be dried and added to make other pleasant drinks.

During the summer she collected cranberries and bilberries and, for this job Cissy soon became a good helper, reducing the amount of bending Alice had to do, which always gave her back ache. Alice cooked some, stored some and sold some. With these, and occasionally other items to trade as well as her wool, she had the means of bartering for, or buying enough other food to supplement the green herbs she could gather, to see them through the winter months.

Seasons followed one upon another and Cissy had been living with Alice for more than two years. She spoke like a little adult, which was very noticeable on the rare occasions she played with Maud's children or encountered other children on their trips to Skipton market. One day in Skipton, on a March day when the sun had decided to shine brightly, Alice finished selling her wares. Cissy, after playing with some children a bit older than herself, came back to Alice and said, "Can we go and see God?"

Alice was startled by the question. "What do you mean, Cissy?"

Cissy pointed. "A boy said that building over there is God's house. Can we go and see God? I can tell him I am a good girl and say my prayers every night before I go to sleep."

"I will take you into the church, God's house, but you will not see him like you see people. You will still need to say prayers to talk to him."

With shame, Alice realised that she had not been to a church since her mother's funeral. She faithfully prayed every night and had taught Cissy to do so, but they had not been to church. To be truthful, she was always glad when she could hear the sound of the Arkenthorpe church bell on the wind, as she could be sure that the day was Sunday. She then tried to keep a record of that and subsequent days so she would know which day of the week it was. So far she had only been wrong twice, and then by only one day. She had intended to go to the church last Christmas but the weather had been too wet and cold to leave the cave.

Now, she took Cissy's hand and they walked up to the church. Alice put her bundles down in the porch and pushed open the heavy door. At first they could see nothing, then their eyes adjusted to the gloom. This church was much bigger than the one at Arkenthorpe, and some of the windows had pictures in coloured glass, which glowed as the sun shone through.

"Look, Alice," Cissy whispered, "there's a sheep." Then, a few seconds later, "Oooh, is that God?" She was pointing to a figure at the altar end of the church, holding a lighted candle.

"No," Alice said quietly, "we can't see God, but that man is a priest who works for God.

"Now, Cissy, we must kneel down and say a prayer. Can you do that?"

"Can I say the prayer I say before I go to sleep?"

"Yes, you say that prayer. Then when you finish, keep your hands together and listen while I say the "Our Father" prayer."

Cissy very seriously knelt with her hands together and asked God to "guard me while I sleep and help me to be a good girl tomorrow, Amen."

When Alice had said the Lord's Prayer, they stood up and walked slowly round the quiet church looking at the pictures and the statues. The priest smiled at them and said "Bless you my child", to Cissy, who smiled back at him. Then, putting a farthing into the box for gifts of money, Alice walked out to the porch and picked up her bundles. They went to the lodgings they had arranged for the night, and after an early supper, went to sleep. Next day, on the long walk home, Alice realised that it was time to do something about Cissy's education, and she began to wonder how to set about it.

Over the next few weeks, Alice showed Cissy her letters. They made a smooth patch of mud, or dust, and used a short stick to make the letters. Cissy learned quickly and could soon write her own name and 'Alice'. She learned to count and on their walks she would keep up a steady chatter. "I just saw three rabbits. Look, two big birds in the sky. How many berries are there on that bush? I can't count them, there's too many."

Alice told her the Bible stories that she herself could remember, hoping that she was getting them right. Cissy was growing up quickly.

Life continued on this pattern for another year. Cissy constantly asked questions about everything around her. They visited Arkenthorpe village every two months or so, but still Alice did not feel confident enough to tell anyone where they were living. Since he was now a married man with a family, it was unlikely that Squire Harald would even notice her, but some instinct had kept her from telling even Maud.

Each time they went to Skipton market, they would go into the church for a short time to look at the pictures in the windows. On some of these visits the priest would be there and would explain the pictures to Cissy in more detail than Alice could.

On one visit the priest talked to Alice while Cissy was absorbed in watching the coloured bands of light as the sunshine outside streamed in through the glass.

"Your daughter is a bright child," he said. "She learns and remembers well."

"Yes, she is a good child, father, but she is not my daughter. Her mother died when she was very young and I have care of her."

"And what of her father?"

"I do not know him. I can only think he was killed in battle as he has not returned for Cissy."

"So, you do not know whose child she is?"

"No. I found her alone on the moor—a very small child, sitting crying by the dead body of her mother. I did the only thing I could at the time, and took her home with me. The fighting was very bad and the woman had obviously been robbed and possibly attacked too. The place I found them was off a main track and very lonely. I went back several times, but no-one had been there."

"How long has she been with you?"

"More than three years."

"Have you asked around the towns and villages?"

"No, father. I know she does not belong anywhere around Arkenthorpe, and Skipton is the only other place we visit. At first it would not have been safe to ask too many questions because it was difficult to know the loyalties of the folk you were speaking to. Then, she just seemed to belong to me. I do worry sometimes that she has a family somewhere who would want her back and are grieving for her loss. Have I done wrong, father? Have I been very selfish?"

"I cannot say, but if you have done wrong it is a minor sin only. You obviously love the child and care for her well. At the time you found her, you did the only thing you could. After those dreadful battles, many people were lost, through death or just separation from their families; I heard of many cases. Now things are quieter, I could enquire of my brothers in the churches around if they have heard of anyone seeking a wife and child. Do you really have no idea at all who she might be?"

"There may be one clue, father. Cissy had a chain with a tiny medallion on when I found her. There is a pattern, or symbol engraved on it. Next time we come to Skipton, I could bring it to show you. You may know what it is. Also, father, the clothes on the dead woman were quality. She was certainly no peasant."

"Yes, Alice, please bring the medal and I will see what I can do to help with your little mystery."

But, as it turned out, it would be some considerable time before Alice could return to Skipton.

Chapter Four

Instead of more clear, bright and frosty Autumn days, from mid-October the weather became foggy, damp and unpleasantly humid. Alice became quite ill. Of course, both she and Cissy had been unwell from time to time or had had nasty cuts or bruises, and at first Alice was not too concerned. But, her illness kept getting worse—sometimes she had difficulty breathing, sometimes she felt too weak to do anything and struggled to keep the fire going or to cook some food.

For a child so young, Cissie was amazingly helpful and took care of herself as much as she could. She would fetch water from the beck and collect kindling and wood from the supply in the cave. She collected berries from the bushes but, of course could not reach many, especially from prickly bushes. She did, however, seem to have learned which ones could be eaten and which would make them ill. They frequently resorted to eating fruit and vegetables without cooking them, as it was too dangerous for Cissy to try to handle hot utensils. When Alice had a good day with some strength, she would set a trap for a dove or a rabbit, but it became clear that they could not go on much longer without fresh supplies.

One day, while Alice was sleeping, Cissy had taken herself down-stream to where the beck became a little wider. Alice was alarmed when she woke and could neither see nor hear the child. She called her. No reply. She got to her feet and called again. Still no reply. Panic was just rising in her when a voice called back, “I’m coming,” and Cissy appeared, struggling up the wet, grassy slope with something in her arms. As she got nearer, Alice saw that the child had something moving around in her skirt, which she had lifted and was holding in the form of a bag. Arriving outside the cot, she dropped the hem of her skirt and a fair-size fish landed, writhing on the ground.

“I tickled it; it jumped out and I caught it!” Cissy was triumphant.

“Well done, Cissy. That was very clever,” Alice said as enthusiastically as she could, while taking a stick and hitting the gasping fish. “We will have it for dinner. Can you manage to fetch some more wood from the pile to make the fire hotter? I will get the fish ready. Then, when the fire is burning better, you must take off your wet clothes and get really dry and warm. We must not let you get sick too.”

Later, as they sat by the fire eating their fish stew, Cissy asked, “Will you be better soon Alice? I don’t like it when you are sick.”

“I don’t like being sick, but I think I am a bit better now. If the sunshine would come back, I think I might be able to get to Arkenthorpe. I will have to go soon because we have only a tiny bit of flour left and a few dried peas.”

Cissy looked at Alice very seriously. “If you can’t go, I will go. I could find my way to Maud’s house if the fog goes away.”

Alice looked at the bedraggled little girl, dressed only in a rabbit-skin cover and with wispy strands of fair hair hanging round her face, but with the expression on that face showing such determination that Alice had to say, “I’m sure you could, Cissy, but if we wait just another day or so, I think we can go together. With you to look after me, I know I could get there.”

As it happened, neither of them had to go to Arkenthorpe; Arkenthorpe came to them.

It was such a long time since Maud had seen Alice that she had become very worried about her friend. Not knowing where Alice and Cissy were living though, she couldn't go to see what was wrong. "Alice must be getting low on food now, and in this dreadful weather, surely Arkenthorpe would be the only village she would travel to," she thought.

Maud's brother, John, had returned from the fighting with a nasty thigh wound but, now, with care from his wife, it had healed and he was working in the Arkenthorpe garden alongside his father again. John had married the young woman who had taken the job of cook at the Manor after Alice had left. They had married when he was home between battles but, although that was now two years ago, John and Mary had no children.

Alice and Mary had met briefly on one of Alice's visits to the village, while John was away, and Maud had told Mary about Alice and Cissy.

On this particular Saturday evening, Mary and John were visiting Maud and her family, and Maud told them how worried she was about Alice. "I wish she had told me where she is living. I would never have told the Squire."

Suddenly Maud's eldest son spoke up, "Cissy told me where she lives."

"Did she? Can you remember?"

"Well, she was not much more 'n a baby when she said, but she said they had two houses. They had a little stone house with a fire but sometimes they lived in a cave."

"But Cissy didn't say where they stone house or the cave were?"

"No, she was only little and I thought she was pretending 'cos she also told me she had a fur blanket."

"Oh dear, that isn't really much help."

John spoke then. "Perhaps you are right lad. I think I know where that place might be. Can you remember anything else that Cissy said?"

"I don't think so . . . . oh, she did follow me to the well when I got some water for Mam. She asked me what was down the big hole and I said, 'water'. She looked surprised, so I said "doesn't Alice go to the well?"

Cissy said, "No, she goes to the little water fall."

"That's it! I do know where they are," John exclaimed. "I could try to find 'em tomorrow. The sky is clearer tonight so t' weather might be better at last. The place is very well hidden. Alice and I found it when we went exploring as children. I hope I can still remember t' way.

"What do you want me to do if I find 'em?"

"You must take them some food, John. It is so long since they came they must be near to starving, and probably sick too. Flour, oatmeal and beans; a turnip or two; whatever we can spare."

"If Alice is likely to be ill," Mary chipped in, "you had better take some bread that is ready to eat. I'll make an extra loaf tomorrow morning and there is a bit of fat bacon that'll not be missed."

"I have some cheese you can take as well," said Maud.

"Whoa! I will have to carry all these things, and I will not be on a track. It'll be across country.

"Oh sorry, John, I'd forgotten your poor leg. Perhaps one of us should go with you."

"No, I'll go alone. If she's still worried about Squire, the fewer of us that know, the better."

"Take my small handcart, John," said the wheelwright. "Alice brings hers when she comes to Arkenthorpe, so it must be possible to pull it, across country or not."

So it was that next morning, John slipped quietly down the Manor garden to the corrie, to try and follow his childhood memory, just as Alice had done before him.

Alice was feeling a bit better when she woke in the morning. She lifted the sheepskin that served as a door and saw for the first time for many days, a watery sun showing through the mist. Cissy was still sleeping when Alice returned from the privy, so she quietly scraped together the ashes of yesterday's fire and added some kindling. Soon a wisp of smoke was followed by a faint glow which, with encouragement was soon strong enough to light the last bits of wood the child had carried from the cave yesterday.

Alice realised that she was hungry, which was a good sign, but it made her realise how hungry the child must be. That fish last night, after she had prepared it for the pot, had only given them two or three spoonsful each. She had saved the small quantity of fish-flavoured water left from boiling it. That, thickened with the last of the flour and some herbs added, would make a broth for today.

With care, and feeling very shaky, Alice made her way to the cave to see just what was left in her store. The barley flour had all gone but there was a handful of oatmeal and a fist full of dried peas. She would have to soak the peas before they could be used, so she took the oatmeal and added it to the pot. She must get well enough to go to Arkenthorpe tomorrow or they would soon be too weak from hunger to go anywhere. She had lost track of the days—how long had Cissy been looking after them both? The child had done amazingly well.

As though Alice's thoughts had penetrated her sleep, Cissy stirred and woke. She looked up and saw Alice by the fire.

"Oh Alice, you are out of bed. Do you feel better?"

"Yes, Cissy, I do feel better today. This time I think I will keep getting better. Have we anything to eat for breakfast, or do we have to wait until this fish broth is ready?"

"There are a few nuts and berries and there is still a drop of the rosehip drink you made."

"Well I think we should have those things now. Now I can cook things again, I can make us a hot drink later from the dried heather flowers. I think the weather is going to be better today too."

"Good. I was so wet after I caught the fish, I felt as if I had been swimming in the beck with it. Are my clothes dry now?"

Alice picked up Cissy's garments and felt them. "Yes, they are dry, but they are not clean. Your skirt still stinks of fish!"

"Never mind. I'll put it on so I can go outside and get more wood for the fire. I'm so glad you are feeling better. I said an extra prayer to God last night asking him to make you better. He must have been listening."

A short while later, the child came quietly into the cot with three small logs clutched to her chest and a worried look on her face. She said very quietly, "I think a man's coming."

"Coming here?"

"I think so."

"Where is he?"

"He was standing on the top edge looking round."

"Did he see you?"

"I don't think so, and I hid in the bushes to get back here."

"I had better go and see," said Alice. "He will see the wisps of smoke from our fire and know someone is here. Give me your cloak to put round my shoulders. You stay here out of sight."

"Are you frightened, Alice? He didn't look like a bad man."

"No, I'm not frightened," Alice lied, "but I wonder why he is here?"

Wrapping the small cloak round her head and shoulders, Alice walked unsteadily out of the cot and looked around. The air was still misty and damp. At first she saw no-one but then the figure of a man appeared around the end of the gargoyle rock on the opposite side of the valley, with the light behind him. Alice could tell immediately that it wasn't the Squire—although why she had even thought it might be him, she didn't know. Again, he didn't look like a wandering villain either. Then the man turned and saw her.

"Alice? Alice, be that you?"

There was something slightly familiar about the voice.

"Who are you?" Her own voice sounded nervous.

The man smiled. "Don't be frightened, Alice, it is me, John, Maud's brother. I am alone. Can I come down?"

"John! Oh yes, please come down."

He came carefully down the track and stood in front of her. Oh yes, it was John, but how he had changed. He had been about twenty years old last time she had seen him, and like Maud he now looked much older, but his smile was the same. He took her hands in his.

"Maud was right, you are ill. How is Cissy? Is she ill too".

"No, Cissy is well, but she is very hungry. Please come inside. We have a fire—you must be cold."

"No, I am warm enough after my walk, but you certainly should be near the fire."

"Cissy," Alice said as she pushed the door curtain aside, "this is a friend called John. He is Maud's brother. He has been away at the fighting but has now come back."

Cissy looked warily at this man invading their home. "Why have you come?"

"Oh Cissy, that sounded rude," said Alice.

"My sister was worried about you both, so I thought I'd better come to find you. Maud was right to worry. I can see Alice is ill and needs some help."

Immediately Cissy was on the defensive. "I have been looking after her; but she wouldn't let me cook things on the fire."

John looked down at the fiercely protective small girl in front of him. "I'm sure you have looked after Alice very well indeed, but even t' best little girls can't make hungry people better when there's no food left and it's winter time. Behind the big rock above the cave I have got a cart with bread and cheese in it. Will you let me bring it down?"

Cissy's eyes opened wide. "Bread and cheese?"

"Aye, and some other things too. Shall I get it?"

Cissy jumped up and down. "Please! Oh please!"

John laughed. "Very well, I'll get it."

In no time at all, Alice and Cissy had a hunk of fresh bread and cheese in front of them and Cissy was eyeing the other good things in the cart. John had included a skin of ale and they mulled some, giving Alice a warm, comforting drink, and she insisted John have some too. Cissy had a sip from Alice's but was not very impressed. It was not long before, with the warmth of the fire outside and good food inside her, Cissy fell asleep.

John went out and cut more wood for the stack in the cave, gathered more kindling, and put the supply of food he had brought into Alice's store.

"You could come back to live in t' village," he said as he was resting before going back to Arkenthorpe.

"Perhaps I could now," Alice agreed, but I would still need to earn money and I don't know what I could do there. I did realise when I was so ill, that I had been foolish not to tell anyone where I was living. When it was just me, it was not so important but with Cissy to think of as well, I should have told Maud at least.

"There really was only you who could guess where we might be, and you found us. I am so grateful John. Please thank Mary and Maud for providing us with so much. I will soon be fit again, and perhaps we will come down to the village for the Christmas Mass.

"How many days is it to Christmas? I fear I have lost track of the days."

"Today is Sunday," said John, "and last Sunday the priest lit t' first Advent candle, so I reckon that there will be two weeks and three days to Christmas Day."

"It is sooner than I thought, but we will try to be there."

"You mun eat with us and stay the night."

"I must put my fear of Squire Harald behind me."

"I don't think you need fear him, Alice. He is nothing like t' old Squire, but he is not a bad master. He works us all hard but, perhaps after he'd treated you and your mother so bad and saw what happened, he learned his lesson."

"I will think about finding somewhere to live in the village for Cissy's sake, but now I must stay here, get better, and organise our move into the cave for the Winter. The cot is fine in the better weather, but we are warmer and drier in the cave."

"Now, John, if you are to get home before dark, you must go. Thank you and God bless you for coming, and please thank everyone else for us too. You may really have saved our lives."

"You both look better than you did when I arrived, but take great care. I'll tell Maud that you'll try to come to us at Christmas. Farewell Alice. Farewell Cissy."

"Farewell. Thank you for bringing the lovely bread and cheese," said Cissy. "May I give you a kiss?"

"'course you can." John bent down and presented his cheek to be kissed. Then, patting Cissy's head, he picked up the shafts of his handcart and set off for home. He turned and waved before disappearing over the ridge.

Chapter Five

Alice kept a careful tally of the days after John's visit, and she and Cissy walked to Arkenthorpe early on Christmas morning.

In the previous two weeks, Alice had made a full recovery, helped by the food and the weather which had become colder, brighter and drier. She had washed their clothes and made the move into the cave.

She wanted to take gifts for Maud's family, after all she had received from them, but had little time and could think of nothing. Then only two days before Christmas, she remembered she still had three good dresses that had belonged to Cissy, long grown out of, which she had collected from the scattered luggage of Cissy's mother. The fabrics were of good quality so Maud, with her needlework skills, would be able to make useful things from them for her own family. The baby dresses were packed in the bag.

They were made very welcome at Maud's and the children were excited to be together. Cissy was wide-eyed at everything and fascinated by the representation of the crib and the stable at the church. She loved the music of the chanting and her obvious pleasure gave pleasure to those around her. John and Mary joined the family after Mary had served Christmas Dinner at the Manor and after they had had their own meal. However, Mary had brought the remains of a plum pudding which was a great treat for everyone. John produced gifts for all the children. His gift to Cissy was a small fishing net—just the right size for her to handle.

"Did you know, John, that I caught a fish all by myself?"

"Aye, Alice told me when you were asleep, and if you remember you had used your skirt to carry it in. I could still smell the fish!"

Everyone laughed, but Cissy didn't mind. "I tickled it and it jumped out; but thank you for my lovely net."

Maud was delighted with the dresses and immediately started to plan what she could make from them. She lovingly fingered the quality fabrics.

The day passed quickly and when the children settled for sleep, Maud's husband, Thomas, took out a set of pipes and played a few tunes. Alice thought to herself what a talented man this wheelwright was, and for a few moments she envied Maud for her husband, her children and her life.

Next morning was frosty and clear as Alice and Cissy left for home. Alice avoided the Manor garden and walked along a track that would bring them out beyond the corrie. They were approaching the last outlying dwellings of Arkenthorpe when two horses came trotting into view, moving towards them from across the moor to the right. The riders were clearly a man and a woman, and the man was very clearly Squire Harald. He brought his horse round so that he came to a halt just ahead of Alice and the child.

"What a beautiful morning Alice. I heard you had been seen in the village with a child. How pleasant to see you again. I hope you are well."

"Yes thank you, Squire," Alice stammered, feeling herself starting to tremble as she dropped a small curtsey. "Cissy, please curtsey to the Squire."

Cissy did as she was asked, staring up at this man who looked so big sitting on the lovely horse, and sensing Alice's nervousness.

"My dear," said the Squire, turning to the lady just behind him, "this is Alice who grew up in our house where her mother was cook for many years. Alice, this is my wife."

Alice and Cissy curtsied again to the lady on the grey horse. "My lady, I hope you are well. May I ask, sir, how Master Edmund and Miss Ellen are faring?"

"You may. Both are well and living at Carlisle, so we rarely meet now. Well, good day to you and the compliments of this season. Come my lady, or our horses will get cold."

The lady nodded to Alice, smiled at Cissy and, as quickly as they had appeared, they had gone. Alice waited until they were out of sight before leading Cissy back towards their usual track home.

"Where do Squire Harald and the lady live?" asked Cissy.

"In the Manor House—you know, the one I showed you before."

"Oh that big house. Did you live there when you were little, Alice?"

"Yes, I lived in a little room at the side of the big kitchen with my mother."

"Where's your mother now?"

"She is dead. She died a long time ago."

"So you couldn't live in the big house any more."

"No, but we have our own little house now."

"Yes," Cissy said cheerfully, "and when I run over that hill, it will be there!"

So saying, she lifted her skirt with one hand and holding her fishing net over her shoulder with the other, she did just that. Her hood fell back and her long fair hair streamed out behind her.

Snow fell soon after the New Year, but not before Alice had gone back once more to Arkenthorpe to sell the last of her wool and buy a few more things for the store cupboard. There was a short, mild spell when the snow melted slowly and Alice and Cissy were able to gather more bits of wool for cleaning and spinning. After that the snow fell again, staying for another three weeks. Then, at last, at the end of February they were able to set off on another visit to Skipton.

The day before, when they were packing things into the cart, Alice remembered that she had promised to show the medallion to the priest at Skipton church. Quietly, so as not to rouse Cissy's curiosity, she went to the small hole in the cave wall where she had hidden the items she had removed from the hem of the petticoat which Cissy had been wearing when found. She unwrapped them from the small bag she had made to keep them in then, removing the medallion from its chain, she re-wrapped the chain, the coin and the buckle, and returned the bundle to the hole. She studied the tiny but intricate design on the medallion, but although she recognised a flower as probably a rose, enclosed in a triangle with branches twisting through it, and a symbol, one in each of the three areas outside the triangle, none of it meant anything to her. She wrapped it carefully in cloth and placed it inside her bodice for tomorrow.

There was a different priest in the church when they first visited late on the afternoon of their arrival, so they moved on to their lodgings. Next morning, Alice sat on some steps, displaying the items she had for sale and, fortunately, by late morning she had sold or bartered all her wares and purchased the essential items they needed.

They returned to the church and this time the priest, whom she came to know as Father Luke, was tending the altar. She and Cissy said their prayers, then, while Cissy was happily wandering around, Alice approached the priest.

"Do you remember me, Father?"

"Of course I remember you and the child. I am glad to see you again. You were going to bring something to show me, I think, to see if I can help in the search for Cissy's father."

"Yes, it is a tiny medallion. I have it here," said Alice, unwrapping it carefully so as not to drop it.

The priest took it and examined it closely, moving across to one of the large candles to get more light on it. "It is certainly made of gold and is beautifully wrought. The design is not one I am familiar with. Will you allow me to soften some candle wax and press the medallion into it so that I have a copy of the design? The wax will not damage gold."

Alice agreed. While the process was taking place, Father Luke told Alice that he would make discreet enquiries to see if anyone recognised the emblem. He assured Alice that, if someone was able to tell him whose emblem it was, he would make no mention of the child without her specific permission.

Cissy had suddenly become aware in her wanderings, that Alice and the priest were 'doing' something, and her curiosity brought her over to see what this was. She surprised them just as the medallion was being eased out of the warm wax.

"What are you doing, please?"

Alice was slightly startled, but Cissy gave no indication that any words she had heard had meant anything. She wanted to see the "coin" and the wax.

"By doing this, I have a way to remember what a particular coin looks like. Look, you can see the pattern pressed in the wax? Now, if

I am careful, when the wax cools, the pattern will stay there for a long time. Before it melts again, I will get someone who is clever at drawing to make a copy on parchment."

"That is very pretty," said Cissy. "Look there is a flower in the middle. Can we use a bit of wax to do that at home, when we have a coin please?"

"Yes, we can try," said Alice, wrapping her cloak around her so that she could conceal the medallion from Cissy as the priest returned it to her. "Thank you for showing us, father. We will come to the church again next time we are in Skipton but now, Cissy, we must leave quickly for home. It is lucky there will be a moon early this evening, as we will not be home before dark.

Soon after darkness fell, the stars were very bright in the sky. It was cold with no wind. Cissy walked beside Alice along the rough track, as Alice pulled the handcart. They still had some way to walk before home, when Cissy took hold of Alice's hand and said, "I'd like to stop for just a little bit."

"Are you very tired?"

"No, I just want us both to stop to look at the sky."

Alice stopped. They were at a high point of the track and there was a shallow, rocky outcrop to one side. They crossed to it, sat down and cuddled together for warmth.

"Look," said Cissy, pointing upwards. "Everywhere there are stars—big ones, sparkly ones, lots of little ones. You are good at counting Alice, but I don't think there are enough numbers to count the stars, do you?"

It was a long time since Alice had really looked at the night sky, and Cissy was right. On a clear night such as this, stars were visible everywhere you looked. "No," said Alice, "no-one can count the stars, but the sky is beautiful tonight. If you look the stars sometimes seem to make patterns and shapes of things."

They sat and looked until Alice began to feel the first shiver. "Come now, we must get home. Oh look there, where the hills touch the sky. What do you see?"

"Oooo! There is a big light behind the hills. Do you think it's an angel?"

"No, not an angel this time. Just watch."

Quickly and smoothly the moon rose from behind the hills and suddenly the path was as bright as day before them as once more they quickened their steps across the moor for home.

Spring came early, as if to make up for the terrible weather before Christmas.

At Christmas, Maud had asked Alice if she could visit, to see where they lived, if she ever got a chance to do so. Alice had readily agreed and so it was only a small surprise, but a pleasant one, when John appeared with Maud early one Sunday morning.

Maud was amazed at the degree of comfort and convenience that Alice had created in this wild, lonely place. The stone cot was open and a fire smouldering in the hearth, although their bed covers and clothing were still in the cave. With a heather drink and an oatmeal biscuit, they sat outside the cot talking, while Cissy dragged John off to show him how good she was at using her fishing net.

"I had wondered how you and Cissy keep so clean and tidy when I knew you did not have a house. But I see you have fresh water right here for drinking and washing."

"Yes, the beck was really what allowed us to stay here, and I enjoy the freedom of being able to do what I want. When I found Cissy, I thought I would have to leave and take lodging somewhere in town. We do stay overnight in lodgings when we go to Skipton market, but I cannot pay for good lodgings. It is always such a pleasure to come home to a bed with almost no fleas, to our own privy and this good water, so I decided to stay here as long as possible."

"It must be very cold and lonely in the winter, though," Maud commented.

"So long as I have plenty of wood for the fire and a stock of flour and beans, we can be cosy. I'll just put the stew pot on the fire now, then I will show you our cave."

Maud was amazed again, this time at the mattress made from heather and bracken stuffed into the cover made for the bed Alice had had at Arkenthorpe Manor, and even more so when she saw a pillow and thin coverlet filled with feathers. Then, when she saw the rabbit skin blanket, she started to laugh.

"So, when Cissy told young Tom that she had a fur blanket, she was telling him the truth. He thought she was playing pretend. Where did you get it, Alice?"

"I made it. There are rabbits here in our little valley. I catch one occasionally and over the years I have cleaned the skins to make things from. I would have liked to sell some but I know I would be suspected of poaching, so I sell the wool and we use the skins ourselves. In fact, you will be having rabbit stew when we eat.

"The feathers come from the stock doves or grouse I catch and from the occasional dead bird we find on the moor. We can gather herbs and, in Summer and Autumn, we gather the fruits from the bushes and, of course, we catch fish."

"Have you not found a way of making something out of fish skins?" Maud teased.

"Not yet, but perhaps one day I might."

One glorious afternoon a few days later, Cissy was fishing down by the reeds and having caught one fish, she had returned to try for another.

Alice was in the cave deciding what to leave there and what to carry across to the cot for the summer, when she suddenly noticed a glow of light further into the cave. She was puzzled.

Picking up a brushwood torch (something she had learned to make the previous year and which saved their precious candles) she lit it and carefully felt her way along the wall on the left as the cave sloped slightly upward. There was a long crack down the left wall. The crack was wide and with only slight hesitation, Alice walked through. A few feet ahead the patch of light widened and she found herself in an area, surrounded by rock on all sides but open to the sky. Under her feet were grass and flowers and, in the walls, some ferns. There were even one or two butterflies flitting about. The walls were quite high—perhaps as high as a church—so although it would always be light in the day time, the sunlight would only stream through the crack in the cave wall when the sun was passing overhead as it was now. On the grass was a scattering of newly broken pieces of rock. High above she could hear a lark singing, and a small trickle of water was splashing down one of the rocks, filling a tiny rock basin at the foot. The overflow disappeared under ground below the basin.

Alice surveyed this wonderful discovery. Why had she suddenly been able to find it? Why hadn't she found it before?

Turning, she looked back at the cleft in the rocks that she had come in through. Outlined against the sky at the top of the cleft, she could see the roots of a tree—a tree that must have fallen recently. From the scars, this must have been where the loose pieces of rock on the ground had come from. The tree's falling must have let the light into the crevice and so into the cave. What a discovery!

Now, though, she must go back to her task and to Cissy. She wouldn't tell Cissy yet; not until she had given it a lot more thought. She was glad the torch was still burning as her eyes had difficulty adjusting to the dim light inside the cave. She felt her way back along the wall to their living quarters.

She got back to the cave entrance in time to see Cissy, with another fish in her net, returning from the stream. They were both having a successful day.

For several days, Alice did not mention her discovery to Cissy. Three times she slipped back again while Cissy was engaged in her own pursuits.

The place, which she now thought of as her garden of Eden, was sheltered from every direction. In places the earth was quite deep and she might be able to grow some vegetables there. It was a very secret place. If they needed a hiding place for things—or for themselves—it would be perfect.

She tried to work out where on the moor she would be if she could have climbed the steep sides to the top. "Of course," she decided, "I must look for the fallen tree." She eventually discovered it and, to her relief, it was high on the rock face and could probably only be reached by a goat, so there was little danger of the garden of Eden being discovered from above.

Eventually, when she had checked that there were no hidden dangers along the way from the cave to the cleft in the rock, she decided to show

Cissy what she had found. She chose another bright, sunny day. As they finished eating the midday meal, she said, “Cissy, there is something special I want to show you. I only found it a few days ago. Come with me into the cave.”

Once again, Alice lit a brushwood torch then, taking Cissy’s hand, she led her to the back of the cave and round a jutting rock. “Look ahead, Cissy. What can you see?”

“Light!” exclaimed Cissy. “Light, with bits dancing in it. Where is it coming from?”

“That’s what I want to show you. Come with me to the light—it is quite safe! A few steps more and they had reached the cleft. “Go through, Cissy. I am coming right behind you.”

Slowly Cissy went through the short, narrow passage to where the big patch of light was, then stepped out on to the soft, flowery grass.

“Where are we?” she whispered.

“Isn’t this a lovely place? I found it quite by chance when I saw the sunbeam in the cave. I hadn’t been this far into the cave before.”

“But we’re not in the cave, Alice. It’s a sort of outside inside, and it is so pretty. Look at those pretty plants. I haven’t seen those before.”

For a few minutes they both wandered around looking at all the familiar and unfamiliar plants. Then they saw some small birds flying around—up to the sky, disappear, come back and land on a ledge. By the excited chattering that happened every time a bird came back to the ledge, there must be a nest up there with babies in it.

After a while, Alice said, “Well, we must go back now, before this torch burns out.”

“Oh!” Cissy sounded disappointed, “but I can come here again can’t I?”

“Yes, we’ll come here often, but we must try to get a proper lantern so that we don’t get lost in the dark bit of the cave.”

It was actually easier to leave the dark part of the cave than to go into it, because they could see a grey patch at the entrance, which got bigger as they went towards it.

Alice returned to the cleaning and drying of her pieces of gathered wool and as she was working, she told Cissy that she must never go into the garden of Eden on her own. The way there was too dark and if she was to go even slightly the wrong way she could get lost in the really, really dark parts of the cave.

Cissy was actually frightened of those dark parts and wouldn't think of going any further in than they had been today, but she began to wonder how she could learn to get through the dark bit without a torch or candle. She would think of something.

Chapter Six

Father Luke had a good drawing made of the engraving from the wax impression. He had taken it to the Priory at Bolton where one of the young brothers was a skilled calligrapher. Several of the brothers had seen the drawing but none of them recognised the device.

Whenever he travelled, which was very occasionally, and then only within a few miles of Skipton, Luke carried the drawing with him and looked carefully at his surroundings to see if the device was repeated anywhere, but in almost a year he had not picked up even the smallest piece of information that might help to find whose child Cissy was.

In early December, as he later reported to Alice, he paid another visit to the Priory to spend a few days in prayer and in discussions with the Prior and brothers about the correct translation of some points of the Christmas story from Latin into the local English. In a brief period of recreation, he was walking in the cloisters with one of the brothers who supervised the hospitality to travellers passing through. Brother Jerome mentioned that a recent visitor was on a sad and almost hopeless journey, seeking his lost wife and child. They had vanished during the time of battles in this and other areas. He had been looking for three years to no avail.

The man, a nobleman, had left the Priory a few days earlier, telling the Prior that if he had still not succeeded in his quest by Easter, he would contemplate entering a monastery and withdrawing from the world.

Luke had not thought about Alice and Cissy for many days, but suddenly they flashed into his mind.

“Brother Jerome, did you see what device this nobleman wore?”

“His device? Now let me think—his name was Michael, Baron Muirhill, but as to his device . . . . I really cannot recall. If it is important we can ask the lay-brother who attended to him during his stay with us. Shall we seek him out?”

“Yes please, brother. I have had a visitor to my church in Skipton. She had found a small medallion with a device engraved upon it. I have promised the woman, Alice, that I will watch out for the device as I travel. I have a drawing in my bag. She lays no claim to it herself but thinks it belongs to a child.”

“Come then, let us find the lay brother; he should be near the kitchen at this time of day.”

The brother was soon found and asked if he recalled the baron’s device.

“Yes, in part. It is complex but has a central flower, a rose I think. A twining vine divides the device into parts and there is an emblem in each section, but the only one I remember is the holy cross.”

Luke was now quite excited. “After evening prayers, brother, please come with me to the dormitory. I have something I wish you to see.”

And so it was that the first clue came into place, for the lay brother indeed confirmed that the device on the drawing was very like, if not identical to, the one the baron had worn, although of course that one had been in colours, whereas the drawing was not.

“Did the traveller say whether he would pass this way again?”

“Yes brother, he thanked me for our courtesy to him and he expects to return this way in early March.”

“Can you give him a message on his return?”

“Yes, but perhaps you should leave your message with Father Prior.”

"Yes, you are right; but take care not to let the baron leave again without getting the message."

"I will, brother, I will. Do you think you can help in his search perhaps?"

"I think that is possible. Now I must see Father Prior."

It was late January when Alice and Cissy made their next visit to Skipton market and the church. When Luke saw them, he signalled to Alice that they should talk.

Alice turned to Cissy. "Please sit here and be good for a few minutes while I talk with Father Luke."

Cissy, who was trying to read some letters in a window picture, muttered, "Yes", and made no attempt to follow.

"I have a little news, Alice. When I last visited Bolton Priory, I heard that they had had a traveller staying who was on a quest to find his wife and child. I asked one of the brothers to describe the man's device and, although a little vague, his description was enough to suggest it was the same as that of the medallion. I then showed the drawing to the monk and he confirmed it to be the same, apart from the colours."

"Did you see the man, Father?"

"No, he had left a few days previously. I was told he is a baron and has said that if he does not soon succeed in his quest, he will retire to a monastery."

"So, what can we do?"

"I have left a message with the Prior that, if the Baron returns, which they think is his intention, he should be given a message requesting him to visit me here at Skipton. I will show him the device and, with your agreement, I will tell him how it is that I have it. Somehow, I will then need to get a message to you."

"That may be difficult, Father. How many weeks will there be before Easter?"

The priest thought for a moment or two. "Ten weeks to Holy Week."

"I will come to the market again in four weeks' time, if the weather is clement. Do you think there will be a message by then?"

"It is possible, but perhaps he will not return to the Priory until March."

"I cannot come to market every week, but do you know of the inn at the cross roads where the road west from Skipton meets the main north-south track through the hills?"

"Yes, I know it—the *Ramshead*, I think is its name."

"If it is possible for you to have a message left there, I think it will reach me within two or three days."

"I can arrange that, but what should the message say?"

"I have friends in Arkenthorpe who can be trusted, and who will ensure that the message reaches me. Just leave a message with the landlord of the inn, to be given to a regular traveller to Arkenthorpe, asking them to tell the wheelwright in Arkenthorpe that "the priest from Skipton Church wishes to make use of his services". I will tell Thomas, the wheelwright, to expect the message. He will then tell me, and I will come to Skipton on the next market day. Perhaps I could meet the baron here in the church, Father, in your presence?"

"Yes that may be best. What will you tell the child?" the priest asked, watching Cissy absorbed in her studies of the window.

"I will not say anything until we are sure this baron is her father. I will find a reason not to bring her with me when I come in answer to your message. Once we are sure Cissy is the child he seeks, I will need a few days to prepare her, and myself, for our separation. It will not be easy for her, or for me."

"No daughter, it will not."

Alice and the priest returned to Cissy.

"Well, have you been able to read any of the letters, Cissy?"

"Yes, Alice, I can read a lot of letters but I cannot read the words. They are very strange."

"That is because they are not English words", said Luke. The words are in a language called 'Latin'. Do you see the word just below the bird with the leaves in its bill? What are the letters?"

"D, E, U, S", Cissy spelled out.

"That is the word 'Deus', which is the Latin word for "God".

"Oh," said Cissy, sounding weary. "Why doesn't it say G, O, D?"

"Well, Cissy, there are many countries and many languages in God's world, so the Pope and the Cardinals in Rome, decided that the church should use Latin, which is a language used by learned men throughout the world. In that way the priests can talk to priests from other countries about the things of God and the Holy Church, wherever they come from. So, if I meet a priest from Italy or from Ireland, we speak Latin and so understand each other."

"Oh", said Cissy again, "but Father, people who aren't priests can't understand."

"That is why you have priests to explain the Bible to you. I explain to people here in English, which they do understand, and in Italy the priests will tell the stories to people there in Italian, which they understand.

"But now I must go and prepare for Mass, so I must leave you. God grant you a safe journey home."

Alice and Cissy returned to Skipton four weeks later, but there was no news of the baron. The weather in early March was wet and the tracks muddy. While this made it more difficult for folk to travel between Arkenthorpe and Skipton, Alice also realised it would mean the baron would have to contend with the same conditions and must be slowed down in his journeying. So she was not surprised when April arrived and there had still been no message.

Alice admitted to herself that she was actually quite fearful of the message arriving. If this man should indeed prove to be Cissy's father, Alice would have to return the child to him. If he had been searching for so long, he must be a good, caring man and she should be happy to be able to bring an end to at least some of his sorrow but, in her heart, Alice knew that she would be sad and very lonely herself when she had to part from Cissy. The thought of life without her was almost unbearable.

She had told Maud and Thomas that an important message might come to them, to say that the wheelwright's services were needed by the priest at Skipton, and that this would really mean that the priest had an important message for Alice and she would need to get to Skipton as soon as possible. She had told them also that the priest thought it was possible that Cissy's father was looking for her, so it was agreed that when Alice went to Skipton, she would leave Cissy in Maud's care.

The message was eventually delivered by an ostler who had come to collect a foal from the Manor. The foal was not of good enough quality to be ridden, so it was being sold to a trader in skins as a pack horse. The ostler delivered the message to the wheelwright then went on to the Manor to conduct his own business.

Thomas did not know how to reach Alice himself and it was decided that John and Maud would take the message after church the next Sunday. There would be a market on Tuesday, so Maud would bring Cissy back to Arkenthorpe, leaving Alice a free day to prepare to travel very early on Tuesday morning.

Alice was both relieved and anxious when she got the message; relieved that the waiting was over, but anxious about the outcome of her visit. Cissy was uneasy about leaving Alice to go with John and Maud, but Alice explained that there was some very important business she had to do in Skipton; that she was not going to sell wool or to buy things, and the business could take two or three days. Eventually, Cissy went quite happily and Alice prepared for her own journey.

It seemed important that she looked respectable so, even though the water in the beck was still cold, wearing only her thin undergown, she stood under the little waterfall and washed herself all over, paying special attention to her hair. Then she danced around in a sunny corner where the breeze still blew, until she was warm and dry again. Her hair was very tangled but patiently she combed it through until she was able to braid it and tie it with a short strand of wool.

Next morning she rose early. She took the bag containing the medallion and the other precious items, from its hiding place and removed the medallion and chain which she bound securely to her body before putting on her cleanest gown, cloak and wimple. She only had one pair of boots that she could wear on the long, rough walk. They were shabby but would have to suffice. She knew she would travel more easily without the handcart so, placing the few items she needed into a square of fabric, she tied the corners of the square across and ran a fabric strap through below the knot so she could carry the bundle slung across her body. As she set out, the morning was cloudy, but breezy and dry.

In the church at Skipton, Luke was anxious. The baron had agreed to stay in Skipton until the end of the week and to visit the church daily around noon. He had already been in the town for five days.

After conducting an early Mass, Luke went out to find bread in the market, then wandered around looking for Alice. However, it was now sunny and the market was bustling with life, so sensibly he retired to the church to wait.

Alice arrived before the baron and, at first, Luke did not recognise her. The woman who appeared could have been the wife of a clerk or a fine craftsman, but he knew her when she spoke.

“I received the message on Sunday, Father. I came as swiftly as I could.”

“I am pleased to see you, Alice. The baron is still in town and will come to the church at midday. You have time for some refreshment after your long walk.”

“I have a little food with me,” said Alice, “but I would welcome a drink.”

“If you sit on the bench by the lychgate, I will fetch us both some fresh milk. I saw a woman milking a cow at the edge of the market only a short time ago. I will take my jug and buy some.”

Alice sat, welcoming the chance to rest her body and organise her thoughts. She had stopped in a secluded spot, just before she reached the town, and had unstrapped the little chain and medallion from her body. It now rested loosely in her bodice. She ate a piece of bread and a little cheese, and when the priest returned she had her first drink of cow’s milk for many years.

As they waited in the spring sunshine, Father Luke said, “Baron Michael certainly recognised the drawing of the device as his own, and he is anxious to hear your story. I have only told him how you and I met in the church and that I have seen the child. He must hear the rest of the story from you.”

“Does he seem a kind man, Father?”

“Have no fear of him. He is a devout gentleman, but has almost despaired of finding his loved ones. He may seem aloof at first, as I know he cannot allow himself to believe that this could be the news he has sought all this time. Ah! Here he comes."

Alice looked up to see a tall man, with greying hair and a short beard, approaching. His tunic and hose were in tones of russet brown. He was accompanied by a young serving man but at the Baron's signal, the servant dropped back to sit on the steps leading to the church gate.

Luke and Alice stood up, and Luke went forward to greet him.

"My lord Baron, the message was delivered, and here is Alice, the woman I told you of."

Alice curtseyed and the baron acknowledged her with an inclination of his head. His brow was deeply furrowed but the face was gentle in expression. "Thank you for coming. I hope the news you bear is good."

"Some good, some bad, my lord."

"Well, whatever, I must hear it. Can we find a quiet corner, Father, where we can talk undisturbed?"

Luke led them into the church and, having made the sign of the cross, they sat in the Lady Chapel.

"Now", said the Baron to Alice, "please tell me everything you can, good and bad."

Alice began rather hesitantly, but the Baron listened without interrupting, and she gradually spoke more fluently. She saw the pain on his face when she told of the cries of a child leading her to the body of a woman, and how there had been no doubt in Alice's mind that the woman was dead. That there was no sign of anyone else around, no horse, just an abandoned cart and strewn luggage.

She told him of carrying the child home with her, and then returning to the scene several times to see if anyone had been looking for the woman and child, but there being no evidence that anyone had.

"Since then, my lord, I have continued to raise the child."

The Baron sat quietly for a few moment before asking, "And the device which Father Luke copied, where was that?"

"It was on a medallion on a chain, which was sewn into the hem of the child's petticoat. I have it here my lord."

Alice reached into her bodice, and removing the chain and medallion, she placed them in the Baron's hand. His hand closed round them and tears sprang to his eyes. Excusing himself, he moved to the altar and knelt in prayer.

When he returned to Alice and Luke, he gave the chain back to Alice. This belongs to my child. It is a girl child. What name do you call her by?"

"I call her Cissy, my lord. She was very young when I found her and only just starting to say words. She seemed to refer to herself as Cissy."

"Her name is actually 'Cecily', so Cissy was a good try." He smiled. "When may I see her?"

Alice was stunned that he asked her permission. "As soon as it can be arranged. I have left her in the care of friends today. I intend lodging in Skipton tonight, so I shall not be able to collect her and return home until late tomorrow. If I may say, my lord, it will also be necessary to prepare Cissy for meeting you. She knows nothing of this current business. I wished to be sure that you were really her father before I said anything to her. I will need to talk to her very carefully. She is a bright child and will be full of questions and concerns."

"Of course, I understand. Today is Tuesday. It would seem I must be patient until Saturday. Will it be acceptable for me to come to your home to meet Cecily? I will need instructions on the way to reach you."

Throughout most of Alice's account and the subsequent conversation, Father Luke had remained silent. He now spoke. "I think, Alice, it would be wise for the Baron to be aware of your situation. Alice, my lord, is unmarried and lives alone with Cissy. They have no servant or hired help and no man at home. They live a simple life. Alice comes to the market in Skipton to sell wool she has spun, and some other items, in order to buy provisions for their store. She left home this morning soon after dawn and walked for perhaps three hours to get here."

"My good woman", the Baron exclaimed, I regret my misunderstanding. You speak well and are of good appearance. It had not occurred to me that your circumstances were such."

Alice blushed, but was relieved that Father Luke had spoken.

"One thing, however," the Baron continued, "that I can do, is provide transport for the return journey to your home. Do you ride at all?"

"No, my lord. As a child I had one short ride on the back of a pack mule, but that is all."

"I have two pack horses but you might find such a ride uncomfortable after many years of not riding. I will hire a small cart and driver, and I shall accompany you. We can start within the hour if you are agreeable."

Alice hesitated wondering how best to deal with the situation.

The Baron saw her hesitation. "My man will travel with us. I swear you will be safe and treated with the utmost respect. I would do nothing to jeopardise my chances of being reunited with my daughter."

Father Luke responded. "I am sure you can trust the Baron's honour, Alice. He is a God-fearing man."

"Thank you," said Alice. "I had no wish to cast doubt on your honour. It is a circumstance I have not had to consider before. To travel home by cart will save time. I will accept gladly."

And so it was that Alice found herself riding in the back of a cart with the Baron and his servant, Colum, and giving instructions to the driver of the route to take.

In between instructions, the Baron asked about his daughter. "Is Cecily well? She must be quite big now. She will be seven years old. Is she pretty?"

Alice laughed. "Yes, she is pretty, but not exactly looking her best at the moment. She is losing her milk teeth. The new teeth are there in the middle of her jaws, but the ones at either side of them on her bottom jaw are missing. She is tall for her years, I think, and very curious about everything."

A little later the Baron asked, "Will we pass the place where you found her, and where my wife died?"

"Yes, we will."

"Will you tell me so that I can stop the cart and see it?"

So they stopped at the point on the track where Alice had heard the cry on that miserably wet day five years ago.

"You cannot see the place from here," said Alice. "We must leave the cart and go through the rocks there."

"Stay here with the cart, Colum," ordered the Baron. "We will not be long." He followed Alice through the rocks.

It was a long time since Alice had last looked into the hollow, and the grass and bushes had grown over the place where the woman's body had lain. She felt very uncomfortable talking about the scene she had come upon with the woman's husband standing next to her.

"She, your wife, was lying there," she pointed, "and Cissy was sitting on the grass, wet, dirty and crying, "Mama, Mama", and sometimes hitting her body."

The Baron made his way forward and carefully parted the vegetation. After a minute or two he said, "Ah, yes. There are bones here."

"I could do nothing for her," Alice said sadly. "I promised to care for her child and asked God to have mercy on her, whoever she was."

After a few moments of quiet, the Baron asked where the cart had been. Its remains were just visible among the bright yellow gorse and, judging by the fuss two linnets were making, they currently had a nest close to it.

"There is little to see now," said the Baron. "I will bring some men to collect the bones that are left and arrange a Christian burial for them. I doubt there will be anything else to retrieve. Let us return to the cart and continue our journey."

It was only a short time later that they reached the oak tree marking the spot where Alice had to leave the main track to reach her home.

"We must stop here," she said. "The cart cannot get nearer, and if you are to return to Skipton before dark, you must start back soon . . . . and, my lord, as your kindness has saved me almost a day, it will be possible for you to meet Cissy on Friday, unless you wish me to bring her to you in Skipton."

"I will come here," said the Baron. "If I come on horseback, can I get nearer to your home?"

"Yes, although you will need to lead the horse some of the way. We will meet you here, my lord, and guide you. What time shall we look for you?"

"Well before noon—shall we say half way between sunrise and noon. I shall wait until you appear."

"We will try not to keep you waiting long."

"I will return now, but thank you Alice for making the journey today. For me it has been a most wonderful day; one of hope after years of unhappiness. God bless you, Alice."

"And you, my lord."

Chapter Seven

Alice did not sleep well after the excitement of the day, and because it was a second night without Cissy curled up against her. She sighed as she thought of having to get used to being without her all the time.

Next morning she had some porage, then set off for Arkenthorpe. Maud was surprised to see her as she was not expected until the following day. Cissy and two of Maud's children were playing near the duck pond and did not immediately see Alice.

"Did you learn anything about Cissy's father from the priest?" Maud asked.

"Oh yes, I met him and talked with him."

"With the priest, or Cissy's father?"

"With Cissy's father. Maud, he is a baron! Baron Michael of Muirhill. There is no doubt that he is Cissy's father. Her name is really Cecily. I am here today instead of tomorrow because he hired a covered cart to bring me home. He has been travelling everywhere trying to find his wife and child."

"The poor man," said Maud, "but he must be a good man to look for them all this time."

"He is a good man, and will certainly care for Cissy but, Maud, what am I going to do without her? It will be so hard to part."

"It will be hard, but you will at least know she is with her family. She could easily have been dead."

This remark seemed cruel to Alice, but then she stopped to think. How could a woman who had given birth to a child bear the pain of losing that child, perhaps at an age between two and eight? So many mothers had to face such a loss, sometimes more than once. Her own loss could not be compared; she must be thankful that she had had Cissy for so long. However, it was not going to be easy to explain the position to Cissy.

As they walked home together, Cissy was at first eager to tell Alice of the games she had played and how she had helped Maud with the care of the youngest child—a boy nearly two years old. Soon, however, she started to ask Alice about her visit to Skipton; why hadn't she been to sell things; why had Father Luke asked her to go, and why couldn't she, Cissy, have gone too?

It wasn't easy to talk seriously while walking across the uneven ground, so Alice asked Cissy to be patient until they reached home, but also whetted the child's curiosity by saying that it was all exciting and important. Even Cissy's imagination could not conceive of what such news could be.

At last, sitting in the afternoon sunshine on the rocks near the cave entrance, Alice began her difficult task.

"Have you ever wondered, Cissy, why you do not have a Mama and Papa like the other children you know?"

"I s'pose a bit, but I have an Alice and you are my Mama, even though I don't call you that."

"Well, you are here with me because, when you were very small, not much bigger than the baby you were playing with today, I found you alone in a rocky valley. You were crying and wet and cold, and you were alone because a lady, who must have been your real Mama, was lying there dead."

Cissy's face showed total bewilderment. "I was a little baby, on my own, with a dead lady?"

"Yes. It was raining and a bit misty and cold. I was walking back from Skipton, and as I walked down a big dip in the track, I thought I heard a cry. I had just decided I had heard the cry of a bird, when I heard another cry and decided to find out where it came from. It came from you.

"It was getting dark so, once I was sure that the lady was dead and I couldn't help her, I picked you up and carried you home with me. You didn't want to come and you cried and struggled, but I couldn't leave you there."

"Why was the lady dead?"

"I think she had been attacked by robbers. She had been travelling in a cart with you. The cart was still there, tipped up in bushes and some travelling bags open with things scattered everywhere. She had a nasty wound on her head too."

"Poor lady. Poor baby," said Cissy.

"Yes, that is what I thought too. I brought you home to look after you and you have lived with me ever since."

"Oh!" Cissy sat quietly for a few moment before asking, "but why did you have to go to Skipton on important business yesterday?"

"Because Father Luke had heard that a gentleman had been travelling around the country for a long time, hoping to find his wife and child. He thought the man might be your Papa and you the child he is looking for. Father Luke and I met the man yesterday and we talked with him. He is your Papa and he is coming to see you."

"Will the man who is my Papa come and live here with us?"

"No, he can't do that. He is an important man, and will have a big house somewhere. He may want you to go to live in his big house."

Cissy looked horrified. "I can't do that. I can't leave my Alice."

"I really don't know what will happen, Cissy." Alice put her arm around the child's shoulders.

"He seems a very kind man and he has been looking for you for a very long time. He has travelled hundreds of miles trying to find you."

"How does he know I am his child? Perhaps he has got the wrong onc."

"That is why I went to see Father Luke. It was very, very important to be sure."

Alice went to her small bag and took out the medallion and chain and handed them to Cissy. "When I found you, you had this."

"Oh," breathed Cissy, "it is beautiful."

"Look at it very carefully, and you can see a pattern on the medallion. What can you see?"

"A flower . . . and some twisty leaves. A Jesus cross . . . and . . . some other things."

"That pattern is the badge of your Papa. The man I met yesterday has the same design on his tunic. He is an important man, Cissy. He is a baron."

"What's a baron?"

"Well, an important man who has a house and land and servants, and does things for the King."

"When is he coming to see me? How will he find us?"

"I have told him how to find us. He gave me a ride in a cart as far as the oak tree. We will go to meet him there."

"Yes, but when, Alice?"

"On Friday—not tomorrow, but the day after tomorrow."

"I don't want him to come. I just want you Alice." Tears shone in Cissy's eyes and she flung her arms around Alice.

Alice held her close, trying to comfort her but feeling the tears pricking her own eyes.

Cissy eventually fell asleep that night, but once Alice awoke to hear and feel her sobbing quietly. After being comforted, she slept again and then did not wake until much later than usual.

It was a beautiful morning, with sky larks rising high into the sky, singing to the small white clouds passing over. At first, neither of them spoke about the baron and his visit, but at last, as she was going to collect some water, Alice said, "We must make you look your very nicest Cissy. When the sun is high and warm, you can take your clothes off and wash in the beck. Your good dress is clean, but I will spread it on a bush to freshen up and stand your sheepskin boots in the air. Then we will wash your hair under the waterfall. How would you like me to do it for you?"

"Why, Alice?" Cissy demanded. "Why make me look nice? I think I should look horrid then the baron won't want me."

"Oh my precious child! You really do belong to this man and I want him to be proud you are his. If you look dirty and horrid he will still take you away because he wants you so much, and he will think I have not taken good care of you. Do you want him to think I do not love you?"

"No, no. I know you love me and I love you too. He must know that."

When, later that day, Cissy splashed naked in the beck and Alice washed her hair, she giggled and enjoyed herself chasing a rabbit that appeared as she was dancing in the sunshine to get dry. Having combed the tangles out of the long hair, which Cissy did not enjoy, Alice braided it to keep it tidy.

"Do you think we can catch some fish to eat tomorrow?" Alice asked as the sun began to go down. Taking their nets, they wandered to where the reeds grew at the edge of the beck and, after a while, quiet patience rewarded them with two good size fish.

It was a peaceful evening and the balmy atmosphere worked its magic on both Alice and Cissy. There were no more tears. When they were ready to sleep, Cissy said her own prayer, then Alice said the Lord's Prayer with Cissy joining in where she could. She knew most of it now.

In their unspoken thoughts they both knew they could do no more, and they would see what the morrow would bring. They slept peacefully.

Alice was up soon after first light, though Cissy slept on for a while. It promised to be another fine day.

"It is just possible," Alice thought, "that I shall need to give the Baron some food. She wandered around their little valley collecting greens to have with the fish, including some leaves to wrap the fishes in so that they could be baked on the hot stones around the fire. In Arkenthorpe, she had bought bread and some goat's milk cheese and a small amount of ale. She and Cissy would have water or a heather flower drink. There were some good herbs today—long dandelion leaves in her vegetable strip and chickweed growing wild in several parts of the valley. Her small willow basket was soon full.

When she returned to the cave, Cissy was awake but was much quieter than usual. They ate an oatcake and had a drink of goat's milk. Then Cissy put on her good dress. It fitted her but was a little short. Maud had already lengthened it once by adding a piece of different coloured fabric to the bottom, but Cissy had grown again. Alice loosened the braids she had put in Cissy's hair yesterday so that her hair fell in waves down her back. She left one braid at either side of her face, then tied them gently back so that they kept much of the loose hair away from her face.

Alice wore her everyday clothes which she had shaken and hung in the breeze for a while. The fire was dying down to glowing red ashes as Alice put the wrapped fish on the hot stones to start cooking. Then, putting on her wimple and checking that all was as tidy as they could make it, they set off to walk to the oak tree. The sun was warm but the breeze was cool. Birds were singing and flitting around between the bushes of blazing yellow gorse. Cissy seemed to have forgotten the reason for their walk and was watching everything around her with pleasure. Alice, though aware that it was a pleasant day, was going over in her mind the different ways that this day could end, with no idea of which ending she favoured.

They reached the oak, which was showing the tender green leaves of Spring among its gnarled branches, all leaning to one side as the prevailing moorland wind dictated. There was no sign of the Baron, so they sat on a rock to watch for his coming. Now Cissy started to be a little anxious and cuddled up to Alice.

"Do you think the Baron has forgotten?" she asked.

"No, I don't think so. We are quite early, but I am sure he will come soon."

It was only a couple of minutes later when Cissy, pointing along the track towards Skipton, asked, "Is that the Baron?"

A horse with rider had just crested the rise and was trotting briskly towards them. As it got nearer it slowed to a walk. Alice and Cissy stood up, while the rider reined his horse to a stop and dismounted.

"Good day, Alice. What a beautiful morning!"

"Yes, my lord, it is beautiful," Alice responded, curtseying.

"I see you have brought the child with you. May we be introduced."

"My lord, this is Cissy, the child we talked about. Cissy, this is Baron Muirhill. Please curtsey to him."

Cissy had been staring at this strange man who was supposed to be her Papa, and who had arrived on a shiny, brown horse; but now she recollected her manners and curtseyed to him.

"Good morning, Cissy, I am so pleased to meet you again at last. It has been such a long time." The deep voice shook a little. "You were still a baby when I last saw you. You are not a baby now."

"No, sir."

The Baron turned to Alice. "Are you still willing for me to visit your home?"

"Yes, my lord. If you will follow us, we will take you there. As I said, some parts of the track might be difficult for your horse."

"I will lead him. Please go ahead."

The little procession wound its way down, then up, then down again along the rocky hillside, with Cissy at the front. The horse was left to select its own way through the difficult and narrow bits, and they reached their tiny valley without mishap. The horse was led to a grassy area and tethered to a hawthorn tree and its saddle and bags removed.

"You are welcome, my lord", said Alice, leading the Baron to the cot.

"How long has this been your home?"

"I lived here for four or five years before I found Cissy. The cot was in a ruined state when I first came, but we have a small cave as well, so we always have a dry shelter."

"Amazing", said the Baron, looking about him.

"As it is a warm day, I suggest we sit outside", said Alice. "There is a bench here, or some of the rocks are quite comfortable. May I offer you some ale, my lord?"

"Thank you. That would be most welcome."

Alice fetched the ale and a drinking horn, filled it with ale and gave it to the Baron. She took a small, pottery vessel for herself and Cissy, filling it with water.

"Now", said the Baron, looking at Cissy, "I would like you to tell me something about your life here with Alice."

Cissy was feeling very unsure of herself and did not answer directly. Instead she said, "I like your horse, my lord. Does it have a name?"

"Of course. His name is Merlin."

"That is a good name," said Cissy, "although it sounds more like a bird than a horse. He is a lovely colour."

"I named him after a wizard who was an adviser and magician to King Arthur of Britain. I think there is a little magic in the horse. He always seems to know what I want him to do."

"I think the sky is magic at night", said Cissy, pleased not to be talking about herself, although without being aware of it, she was beginning to paint a picture in the Baron's mind. "There are more stars than anyone can count and they seem to make patterns in the sky if you look carefully. Do you like the sky, my lord?"

"Oh yes, I have spent many nights watching the stars. Have you ever seen a shooting star, Cissy?"

"I don't think so. What is a shooting star?"

"It is a star that moves very swiftly across the sky, just as if it was an arrow fired from an archer's bow. It appears suddenly, travelling very fast, and then vanishes."

"Oh no, I haven't seen one of those. I would like to see one."

"I'm sure you will one night. Do you like doing other things too?"

"Oh yes, many things. The birds and the rabbits are fun to watch, and the butterflies when we go to gather berries. I like looking at the colours when the sun shines through the windows in the church at Skipton. You can see lots of tiny bits dancing in the bands of coloured light."

Cissy was beginning to relax a little and sat down on a boulder between the Baron's and the one Alice was sitting on. "Alice told me you will live in a big house somewhere. Do you . . . . my lord?," she added as an afterthought.

"I live in a castle. It is north and east from here, about a four day journey."

"A castle!" Cissy had seen Skipton Castle and knew how big that was. "Is it like Skipton Castle?"

"No," the Baron smiled, "it is not as big or as grand as Skipton. It is much smaller, but it does have turrets and battlements."

"And does it have dungeons for bad people?"

"Yes, it has a dungeon, but I have never had to put bad people in it, though my father did."

When Alice realised that Cissy and the Baron were likely to continue their conversation without her help, she excused herself to finish preparing the food. Of course, she could still hear what they were saying most of the time. As she worked she thought, "I don't think he is going to take Cissy today. He has come as a rider and not with a cart or packhorse. Although, he might have asked Colum to bring one later."

The conversation between father and daughter had moved on to the visits to Skipton, Father Luke and the church. Alice, of course, was used to talking with Cissy, but she realised now how Cissy was expressing opinions to the Baron, and asking him questions in a strange mixture of childhood innocence and adult expression. To do him justice, the Baron was listening to her and answering her seriously.

Suddenly, Cissy smoothed out the dust on the ground in front of where they were sitting and, taking a short piece of stick, started to draw letters. " . . . . I could read the letters in the window, but they didn't make a real word. These were the letters, D, E, U, S. When I asked Father

Luke why they didn't make a real word, he said they did, but it wasn't in English, and what it said, Deus, was another word for God."

"Yes, that is right, Cissy. It is a Latin word. You are clever to be able to remember that. Can you write other letters too?"

"I can write all the letters and the numbers."

"So you can count too? How many pebbles are there here?"

The baron arranged some small stones in two groups, one of four and one of three.

Cissy looked and without hesitation said, "Seven, 'cos there are four there and three there. That makes seven."

"And what if I take one stone from that group and one from the other? Now how many?"

"Three and two—that makes five."

"Very good. How did you learn all this?"

"Alice showed me. I like counting things. I count the rabbits and the number of steps we have to walk in the dark to get to Eden and the birds . . . ."

"Where is Eden?" asked the Baron.

Cissy suddenly stopped and looked flustered. "Sorry, I didn't mean to say that. It's just a game I play."

Alice decided that this was a good time to offer food to their guest. "Will you eat with us, my lord? We have fish and greens, and a little bread and cheese."

The Baron smiled, and seeing that Alice's offer was genuine, he accepted. Alice suddenly realised she had removed her wimple for safety when she was tending the cooking, and was now bare-headed. "Ah well," she thought, he has seen me now. I hope he is not offended."

She served the fish and blanched greens on a wooden platter and they each had a piece of bread. The Baron served himself first, then Cissy and Alice followed. The fish tasted very good and Alice was relieved that, while it might not be up to the usual standard for the Baron, it was acceptable. They followed with some cheese.

"Perhaps," said the Baron as they finished eating, "you will allow me to add something to the meal." He walked across to his saddle bag and returned with a handful of dried grapes.

Alice had only seen them used in plum puddings before, so she was surprised when the Baron said they could be eaten just as they were. He went on to explain that, while he had been travelling, he had tried to ensure that he always had a supply of them, as they were light to carry and rarely went bad. Alice and Cissy both agreed that they made a tasty end to the meal.

"The fish was good, Alice. Did you buy it or catch it?"

"We caught it, my lord. It came out of our beck."

"You are fortunate to have the beck so close. It must be of great use to you."

"It would be impossible to live here without it. It is good to drink, for cooking, and of course we use it for washing ourselves and our clothes. As you see, there is even a small waterfall where we can fill pots easily. The fish are useful too, as are some of the reeds. It is a real gift from God."

"I caught one of the fish," said Cissy. "I am good at catching fish and I have my own net that John gave me. Shall I show you?"

"I would like to see your net and how you catch fish."

"I will fetch it."

"Cissy," said Alice, "you are wearing your good dress. Please do not get it wet."

"May I put my other one on instead? I might get a *bit* wet."

Alice hesitated, then said, "Very well. Go into the cave and change."

Cissy trotted off happily.

"I am sorry, my lord, I am afraid that Cissy is happiest when she can do things without worrying about her clothes. If she is trying hard to stay clean and tidy, that is the time she is most likely to slip in the mud or catch her cloak or dress on gorse or brambles."

"I understand, Alice. She is a lively child. May I ask who is John who gave her the fishing net?"

"John is a very good friend, my lord. He is brother to Maud who cared for Cissy when I came to meet you in Skipton. In the winter, two winters ago, the weather was dreadful and I became ill. I was ill for many days and was unable to go to buy food. Maud was concerned that she had not seen us, so she and John's wife, Mary, gathered together some food and John found his way to us from Arkenthorpe. He may truly have saved our lives as, although I was recovering from the illness, Cissy and I were both so weak from hunger, I doubt we would have reached Arkenthorpe ourselves."

"A good friend indeed."

Alice decided that before Cissy came back, she must ask the Baron the question that had been worrying her all day. "My lord," she said hesitantly, "may I ask if you will be taking Cissy away with you today?"

The baron looked surprised. "That is not my intention. I know you will probably see me as a man who is used to getting what he wants immediately and, of course, in many things I do, but I could not be so cruel to a child. I want her to trust me and like me before I take her to my home."

"Oh, thank you, thank you my lord. I know she will come to you but she is not ready yet." Alice almost wept with relief.

"I also have arrangements to make," continued the baron. "There is the need to give the bones of my wife a Christian burial. I have arranged for them to be collected in a seemly fashion tomorrow; then I will transport them home. For me it will be a sad duty but there is no need to involve the child in any way. I will also make appropriate arrangements for my home to receive Cissy before returning. I think perhaps in one month I will collect her.

"Ah, here comes the little fisherwoman. I must now go to be instructed in the art of beck fishing."

As the baron and Cissy wandered along the edge of the beck to the reed bed at its bend, Alice watched and marvelled that a man of such power and position could be so sensitive to the needs of a child.

However, she soon became aware of something else; the weather was changing. Clouds were building up beyond the hills to the West. The baron would need to start back to Skipton if he was not to be caught in the rain squalls that were no doubt coming. She had been into the cave to collect the small bag which still contained the buckle and the gold coin, but now she walked briskly down to where Cissy and her father were hunting along the beck together. "My lord, I fear the weather is changing and we will have rain within the hour. You are welcome to remain here until it passes, but that might not be for several hours."

The baron glanced to the West but the view from the beck was not as good as from the cave. "Thank you, Alice. I had not noticed the change.

"Well Cissy, I think you and I must continue our conversation another day. I have no wish to get a soaking, so it is time for me to return to Skipton. I will come here again soon."

Cissy looked at Alice and smiled. Then she turned to the baron and said, "We would like you to come again, my lord."

The baron carried his saddle and bags across to where his horse was tethered. It whinnied softly in greeting. Once the saddle was in place, and while Cissy was talking to the horse and daring herself to stroke it, Alice spoke to the baron.

"My lord, I have two other items here which must be yours. They were also stitched into the hem of Cissy's petticoat, with the medallion and chain." Reaching into the bag, she handed the items to him.

When he saw the buckle he gasped, then smiled at Alice. “This confirms that the lady you found was my wife. I gave her this buckle on the day after Cissy was born.”

“It is very pretty. What are the stones?”

“They are garnets and sapphires. I thought the robbers would have taken this, but you say these things were in the petticoat Cissy was wearing. How strange!”

“I thought perhaps the lady had realised her journey might be dangerous and had therefore selected the unusual hiding place.”

“Yes, I suppose that is possible, but Alice, why do you still have this coin? Why have you not used it to purchase things?”

Alice looked surprised. “Because it wasn’t mine, my lord!”

“But you have used your own money to care for my daughter. You have gathered or made things for sale. Surely you could have used this money with a good conscience?”

“Once or twice, my lord, when things were very hard, I did consider whether I should. But even if I had decided it would not be stealing to use it, I knew I would be suspected of stealing if I presented it in payment, or tried to get it changed for smaller coins. No-one would think that a woman in my position could have come by such a valuable coin honestly.”

“Ah yes, I see.”

“My intention was to keep the coin and the buckle for Cissy to have when she is grown to womanhood, but now you are here, I must give them to you.

“Now you must go my lord. The clouds are much nearer. Can you find your way to the main track?”

“Yes, I am sure I can. As I said, it will probably be a month before I return for Cissy, but I will call again tomorrow for a short while if I may.”

"Of course, you will be very welcome."

"Well, Merlin," said the baron, addressing his horse, "we must leave the ladies now. Farewell Cissy, I will see you again soon. Perhaps even tomorrow for a short time. Farewell Alice. I thank you for everything you have done. Please continue to care for my daughter for a little longer."

"I will," said Alice.

Chapter Eight

The baron did return the following afternoon. Again he was alone. After giving him a friendly greeting, Cissy went to admire and talk to Merlin, getting bold enough to pat the horse gently on the flank. The baron called Alice to come and sit on the boulders near the cave.

"My main task today, Alice, as you know, is to remove the bones of my wife from their current resting place. In doing so, we have also found a few other small items which I recognise, and these confirm both the identity of my wife and therefore of my daughter."

"My lord, I have had no doubt about it since the day we first met. I know I must surrender Cissy to your care, and I thank you for the consideration you are giving to her feelings in the matter."

"I must consider your feelings too, Alice. It is clear that you love the child and I could have wished for no-one better to take care of her after her mother's death. It is because of this that I would like you to give thought to coming with us when I take Cissy to my home."

Alice gasped! "Oh, my lord, I . . . . , I . . . . "

"I don't need your decision now. You must think about it carefully, but if you do decide to come with us, then later find you are unhappy, I swear you will be able to return here if you so desire."

"I will consider it, my lord."

"I must return to my men now, but before I do, I wish you to take this."

The baron removed a small leather pouch from his doublet and handed it to Alice. Inside was a large number of coins.

"Those coins," said the baron, "are equal in value to the gold coin which you gave to me yesterday. These you will be able to use for purchasing goods without any suspicion falling on you.

"Also, you may feel more comfortable about travelling with us if you have a new gown and shoes and a travelling bag. Use the money to obtain whatever you need. When I return I will come to hear your decision, and there will be several days for you to make your arrangements if you decide to come. The journey will take about four days, if the weather is fair."

Alice was rendered almost speechless by the proposals being put to her and by the amount of money in the pouch she was holding. The baron smiled, "Don't worry, Alice, you have time to think. Talk to your friends at Arkenthorpe. If you decide not to come, the money is still yours. You have earned it and more since you saved Cissy's life. Now, after a few words with Cissy, I must return to my other duty."

Alice dropped a deep curtsey as the baron turned and walked to his horse. Cissy had watched the last few minutes of the talk between the two adults and was aware that Alice's manner had changed to something that she, Cissy, did not recognise. She therefore challenged the baron.

"My lord, I hope you have not made my Alice cry. She does not look happy."

"I think you will find that she is not unhappy, my child. We have had a serious talk and she has things to think about."

"Is it because you want to take me away?"

"Yes, that is part of the reason, and I know that you would find it hard to leave her. But we have talked of other things as well. Believe me Cissy, I have no wish to make Alice cry.

"But now, I must take Merlin and leave. It will be about a month before I return. May I ask my daughter for a parting kiss?"

Cissy looked at the kind eyes gazing down at her and decided that she did like the baron. "Yes, I will kiss you Papa."

As he bent to receive the kiss, it was the baron who was in danger of weeping with joy.

That evening, Cissy was full of the new interests in her life. The Baron, whom she occasionally referred to as 'Papa', the horse, and the Baron's castle which she was trying to imagine.

Alice was also trying to imagine what life would be like in a castle. Of course she knew what life in a squire's manor was like, but she would surely feel strange and out of place in a baron's castle. What work could she do? There would already be a cook, maid servants and, as the Baron had no wife, there would be a steward managing the household. There would be no place for her other than some very menial work. Could she give up her hard won freedoms?

But then, could she let Cissy be taken to **her** new life without the comfort and familiarity of Alice to help her, now that the opportunity had been offered? The Baron had said that he would allow her to return home if she wasn't happy, so perhaps she should go for a while, accepting whatever task she was given, at least until Cissy had settled.

The journey would also take Alice out of the Dales for the first time in her life. She had never thought much about the outside world and had had no wish to go there, but now curiosity began to stir inside her at the thought of such an adventure.

Two days later she went to visit Maud to have someone else to talk to about it.

"Oh Alice," gasped Maud when told of the Baron's request that she should go too. "Would you be bold enough to travel so far? Are you sure he would keep his promise to let you return if you want to?"

"Yes, I'm sure of that. He is a good and honourable man; but I am not sure if the strange feeling inside me is fear or excitement."

"Maud's husband, Thomas, came in and was told Alice's news. His view was that she should go. He had seen a little of the world outside the dale when he was younger. "It will give you a chance to see some wonderful things Alice. You might get the chance to see the sea—a more awesome sight you cannot imagine. Great areas of moving water, rushing towards you and pulling away again. I saw it once a long time ago when travelling with the Squire's soldiers. I'll never forget it."

Later Alice asked, "Maud, could you make a new dress for Cissy to travel in. The Baron gave me money to use to prepare her for the journey and she must have a new dress and shoes."

Maud readily agreed, but was worried that the cloth merchant might not come soon enough to give her time to make the dress.

"I could get the fabric in Skipton," Alice volunteered, "but perhaps you could come with me as you will know better than me what to buy and how much of it."

"I would like to go with you. I haven't been for many years. I will need to find someone to watch the children. Young Tom is old enough to watch the younger ones, but I would worry about the baby?"

"Perhaps you can bring him. He could ride in the handcart like Cissy used to."

So they agreed that next market day, Maud, Alice, Cissy and the baby would go to Skipton.

Once more the weather was kind. Maud and the baby had stayed with Alice and Cissy overnight, so they set out early. The baby, Jack, was happy in the cart and laughing when the way was bumpy. The long walk passed quickly as they chatted together. Alice had told Cissy that the Baron had asked her to travel with them when he came for her, and this had turned Cissy's reluctance to think about leaving into excitement at the promise of adventure. The thought that Alice might not go never entered her mind.

As they reached a high point on the track, Cissy pointed across the near hills to the ones just visible beyond them on the horizon. "Do you think the Baron's castle is as far as that? Can we see it from up here?"

"I don't think we can see it, but it could be as far as those hills. It might even be further."

"Oh, that would be a very long way!"

The market, when they reached Skipton, was bustling. Alice had told Maud that she was to have a new gown too. Maud had agreed to make that as well and was eager to start looking for the cloth merchants. She remembered that one had a shop in the town, and there would certainly be one or two in the market today.

"Before I buy anything," Alice said, "Cissy and I must go to the church to see Father Luke."

"I'll look around and see what's here, and then wait for you by the gate to the church. You don't need to hurry. It is so long since I was last here, I'll enjoy seeing everything. I'll get a honey cake for Jack and that will keep him happy."

So Alice and Cissy made their way into the church. Father Luke was not immediately visible, but eventually he appeared from a side room.

Alice went straight to him.

"Father Luke, Cissy and I are here to thank you for your help in finding her Papa. You have done so much and we are grateful."

The priest smiled and looked at Cissy. "It is good that your father has found you, child. He is a very happy man now, although, of course he is sad that your mother died in such a way."

Alice removed the leather pouch from her bosom and removed two coins. “I wish to give these coins to you Father, one for yourself and one for the church. Please accept them.”

“I will gratefully accept the gift for the church, Alice, but as for myself, I will not take it. Baron Muirhill has already been most generous to the church and to me. Let us all kneel and I will ask God to bless the gift and to bless you both as your lives change.”

With their duty done, and the priest’s blessing, Alice and Cissy left to find Maud.

“There is a merchant by the steps with a good Kersey cloth which would make your gown, Alice, but I think we should see what the merchant’s shop in River Street has. As Cissy is a Baron’s daughter, her dress must be a good one. A worsted would be best for the warmer weather.”

Maud chattered on about the things she had seen in the market. She had, of course, bought fabrics and made clothing for the old squire and his family in the past, and when they reached the shop, her touch was still sure as she assessed the available fabrics. Before purchasing a good worsted for Cissy, she took Alice to one side. “If you have enough money, Alice, there is this good Kendall cloth which would make your gown. You would look good in green too.”

“Oh Maud, it is lovely and I do have enough money, but I must not dress like a gentlewoman. It wouldn’t be right.”

“I don’t see why you shouldn’t have a dress as good as the ones I made for Miss Ellen. The fabric will stand up to the journey better than the Kersey. If I make it in a simple style, I’m sure it will be appropriate.”

After a few moments of hesitation, Alice agreed and the purchases were made, together with the threads and pins that Maud would need to make the gowns, and some light fabric for a wimple too.

Next, new boots were purchased for Cissy and Alice, and a travel bag, and finally some items of food. Maud and Alice had agreed that they would return home on the same day, but now the weight and bulk of their purchases made them doubt that they could make the journey in good time.

Alice insisted that, to give them strength, they must have a good bowl of broth each at one of the inns on the market place. Then, having finished her own, she left the others to finish, and made an excuse to return to the market for a few minutes. She had remembered that on previous visits, one of the men who brought cheeses to market from an abbey, had sometimes passed them in his horse-drawn cart as they walked along the main track home. "If he is here today," she thought, "perhaps we can ride with him part of the way."

She soon found him, and he agreed, for a modest charge, to take them as far as the Ramshead cross roads, if they could be ready within the hour. She assured him they would be.

Back at the inn, baby Jack was asleep, with a sticky face and a full belly. Cissy was looking at the castle and asking Maud whether she thought the Baron's would be as big as 'this bit' or, perhaps, 'that bit'. Maud was wondering where Alice had gone. However, the news of a cart ride for half their journey was very welcome. They made their way slowly to the cart, which sure enough was waiting for them. The carter had been buying a few items for himself, but well before the hour had passed, Alice had handed over the fare, and they were on their way.

The journey was uneventful. At the *Ramshead* Alice and Maud lifted the baby, the handcart and all their purchases from the cart. Maud decided it would be easier to carry the baby and put the fabrics and some food packages in the handcart. This left two small packages. Cissy thought she could carry those, which left Alice free to pull the handcart.

They were all too tired to talk now, except the baby, who prattled and wriggled in his mother's arms, but they reached the little valley without mishap. After a drink and a short rest, Maud declared she would continue to her own home. The evenings were light now and with Alice's goods removed, except for the fabrics, and with some of Maud's own purchases in a bag slung across her body, there was room in the handcart for Jack. Maud said farewell and set off, promising to start work on the gowns the next day.

Alice and Cissy paddled in the stream to relieve their tired, dusty feet. As they ate a little bread and cheese, Cissy said, "I know we are going to the Baron's castle, and now that you are coming with me, I don't mind so much, but it can't be in as nice a place as here, can it, Alice?"

"There must be a lot of nice places to live, and the castle might be in a beautiful one. I think what I will find hard will be living inside a building with a lot of other people. We are not accustomed to having people around us all the time."

"It will be better than when we have stayed in lodgings though, won't it? I never like doing that."

"Oh, I am sure it will be much better than that, and I'm sure you will come to like living there. There will be horses and chickens and probably pigs as well. There might be cows and sheep, and you will be able to have milk whenever you want it."

"It is exciting, Alice, but I am a bit afraid too. I'm so glad you are coming with me."

"Well," thought Alice, "I do have to go. Cissy will be heartbroken if I do not."

The month passed quickly. Two visits to Arkenthorpe—one to try the gowns, which Maud made beautifully, and second to collect them when finished. Alice had asked Thomas what Maud was paid for making a gown. Thomas wasn't too sure as she was often paid in goods rather than money, so Alice had to decide for herself.

Maud was thrilled by the amount Alice gave her and, at first protested that it was too much. However, Alice said that the Baron would be very happy with such an amount as it would partly recompense Maud for the food that she and Mary had provided when Alice had been ill.

Deciding which of their few possessions to take with them was not difficult, and the travel bag Alice had purchased would easily hold them all, except for Cissy's fishing net, which she insisted she must take. There would be one other bundle of the thin feather quilt and the rabbit skin cover from their bed, which Alice assumed they would need on the journey. She had no idea when she would return, so she would leave her cooking pot, tinderbox and utensils in a recess in the cave. The spinning wheel, the handcart and a few other possessions, she would store in the walls of the garden of Eden. She could put everything there, but as John had said he would visit the valley occasionally to keep the briars and nettles from taking over again, she would leave anything he might need in the main cave. She had told him that there was a hiding place at the back of the cave where she would leave her other things, so that he would not think they had been stolen.

Cissy had taken on the task of keeping a record of the days. She had found a piece of sandstone with which she could write a little, and every morning after she had visited the privy, she would pick up the stone and make a mark on a small rock then, below the mark, would write an 'M' if it was Monday, and so on. She had three complete weeks marked off so now, each day as she made the mark she would say, "I wonder if he will come today?"

It was on the afternoon of the fifth 'M' for Monday when she looked up from helping Alice to gather greens and saw the Baron leading Merlin carefully along the narrow track down into the valley.

"Alice," she shrieked, "he's here! The Baron has come."

Putting down her basket, she ran to meet him. Remembering her manners just in time, she stopped a few feet in front of him and dropped a curtsey.

The Baron put out his hand and raised her. "You seem happy to see me, Cecily. Are you well?"

"Yes, my lord."

"Are you ready for your big adventure?"

"Yes. I have a new gown and boots and so does Alice. I think it is going to be a very long walk to your castle."

"Oh, you will not have to walk all the way, my child. For much of the journey you will be riding on Merlin with me."

Cissy's mouth opened wide. "Ohhhh . . . right up there on Merlin?"

"Yes. Do you think you are brave enough?"

"Oh yes, my lord."

As the Baron tethered Merlin to the hawthorn tree, Alice came to join them.

"Welcome, my lord. Have you had a good journey?"

"Thank you, yes. The wind was strong in places, but with only an occasional shower, we have remained dry and made good progress. We arrived in Skipton, from the abbey, this morning.

"Cissy tells me she is ready for the adventure, but what about you Alice? Will you come with us?"

"Yes, my lord. I will come."

"I am pleased, Alice. It will help Cecily a great deal to have you with her. Also, I will not have to hire a companion for her for the journey."

"Perhaps I can offer you a drink while we talk, my lord."

They sat, once more, outside the cave. Cissy sometimes came to ask a question but was more interested in talking to Merlin, excited, but slightly nervous, that she would be riding on him.

"I plan to leave in three days, Alice, and I would like to complete the journey in four days. I had thought about hiring a cart again, but there are a number of small bridges over the many rivers and streams, which are too narrow for a cart to pass over. I do not want to have to stay on the larger roads, as it will add many miles to our journey. Colum is with me and we have brought an extra pony with us. It is steady and reliable, so I hope you will be able to ride it. We will not hurry you and I am certain you will not find riding it difficult or uncomfortable after a few miles."

Alice herself wasn't so certain but it was clear that she must try, otherwise the journey would be interminable.

"Thank you, my lord. I will do my best."

They continued to talk about the journey, her luggage and Cissy's excitement.

The Baron then spoke seriously. "Alice, as you know I am grateful that you are coming with us, and I have gathered from conversations with you and Cissy that you do not have a family around you—only good friends. Will you be leaving anyone here who is important to you?"

"Only my friends—Maud and Thomas, John and Mary. I have no kinsfolk."

"How is that? What is your surname?"

"My surname is Moore. My mother was Agnes Moore and I have kept her name." Alice saw a quickly concealed look of surprise in the Baron's eyes. "I do not know who my father was. My mother had promised to tell me some day, but she died in an accident before she had done so.

"My mother was cook to Squire Thorpe—not the present squire, but his father. We lived at the Manor in Arkenthorpe, in a small room off the kitchen. The old Squire was good to us, and I often played with his younger son, Edmund, who was close to me in age. Sometimes, when Edmund was being tutored, I was allowed to sit in with him, which is how I learned to read and write. Outside the house I played with Maud and John who were the children of the gardener at the Manor. Maud became a seamstress and John followed his father into the garden.

"After my mother died, I could have stayed at the manor as the cook, but certain things were said which made me decide to leave. I have lived here ever since."

"Your life has not been an easy one, Alice, but I can see how you would have compassion for my child. She too had lost her mother through death and had no means of knowing who her father was."

Alice smiled. "But at least, my lord, that mystery has now been solved for Cissy."

"Yes, it has. Would you wish to discover who your own father was?"

"I don't know, my lord. All my mother said was that he was a good man and had died many years ago. No-one at the Manor ever mentioned the matter in my hearing. Sometimes I think it would be good to know. Most times, though, I am content to be Alice Moore and not concern myself with the past."

"You are right, and now we must return to our discussions of the immediate future. Today is Monday. We will start our journey on Thursday. Colum will bring the horses to the oak tree and wait there while I come here to help you and Cecily to carry your possessions. We will only travel as far as Bolton Priory on the first day, so that you can become accustomed to riding. On each of the following days we will travel further, if all goes well. We have many hours of daylight and if this weather holds, the tracks will be firm.

"Will you be going to Arkenthorpe to take leave of your friends? Do they know your plans?"

"Yes, my lord. We will go tomorrow. If we are to see John and Mary, we must be there for midday when John breaks for his meal, and then see Mary when she has finished serving at the Manor. We can see Maud and Thomas at any time of day. Thomas is a wheelwright and has his own workshop behind their cottage."

After a few more minutes, the Baron walked across to Cissy, and father and child wandered around the small valley together, then climbed to a vantage point to look out at the wider world.

"That is the way to Arkenthorpe," Cissy pointed, "and that way we go to gather berries. Which way is the way to your castle?"

"We will go towards Skipton at the start of the journey. We will continue eastwards, then after a while we will turn northwards, which is that way," said the Baron, pointing away from the sun. "Then later, we will again turn to the East. The journey will take about four days."

"I do like our home here, Papa. Is your castle in such a pretty place?"

"Perhaps not a pretty place, but I still think you will like it. From a turret roof you can see a very long way. You can see hills and woods and part of a river all from the same point. If you watch for a while you will often see deer or foxes."

"Do you have rabbits too?"

"Yes, I keep rabbits, so you can always see them."

A puzzled look crossed Cissy's face, but passed unnoticed.

Well Cecily, it is almost evening and I must return to Skipton, but I will come on Thursday to collect you and Alice, and we will start our journey to your other home."

A few minutes later the Baron departed, but unknown to Alice he made a short detour to Arkenthorpe.

When Alice and Cissy reached Arkenthorpe village next morning, they soon realised they were attracting more attention than usual but, apart from the usual greetings, nothing was said until they reached the wheelwright's. Young Tom was first to rush to them.

"Cissy, I've seen your Pa. He came here yesterday. Everyone in the village saw him. He's got a magnici . . . . well, a great horse!"

"Yes," Cissy acknowledged, "that's Merlin, and I'll be riding on him with my Papa when we go to his castle."

"We didn't know the Baron was coming to Arkenthorpe yesterday," Alice said with surprise.

"Yes, he came to see us," and Tom launched into a report of the excitement the Baron's visit had caused.

Cissy and Alice both had difficulties working out just what the excited boy was telling them, but it seemed to be that, in the late afternoon, the Baron, riding on Merlin, had moved slowly down the village street, attracting a group of children as he went. He stopped and asked if one of them could tell him where to find Thomas the wheelwright, whereupon they had all told him at once. He had taken out his purse and removed some small coins. Then he had spoken to one of the group, called Ned, and asking if he could be trusted, had given him the coins to share with the others. There had been one for each of them.

"The Baron thanked the boys, then came to see Dad and Mam," Tom said triumphantly.

"Pa'll tell you the rest. I'll tell him you're here."

Thomas came out of the workshop to join them and by now Maud had come out of the cottage. They were obviously thrilled too, and Thomas, with occasional interruptions from Maud, took up the story.

"I was shaving a spoke to fit into a damaged wheel when I heard a horse blowing through his nostrils; I put down my tools and came forward as the rider dismounted.

"Good evening, sir, I said. Can I be of service?"

"Are you Thomas, whose wife is called Maud?"

"I am sir."

"You are friends of Alice and Cissy?"

"Indeed we are." Then I suddenly realised who this fine gentleman must be, "And you, my lord, must be Cissy's father," I said.

"'I am,' said the Baron 'and I am pleased to meet you Thomas. Is your wife about?'"

Maud interrupted. "The rest of us in the cottage had heard the horse and the voices and came out to see what was happening.

"I am, my lord," I said, and curtseyed, as best I could with Jack in my arms."

"'It is good to meet you too, Maud,' he said. The bairns were all staring at this fine gentleman and his beautiful horse.

"'I think Alice has told you, she has agreed to travel with Cissy to her new home. We will start the journey on Thursday.' "Then he said you would be coming today to say farewell."

"We told him that we will be sad to see you go, but that we are pleased that he has found his daughter."

"Then he said that he knew that we were your good friends and that as you, Alice, have no family, he thought he should present himself to us so that we know who you're travelling with. He told us that he will care for you while ever you are with him and that he had promised that you can return here any time you want. He said he is really grateful to you for your care of Cissy and to us for helping you.

"He asked if he could meet John and Mary too. I told him that John would have finished in the Manor garden but Mary would be busy until after the evening meal at the Manor. John would most likely be working on his strip of land down towards the river. 'Perhaps one of you would guide me there' he said."

"Perhaps you will let me tell the story now," chipped in Thomas. "I will take you myself, my lord, I said. So he said farewell to Maud and the children and leading his horse, he walked down the village with me. The news that a great gentleman was in the village had spread like fire. Everyone seemed to be busy at their doors or had some errand that brought them into the street. I could feel everyone's eyes on me as I escorted the Baron down to the field strips.

"Most folk had returned home for the evening, so only two or three figures were in view when me and the Baron reached the field.

"'That be John over there, my lord,' I said, pointing to where John was busy hoeing. The Baron tethered his horse to a nearby tree and asked me to walk down with 'im.

"As we walked carefully down the field, I called to John. He straightened up, stretching to ease his back, then seeing us coming, he turned and walked towards us.

"'John is crippled, I see', said the Baron, so I told 'im about John being wounded fighting for the Yorkists in one of them big battles, and 'ow he's tired by the evening so 'is limp is worse.

"This be the Baron, John. The one that's Cissy's father, I said."

"My lord," said John, and touched his forelock.

"The Baron greeted him and told 'im he wished to meet 'im for two reasons. Alice and Cissy, he said, have told me of your being a good friend and of the help you have given them. Then he said something like 'you know, I am taking my daughter to my home now, and Alice will come with us for a while at least. I understand also that you will be keeping an eye on her home while she is away. I know that you and your wife, and Thomas and Maud will be concerned for Alice, so I thought it right that you should meet the man who is taking her from you. I wish you to have quiet minds, knowing that she will be respected and cared for.'

"'That's real kind of you, my lord,' said John. 'We're all fond of Alice and young Cissy—she's a bright little thing, and very good at telling you what she thinks, as I am sure you will find.'"

Here, Cissy pulled a face at Thomas.

"And your Pa said 'I think I have discovered that already, John. She absolutely insists that the fishing net you made for her goes with us. She has already shown me how well she can use it.'

"We were stunned, Alice, that such a great man would consider how we felt, but we thanked him for his assurances. We had all been walking slowly back to where the 'orse was tethered. Before mounting, the Baron opened his saddlebag and removed a small pouch. He mounted, then turned to John and said, 'I am sorry not to have met your wife, John, but offer her my regards. Here, take this pouch. You and Thomas share its contents between you as you think fit.'

"He clicked to the 'orse and, raising his hand in farewell, he trotted briskly back towards the village and on his way.

"When John opened the pouch he gave a whistle. 'Phew, Thomas lad, there's good money in here.'

"So on Sunday afternoon, John and Mary, Maud and me are going to meet and decide on the best way to use the money."

Maud had managed to stay silent through her husband's telling of the great event, but now she turned to Alice.

"Yesterday was a strange day, I can tell you. It'll be a while, I think, before we decide what to do with the money, but it will make life a lot more comfortable for all of us. Cissy, your father is a very kind and great man. Not many great folk think about such as us. We will miss you and Alice 'til she comes back, but you will grow up to be an important lady. Try to be as kind as your Papa, won't you."

"I will try," said Cissy, very bemused by all this. Then as the adults returned to their various duties, and Alice went into the cottage with Maud and Joan, she ran off with Tom to the duck pond, with Lucas trailing after them.

Chapter Nine

The pony Alice was riding was a Dales pony, such as roamed wild in the area, and was a gentle, steady beast named Freya. Alice discovered that Freya happily followed Colum's horse with no instructions from her. Another pony, almost identical to Freya, and with the unimaginative name of Bags, carried the party's luggage. Merlin, and Colum's horse, Acorn, would often chafe at the bit, but for the first day, Freya was allowed to set the pace and Alice soon learned how to sit comfortably.

Dismounting at the Priory for their night's rest, her legs almost gave way beneath her, but she soon recovered. She ached on rising next morning, but by midday the ill effects were wearing off and the pace of their journey picked up. Cissy was very pleased with her vantage point, sitting up in front of her father on Merlin, frequently questioning him about things she saw.

As soon as Skipton had been left behind, Alice was on strange territory, and as her confidence in Freya grew, she was able to look about her more. For a while the land around was the familiar mixture of green valleys, woods and rocky outcrops on the hillsides, with the occasional small village. Then the valleys became wider and flatter, with frequent small streams to be crossed. Fortunately, most of them were clear and shallow, with the water rippling across stony beds and the horses crossed willingly and with ease. The high ground they next rode across was less wooded and it was frequently possible to see great distances.

This moorland seemed so open that Alice at first felt nervous but Colum explained that, in many ways, it was safer than the dales because there were fewer hiding places from where travellers could be ambushed. Alice had not thought about such dangers until now, but after Colum's comment she realised that there could still be vagabonds and disgruntled soldiers roaming the area. No wonder the Baron wanted Cissy on his own horse. He could not risk being parted from her again.

Fortunately, their day was not troubled by any ill-doers.

The second night was spent in a town called Knaresborough, at an inn. The Baron's presence and money secured them decent lodging and food, and the horses were cared for too. But conditions had been better the previous night at the Priory. The town's buildings were clustered along the banks of the river and up the side of the lower slopes. A ferryman plied his trade and Alice imagined that he would not be a poor man, as even in the short time she was watching him, it was clear he had a constant queue of customers on both banks.

Before the evening meal, the Baron took them to see the cave on the banks of the River Nidd, where the hermit, Robert the healer, had lived three hundred years ago. Robert had been a White Monk, as the Cistercians were known, because they wore habits of undyed sheep's wool. Although he had lived a very simple life in his cave, his fame as a healer had spread far and wide, and pilgrims still came from many parts of Britain and from countries in Europe to Knaresborough to see where the holy man had lived.

On the third day of the journey they travelled more easily. They met the old Roman road, Dere Street, and turned northwards along it. They met other travellers, all ranks of persons, taking advantage of the bright, June day. Before the end of the day they had left Dere Street again, turning eastward, and once more found themselves surrounded by uplands of wild moors and forested slopes. That night they were accommodated by a small Abbey where the food was good, and where they slept well, waking fully refreshed for what would hopefully be the final day of the journey.

Alice had so far enjoyed the journey and Freya had been very well-behaved. Today they were riding on fairly high level ground, with extensive woodlands on the slopes to their left. After a while it became clear that the horses were uneasy, but there seemed no reason for their uncasc.

"Perhaps a storm is on the way, my lord," said Colum.

"Perhaps. Let us quicken our pace a little."

They urged the horses forward but had gone only a short distance when, without warning, a red deer came bounding out of the woodland, straight in front of Colum's horse. Acorn reared violently, almost unseating Colum and startling Freya, who turned and bolted back along the way they had just come. Alice flung her arms round the animal's neck and hung on. Fortunately, Colum had quickly regained control of Acorn and he came galloping to the rescue—Freya's fastest speed being no match for the larger, younger animal. Leaning over, Colum grabbed Freya's rein, which Alice had let go of in her desperation to hold on to something more substantial. With his firm pull on the reign as Acorn slowed, and Colum's calm if breathless voice, Freya quickly slowed too. She came to a halt, blowing heavily, with Alice shaken but still on her back.

Colum had turned the horses and started to walk them slowly back, when he heard the Baron shout, "Hold! Hold it there!"

Alice and Colum were horrified to see the Baron, one arm still holding on to Cissy, reaching for his sword as a man, dagger in hand was backing towards the trees, pulling Bags the packhorse after him. At the same moment they saw a second man emerging from the trees just behind the Baron, also with dagger in hand.

"Stay here", Colum ordered Alice, as he dropped Freya's rein and spurred Acorn forward.

Alice watched the scene in front of her. As Colum reached the group, he drew his dagger, whereupon the man holding Bags let go of the horse and backed away. Colum called Bags and the pony came slowly to him. The second man now edged towards the first and Colum called, "Behind you, my lord!"

The Baron wheeled Merlin with a word of command, and faced the second ruffian. At once the man sheathed his dagger, putting his arms up in surrender. The other did the same.

The Baron returned his sword to its scabbard, but Colum still held his dagger. Alice judged it was safe to rejoin the others and moved Freya slowly forward. She was very shaken.

The two ruffians were an abject and sorry sight as the Baron, on Merlin, towered over them.

"Colum."

"My lord?"

"Is Alice safe?"

"Yes, my lord, she is coming to join us now. She is shaken but not hurt."

"Good. Take Cecily from me and let her go to Alice."

Colum dismounted and lifted Cissy from her father's arm. He placed her on the ground and she ran to meet Alice.

The Baron now dismounted and stood in front of the two men. "What do you have to say for yourselves?" he demanded. "Why try to attack us? You must surely have known you could not win such an encounter."

The larger of the two men spoke. "We was not attacking you, sir. We was trying to catch a wild boar piglet in the forest, but me and Rob aren't good at hunting. It ran everywhere, going one way then t'other, then disappeared. We'd got nearer the edge of the forest than we knowed. Then either us or t'wee piggy startled the deer, which ran out and frightened your horses. Till then we didn't know you was there, sir."

"Then why draw your daggers and try to steal my packhorse?"

"Wasn't going to steal the horse, sir," chipped in the one referred to as Rob. "I thought a pack might have victuals in and my dagger was to cut the strap."

"And you," said the Baron, turning to the first man, "why did you draw your dagger?"

"We've been in the fighting, sir. I guess I just did it, 'cos that's what you do when there's trouble."

To Alice's surprise, the Baron suddenly gave a fleeting smile. "So, you are not footpads out to steal from passing travellers?"

"No, sir, no," they protested.

"You are hungry men?"

"Yes, sir. That's why we went after the wee piggy."

"You were very fortunate that the piggy's mother did not come after you. You would not have won that encounter either. When did you last eat?"

"T'wern't yesterday, were it Dickon? Must have been day afore that when we caught the fish."

"Where are you going?"

"Home, sir. We want to get to the sea, then we can follow the shore till we reach home."

"On the shore there's allus food."

"Are you fishermen?"

"Rob is, but I make nets", said Dickon. "We had to go with the maister to the fighting. with a lot of other men from our village. Maister was killed and so were a lot of others."

"Aye, my brother too," said Rob sadly.

"Are you family men?"

"I am," said Dickon. "I've a wife and three bairns".

"No, sir," said Rob, but my brother was. I've got to go home and tell his wife that he won't be coming back. There's just one bairn."

"Sir, ... my lord," said Dickon, looking very uncomfortable, "we're real sorry about what just happened, and real glad that the lady and the bairn are not hurt."

"I believe you are," said the Baron. "Alice, I think you know which of our packs has our food for the journey. Will you open it please?"

Alice crossed to Bags, leaving Cissy holding Freya's rein. She unfastened a pack and opened the thong tying it.

"What do we have, Alice?"

"Bread, a ham and cheese; oh, and some oat and honey cakes."

"Very well. Please take a knife—Colum's dagger will do—and cut the bread in half, and the cheese too."

"Do you have a pack?" he asked the men.

"Yes, I dropped it in t' bushes when I tried to grab the 'orse."

"Fetch it."

The man swiftly collected a very dirty sack, tied with coarse twine.

"Have you a skin for ale?"

"Yes, my lord." He produced a very empty, scruffy skin from inside the sack.

"What do you have that food can be wrapped in?"

"Nothing, my lord."

"Alice, do you think the cloth around our food can be torn into two pieces which will still be of usable size?"

"It would be difficult, my lord, but we could wrap our bread and our cheese in the same cloth and we would then have an empty cloth."

"Of course. Do that, please, Alice, then wrap half the bread and half the cheese in the spare cloth and, if there is room, some thick pieces of ham. Colum, take the skin and pour some ale from our skin into it."

He turned to Rob and Dickon. "I have accepted your story as the truth. I do not think you are evil men. When you reach the coast, will you be travelling North or South to reach your home?"

"North."

"We should reach our destination, the castle at Muirhill, before nightfall and food and drink will await us there. Take this food to assuage your hunger—it should be sufficient for two days. If you follow this track by the edge of the forest, in the same direction as we are going, sometime tomorrow you will come to a very tall pine tree at a place where the track becomes two. Follow the left track, which goes slightly towards the West, and in a few miles a castle will come into view.

"Come to the castle gate and say Baron Muirhill told you to ask for Simon the Factor. He will be expecting you. I do not have need of a net maker or a fisherman but, if you are willing to turn your hands to other tasks, you can work for me for three weeks. There is building work in progress and many things to be loaded or carried from place to place. For those three weeks you will eat with the other labourers and sleep where they sleep. At the end of that time, if you have worked well, you will be paid in coins. You will then be shown the way to the coast to complete your journey home. Is this plan agreeable to you?"

The two men were standing open-mouthed and seemed struck dumb. Eventually Dickon stammered, "Yes, my lord . . . . very agreeable . . . . yes, very agreeable."

"Then we will mount and continue our journey. Come Cecily, let me put you up on Merlin. Alice, are you ready to ride Freya again?"

"Yes, my lord."

"Good. Only a few hours more and our journey will be over."

As the little party started to move away, Rob suddenly found his tongue and called out, "Thank you, my lord. May God bless you."

The Baron raised his hand in acknowledgement.

The rest of the journey passed peacefully. They reached the pine tree by late afternoon and soon after taking the left track, a castle came into view. The Baron stopped on the brow of a hill and pointed across the open countryside.

"There, Cecily, there is your new home."

"It is a real castle, Papa. I can see the turrets. It still looks a long way away."

"It is not so far. It will disappear from view as we drop down into the valley ahead, but when we next see it, it will be very close. While we are here on top of this hill, Colum will light a small fire in that brazier. Someone at the castle will see it and light one on the castle roof. That way they know that we will be home tonight and everything will be made ready for us."

Colum had been busy filling the brazier with dry twigs and now he got out the tinderbox and some kindling and struck a stream of sparks. As soon as he was sure the kindling was alight, he pushed it in near the bottom of the heap of twigs and in seconds there was a loud crackling sound and a flame shot up. For a minute or two the flame burnt brightly, then began to die down. Colum put some damp moss and wood on to the glowing embers and a cloud of smoke replaced the flames.

"Now, watch the castle roof, Cecily," said Colum, "and tell me when you see a flame or some smoke."

Cissy watched and watched, then suddenly with great excitement, she pointed. "Look, there's a flame; there's a flame!"

Sure enough, Alice could see it too. Again the flames turned to smoke, and Colum began to put out their own fire by covering the embers with more damp moss. Only when he was sure that the fire was completely out did they mount the horses and start the final part of their journey.

Chapter Ten

Seen from the outside, Muirhill Castle was grim and had clearly been built at a time when fear of attack was very real. It was surrounded by a moat, but the drawbridge was down and the portcullis up to welcome its lord.

Once inside the curtain wall, however, everything became more friendly. There were many people going about their business, but all stopped to bow or curtsey to the Baron and regarded Cissy and Alice with curiosity.

As they dismounted, people appeared to unload the pack pony and take the saddlebags from the other horses, while the Baron, taking Cissy by the hand, led the little group through a wide doorway. A man and woman were waiting to greet them.

"Welcome home, brother," said the man, who had a strong look of the Baron about him.

"Thank you, Stephen. It is good to be home again and this time it is a joyful homecoming, as I bring my daughter with me. Cecily, this is my brother and your uncle, Stephen. He looks after the business of the castle for me when I am away from home.

Cecily curtseyed solemnly.

"This lady is his wife, your Aunt Olivia."

Again, Cecily curtseyed.

"I also present Alice Moore to you both. It is to Alice that I owe a great debt, for since finding Cecily and saving her life, she has cared for her as her own."

Alice curtsied deeply and felt very thankful that she was dressed appropriately in her new gown and boots.

"Welcome, Alice," said Stephen. Olivia simply acknowledged her with an inclination of her head.

They all now entered the great hall where a huge table was being prepared for the evening meal. On a raised daïs at the far end of the hall, a shorter table was already prepared and some chairs and long benches set at it.

"We can eat as soon as you are ready, brother Michael," said Olivia, addressing the Baron.

"Allow us a short time to remove the dust of our journey, then we will be glad to eat.

"Come Cecily, come Alice. Our quarters are on the floor above here, up the stairs in the corner of the daïs."

A stone, spiral stairway led to a narrow passage with rooms along one side.

"The first chamber is mine and the next one was your Mama's. This third one has been prepared for you, and the one beyond is being used to store things at present."

The heavy curtain across the doorway was pushed back and as the Baron ushered them gently into the room, a young servant girl, looking no more than twelve years old, dropped a deep curtsey.

"Ah, you must be the new chamber maid. What is your name, child?"

"Tilly, my lord," she whispered.

"Well Tilly, this lady is Miss Alice and this is my daughter, Cecily. They have had a long journey and are tired. I will leave you to help them to refresh themselves before we all eat. I will come back soon to take them to dine."

The Baron turned and left for his own chamber.

"I would like to greet you properly," Cissy said anxiously to Tilly, "but first tell me where is the privy?"

"It's right at the end of the passage. Come, I'll show you."

Alice watched them go, so that she would know where it was herself, then she looked around their room. Someone had brought their travelling bag up and Tilly had obviously been starting to sort their things out. There was a good, thick mattress and a feather pillow on a raised, wooden frame, criss-crossed with bands and covered with a woollen blanket. It was not as wide as the bed they had had at the cot, but it would suffice. A wooden bowl and a small pail of water stood on a table and a towel lay on the back of a chair. A clothes chest stood open with Cecily's few things already in it.

Alice removed her travelling shawl and looked for somewhere to put it, finally laying it on a wooden stool set just below the window. She then tipped some water into the bowl and splashed her hands and face. She was using the towel when the girls returned.

Tilly stopped in the doorway when she saw Alice, blushed, and looked uncomfortable. "I'm sorry Miss Alice, but this is not your room. I was just putting your things back into the travel bag for you to take downstairs."

Cissy stared at the girl. "Of course this is Alice's room. We have the same room."

Tilly looked even more uncomfortable. "That isn't what I was told, Miss."

"But Alice has got to be here with me," Cissy's lip trembled and her eyes filled with tears. "We are always together. She is my Alice."

"Hush, Cissy, it is not Tilly's fault. We will sort it out. Wash your face and hands. Papa will be here in a minute to take us down to dinner."

Alice smiled at the frightened maid servant. "Don't worry, Tilly. You have not done wrong. It will be alright."

"Oh, Miss Alice, the Baron's coming back." Tilly made herself as small as possible at the end of the room.

"May I enter?" asked the Baron.

Cissy wiped her face and her eyes with the towel, but it was still clear that she was weeping.

"Oh, what is this?" asked the Baron. "I did not expect you to be unhappy tonight child. What has upset you?"

"Tilly says this room is only for me and that Alice has to go downstairs. I want Alice here with me Papa. Please Papa, we must be together."

"Of course Alice should be here with you. There has been a misunderstanding which will be put right straight way. I will speak to your Aunt Olivia."

By now, Tilly was weeping quietly in the corner. As Cissy wiped her arm across her eyes, she turned to Tilly. "Don't cry, Tilly. Papa will make things right."

"Why don't we go to the Great Hall and eat. I am sure we must all be hungry."

Alice and Cissy followed the Baron down the spiral stairs and to the table on the daïs. Stephen, Olivia and their two boys were already standing there. A servant was about to pull out the large, central chair for the Baron when, with a hand gesture, the Baron motioned him to wait.

"Olivia, a word please."

"My lord, Baron."

Quietly the Baron said, "You seem to have misunderstood my instructions, sister. The chamber you have had prepared for Cecily has no provision for Alice, and I also see that a chair has not been provided for her here at this table."

"My lord, Baron," hissed Olivia, "it hardly seemed meet to put Alice with the family. I have placed her there at the top of the long table, next to your manservant, Colum."

The Baron felt anger rising in him, but coldly and quietly he said, "I will say it now, and I expect to be obeyed. Alice is not a servant. She may not be family in the accepted sense, but she has loved and cared for my daughter, as a mother, for five years, and that entitles her to a seat at this table. You will give immediate instructions for another chair to be brought and for a good bed to be provided in Cecily's room. See to it!"

The colour had risen in Olivia's cheeks and her eyes flashed, but she turned and beckoned a servant to her. A chair was found and placed to the Baron's left, with Cecily's chair between. Stephen, Olivia and their children were to the Baron's right. The Baron took his place and everyone in the hall sat down. The meal was served.

The noise level was tremendous as everyone talked and laughed, and with the sounds of wooden and metal serving dishes being moved around the tables. When Alice and Cissy tried to talk, they found it difficult to hear one another. The food was good and plentiful but neither of them was able to eat much. The Baron smiled at Cissy when she said, "There is too much food, Papa. I will try harder tomorrow."

A short time afterwards the Baron observed her eyelids closing, then jerking open again as she started to fall forward.

"Are you very tired, my child? Do you wish to go to your room and sleep?"

"Yes, please, Papa."

"Very well, but just wait a few moments more. I must introduce you to all my people here."

The Baron signalled to the Steward in charge of the dining room. The man took a heavy stick and banged it loudly against a metal plate hanging from a chain. The loud ringing sound it produced made Cissy put her hands over her ears but, in only a few seconds, everyone in the Great Hall was quiet and turning to look at the Baron.

He got to his feet and addressed everyone.

"My people, it is good to be back home. As most of you will now know, my long search has been rewarded. My lost child has been found and has returned with me today. Here she is."

He bent and picked Cissy up, standing her on the seat of her chair. "I introduce my daughter Cecily to you."

Loud applause and cheers erupted from the floor of the hall as Cissy stood, bewildered, in front of them all. Not knowing what else to do, she curtseyed, which brought more cheers. The Baron held up his hand for quiet.

"Cecily is only young and after her long journey is very tired and now wishes to retire to bed. But, before she does, there is another person I must introduce. Miss Alice Moore found Cecily as a tiny child, alongside the body of her mother, my wife, whose remains we buried earlier this year. Alice rescued the child, having no idea whose child she was. She took her home and has cared for her lovingly ever since. Eventually, with the help of a priest, a link was established between the child Alice had found and my searching, and by God's grace, we were re-united."

He turned to Alice. "Alice, please stand."

Alice stood, her head slightly bowed.

"I present to you Miss Alice, who is to be a member of my household for as long as she wishes."

Again, there was applause. Alice could not curtsey because of the table in front of her, but she blushed, raised her head, then bent it in acknowledgement. The Baron sat down and, as people turned their attention once more to their food, Alice took Cissy by the hand.

"Say goodnight to your Papa, and to your Uncle and Aunt. I think we both need sleep."

"Goodnight Papa. Goodnight Uncle and Aunt."

The Baron smiled at his daughter. "Goodnight Cecily. I hope you sleep well. The room should now be ready for both you and Alice. Tomorrow I will show you around your new home. God bless you both."

"Goodnight, my lord," said Alice.

The room was indeed ready. Another wooden base had been laid at the side of the first, with mattress, pillow and blanket. Another clothes chest had appeared and Tilly was there waiting for them, smiling.

"I hope everything is alright now, Miss Cecily, Miss Alice. I have now been told the room is to be for both of you."

"It looks fine, Tilly," Alice said. "I am sure we will both soon be asleep."

"If you need anything Miss, anything at all, you must call me."

"Where do you sleep?" asked Cissy.

"Across the passage, Miss."

Cissy looked out of the doorway. "Across the passage—where?"

"Here," said Tilly, going to a recess in the opposite wall of the passage.

"Oh, yes. Look Alice, it is a bit like the cave. Won't you be frightened, sleeping there on your own? Where is your mattress?"

"I won't be frightened. It will be good sleeping here on my own, instead of with lots of others in the hall. My sleeping mat is rolled up in the corner here."

She came back into the room. "Now, let me help you to unfasten your dress. There is a new bed-gown here for you."

"I can undress myself," said Cissy proudly, "but as I am very tired, I would like your help tonight."

"There is a bedgown for you too, Miss Alice," said Tilly, pointing to the second clothes chest.

"That is kind of them," said Alice, wondering who had made this gesture.

Minutes later, Tilly, drawing the door curtain after her, withdrew to set up her own little domain, while Alice and Cissy sank gratefully down into their mattresses.

Cissy gave a big yawn and stretched out her hand to grasp Alice's. "I like Papa, but I don't think I like his castle. I wish we were back at home."

"I am sure things will seem better after you have had a long sleep," Alice replied, trying to reassure herself as much as Cissy.

"G'night, Alice".

"Goodnight Cissy."

Sometime later, the Baron, before going to his own bed, drew the curtain gently to one side. By the light of his candle, he could see his daughter, her face now serene as she slept. One arm was flung out to one side, while the other was stretched across to rest on Alice. The tired look had gone from Alice's face and she too was sound asleep. Quietly, he replaced the curtain, noticed that Tilly was at her post, and retired to his chamber with a joyful heart, thanking God for his great mercy.

A shaft of sunlight was streaming across the room from the high, narrow window, when Alice awoke next morning. It was a few seconds before she remembered where she was. Cissy was still sleeping soundly as Alice slipped through the curtain to visit the privy. The smell from it was strong, although not as bad as from the one at the lodgings in Skipton, but she was glad to replace the lid over the hole.

Tilly woke as Alice returned to the bedchamber. "Good morning, Miss Alice, can I help you at all?"

"Good morning, Tilly. No, I think there is nothing I need for now. When Cissy wakes we will have something to eat. Will there be food in the Hall?"

"Yes, Miss, but I can bring some to you here if you would like."

"What will there be to drink?"

"Ale or milk, Miss, and there'll be bread, or oatcakes, or porage."

"Milk would be lovely. Could you bring some for Cissy and me to share, and an oatcake each? It will be nice to start today quietly—more like we are used to."

"Yes Miss. Shall I go now?"

"No, wait a while until Cissy is awake. Why don't you go and break your fast, Tilly, then bring our food? That will be soon enough."

"Thank you, Miss. I won't take long."

Tilly disappeared down the winding stairs. Alice sat on the chair wondering what the day would bring. People were already moving in the castle, so she dressed and tidied her hair. Some jackdaws were calling noisily outside the window and Cissy stirred, and opened her eyes.

"Is it morning?"

"Yes, it's morning. I think you have slept well."

"I'm awake now and my belly is making noises. I'm hungry."

"Tilly is going to bring us some oatcakes and milk. I thought it would be nice to have a quiet breakfast. Get dressed and I will comb your hair. Your Papa might want to see you soon."

They had eaten and had just decided to go down to the hall, when the Baron appeared.

"Good morning, Alice. Good morning Cecily. Did you both sleep well?"

"Yes thank you, my lord. I hope you are well this morning."

"I am indeed well. Now, Cecily, do you have a kiss for your Papa before he takes you around his castle?"

"Of course, Papa." Cissy allowed herself to be lifted up to kiss him.

"You must come with us, Alice. There are many things to see but, first Cecily, you must meet your cousins. We will just be in time to see Harry before he starts his morning lessons with his tutor."

They went downstairs to the daïs at the end of the Great Hall, then up the steps at the other side. The passage and rooms were like the ones they had just left.

"This first one," said the Baron, "is the schoolroom where Harry studies. The next one is the bedchamber of your Uncle Stephen and Aunt Olivia. The next one is the nursery where your youngest cousin, baby Eleanor and her nursemaid live, and the one at the end is the bedchamber of Harry and Edward. Edward is only four years of age and has not started lessons yet. Of course, Cecily, you must not go into these rooms unless invited to do so, but you may go into the schoolroom when Harry is not having a lesson.

"Now, let us see if he is here."

"Yes, my lord," said a child's voice. "I am here, but Brother James has not yet come."

Cissy got a better look at the bigger of the two boys she had seen last night at dinner. Harry was a nice-looking boy. He had straight, dark hair, cut short and with a fringe. He was dressed in hose of a grey-green colour and a white shirt with green lacing. He was a few inches taller than her, so she guessed he must be older too.

"As you know, Harry, this is Cecily, your cousin. She is seven years old. Today, I am showing her around her home, but in a few days' time, if Brother James is agreeable, I hope she will join you for some of your lessons."

"But, my lord, she is a girl. I didn't think girls had lessons."

"Some girls like to learn, Harry. Cecily already knows her letters and can do simple arithmetic. I think she will enjoy learning.

"Ah, here is Brother James."

"Good morning, Baron. I fear I am a little late on this beautiful morning. My donkey is unwell and I have walked from the monastery.

"I see, my lord, that your daughter is here at last. God be praised."

"Yes, Brother, God be praised indeed. I am giving today to showing her around her home. This woman is Alice, of whom I have told you."

"It is good to meet you both," said the monk. "The Baron and I have offered prayers for you both many times."

"Now," said the Baron, "we must leave you to your pupil, but perhaps we may speak together before you return to the monastery."

They left Harry to his lesson and went towards the room where Edward was likely to be, but as they passed the nursery, it was clear that he was in there, arguing with someone.

"Good morning," called the Baron. "May we enter?"

The curtain was drawn back and inside young Edward, with an angry look on his face, was telling a servant in no uncertain terms that she should be fastening his clothes for him and not dressing the baby.

The servant, hearing the Baron and seeing the little group outside the curtain, looked flustered as she sat with the part-dressed baby on her lap. "Oh, my lord, forgive me, I cannot rise."

"Of course not. Do not concern yourself. What is all the noise about, Edward?"

"Want my clothes fastened! Want to go down!"

"Getting so angry is not a good way to get people to help you," said his uncle.

Cissy looked at her cross young cousin. "Shall I fasten your clothes for you?" Without waiting for an answer, she walked over to him and started to sort out the lacing on his shirt. Edward was stunned into silence.

"There," said Cissy a minute or so later, "I think that's right."

Edward looked at his cousin and smiled. "I am going down now. Do you want to come with me?"

"I can't just now," said Cissy. "Papa is showing me round the castle. Perhaps we can play later."

"Master Edward, you must ask your Mama before you go downstairs," said the nursery maid. "You must!"

Edward rushed out into the passage and was about to go straight past the door of his mother's chamber, when the Baron called sternly, "Edward, stop! Edward . . ."

The boy stopped. The Baron just looked down at him. Slowly, he came back a few steps and disappeared into his mother's room.

"Can I see the baby, please?" Cissy asked the maid.

"Yes Miss, you can." The maid sat the child up on her knee. The baby looked solemnly at her visitors and put her chubby fingers in her mouth. Alice guessed she was about a year old.

Cissy touched the other hand and stroked it gently. "Hello, baby cousin. You are pretty, aren't you?"

Slowly the baby removed her hand from her mouth, took hold of a strand of Cissy's hair with her wet little fingers and pulled hard.

"Ow!" said Cissy, disentangling it. Baby Eleanor laughed.

"Sorry, Miss," said the maid. "I'm afraid she loves to pull hair at the present. It was noses last week."

"It didn't hurt very much," said Cissy. "'bye baby. I'll see you again soon"

"Come along," said the Baron, "we will go down to the hall."

The hall looked even bigger now there were few people in it. Because it was a warm day the fire in the huge hearth had not been lit. They stood with their backs to the empty hearth while the Baron explained the layout of the room and pointed to the gallery where, on feast days, minstrels would play. The strong light from the morning sun shone in bright shafts from the narrow windows, highlighting whatever it struck, but causing other areas to be in deep shadow. It gave the hall a strange, unreal air, but also it reminded Alice of the shaft of light in the cave that had caused her to find her little Eden.

Next they visited the kitchens. Here a big fire was glowing and above it a huge spit was being turned by a boy who looked about ten years old. Cissy was amazed by the size of everything, especially the meat on the spit! It seemed to be the whole body of an animal.

"What is that, Papa?"

"It is a sheep. We will be eating roast mutton for dinner."

"It is so big! It must be heavy for that boy to turn. Did you know, Alice, that people eat sheep?"

"Yes," said Alice, "I did know. Remember that I told you my mother was cook to the Squire, and we lived in a room off the kitchen. That kitchen was much smaller, but there was a spit on which sheep and pigs were roasted."

"Have you not eaten mutton before, Cecily," her father asked?

Alice replied. "No my lord, she hasn't. Our meat was always rabbit, stock dove or, very occasionally, grouse. Just once, at market, we ate mutton with our bread, but Cissy would not have known it was sheep meat, and once or twice we have eaten a little fat bacon."

"Well, Cecily, there will be many new foods for you to try now."

They were glad to leave the heat and noise of the kitchen as the Baron led them outside.

Sitting on a large, stone bench, Alice and Cissy were at first confused by what they could see. The Baron explained that parts of the castle were very old indeed, but his father, his grandfather and, probably his father before him, had changed and added bits to the buildings and walls. At first they had done it to make the castle easier to defend, and to provide more room to shelter the peasants and other village people at times of attack. Then, in times of peace, parts had been made more comfortable for the Baron and his family to live in. Now, the Baron explained, he himself was making changes and soon there would be a kind of manor house, within the castle walls, where the family would live. The great hall would still be used for feasts but a smaller hall with a fire-place and a flue to remove the smoke, would form part of the new house and on most days they would eat there. There would be a solar with bedchambers and rooms for use during the day. There would be more light from larger windows with fine bone in them. There would be new kitchens and a buttery to store food, and there would be a small, private chapel for personal and family devotions. Its windows would have stained glass.

"Come," said the Baron, rising from the bench, "come and see the place where it is being built."

As they followed the Baron, the tapping of hammers against chisels could be heard and the voices of men calling to each other. Walking around the end of a stone barn, they came to an area where walls were being built. Men were moving large pieces of stone to masons who were cutting them into smaller pieces and shaping them ready for building. Two walls were almost complete and beautiful arched spaces for the windows could be seen.

As they approached, a man came over to them, bowing slightly to the Baron.

"Good day, my lord."

"Good day, Simon. All seems to be going well."

"Yes, my lord. The stone-masons are all skilled and most of the men are working well. There is a problem with the ropes on some of the hoists and we need more rope, but your brother is seeking a supply."

"Good. He will tell me if he has difficulty. I have not yet met with him since my return. Oh, and Simon, it is probable that two very shabby men will be asking at the gate for you. We met them on our return journey. They have been in the fighting and are now making their way northwards to their homes. They have had little to sustain them on their journey. I have offered them three weeks' work. They will be fed and housed with the men who do not return daily to their homes. If they work well, they will be paid in coin at the end of three weeks and will continue on their way. Their names are Dickon and Rob. They look very rough and have clearly had little to eat in recent days, but I think they will be willing labourers. Do not expect too much heavy work of them for the first few days, but Dickon is a net maker so could be useful when the new ropes come. Let me know if they do not prove satisfactory."

"Yes, my lord. Two extra men will be useful, especially if this weather holds."

"Good. We will leave you now. I am showing Cecily and Alice around their new home today and will return to my own duties tomorrow."

The next stop of their tour was at the stables. The horses that had carried them and their bags were resting today. Cissy ran to greet them all. A stable-lad came out and, seeing the Baron, disappeared to find the head groom, who duly presented himself.

As they wandered around, the Baron turned to Cissy and said, "You must learn to ride, Cecily. I am sure we can find a small pony for you—and you too, Alice. You managed well on our journey but you would do well to be able to ride a slightly larger and faster beast. I will arrange for you both to have instruction."

He turned to the groom. "I will come again tomorrow. Will you have suitable beasts ready, or tell me if we need to look for new ones?"

"Of course, my lord."

The sun became quite strong and eventually Cissy asked, "Papa, may we find somewhere cool to rest for a while? I'm sure Alice must be getting tired."

The baron looked with amusement at his now flushed daughter. "Of course she must. I think we should all rest and have a cool drink."

He led them to a patch of dappled shade cast by some blackthorn trees growing below the castle wall on the edge of the moat. Spying a young boy coming into the castle with a sack of vegetables, he called him over.

"When you reach the buttery, boy, would you tell a cook that the Baron wishes for cool drinks for Miss Cecily, Miss Alice and himself to be brought here?"

The boy assured him he would and, heaving his sack slightly higher, he increased his pace towards the keep.

Their drinks arrived in no time and, later, the boy was rewarded with a farthing on his way out.

Cissy finished her drink quickly and, having been warned that the water in the moat was very deep, she wandered off along its edge, looking for signs of fish in the water. Alice, sensing that her time with the Baron would be very limited in the future, took the opportunity to ask him a question that had puzzled her for a long time.

"My lord, may I ask a question?"

"Of course, Alice. What is it?"

"I have often wondered, my lord, how your wife came to be travelling, apparently alone except for Cissy, at that time of fighting, and why she was on the Skipton road?"

"Oh, Alice, I have asked myself that question so many times. I have made enquiries of many people, but have never had a good explanation.

"I had been summoned to London for a gathering of the barons to discuss the serious political situation. Belle wished to visit her elder sister and her family in Nottinghamshire, so we travelled together, and I left them safely with her family when I continued on to London two days later.

"The plan was that Belle and Cecily would stay there until I collected them on my return journey, but it seems that, only a few days before I returned, a messenger arrived, claiming that I had sent him. I would be delayed because of serious political problems, and for the same reason I wished Belle to start her journey home. The messenger, calling himself Daniel of Whitby, would arrange a cart for their transport and escort them himself back here to the castle.

"I, of course, only discovered this when I arrived at my wife's kinsfolk's house on my return journey. I was immediately anxious, as I had sent no messenger, and the name the man had given meant nothing to me."

"How strange," said Alice.

"I made the journey home as swiftly as possible and was distraught when I found they had not reached here, and, of course, there had been no reason for anyone here to think anything was amiss.

"I prepared to search for them immediately, taking only Colum with me. We returned along the route I would have expected them to take, asking for news at every abbey, inn and hamlet on the way, but we reached Belle's kinsfolk again without a single piece of news.

"But, her kinsfolk did have some news. Their nursery maid had been travelling with Belle and Cecily and had succeeded in making her way back to her mistress. Kathy was able to tell me some of the story.

"The man, calling himself Daniel of Whitby, seemed pleasant but Belle had not been happy about changing her plans. She had asked him to show her his authority from me. He produced a token with my emblem, saying that, as he understood she was unable to read, I had said that this would suffice. How did this man know that my wife had not been taught to read?"

"Eventually he convinced her and just two days' after first calling on her, he arrived with a cart and driver. He settled Belle, Cecily and Kathy comfortably enough in the cart. They travelled for three days along a good road and all was going well. Each night they had left the main road and stayed in some small village inn. Daniel said these inns were more suited to the needs of a lady and child. The inns on the main road would be full of all kinds of travellers, whereas a lady would be treated royally at small inns whose landlords could then boast of their patronage. Apparently though, as I would expect, the comfort, cleanliness and food were of poor standard."

The baron paused. He had risen and been walking up and down restlessly in front of Alice as he spoke.

"I am sorry, Alice. Telling you the story is bringing back the feelings I had at the time I heard it myself."

"No, I am sorry my lord. I had no right to ask."

"You had every right to ask, and I shall continue. The feelings are strong but you are the only person who can understand. You were there at the scene of Belle's death. You told me what I needed to know. You gave me the end of the story; I shall give you the beginning. I think neither of us will ever know the whole story.

"Now, on the fourth day, Kathy said, they had returned to the main road and, before midday, had arrived at the town of Doncaster on market day. Cecily had been fretting and crying at being restricted in the cart again. Daniel suggested that Kathy be given a coin to go to see if she could quickly find something that would amuse the child for a while. Belle had produced a coin and, promising to be very quick, Kathy went. She was not away from the cart long but, when she returned to the place she had left it, it had gone. Daniel on his horse had gone too. She searched and searched in case she had mistaken the place. She asked everyone around if they had seen the cart leaving. Which way had it gone? Had anyone left a message?

"Two or three women claimed to have seen the cart drive away and they agreed about the direction it had taken but, although Kathy walked along the way pointed out to her, she never saw the cart or its occupants and escort again.

"Eventually, the poor girl, who was little more than a child, decided she must make her way back to her mistress. She had the wit to follow the main road. Fortunately, the coin which Belle had given to her was of modest value and Kathy had been given several coins in change from her purchase. Thus she was able to buy a little food each day. At night she slept under whatever shelter she could find and, praise God, she was not attacked or molested by anyone. On two occasions a good Christian soul took pity on her. One gave her a shawl for warmth at night, and another gave her shelter when it was raining so that she could get dry in front of the fire and take a bowl of broth. When she arrived back at Belle's sister's house she was barely able to stand, being weak from hunger and barefoot. Her feet were bleeding as her boots had soon worn through and her few possessions had, of course, gone with the cart.

"She was tended to and put to bed, where she stayed for three days, but thankfully she made a full recovery of body. She was, however, beset by fears for Belle and Cecily, and frequently wept and woke from terrible dreams.

"After learning all that Kathy could tell me, once again I set off to look for them. Now that we knew that they had travelled to Doncaster, my new search started there, but all our enquiries came to nought. All that Colum and I could do was to follow the roads which ran out of that town, first in one direction, then another. As you already know, Alice, our searches lasted more than three years before that ray of light was given to me at Bolton Priory. I do not think we will ever know how the cart came to be where you found Cecily."

"No, my lord, I don't think we will. But, Cecily is coming back. Thank you for telling me. I have wondered so often."

The rest of the day passed pleasantly, although they stayed within the castle walls. In quiet moments, and after she was in bed that night, the strange episode that had brought Cissy into Alice's life went round and round in her mind.

Who was this Daniel of Whitby? Why had he wanted to kidnap and kill the lady Belle? Perhaps he had intended to extract a ransom from the baron but his plan had gone wrong. Nothing seemed to make much sense.

Cissy slept soundly, exhausted by all the new things she had seen during the day.

Next day, the Baron returned to his duties, spending time with his brother Stephen, who informed him of matters which had taken place in his absence. Later he rode out of the castle to visit his demesne and check on the farms. Alice and Cissy spent most of the morning together then, after his lessons, Harry came looking for his cousin, having permission from the Baron to amuse her, so long as he took care of her. Alice watched from a distance but enjoyed having some time to herself.

On Sunday, the whole family and many of the servants joined the village folk at Mass in the quite grand village church. Cissy sat with her father, Stephen and Olivia, while Alice sat behind with Harry, Edward and the nursery maid who was holding Eleanor. Alice enjoyed the Mass and the walk back to the castle in the warm sunshine. The Baron was able to spend more time with Cissy and asked Alice to accompany them.

He asked Alice whether she found her new surroundings agreeable.

She assured him the surroundings were fine, but she did find the confinement and bustle a little difficult. "But, my lord," she added, "I need to know what is expected of me. What work should I undertake, as I cannot be idle all day?"

"Tomorrow," said the Baron, "Cecily will join Harry for lessons. I think it would be a good idea for you to sit in with her, as Brother James will feel more comfortable teaching a young girl if there is a woman present. Also, in the next few days you must begin riding lessons. If there is some other task you feel you would like to undertake, I am sure it can be arranged. You would need to consult Olivia, as she oversees most domestic matters. In a few weeks' time we will start harvesting; then there will be work for everyone, even the children."

Cissy was happy to start lessons and Harry didn't seem to mind her presence. She only stayed for the first part of the morning, while Harry spent the whole morning studying.

Brother James found his new pupil a little undisciplined, as Cissy would interrupt to ask questions as soon as anything puzzled her, and she would make comments about things the monk was saying. However, by the end of the first week, she was beginning to wait until the monk had finished what he was saying before having her own say.

Alice had a role in helping Cissy to adjust and develop some discipline, but she also realised that the Baron had given her a great opportunity to improve her own education. She guessed that Brother James had been instructed by the Baron to include her needs in his teaching, without treating her as a child. In his youth, Brother James had travelled to the Holy Land and was able to describe Nazareth and Bethlehem, the Sea of Galilee and even Jerusalem, with the Garden of Gethsemane and the Mount of Olives. He had some talent for drawing and showed them charcoal drawings of some of the things he had seen, such as an olive tree and its fruit, the lilies of the field, a locust, palm branches, water pots and many other things mentioned in the scriptures. It was very interesting.

When the children were practising their letters, Brother James would say, "Perhaps, Miss Alice, while Cissy is busy with her letters, you would like to look at this passage", and she would quietly read the words on a beautifully scribed piece of vellum. She really enjoyed this part of her day.

After lessons, when the weather was fine, Alice and Cissy would go exploring within the castle walls, or have a riding lesson. Strangely, Cissy was not enthusiastic about riding, but Alice soon gained in confidence. Her horse was taller than Freya but very little wider, so once she was used to being further from the ground, she felt comfortable most of the time. Of course, apart from the time that Freya had bolted, Alice had never gone faster than a trot before. Now she found a short period of cantering quite exhilarating.

Half-way through the second week, however, the weather changed. Dark clouds brought frequent, heavy showers of rain and some thunder and lightning. On these days both Alice and Cissy found the castle a dark, depressing place. It had been much better to sit near the entrance to the cave and watch the sky lighting up in the flashes and listen to the rain pelting down just outside. There had been the smell of wet earth and refreshed plants and trees when the storm had passed. Then, when the sun came out, everything dripped and sparkled. Now, the castle just felt damp. The windows were too small and high to see the storm properly and the plants and trees were too far away to smell.

One afternoon, they had endured a grumbling storm, then a blowing curtain of rain obscuring all attempts to see out and they were both lying on their beds thinking.

"Alice, are you awake," Cissy asked quietly.

"Mmm, I'm awake."

"I wish we were at home, don't you?"

"This is your home now, Cissy but, yes, today I would like to be back in our Home Valley."

"Won't we ever go back again?" Cissy's voice was wistful.

"You won't go back to live there," Alice said gently. "You may visit it sometime."

There was a pause before Cissy spoke again. "You just said the castle is **my** home now, but it is yours too Alice. You're not going back, are you?"

"I may have to go back. Your Papa asked me to come because he didn't want you to be sad or frightened when he brought you here. So I said I would come for a while, and I am not planning to go home yet. This was your home before, you know. You were born here and lived here for two years when you were a baby, even though you do not remember it.

"In so many ways, Cissy, it is better for you here. You are with your Papa, who loves you very much. You are learning new things which I could not have taught you, and you are eating good food."

"But we are not going fishing and we are not going out and collecting the herbs and berries. We're not watching the birds and the rabbits, and we're not going to the market or to see our friends. I liked doing those things."

"I know you did and I did too. We will try to do some of those things again. We will ask your Papa if we can go outside the castle and walk down to the village. We'll find a stream to fish in, and go looking for butterflies and dragonflies. The rain will soon go away.

"Your Papa was telling me that, in a few weeks, it will be time to harvest the crops growing on the farms. Everyone will have to work, even the children, so we will both be busy then."

Next day the storms had passed and things seemed brighter again. After lessons, Cissy went to find her Papa and asked him where she could go fishing.

"You will have to go outside the castle and down the hill towards the village. You must not go alone—it is too far."

"Alice will come too Papa, if you tell us where we should go."

"Yes, I'm sure she will, but I think that today, perhaps I will come too."

"Oh yes, please Papa; we would like you to come."

Cissy kissed her Papa and was rushing to tell Alice the news when Harry appeared.

"We're going fishing," Cissy told him with delight.

"Fishing!" exclaimed Harry. "Girls don't go fishing."

"I do," said Cissy. "I've got my own net. I'm good at catching fish."

"Can I come?" asked Harry.

"I suppose so. Papa won't mind."

"Is Uncle Michael going too?"

"Yes, he is going to show Alice and me where the stream is."

"I must find my Papa and ask if I may go. Please don't go without me." Harry sped away.

So it was that, half-an-hour later, the little group crossed the drawbridge. Cissy, armed with her net, and Harry holding one borrowed from Simon the Factor's son, followed the Baron along the track towards the village. Alice followed the children, carrying a small basket that had been hastily packed with bread, cheese and fruit-cake.

It was not long before the Baron led them away from the well-worn track to follow an almost invisible, narrow track through the grass between the trees, down to a stream. The stream could be heard tumbling along well before it came into sight. In a small clearing in the trees, the Baron stopped.

"Here you are Cecily. You should be able to fish here."

"Oh yes, Papa, this is a lovely stream."

At this point the stream came rushing down from the hills but was broken up and slowed by several rocky ledges across its width. After the last ledge, at the centre of the stream the water was quite fast-flowing, while towards the banks, slightly deeper, quieter pools had formed.

Cissy now spoke in a firm, calm voice to Harry. "Now we must be quiet and move slowly. Don't let your shadow fall on the water or you'll scare the fish away."

The two children were soon absorbed in trying to spot a fish and then entice it into a net. Alice sat on the soft grass with the food basket. Soon the Baron sat beside her.

"I used to come here with Stephen when we were boys, but it is a very long time since I last came. It is so easy to forget the delights of childhood. It will be good to have Cecily around to bring some of them back."

"Cecily may want to take any fish they catch back to the castle and cook them."

"I think we must dissuade her today. This time the fish should go back in the water to live a little longer.

"Now, I am ready to eat. What do you have in the basket there?"

Alice had just spread the contents of her basket, when an excited cry came from Cissy. "I've got one! I've got one!" Before the adults reached the stream bank, Harry exclaimed, "I've got one too!"

Both children had indeed caught fishes. Laying the nets gently on the grass, they looked at their prizes.

"Mine's bigger than yours," said Harry.

"Mine's wriggling so much I can't see how long it is," Cissy asserted. "It might be longer than yours."

"I am sure it doesn't matter whose is biggest," said the Baron, knowing full well that to the children it did. "You have both done very well to catch one so soon. What do you say, Alice?"

"They have both done well, my lord, but which of the two is the larger is hard to tell and, as both are still quite small, I think it would be best to put them back to grow bigger. If you were to try to eat either, after gutting and cooking, there would hardly be a mouthful each."

"Yes," said Harry, "I see what you mean. I'll let mine go back to grow bigger, if you will put yours back Cecily."

"Of course I will," said Cissy, "I was going to anyway. If we go a bit further down-stream, we might catch some really big ones. Back you go little fishy. Swim away."

"There is food when you are hungry," said Alice.

"I'm hungry now," said Harry. "Let's have some food before we go further down-stream."

Everyone sat on the grass to eat, but the children sometimes wandered to look at something as they ate, finding lots of things to interest them, especially by the bubbling water. Alice and the Baron took more time over the food, then both leaned back against tree trunks, enjoying the sunshine and the peace.

"I had forgotten how pleasant it is to just sit for a while and appreciate creation," said the Baron. "I felt a similar peace in your valley. Cecily talked to me most easily when she and I were wandering together."

"You seem to enjoy the company of children, my lord. I think it is rare for people of rank to spend time with them."

"Perhaps, but I clearly remember days spent exploring with our father and our grandfather. Those were some of the high points of my childhood. I will not be able to do this often, but I promise myself I will make some time for such things. I have lost so much time with Cecily already."

The afternoon passed lazily for Alice. She slept for a short time. She roused and was about to ask the Baron if it was time to collect the children and return to the castle, when a figure emerged from the wood into the clearing.

"So, brother, here you are!" the new arrival exclaimed. "When Harry told me fishing was the plan, I guessed you might bring the children here."

"Yes, we had some good times here, did we not?"

"We did. But, where are Harry and Cecily?"

"Just beyond the bend in the stream. Tread quietly or you will be scolded by Cecily, I'm afraid."

Stephen made his way quietly towards the children.

"I think, my lord," said Alice, standing up and stretching a little, "that we will need to return to the castle soon."

"Yes, the sun has moved westward. The evening meal will be served 'ere long. I will go to tell the children. I think they have enjoyed themselves." The baron rose and wandered slowly after his brother.

Alice took a few sips of ale from the skin, then covered the remaining food morsels in her basket. She had really enjoyed the last few hours and felt relaxed. She was truly an outdoor person, and while she realised that the strong walls of the castle and the large fires would make the worst days of winter more bearable, life in her cot and cave had been really sweet most of the time. Cecily, being very young, would soon adjust to castle life. The time would come when Alice could return to her own home with a good conscience.

Chapter Eleven

The weather for the rest of the month of July was settled and warm. Alice and Cecily were able to spend most afternoons exploring and enjoying the open air. Sometimes, with a groom in attendance, they would test their new riding skills outside the castle walls and so explore further than they could on foot. Cecily became quite attached to her small hill pony and decided that riding was pleasant after all. She had enjoyed riding high on Merlin, firmly settled against her Papa and, at first, had felt very insecure sitting alone on her pony, knowing that she had to control it. But now, that feeling had passed and her pony, which she called Amber, because of the colour of its eyes, was now her friend. At the end of every ride she would go to the stable with the groom to be shown how to look after Amber, and Alice went along too. Alice's pony was called Misty, as there were flecks of white on her dark brown coat, which gave her a 'misty' look.

August came and harvesting began. As the Baron had predicted, everyone was kept very busy. The crops were grown on the farms worked by the tenant farmers, but now the harvesters, whoever they were, worked where they were needed. Beans and peas were picked and barley and oats were scythed, raked, bundled and stooked. It was hot, hard work but generally everyone worked cheerfully. Alice, Cecily and Harry joined in. The Baron and Stephen gave the orders and agreed with each farmer the amount of each crop to go to the castle's barns, and the tithe for the church.

On some days, Alice stayed at the castle to assist Olivia. The castle kitchen provided a midday lunch for all the harvesters and Alice found herself doing several different tasks in the preparation. Then she would go with the servants to carry the food to the fields.

Olivia saw her own work as organising others, which she did efficiently, but she rarely worked herself. She was very skilled at embroidery, making some beautiful wall hangings, and panels for garments or belts. She organised the dinner each day with the cook and head steward, and, of course, she supervised the nursery-maid. Olivia loved her children but felt little need to spend time with them, and she did not approve of the time the Baron was spending with Cecily. He was certainly not, in Olivia's opinion, giving her a suitable up-bringing for a Baron's daughter.

Alice was aware that Olivia did not approve of her. She clearly resented the Baron treating Alice as a member of the family and during this time of harvest, Olivia made the most of the opportunity to use Alice as a servant without bringing the Baron's wrath down on her.

Alice felt all this in the reserve which Olivia showed towards her, and the look on her face when Alice joined the family at meals. She admired Olivia's ability to organise the household and she especially admired her beautiful embroidery. She had expressed her admiration too. However, she was aware of a hostility that wasn't there in her dealings with the Baron or Stephen. Alice, however, was pleased at last to be doing something other than just being there for Cissy, and she did not resent doing her share towards the harvest and having the chance to know more of the local people.

Harry and Cecily worked hard. Harry was tall enough and strong enough to help with stooking. Cecily had done well with picking beans.

She had sorted the pods—some for immediate use, some to be stored for winter use and some to be dried to become seeds for a new crop next year. She was still not tall enough or strong enough to make the stooks. She worked with other groups of children gathering small armfuls of the cut grain for others to tie and stook, or she took bundles of cut twine to the stookers. She loved watching for the small creatures that ran out of the corn as the reapers worked across the field and, although she got very hot and dusty, she was happy and soon became friends with some of the village children. She was pleased when Alice was one of the people bringing food around at midday, and they could find a shady spot to sit and eat together. Some days Harry joined them but on others he stayed with a group of young boys.

The days went by, broken only by the occasional shower of rain until, at last, the harvest was all gathered in. There was a dinner in the great hall for everyone then, on the next Sunday there was a service of thanksgiving for the harvest in the village church. As the family worshipped together, Harry and Cissy looked very brown in contrast with Edward, Eleanor and Olivia, and as the family walked back to the castle, Olivia remarked to Stephen that they looked like the children of peasants.

Stephen laughed. "You should have seen Michael and I when we were that age. In a good summer we were rarely inside and were the colour of acorns."

Alice, who had overheard the comments, just thought how healthy Cissy looked and that, browned by the sun or not, one look at the child's bright, intelligent face would tell she was no peasant.

The weeks went by and life in the castle fell into a fairly regular pattern. Cissy was usually happy to attend her morning lessons and

Alice continued to accompany her. Alice found her own reading was now good and her writing had improved greatly. Cissy learned very quickly and was soon good at both.

After her morning lessons, Cissy would usually go to play with Edward or to amuse baby Eleanor. After the midday meal, which was a light one, Alice and Cissy would go out for a ride or down to the village. Sometimes on the sunny, autumn days they would gather berries and nuts as they used to do and take them to the castle kitchen. On days when the weather was wild, which it frequently was, Cissy would spend time with her Aunt Olivia, learning to stitch or embroider. Olivia would also use these occasions to instruct Cecily in the manners and behaviour expected of the daughter of a Baron.

Cecily had become very friendly with Tilly, her young maid-servant, and would have liked to include her in some of her outings with Alice. Olivia had carefully explained that this was not possible, as Tilly had duties to do all day. Cissy thought this was unfair but had to accept it, especially when Alice assured her that, on this occasion, Olivia was right. Alice had explained to Tilly that she was not required to look after her. Alice would care for her own clothes, her bed and getting her things to the laundry. However, she often found that Tilly had done small tasks for her, and that she enjoyed caring for her hair. Alice found it quite soothing to have her hair brushed and combed and Tilly was glad that it pleased her.

With time on her hands, Alice would sometimes offer her services to the cook, helping wherever she was needed. Most of the domestic servants found no difficulty in accepting Alice. She wasn't one of the family, nor was she one of them, but they trusted her, accepted her friendship and gave theirs in return.

Christmas came and it was a wonderful time. The Baron insisted that every member of the household should have the opportunity to attend Christmas Day Mass, so the priest of the village church conducted two services, before joining the Baron's household for the feast. All servants were allowed to spend either Christmas Day or St. Stephen's Day with their own families, so they willingly performed their duties. On St. Stephen's Day the Baron, accompanied by Cissy, toured his demesne, distributing gifts to the peasant families. As Cissy reported to Alice afterwards, she really enjoyed this, her first duty as the Baron's daughter.

Before they set out, her Papa had explained to her that rich families, such as theirs, who had wealth and land, had a duty of care to the less fortunate, and a responsibility to those who worked for them.

"I told him that I thought it is a good thing, but that when I was living with you, Alice, we didn't get our help from rich people, it was our friends who came to help us. Perhaps there weren't any rich people at Arkenthorpe, and of course you didn't work for anyone any more."

"Papa said that our friends in Arkenthorpe are good Christian people and so, although they are not rich people, they shared what they had with us when we needed help."

"Papa also told me," Cecily reported, "that when he was travelling the countryside, just with Colum, looking for me and my Mama, he mixed with the ordinary people more and came to respect many of them. He also said that the way you had made such a good home for me, Alice, was almost a miracle!"

Soon after Christmas, the snow came. It came and it stayed!

At first it looked beautiful and the children took great pleasure in playing in it, but then more and more came and strong winds blew it into great drifts. No-one could play in it—it came over the top of boots and, however well leather wrappings were bound to the legs, the snow got through and feet became swollen with chilblains. Everyone stayed indoors as much as possible, but even there only the kitchen and the great hall were warm.

Alice and Cecily's bedchamber was cold, but their woollen blankets and sheepskin covers kept them warm once they were in bed. They pushed the wooden bases of their beds together so they could cuddle up too. Visits to the *garde loo* (as they had learned to call a castle privy) were as short and infrequent as possible. It was on returning from one such visit, that Cissy glanced at Tilly, lying in her alcove opposite the chamber door. The girl was trembling all over.

"Tilly," Cissy whispered, "Tilly, are you crying?"

"No, Miss."

"But you're shaking all over."

"It's j-j-j-just the c-c-cold Miss."

"You must have another blanket. I'll get you one."

Cissy went into the chamber and opened the chest she kept her clothes in. At the bottom, she knew, was the rabbit skin cover she had brought with her to the castle. Alice roused as Cissy delved into the chest.

"What are you doing, Cissy?"

"Trying to find my rabbit skin cover."

"Why? Are you cold?"

"No, not when I'm in bed, but Tilly is so cold she is shaking all over."

Alice immediately roused fully. "I'll go to look at her while you find the cover."

Alice was horrified to see the state Tilly was in. "Goodness, child, you are like ice. We must get you warmed up now. Come into the bedchamber."

"I can't, Miss Alice," Tilly stammered through chattering teeth.

"You must."

"I don't think I c-c-can s-s-stand up."

Alice bent and lifted the girl into her arms, still wrapped in her woollen blanket. She carried her into the bedchamber and laid her in the middle of their bed.

Cissy had found the rabbit skin. "Here it is. Shall I cover her up with it?"

"Tilly needs more than another cover. I will go down to the kitchen to get her a warm drink. You must get back into bed, pull the covers over you and Tilly and cuddle her until I get back. Oh, and can you take each of her hands in turn and rub them gently to help to warm them up. I'll be as quick as I can."

Wrapping her heavy cloak around her, Alice lit another candle and made her way down to the kitchens. Icy blasts of air were coming in at every window slit and turret stair. Several times she thought her candle would blow out, but she reached the kitchen safely. The kitchen was still warm, and many of the household servants were sleeping there. Carefully making her way to the buttery, Alice found a ewer of milk and ladled some into a small iron pot. She took the pot to the fire and, placing it on a trivet near the glowing embers, she picked up some bellows and began to encourage the embers to flame.

At the noise of the bellows, Cook awoke. Seeing Alice, she asked anxiously, "What's wrong, Alice? Is it Miss Cecily?"

"No, not Cecily. It is Tilly. We have just found her, in her bed, but as cold as death. I will take her this milk to try to warm her through. Cecily is trying to cuddle some warmth into her."

"Right, Miss," said Cook. "You do the milk. I'll wrap one of these hearth stones in a towel and bring it up in a basket. It will help to warm her feet. Trouble with Tilly is she's no flesh on her to keep out the cold."

A few minutes later, followed by Cook, Alice carefully carried the cup of hot milk in one hand, and with her candle in the other, made her way back to the bedchamber.

"I'm glad you're back, Alice," said Cissy. "I can't warm her up and she is making me cold. I'm trying to warm her hands like you told me, but it isn't working."

"Oh, the Lord have mercy!" exclaimed Cook as she saw Tilly. She bent down and quickly lifting back the bedclothes, she took the hot stone, wrapped in the thick towel, from her basket and put it just below where Tilly's feet lay, blue and cold." She swiftly drew the bedding back up again.

"Now we must get her teeth to stop chattering so she can drink some milk. And you must get back into bed, Miss Cecily, else you'll be freezing too."

"Yes, Cissy," added Alice. "Here, you have a couple of sips of the milk. There's enough."

Cissy had the milk, which was lovely and warm, and as she snuggled into the bed again, she could feel the gentle warmth coming from the hot stone.

"That's much better," she said.

Alice and Cook sat in the bed, lifting Tilly so that she nestled between them. Gradually Tilly's teeth slowed their chattering and she was able to take small sips of the milk. Then, with Alice taking her hands and Cook her feet, they gently rubbed and stroked some life back into them. At last the shivering stopped and Tilly's body relaxed. She was given the last of the milk and laid back down against the pillows.

"Oh, thank God," said cook, "she'll live."

"Yes, I think she will be better in the morning. Thank you for your help, Josse," Alice said to Cook. "I am grateful."

"I'll return to my own bed now," said Josse, heaving herself to her feet. That's one good thing about working in a kitchen, you rarely suffer from the cold!"

"No," said Alice, "I know. Goodnight my friend."

"Goodnight, Miss Alice, and goodnight Miss Ceci . . . . oh, bless her, she's asleep already."

"Oh, take the candle," said Alice. "We have another if we need it."

So Cook departed. Alice slipped down into the bedclothes. Tilly wasn't giving out any warmth, but she was no longer cold to touch. Hopefully, with Alice on one side, Cissy on the other and a thick mattress beneath her, she would soon be warmed right through.

"This must not happen again," thought Alice. "Tomorrow I must find warmer clothes and covers for this child."

When Tilly awoke next morning, she was horrified to find herself sleeping in her mistress's bed. She had almost no memory of what had happened during the night. She insisted on rising to perform her duties, but later in the morning Alice went to talk with her. She soon realised that Tilly had little clothing except the things she was wearing and only had a thin mattress and one blanket.

Alice was furious with herself for not having noticed this, her only excuse being that she had no real authority and had assumed the "someone" would look after such things. She now took it on herself to remedy the situation.

She went to see Olivia and could tell that Olivia was truly concerned when she explained what had happened. She authorised Alice to go to various staff of the household who could help. Before the evening meal, Alice had procured a new, thick straw mattress and wooden boards to put on top of the stone of the alcove for the mattress to lie on. A few extra items of clothing, including a shawl and a thicker pair of boots had also been found. Alice herself made a small curtain to hang across the alcove to keep out draughts and found one of the men who was usually involved in the building work to come to drive some pegs into the wall so that the curtain could be fixed. Cissy also insisted that Tilly must have the rabbit-skin cover.

Tilly was embarrassed to have so much fuss made of her. Her family was one of the poorest in the village. Her father was a woodcutter. Her mother had died giving birth to their fifth child. Tilly's older sister looked after the family so, when the chance had come to work at the castle, Tilly had gladly taken it and had felt that she was living in luxury. It had never occurred to her to ask for anything more for herself. That night, as she retired into her now snug little alcove, she felt like a queen.

Alice checked on her twice during the night hours and was relieved to see her sleeping soundly with even a hint of pink in her cheeks.

Finally, Alice approached the Baron and, having told him briefly what had happened, she suggested that perhaps someone should try to discover how Tilly's family was faring in this very cold weather. A path had been made through the snow between the castle and the village, so the Baron ordered that a check should be made on all the families in the village to ensure that everyone had enough fuel and bedding to keep out the worst of the cold. Several families were found to have exhausted their fuel supplies, so enough was taken from the castle stores to meet the need and some folk were provided with extra blankets.

Three days later, the wind changed direction and a slow thaw started, but there were another two weeks of damp, clammy weather before the dreadful chill went away. There had been two deaths in the village, both of old people, but everyone else had survived the longest period of bitter weather these hardy folk could remember.

Chapter Twelve

With the arrival of March, the weather turned brighter and breezy with the occasional heavy shower of rain, but Cissy was able to spend most afternoons outside, either in the company of Harry or with Alice. Riding and fishing, or just simply exploring the surrounding moorland and valleys were the main activities.

If they were staying within the walls or near to the castle, Alice would offer to take Edward too. He was a very wilful boy, but he enjoyed these outings and gradually he became more manageable. For a short time, Harry and Cissy would include him in what they were doing, but then they would leave him with Alice while they went exploring.

Alice gathered that a lot of the time Cissy was passing on her knowledge of the plants and animals to her cousin. Harry was amazed how much Cissy knew about these things, although he did not tell her so. One day he had slipped over and stung his hand on a very unpleasant plant and Cissy had immediately searched for and found another plant which soothed the rash that was rapidly appearing on his hand.

That evening Harry took Alice to one side and told her what had happened. "Why does Cecily know such a lot about these things, even though she is only eight years old?"

"Our lives before we came here depended on learning such things, Harry. Cecily and I lived alone, with no servants; even our nearest friends were an hour's walk away. We occasionally bought flour, oatmeal and honey at a market a few miles from where we were living, but we had little money and caught or gathered everything else we ate. When Cecily went fishing, it was to catch fish to eat. I had to teach her which plants could be eaten and which berries were safe. For meat we had to trap stock doves or rabbits, and we had to collect wood for the fire so we could cook food and keep warm. Some wood burns well, while some only makes a lot of unpleasant smoke. We had to know which to collect. Cecily learned because she had to learn."

"Were you really so poor, Alice?"

"I am afraid so."

"I've been thinking about Cecily a lot. I can just remember a few little things of the time when Aunt Belle and baby Cecily went missing, but I was very small. After that Uncle Michael was away from the castle most of the time and, whenever he was here he was a very sad, unhappy person.

"It was so different, though, when Uncle Michael returned last year, saying that Cecily was alive and well and he was going to bring her home soon. The day we buried the bones of Aunt Belle was a strangely sad but also happy day. After that Uncle Michael became much more cheerful and started to share some of the work with my father. The whole castle became a nicer place to live. Mother didn't seem very happy but I think that was because baby Eleanor had just been born and she cried a lot, so that probably made mother cross and tired.

"I'm glad you are both here now," Harry added. "Cecily's quite fun for a girl."

The battles and skirmishes of the war between the houses of Lancaster and York had mostly moved away to other parts of England.

Life was more settled and the countryside less dangerous. The Baron decided that Cecily and Alice should have their experiences widened by some travel to interesting places. He consulted with Stephen and they decided that the Baron would take a small party to the city of York and then, later, Stephen would lead an expedition to the coast. Young Harry had not travelled far either, as since he had been old enough to travel, the war had made such journeys too hazardous.

The children were excited by the prospect and Alice looked forward to getting away from the castle for a while. She had been thinking that it was time for her to return home, but she decided she would regret not taking these chances to see new places, as she would not get such again.

The party that set off for York in early April comprised the Baron, attended by Colum, Harry, Cecily, Alice and a young groom, Cerdic, who would lead the pack-horse and care for the other horses.

The journey, through pleasant, hilly land, was shorter than Alice had expected and, to her surprise, early on the third day, there suddenly appeared below them a vast area of flat land, with a walled city in its midst. Above the walls of the city arose a building larger than she could ever imagine. It was clearly the Minster church which the Baron had spoken of on more than one occasion. The party reigned in the horses on a high point, to gaze at the scene below them. They could see the city walls and other large buildings, but all were dominated by the great Minster.

"I have seen the Minster on a number of occasions", said the Baron, "but its magnificence never ceases to impress me."

"I have never been able to understand how a building could be made so tall," said Colum. "It must be possible to see for many, many miles from the top of the main tower." Colum had, of course, visited before when travelling with his master.

Harry, Cissy, Alice and the groom all stared dumb-struck at the ancient city in front of them—ancient, but with new buildings rising everywhere among the old.

"When the Roman Empire ruled Britain," said the Baron, "this place was called Eboracum. Later, the Viking invaders claimed it and called it Jørvik. This city, which we now call York, has been of great importance for hundreds of years and will, no doubt, continue to be so. It is over two hundred years since Archbishop Walter de Grey began the building of the Minster. Surely even he could not have imagined the splendour of the completed work."

"Please let us ride on," said Harry eagerly. "I can't wait to see inside the city walls. Look at all the people coming out and going in. I have never seen so many people all in one place."

"Yes, we will ride on now, but we must all stay together. When we enter the city, I will lead. The streets are narrow so, Harry and Cecily, you must follow me, with Alice behind you and Colum and Cerdic at the rear. Stay close together.

"We will go to the hostelry which I hope will have room for us to stay tonight. There, if we are fortunate, we will leave our horses, refresh ourselves, then walk to the Minster to see it in all its magnificence."

In a short time, they were entering the city through Bootham Bar and slowly making their way through thronging humanity. It was just after midday as they reached the inn that the Baron was seeking. They had no difficulty securing accommodation for the coming night. Cerdic was despatched to the stables to see to the horses and a young boy was hired to guard their room and their bags.

The Innkeeper's wife brought them refreshment. As they ate, Cecily and Harry could not sit still for excitement. They had had glimpses of so many other enticing things besides the Minster. An old guard tower; the city walls themselves; streets full of workshops, and also, from the viewpoint before they had come down into the city, they had seen a curve of river, deep and wide with boats on it. It was not at all like the swift, shallow rivers and streams they were used to.

At last they finished eating and set off through the narrow, busy streets. It was noisy. People were carrying the strangest things and pushing carts. Most buildings had a shop or workshop at ground level with rooms for people to live in, jutting out over the shops. Some buildings must have been owned by rich people as the whole building was a house. The cobbles were not very comfortable to walk on and it was difficult to look around properly without being in danger of stubbing a toe, bumping into someone, or walking through something unpleasant. Soon, however, they reached the end of one of the narrow streets and, suddenly, there was a wide open space ahead, and at its centre rose the Minster. It was enormous; soaring high into the sky and stretching to right and left.

Alice gasped. "Oh! Oh, my lord, how can men build something so big and so beautiful?"

"It is wonderful, is it not," replied the Baron. "It is one of the finest buildings in the country. There are others which some would claim to be at least as fine, and I have heard tell of buildings of equal splendour in Italy and France."

"But this one is here. It is here for us to see. I could not conceive of a finer building anywhere," Alice breathed.

"Well, let us go to give thanks to God and to admire the craftsmanship that has gone into beautifying the interior."

If the outside had impressed, inside it was awesome. As they gazed up into the beams of the roof and at the top of stained-glass windows, Cissy touched Alice's hand.

"Now I know what a mouse must feel like—no, not a mouse, a beetle—when it is standing on the ground and looking at me. I feel so very, very small."

"So do I," said Alice, "and look at all the wonderful pictures in the windows. The colours are glowing, especially over there where the sun is shining through."

Slowly the party walked down the nave towards the main altar. On the altar were beautiful vessels in gold or silver, with jewels glinting in them. On the wall behind hung a carved stone cross with the crucified figure of Christ, wounded and crowned with thorns. Carving was everywhere, sometimes in the stone around the windows or doorways, or in wood on screens and on the doors themselves. There were smaller side chapels with altars for private devotions, and for a time the Baron knelt in prayer while the others gazed around reverently. Even Harry was awe-struck, although previously he had shown little interest in things religious. Some of the statues of saints showed men in armour and these attracted his attention. There was a beautiful statue of the Virgin and Child, and many alcoves without statues, for which figures would be made in the future.

For a while there were just small groups of people, like themselves, wandering through the vast building, admiring the skills that had produced such a powerful, awe-inspiring place, but then a party of robed monks entered, chanting the appointed office for that afternoon. The Baron's party moved to stand behind the monks in one of the side chapels, where they remained reverently throughout. The chanting echoed strangely from the high vaulted roof as the monks passed through the nave, and the whole building seemed to be filled by the singing.

When the monks had returned, still chanting, to their living quarters, the party went back to the streets to explore further, having been assured that they would all come back to the Minster again during their visit to the city. In the crowds, Cissy clung firmly to her Papa or to Alice, while Harry walked mostly with Colum. They found a point where soldiers, keeping watch from the massive walls over the comings and goings through the city gates, allowed them to mount the steps and walk a short way along the inside of the walls. From there they could see into the courtyards of buildings, some very grand where there was a garden as well as a courtyard.

From another point where the guards allowed them to mount the steps, they could look outside and see the River Ouse with its boats, large and small. The Baron told them that some of the bigger sailing boats would follow the river until it joined an even wider river, which would take it to the sea. The boats could then sail to a foreign country. This idea was difficult to grasp, as only the Baron and Colum had seen the sea.

Alice remembered Thomas the wheelwright trying to describe the sea to her. What had he said? "Great areas of moving water rushing towards you and going away again." A more awesome sight he couldn't imagine. But then, of course, Thomas had not seen York Minster. Could the sea be a greater sight?

The rest of that day, the party wandered through the city, watching craftsmen at work. Weavers, metal workers, silver smiths, candle makers, apothecaries and shoe-makers. However, the street which was most imprinted on their minds, for all the wrong reasons, was the street of the butchers. The noise from squealing and bellowing animals, the smells and the rivulets of blood running along the gutters, made both Cissy and Alice feel ill. Even Harry thought the Shambles the foulest area he had ever seen.

They left that street as quickly as they could and went out of the nearest gate to breathe fresh air outside the walls before it was time for the gates to be closed for the night.

In the early evening, as they entered their inn to prepare for supper, it was obvious from the bustle that someone else of importance had arrived. The innkeeper was looking flustered as he addressed a liveried servant. "Please give his lordship my sincere regrets, but my best room is already taken for tonight and tomorrow night. I have one smaller room. If, as you say, your master travels alone with only yourself and a groom, I am sure we can make him comfortable." The servant departed.

When the Baron's party descended to the main room of the inn for their supper, a large, richly attired gentleman, quaffing ale, was waiting to be served with food. He looked up as they entered the room.

"Aha! Muirhead is it? You're the one who's taken the best room. Wouldn't have expected to see you in a hostelry—thought you only stayed in religious houses."

"Good evening to you, Derwent. My apologies if we have inconvenienced you, but one of the purposes of this visit to York was to broaden the experiences of my daughter and my nephew, so a hostelry seemed more appropriate."

"Thought your daughter had disappeared with your wife. Did you perhaps find 'em both?" Derwent looked across at Alice and Cissy.

"I found only my daughter alive. Come, Cecily."

Cecily moved to stand at the side of her Papa.

"My Lord Derwent, may I present my daughter, Cecily. Cecily, this is Baron Rufus of Derwent."

"My lord," said Cecily, curtseying.

"Unfortunately," continued her father, "I found only the bones of my wife, but I am most grateful to God for my daughter."

"Well," boomed Derwent, looking Cecily up and down, "she is a comely enough child, but you'll need to set about begetting yourself an heir soon."

"That does not concern me overmuch," replied the Baron. "My brother is my heir, and in turn his heir is young Harry here." He signalled Harry to come forward.

"This is Harry, elder son of my brother Stephen."

Harry gave a small bow, while candidly appraising this rather unpleasant man. He glanced at Cecily and, reading her expression, grinned at her.

Alice and Colum had moved away to the table prepared for their meal. Cecily pulled gently on her father's hand. "I'm hungry, Papa. May I join Alice at the table?"

"Yes you may, and you too Harry. I will join you presently."

The children gave a perfunctory curtsey or bow to Baron Derwent and scuttled across the room.

Derwent's eyes followed them and studied Alice. "Ah, I see now why an abbey was not appropriate on this trip, Muirhill. A fair looking woman. Perhaps the idea of a son and heir is not as far from your mind as you would have me believe."

The Baron bristled. "That woman, Derwent, has care of my daughter, and is her constant companion. She would be most offended by your implications."

Derwent guffawed again. "As it's you, Muirhill, I'm inclined to believe you, but few men could get away with such a claim. You always were a strange fellow."

The Baron gave a curt nod, turned and withdrew to the table. He looked quite annoyed as he took his place. Fortunately their food was brought almost immediately and it was a while before anyone wanted to talk as they were all hungry after their day seeing the sights. Baron Derwent was also served soon after them and he too was more interested in his meal than in his fellow guests. However, they had to pass him as they retired to their chamber.

"I wish you a good night, Muirhill," he called, looking first at the baron and then at Alice, with a suggestive wink and a leer.

The Baron wished him a curt "Goodnight" and ushered his party out of the room.

"I don't think you like Baron Derwent, do you Papa?"

"No, Cecily. He is not a friend of mine."

"Why does he know you?" asked Harry.

"We have met several times when I have had to go to London, or elsewhere, at the behest of the King. There are times when many barons are called together to discuss the military or political situation and to show their loyalty to the King. This war between the Yorkists and Lancastrians has been damaging the country for many years now. I detest war and have expressed my wish for peace on several occasions. Rufus of Derwent thinks I am a coward. He is at his best leading a troop of men into battle and he has led some very successful forays in major battles. No-one can deny he is an excellent soldier."

"Have you led men into battle, Uncle?"

"Yes, Harry. I have had to do so a number of times."

"And have you been successful too?"

"Yes, but I only get a great sense of relief that a skirmish is over. I do not feel like celebrating a success."

"Why do you feel that? I'm sure I would want to shout and shout 'We've won! We've won! Hurrah!' I feel like that when I've hit the bull in my archery from a longer distance than my previous best."

"Of course it is good to celebrate an improvement in your prowess, Harry. Your father and I used to shout and prance around in happiness when we had beaten one another in a horse race or a joust. But, the duty of a Baron is to supply men to fight when the King calls. This means that I have to take numbers of men from the villages and the estates around the castle to follow me into battle and fight in the King's cause. They have to come because they have a duty to me. I am calling these men, whom I know, to leave their wives and children, whom I also know, to fight against other men who have also had to leave their families because they owe duty to a Baron or Squire who is fighting for the other side. I know that some of these men will never return home again."

Throughout this conversation, Cecily had been listening. Now she commented, "That's what Rob and Dickon had been doing, wasn't it Papa?"

"Yes, Cecily, they had been fighting. I did not ask them which side they had been fighting for, because when we met them it was no longer important. They were just exhausted men making the long journey back to their homes unaided, as their Master had been killed in the battle.

"Rob was going to have to tell his brother's wife that her husband was dead. A dreadful job for him."

Harry was now looking thoughtful. "I see, my lord, why you think war is a bad thing. You're sure your side will win and you'll be a champion for killing as many of the enemy as you can. You don't think that the people you have killed or injured are fathers with children and wives at home who will be sad and poor without them."

At this point Cecily yawned, although she tried not to show it.

"Come along," said Alice, "we must go to our beds if we are to be ready to explore again tomorrow."

"Colum and I will check on Cerdic and the horses before we sleep," said the Baron. "Goodnight, Cecily, goodnight, Harry. Sleep well. Good night, Alice."

"Goodnight my lord, and thank you. Today has been a wonderful day."

Alice expected to lie awake thinking about all the things she had seen that day, but it was only a few minutes after the children had fallen asleep when she succumbed to her own tiredness. She did not hear the Baron and Colum return to the room.

The next morning they started their exploring early, but without Colum. He was to stay with the horses. The Baron had asked him to do so for a few hours, to give Cerdic the opportunity to see something of the city. At first Cerdic joined their party to visit the Minster, as the Baron thought he might be too over-awed to enter it alone, but after a short time, he was left to his own devices, with instructions to return to the inn to relieve Colum by midday.

After the Minster, the party wandered to the river to watch the boats before re-entering the city for food, then went to explore the areas they had not visited yesterday. It was a breezy day and the wind was quite cold, so they returned to their lodgings early to rest before the evening meal. There was no sign of Baron Derwent, so he had presumably continued on his journey.

Next morning the party ate breakfast early and started their journey home immediately after. As the morning progressed the sun shone and the wind had quietened from the previous day. Trees were coming into leaf and birds were singing—the larks rising high in the sky, their songs clear and beautiful. Alice's thoughts were full of the wonders she had seen on this trip. The children, riding ahead of her, behind the Baron, were chattering and arguing in a friendly way. Colum kept a general eye on the whole party, sometimes riding ahead with his master and at other times riding behind with Alice or Cerdic.

Cerdic was looking very cheerful. He told Colum and Alice that he had always had a high regard for the Baron, but since talking to Baron Derwent's groom, he had realised just how fortunate he was to have such a master. Derwent's groom had never had a chance to look round the places he went to on his master's travels. Obviously he saw things as they rode along, but after that, all he ever saw was a stable or stable-yard. He was given his orders by the servant in livery, and the only times Baron Derwent addressed him was if he was in trouble.

All-in-all, the visit had been a great experience for everyone, and they talked about it for many days afterwards.

It was late June when the second promised journey took place. This time Stephen led the party. Olivia came with Edward, leaving Eleanor with the nursery-maid. Stephen's man-servant, Joseph, replaced Colum, who stayed with the Baron. Olivia and Edward travelled in a partly-covered waggon, driven by Cerdic, and to her chagrin, Alice had to ride with them. Originally Olivia had told Cecily she must be in the waggon too, but she kicked up such a fuss that, in the end, she got her way and rode alongside Harry.

It soon became very clear that, on this occasion, Alice was definitely in the role of servant. She ensured always that her first responsibility was Cissy, but after that she was at Olivia's beck and call. However, she decided that she was going to make the most of this opportunity, even if it meant holding her tongue when Olivia was ordering her around. She was surprised to find that her calm acceptance and efforts at staying pleasant seemed, perversely, to irritate Olivia, but she shrugged it off and gave attention to Edward. She pointed out things of interest to him as they travelled—a big bird of prey high in the sky; a stoat or weasel running in and out of the rocks; various folk going about their business as they passed through a village.

When they stopped for the night at a hostelry, Alice had the chance to chat with Cecily and Harry about the experiences of the day. Stephen was a good host and joined in the conversation. In many ways he was like his brother. He was a God-fearing man, but not as dedicated to the church as the Baron. He was interested in the children, even spending short periods of time playing with Edward, and it was clear that Cecily was comfortable in her uncle's company. Joseph, Stephen's man-servant, was a married man, older than Colum by many years. He was quiet and respectful to Stephen and Olivia, and he willingly gave his help to Harry if required. Alice did not have an opportunity to talk with him on the journey, but he was in no way unfriendly.

"Today, we should reach the sea," announced Stephen as he helped Olivia into the cart while Alice and Cerdic loaded the bags. Harry and Cecily were already mounted. "How will we know it is the sea?" asked Harry. "What does it look like?"

"I am not going to try to tell you," replied Stephen. "You will know when you see it."

The morning was warm but with a brisk breeze blowing into their faces as they rode along. The land was high with fewer trees than there had been on the earlier part of the journey. They stopped for a midday meal and had ridden on for a while afterwards, when Cecily called out, "Uncle, what is that strange noise? It's a bit like thunder but there is no storm."

"You can hear the sea, Cecily. When we get round that small hill ahead, you will see it."

"Why is it so noisy?"

"Stop asking questions. Just have patience for a little longer."

Harry, Cecily, Stephen and Joseph encouraged their horses into a brisker trot and got well ahead of the waggon. Alice so wished she was with them as the waggon trundled on behind.

When eventually the waggon rounded the end of the hill, the four horses were standing still, and a good thing too!

"Oh, we're at the end of the earth!" Alice thought, completely stunned. The land just stopped somewhere below them. There was nothing but water and sky as far as the eye could see. Even Olivia let out a cry of surprise, while Edward grabbed Alice's arm and hung on tight.

Stephen rode over to them. "Don't be afraid, we are a long way from the edge of the land, but this is a good place to look from. That is the sea!"

The noise that Cecily had heard earlier was loud now, but although they could see water rolling in towards the land, Alice could not think why it was making such a noise. The wind was still strong and, suddenly, she remembered the slapping noise that a full stream or river made when it hit the bank. Perhaps the sea made such a noise but much louder.

"Come now," said Stephen, "we must get down lower where we will be sheltered from the wind, but can get even closer to the sea."

He led the group along a path which sloped gently downwards into a village where the houses seemed to be built into a steep rock face. The narrow road twisted and turned until, rounding one bend, it suddenly stopped at a wall. The noise from the sea was deafening here, and every so often there was a loud slapping sound and a spray of water shot into the air above the wall and fell, wetting the road.

Stephen dismounted at several yards distance from the wall and passed his horse's rein to Joseph.

"Cecily, Harry, dismount and give your horses to Cerdic and come here to me. Olivia, Alice, come here too, and you Edward."

Once they were all standing around Stephen, he told the children to each hold the hand of an adult. Cecily immediately came to Alice, so Edward went to his mother and Harry to his father.

"Now," said Stephen, "if we stand over there to the right, we will be sheltered from the wind, but still have a good view of the sea. Follow me and keep near to the side of the cliff."

They did, and then turned to look back at the wall to find that its seaward side was now in view. Great swells of water were rushing in from the sea and crashing against the rocks below the wall. After hitting the rocks, and sometimes the wall too, the water would start rolling back again towards the sea, only to have other waves of water rolling in and curving over the top if it.

"Now I can see why it makes such a loud noise," Cissy shouted to Alice. "It looks very fierce and frightening."

"Yow!" Harry shrieked, "it looks like an ogre's cauldron. Look at all the froth."

Alice looked beyond the furious water just below them, which was in shadow, to admire the curve of the high cliffs stretching away from them bathed in sunshine. Across there the sea was a clear blue colour and sparkled like snow. A large castle had been built on top of the farthest cliff and that was glowing in the sun too. All around them, white birds screamed, flying and soaring, and even landing on the heaving surface of the water.

Olivia spoke. "I have seen the sea once before, but that was not here and it certainly wasn't as fierce as this. It must be dreadful to live with this noise all the time."

"It isn't like this all the time, my dear. It has what is called a tide. For some hours the tide is high, as it is now, but at low tide the water retreats and is much quieter."

"Ah, good."

Edward started to whimper. "Let's go home. I don't like the sea Papa. Let's go home."

"We can't go home tonight," said his father. "We must have some food and go to bed to sleep. The horses must rest too. And, I think you will like the sea tomorrow."

"I won't. I won't."

"Well, we must find somewhere to sleep tonight. I'll get Joseph to find a place for us."

Joseph returned quite swiftly with news that there was an inn which could provide two rooms and food just a short-distance away. It was old and very plain, but had the benefit of being further away from where the fishermen brought in their catch than its only rival.

They found the inn, which displayed a sign showing a sailing vessel. The ceilings were low and windows small, making the interior quite dark, but there was clean sand on the floors downstairs and fresh rushes upstairs. Their rooms were small, so it was decided that Stephen, Harry and Joseph would take one, while Olivia, Cecily, Edward and Alice would share the other.

The meal provided was a kind of fish stew, served with thick, fresh bread. It was very tasty but was made from kinds of fish that Alice had never seen before. Stephen explained that the fish came from the sea and the seashore, and were different from the ones which were found in rivers and streams.

After the meal the children were all ready to sleep. It was still light outside because of the long, light evenings, but the journey, the wind and the excitement of the day had made everyone tired and, in the darkness of the rooms, sleep seemed a good idea. The noise of the sea could still be heard, though it was muffled, and the gulls, the white birds that Alice had watched, were still calling. But soon sleep came to them all.

Cecily woke first and after lying still for a while, she turned to Alice and prodded her gently.

"Alice, are you awake?"

"Mmm, nearly."

"Alice," she whispered.

"What is it?"

"It's quiet. I can't hear the sea. I can hear the birds, but not the sea."

Alice sat up. "Yes, you're right, it is quiet," she said softly.

"Can we go and look?"

"Yes, but we must be very quiet. Olivia and Edward are still asleep."

They tip-toed around as they put on their shoes and tidied themselves, then made their way down to the door of the inn. The heavy wooden bar was in place, but Alice was able to lift it. As she did so, the inn-keeper's wife appeared, looking dishevelled from sleep.

"Can I get you anything?" she yawned.

"No thank you," said Alice. "I am sorry we have disturbed you. We just wish to go and find out why the sea is so quiet."

"What, have you never seen t' sea afore?"

"No, never."

"It's low tide now. That's why it's quiet. Menfolk are out already combing the shore. You go and look if you want. When you come back, I'll get you summat to eat. Door won't be locked."

"Thank you. Come along Cissy, let's see what low tide is."

"Wait for me," hissed Harry, coming out still lacing up his boots and with his hair standing up in tufts. "Wait for me."

It was a beautiful morning. The sun was shining and already feeling warm. The breeze was gentle and the gulls were swooping everywhere as the three of them made their way down the steep, narrow lane to where the wall was. Then, moving to the place from where they had watched the sea the night before, they took in the new scene with amazement.

The sea had gone! Where it had been slapping and crashing on the rocks last night, there was now wet sand and rocks covered in green slime, with pools of water among them. The sand stretched to left and right, even over to the cliffs where the castle stood. Just below them a couple of boys were fishing in the rock pools and Alice saw they were working in bare feet. Further along, men were putting rope nets into small boats. The sea was now a long way from them and looked very smooth and quiet.

Alice and the children watched the boys working the rocks, and as they came a bit nearer Harry called to them.

"Hello, there. Can I come to see what you are doing?"

They looked surprised, but the taller of the two spoke. “Yeah, if you want.” Then looking at Harry’s boots, he said, “You’d best take yer boots off. Sand and salt wrecks ’em.”

“Can I, Alice?” Harry asked.

“Yes, but take care.”

“Can I go too?” pleaded Cissy.

“Yes, I think we will all go down,” said Alice.

They found a dry rock and sat on it to remove their footware. Cissy tried to kilt up her skirt, as she used to do when she fished in thc stream, and leaving their shoes by the rock, they ventured on to the wet sand. It was firm and cool under their bare feet, and they left a clear trail of foot marks behind them. They reached the rocks where the boys were and, as they were about to step on to them, the boy who had spoken said, “Beware, t’rocks are slippy. Walk where there’s no weed.”

Cautiously they made their way to a flattish rock where they could stand and watch. One boy had a net while the other had a leather bucket. In the bucket some very strange creatures were moving around.

“Don’t put yer fingers in. They’ll pinch you,” warned the younger boy.

“What are they?” asked Harry.

“Crabs mostly.”

As Harry moved over to look more closely, his shadow fell across the pool where the older boy was fishing.

“Harry, your shadow just frightened a fish. Be more careful,” ordered Cissy, who was resting on her belly to look into the pool.

“Yer know summat about fishin’ then?” said the older boy.

“Oh yes”, Cissy assured him, “but in rivers and streams. Not in rocks or the sea. We’ve never seen the sea before.”

The boy turned his attention to Cissy. “You’ve never seen t’ sea afore? D’ yer keep yer eyes shut?”

“No,” said Cissy indignantly, “there just isn’t sea were we live.”

"No sea? Sea's everywhere."

"No it isn't. We've travelled across the land for two days on horses to get here. We've seen a few rivers and a lot of streams, and some lakes, but there was no sea till we got here."

The boy called to the younger one. "Wat, this lass sez there's no sea where they live."

"No sea!" exclaimed Wat. "Must be a strange place where you live," he said to Harry.

"We live in a castle, a bit like that one over there, but we don't have sea. We have hills and valleys and rivers and villages, but no sea."

"Your Pa a lord then?"

"No, my uncle, her Papa, is the lord, but we all live in the castle."

"Got it!" exclaimed the other boy.

"What yer got, Ranald?"

"A big shanny."

Cissy and Harry watched as Ranald tipped his fish into Wat's bucket. "That's a good one," said Harry.

"Hallo!" A call came from the end of the road, and everyone looked up to see Stephen standing there.

"My Pa," said Harry to Wat.

"Alice"," Stephen called, "come here please?"

Warning Cissy and Harry to be careful, Alice went back across the sand.

"The children seem very interested in the rock pools," Stephen said as Alice reached the rocks below where he was standing.

"Yes, and so am I," said Alice. "The pools are full of many interesting and pretty creatures. I can't believe that we are in the same place that the tossing waves were last night."

"I agree, it is amazing. I am sorry to call you away, but Olivia wishes to get up and Edward is whining, I'm afraid."

"I will come, of course," said Alice, but I must call Cissy and Harry back first."

"No, don't call them. I will watch over them. I will go down there to them. I like rock pools too, and they will disappear under water again soon."

"Why?" asked Alice, as she attempted to rub the sand from her feet.

"Because the tide will come in again."

"When?"

"I'm not sure exactly, but it comes in and goes out twice every day."

"Twice every day, it changes so much?"

"Yes, every day. The people here have their lives ruled by it."

"Now, I must remove my boots and go to the children. When he is ready, try to persuade Edward to come here. He must not miss this."

"I will, sir."

When Alice returned to the shore with Edward, Olivia came too. She had insisted that they ate before they left the inn, and was irritated that Harry and Cissy had not come back for breakfast. Alice had therefore had a word with the inn-keeper's wife and a basket of food had been prepared to take to the shore.

"I don't like the sea," Edward protested as they left the inn. "I want to go home."

"Wait a little bit until you have seen what the sea looks like today. Your Papa, Harry and Cissy are having fun."

They reached the wall and walked past it to the edge of the rocks.

"Not the same place," said Edward, "the sea's gone away. What's Harry doing down there?"

"Looking at fishes and things in rock pools."

"Want to go to Harry."

"Do you? If you do you must take your shoes off and leave them here."

"He must not remove his shoes, Alice. We are not peasants."

"I'm sorry, Olivia, but if he does not take them off they will be damaged by the sand."

"In that case, we must stay here."

"No, Mama! No! Want to go down." Edward sat down and started to remove his shoes.

Stephen, hearing the familiar, frustrated cries of his younger son, turned to come and join them.

"What is all this fuss about now, Edward? You must learn not to get so cross."

"Want to take my shoes off and go to Harry."

"So, can't you unfasten your shoes? Alice will help if you ask her nicely."

"Mama said 'no', must keep my shoes on and stay here."

"Oh, I see. Well my dear, I think this time we should let Edward remove his shoes. I do not want him to miss all the interesting things in the rocks. His shoes would suffer damage from the sand and salt. See, I have removed mine. Why don't you come and join us too?"

"No, thank you. If you will walk with me to that grassy ledge on the cliff there, I will sit and watch you all playing. But don't leave me for too long.

"Alice, care for Edward while Stephen walks me to my seat."

Alice helped Edward with his shoes, then asked him to stand still while she removed her own again. Then she lifted him across the first stones and rock until they were on firm sand, where she put him down.

"Oooh, that feels funny—but I like it. Oh look, my foot has made a mark."

He first walked slowly, watching his feet and the line of footprints behind him then, suddenly gaining confidence, he started to run along beside Alice. She restrained him as they reached the slippery green rocks, but he was soon safely lying on his belly, staring into the pool. Harry and Cecily were chatting happily with Wat and Ranald, although they at times had difficulty understanding the boys' speech, and the boys their's. Cecily was fascinated by the pools which provided such easy catches, but also she was amazed at the strange creatures they were finding. Crabs, which could be no bigger than a thumb-nail or bigger than the palm of her hand, which seemed to look straight-ahead, then walk off sideways. Harry, forgetting the warning from Wat, put his hand into the pool and tried to pick up a crab, which immediately attached itself to his finger with its big claws and hung on tight as Harry pulled his hand out.

"Ow!"

"Told you they nip", said Wat, coming over to Harry and carefully detaching the crab. "Yer lucky it was a little'un."

"But you pick them up," said Harry. "You picked up a big one to put in the bucket."

"Yeah, but I pick 'em up from behind. Look."

Harry watched Wat pick one up, bringing his hand round the creature's shell from the back, away from the claws, so the crab's waving claws could not reach his fingers.

"I see," said Harry. "Can I try again?"

Harry's next try was successful and he added a crab to Wat's bucket. He then sucked his finger which was still uncomfortable from the nip the first crab had given him. He was surprised to find it tasted very salty. He dipped his finger in the pool again and tasted the water. "Hey, Cissy, sea water tastes salty. Try it."

Cissy did, and agreed.

"'course it does," said Wat. "That's 'ow yer get salt. Yer boil a cauldron of sea watter until all the watter boils off and you've got salt left in t' bottom of t'cauldron."

Time passed and the children were having a wonderful time. Cecily discovered lots of pretty coloured things on the sand which Ranald explained were the empty shells of dead shell-fish. He showed her live ones which were so firmly stuck to the rocks that they couldn't be moved, and others which had two parts to their shell, stuck together all along one side, so that the creature could hide itself completely inside. But when the fish had died or been caught and eaten by the sea birds, which could open up the shell, the empty shell parts were washed by the sea and often left on the sand. Cecily started to gather a small pile of the prettiest or strangest.

Harry found a flattish piece of wood among the long brown straps of a plant lying on the sand. The plant looked like a leather tawse used for punishing people, but Wat assured him it was a kind of sea weed. With the piece of wood, he started to draw on the flat, smooth sand. He had been doing this for a while, when Wat looked towards the sea and called to Ranald.

"No much longer, Ran. Tide's well on its way in."

Alice's eyes followed Ranald as he looked out away from the land. The edge of the sea was coming nearer, and there were small waves curving, breaking and rushing up the sand.

"We mun stop fishing and playing now," said Ranald, addressing Alice. "Once it gets past Pillar Rock there, tide runs in fast."

"Thank you," said Alice. "Harry, Cecily, we must go back on to the land. The sea is coming back again. Come along Edward, we must go and put our shoes on before the sea makes them all wet."

Cecily gathered up her pile of pretty shells, carrying them in her skirt. Harry brought his "tawse" and Edward had fistful of smooth coloured pebbles.

Stephen, who had stayed with Olivia at the viewpoint on the cliff, saw the little procession leaving the shore, and came down to the sea wall. He retrieved his own boots then admired the treasures the children were carrying. Now, as they all looked at the sea from the wall, they could see the boats of the fishermen who had gone to the sea earlier, bringing their catch back. The water was carrying their boats toward the shore, but they needed skill to make sure they were not carried on to the rocks. Each wave seemed to bring the sea nearer and nearer.

Wat and Ranald were looking at the contents of their bucket with less than pleasure.

"Our Mam will not be 'appy," said Wat. "It's not as good as yesterday."

Stephen overheard the remark and went over to the boys. "Do I understand that you have not caught enough to please your mother this morning?"

"That's right, sir. I think we might get a whipping today. 'S enough for dinner but not much left to sell for bread."

"I think that my family may be the reason for your poor catch, but you were kind to let them see what you do and tell them about the sea creatures. I am grateful and do not wish you to suffer for your kindness. Here, take these coins, Ranald. Your mother can use them to buy bread and whatever else she will be short of because of your poor catch."

The boys stared at the coins, then at Stephen.

"God bless you, sir," said Ranald. "These will more than spare us a beating. Mam's laying-in with a new babby and can't make bread at present. Now our sister Meg can go and buy some good bread and Pa won't need to beat us."

Alice, watching Edward and keeping him from scattering Cissy's shell collection, heard the exchange between Stephen and the two boys. She marvelled that Stephen and the Baron were so considerate of others, whether servants, peasants or humble strangers such as these boys. She had not had dealings with many people from the wealthy classes but she had heard many tales which suggested that most were not so considerate.

Now that they had left the shore, Harry, Cecily and Alice became aware of their hunger. They joined Olivia on the cliff side and tucked into the basket of food Alice had organised. While they ate, they watched the steady progress of the sea, rushing in, then pulling back again, but getting nearer with each big wave. They saw the fishermen pulling their boats up out of the reach of the sea and selling the fish they had caught along the water front. Then the sea started battering the rocks again and they came down from the cliff to explore the land around the village.

Chapter Thirteen

It was harvest time again. The weather was not as kind as it had been the previous year and the grain had to be harvested in short dry spells between days of heavy rain. It was going to be difficult to get it dry enough for safe storage.

In one of the rainy periods, the Baron and Stephen had the men build special wooden racks in the barns so that, after threshing, the straw and grain could be stored off the floor. The women wove rush mats to lay on the racks so the grain would not fall through, then both ends of the barns were left open for the wind to blow through and help to dry the crop.

The political situation had been quieter for a while, but in some circles unrest was building again. The deranged old king, Henry, was still imprisoned and his wife, Queen Margaret, whose army had fought and defeated the Yorkists at Wakefield and at Towton, was still at the spearhead of plotting against King Edward, and problems were arising in Burgundy also. The Baron did not like the constant scheming that was going on. He wanted a settled, peaceful, Christian land where Kings (or Queens) were not demanding money from the wealthy to spend on war. However, his status and duty demanded that he obey summonses to councils called by the King or by the Royal Dukes, and one such summons came just before the end of harvest celebrations. He headed South in early October.

It was strange to Alice to be living in the castle without the Baron's presence. Cecily missed him very much but, at first, their lives continued in the usual routines. Things started to change when Olivia found she was pregnant again. She became very quick-tempered and began to complain about Alice's privileged position in the household. She should not still be attending lessons with Brother James. Cecily was quite old enough now for Alice's presence not to be required in the schoolroom. The girl had enough book-learning now, and should be concentrating her time on sewing, embroidery, genteel deportment and behaviour, and other such skills which would turn her into a suitable wife for a rich husband.

Alice was therefore called out of the schoolroom frequently to attend Olivia, or to help Cook, or the launderess.

Alice knew that Cecily no longer needed her constant care, but still felt like the child's mother and therefore responsible for her well-being. However, she had no wish to cause trouble between Cecily and her aunt, so she generally did as requested without fuss, hoping that Cecily would not notice.

However, things came to a head about three weeks after the Baron's departure. The weather was once more clement and Harry and Cecily were keen to spend the afternoons out on the moors. Alice had planned to go with them to collect hazel nuts and some late blackberries. Baskets had been assembled and they had a hook on the end of a long pole for pulling down the bramble branches to within reach. Just as they were leaving, Olivia's maid came running after them.

"Miss Alice, Miss Alice, the Mistress wants you now. She said to tell you to come right away."

Alice sighed. "Oh, dear, we are just leaving for the hill above Owls Copse, but I had better see what Olivia wants."

"We'll walk on," said Harry. "You can catch us up when you have seen Mama."

"Very well, but don't go beyond this edge of the copse. If you reach it before I catch up with you, wait there. You will find brambles a-plenty for picking, but be careful."

"We will," said Cissy, but please don't be long."

Alice turned back into the castle, and passing through the main hall, went up the stair to Olivia's rooms. Olivia sat on a bench by the window doing her embroidery.

"Ah, Alice, sit down. I think it is time we had another talk about your duties here."

Alice did not sit. "I cannot stay now, Olivia. We are going to pick blackberries."

"Nonsense," Olivia snapped, "blackberry picking can wait, and I would prefer you to call me 'Mistress Olivia', or 'Mistress'".

"No, I cannot stay now. Cecily and Harry are already on their way. I must go to them."

"Cecily AND Harry."

"Yes, we were leaving by the lower gate when your maid called me back. I cannot leave the children alone on the moor for more than a few minutes."

"Oh, very well. Go if you must but be sure you do not arrange to go out tomorrow afternoon. We will meet then to discuss the terms of your continuing to stay here. Go, then. Go!"

Alice, gasping at what she had just heard, hurriedly went from the chamber and dashed through the castle, out on to the moor. With the words Olivia had just spoken going round in her head, 'terms of your continuing', 'continuing to stay here', 'must discuss', she walked quickly in the direction of Owls Copse.

Instead of enjoying the warmth of the mellow afternoon, Alice walked on oblivious of her surroundings, wondering why suddenly Olivia should want such a discussion. Alice knew that whether she should remain at the castle or not was her own choice, unless the Baron told her otherwise. Perhaps it was just the strain of this early stage in her pregnancy that was making Olivia behave in this way. She must think carefully about what she would say tomorrow, but she certainly could not leave until after the Baron's return, and she must not let Cissy suspect that anything was afoot.

She now reached the top of a slope and Owls Copse was immediately below her. But where were the children?

They were nowhere in sight. Surely she couldn't have gone past them without seeing them. She turned to look back the way she had come. No, they were not behind her.

"Oh, they have disobeyed me and gone into the copse after all." She decided to call them before entering the wood.

"Haarree! Haaaree! Cisseee! Where are you?"

There was no answering call. She called again and again.

Now she started to worry. Surely, if they were in the wood they must have heard her calling. She stood there on the crest of the hill, anxiously wondering which way to look. They wouldn't be deliberately hiding now. Something must be wrong. Then she heard a faint call, which sounded like her name. It was coming from her left.

A small figure was running towards her along the top of the ridge. It was Harry.

Fear grabbing at her throat, she ran to meet him.

"Harry, what is it? Is Cissy hurt?"

Harry was out of breath, but shook his head. "No, Cis's alright . . . . it's a village child who's fallen."

"Take a minute to get your breath, then tell me slowly."

"Well . . . . we got to Owls Copse and started to pick berries. We walked . . . . over that way 'cos we could see . . . . the big bushes." He took a long, deep breath. "Then we heard someone shouting, 'Help! Help!' It came from over there." He pointed back along the way he had come.

"We ran towards the shouting and found two village children—a brother and sister. They had been gathering blackberries too, with their other sister who is an idiot child. Her name is Mary. She had seen some big juicy berries and gone to get them, but they were right at the edge of a cliff and the ground broke under her feet and she fell down the cliff."

Harry had now recovered his breath.

"She didn't fall to the bottom but landed on a sort of shelf part way down. No-one can reach her from above, or from below, and she is just sitting there. We don't think she is very hurt, but her hands are bleeding and she hasn't the wit to do anything for herself."

"Will I be able to reach her, Harry?"

"No, we'll need some men and some rope, I think."

"Can you still run?"

"Oh yes. I was going to run to the castle. It's nearer than the village."

"Very well. You run on to the castle. Get at least two men to come with long ropes. Tell them to come on horses for speed. I'll go on to see if there is anything I can do, and to make sure Cissy's alright. How do I get to them?"

"Along the top here then, when you're level with the end of the copse, go down to the bottom of the slope. You'll see them from there."

"Tell the men to hurry, and take care you don't fall."

Harry side-stepped down the slope and set off at a run back to the castle. Alice ran as best she could along the uneven top of the ridge. She found the way down to the bottom near the edge of Owls Copse, and looked anxiously around. She heard voices calling, and to her left she saw two children, but she could not see Cissy. She ran across to them.

"Can I help you?" she called as she approached from behind. The children turned. There was a boy about eleven and a girl perhaps eight. Alice had a vague memory of having seen them at harvest time.

"Our Mary's fallen down there," said the lad pointing.

Alice looked over the edge of the small cliff, from a safe rock at one side. The child was perhaps fifteen feet below and, as Harry had said, sitting on a narrow ledge. But to her horror, Alice also saw Cissy down there, carefully working her way along the same ledge about thirty feet to the child's left.

Cissy had heard Alice's voice and, without looking up, called, "Oh, I'm glad you are here Alice."

"What are you doing, Cissy? You shouldn't have gone down there."

"I didn't climb down from the top. I got on to the ledge easily at the end of it, but it's getting narrower now, so I've got to be careful."

"Yes, please be very careful. Harry has gone to get men with ropes, so you don't need to go any further."

"I'm just going on to that next bit, so I can sit and talk to her, so she won't be so frightened."

Alice was about to forbid Cissy to go any further, then realised that she was in mid-manoevre, so didn't risk breaking her concentration and, seconds later, Cissy was on the widest bit of the ledge and only a few feet from the child. She sat down carefully with her back against the cliff.

Alice let out a sigh of relief.

The child was watching Cissy with a blank stare from eyes in a dirty little face, which had little cleaner rivulets down it where her tears had trickled.

"Hello, Mary," Cissy said softly. "I'm Cissy. Don't be frightened. People are coming to rescue you."

The child sat.

"Why don't you come very carefully towards me," said Cissy. "It's wider and more comfortable here. Just shuffle a bit at a time on your buttocks."

The child still stared. Then, suddenly, she looked at Cissy and smiled.

"Pretty", she said.

"That's good, Cissy," said Alice. "Just keep talking to her softly like that. She seems calmer."

"I think you're pretty too, Mary."

Mary smiled, then seemed to remember why she was sitting there. "Fell. Hands hurt," and she held her palms up for Cissy's inspection.

"Oh dear. Never mind. When we get you out of here, they can be made better. Someone will be here to rescue you soon."

"Soon," said Mary.

Alice questioned the older children, who were called Jonah and Gertie. They knew who she was as she had brought them dinner in the harvest field.

"Our Mary's usually good," said Gertie. "She only understands simple things but she can be good at helping. She likes picking the berries, but I think she hurt her hands on the bramble. She got upset and went too near the edge."

"If I'd seen the end of the ledge," said Jonah, "I would've gone to Mary, but Cissy saw it and went."

"Yes," said Alice, "Cissy would. Oh, I do wish someone would come with help."

Things were still calm on the ledge and, as Alice watched from above, she saw that with imperceptible movements, Mary was getting nearer to Cissy.

Not knowing who would arrive first with help, Alice suddenly thought, "One of us should be on the ridge up there to signal to the rescuers."

"Jonah, go up to the top of the ridge over there. When help comes it will come from the other side of the ridge. If you stand on top you can signal to them."

"Yes, Miss Alice; that's a good idea." He ran off. He was soon out of their sight, but only minutes later they heard him shout, "They're coming."

"Thank God," thought Alice. "That means Harry got there safely."

She looked over the cliff edge. "Help is in sight, Cissy. Harry must have raised the alarm."

"Good," Cissy called back. "I'm beginning to get numb buttocks."

Two men on ponies suddenly appeared, coming down the steep slope from the ridge very carefully. Alice could see that one was the groom, Cerdic, and the other was a man she did not know by name, but he was a worker on the new building. They both had ropes with them and one had a pannier with tools in.

Cerdic joined Alice and looked over the cliff edge. "What's Miss Cecily doing down there too?" he exclaimed.

"She went down to help the child before I got here," said Alice.

"She's a bold little thing, that one. It's a good job we've got two good long ropes. Though how she got there safely, beats me.

"Dirk, bring t'ropes and come here."

The builder came over.

"Now, how best d'ye think we should do this?" asked Cerdic.

The man pondered, then said, "You say t'little un is simple-minded; we should get t'bright un to rope hersen and then she can help t'other un. I'll make loops, then she don't have to tie knots."

"Right," said Alice. "I'll explain to Cissy what she must do. Cissy, can you hear me clearly?"

"Yes."

"Listen carefully. In a few minutes a rope will be lowered over the edge and come down to you, slowly. You must take the first rope. It will have a big loop in it. You must put it over your head and shoulders until it is under your arms."

"But, Alice, they're supposed to be rescuing Mary."

"Cissy," Alice said sharply, "listen. This is not the time to argue. I am telling you what the men say must be done. Once there is a rope around you, you can put the second rope round Mary. She may not understand what is happening, so if she secs you do something first, she may know better what to do herself."

"Oh, I see. Sorry, Alice."

The first rope was gently lowered down to the ledge and Cissy caught the loop and put it over her head and shoulders. When the second one came down, she spoke softly to the child.

"Look, Mary. I've got my rope on. Now I'll put this rope on you. Don't be frightened."

She lifted the loop over Mary's head and shoulders, but then called up to Alice, "Alice, tell the men not to pull yet. The loop is too loose. Mary will slip straight through it. She's very thin."

"Oh. You'd better take it off her again and we'll pull it back up."

"Up-a-daisy," said Cissy. "It's got to come off again," and she carefully removed the rope. "You can pull it up now."

Dirk looked at his rope, then looked down again at Mary. "Can't make it much smaller," he said. "We'll have to wrap summat round it; 'ave we got owt?"

Because the afternoon had been a warm one, no-one had a cloak or a muffler, but Alice had a small woollen shawl.

"Here, try this".

Dirk wound it tightly round the rope, but its shape was not right.

"Let me tear it or cut it along its length," said Alice. "Have you a tool I can use?"

A sharp knife was produced from the pannier and with Alice and Cerdic pulling the fabric taut, Dirk slit it in half. The two pieces then rejoined lengthwise made it possible to wrap it around the rope securely, reducing the size of the loop.

Back down came the rope and Cissy tried again to fit it over Mary. "That's better. She won't slip through now."

All this time the other ends of the ropes had been tied to bushes near the top of the cliff. Just as Cerdic and Dirk straightened up from lowering the ropes, there was a shout from Jonah. "More people coming."

Alice looked down at Cissie. "Don't move yet, Cissy. Just a few more minutes. Someone else is coming."

The someone else was Stephen on his fine horse, closely followed by Harry on his pony. Stephen dismounted and came over to assess the situation.

"Glad you've come Master Stephen. We're just about to pull them up, and an extra pair of hands will be useful."

"Them?"

"Yes, Stephen, Mary and Cissy. Don't ask now. I'll tell you about it later."

Stephen nodded. He looked over and saw the arrangement of ropes. "You've done well here, but can I make one suggestion?"

"Of course, sir," said Cerdic.

"If we tie the ropes to the harness on my horse, I will hold him and get him to take the strain. You men can then watch the girls and hold the ropes to prevent them being chafed by the top edge of the cliff."

"Can t'horse be trusted not to panic?" asked Dirk.

"He can," said Cerdic firmly. "He'll do just what Master Stephen wants."

So minutes later the two girls were being raised, slowly, side-by-side, up to the top of the cliff. They were close enough together for Cissy to steady Mary and stop her from spinning at the end of her rope. Cissy stopped herself from spinning by bracing her feet against the cliff-face.

At last, they were hauled safely on to firm ground. Mary was grabbed and held by her brother, while Cissy was held close by Alice. Cissy, for all her apparent calm and competence, was trembling after the ordeal.

"Well done, Cissy," said Alice, hugging her tightly. "Well done!"

Mary looked across to Cissy and pointed at her, smiling.

"Pretty," she said, "pretty."

By now it was getting quite dark.

"It's going to be tricky crossing the moor to get home, Master," said Cerdic. "There's no moon 'til late."

"I've got torches," called Harry. "Papa guessed we might need them."

"Have you anything to light them with?"

"Of course," Harry responded proudly. "I've brought a tinder-box and a pouch of dry tinder."

"Good lad, Harry. It's a tricky job but we'll do it," said Cerdic.

"Give the tinder-box and tinder to me," said Alice, taking them from Harry, "then bring me the first torch."

With her years of practice, it took Alice no time at all to coax the tinder to a red glow, then to a small, steady flame. The first torch was lit, and the second and third torches were lit from that one.

Stephen organised the procession back.

"I will lead and Cissie will ride with me. We will carry one torch. Harry, you will follow me, and I'm afraid Alice and Jonah will have to walk along side you. Alice, you will carry another torch. Dirk, will you put Gertie in front of you and Cerdic bring Mary. Perhaps, Dirk, you will carry the third torch and bring up the rear."

It was a very weary group that eventually arrived back inside the castle gate after negotiating the undulating moor in the near dark. Torches had been lit on the drawbridge and inside the wall, the worried parents of the three village children were waiting.

They could not thank everyone enough and were desperate to know just what had happened.

"Your son will tell you," said Stephen. "Go home now. It is late and your children will be hungry. Good night."

As the family left, Mary turned to smile at Cissy again.

"Pretty," she said, "pretty."

The horses were led away by the grooms; Alice and Cissy walked into the great hall together and Tilly ran to greet them.

"Oh, Tilly, can I please have a bath and change my clothes," Cissy asked. "That little Mary stank horribly! Now I stink too."

"I'll get your bath ready right now," Tilly offered, and raced to the kitchen to order hot water to be taken to the bedchamber.

Later, clean and fed, Cissy sat and explained to her Uncle, cousin Harry and Alice, why she had gone down the cliff to Mary.

"But why did YOU go down?" Harry persisted. "When I left to get help, I thought you were just staying there to look after our baskets and things and wait for Alice."

"Well, I was," Cissy replied, "but Mary was getting scared and I remembered Papa telling me that people like us, with money and land, have a duty to look after the people who work for us and those who are poor and have very little, so I knew I had to do it. It was my duty."

Stephen looked across at Alice, who was sitting opposite him at this very informal meal, and he grinned conspiritorially.

"And my wife worries that Cecily is not being brought up to behave like a Baron's daughter!"

Chapter Fourteen

The next afternoon, Alice presented herself in Olivia's room. She had spent most of the morning wondering either, what would be said and how she would respond, or, recalling the adventure of yesterday and cold shivers going down her spine as she thought of what could have happened to Cissy. Now she must concentrate on the former.

Olivia was once again sitting with her embroidery, and she continued stitching as she instructed Alice to sit down. For a moment or two she looked slightly unsure of herself, but then turned to face Alice.

"I have been meaning to talk to you for some time. You have been here for more than a year now, and with Cecily growing up quickly, your role in her life is coming to an end. It is most important that she begins proper training for her position in life, which is something that you cannot give her.

"I have been trying to think of a suitable position for you to take up in the household but, in truth, I cannot think of one. I understand that your own home is there for you to return to, so I feel that is the course you should take."

"Yes, Mistress Olivia," Alice said thoughtfully, putting a subtle stress on the 'Mistress', "my old home is there for me to return to and I do miss my friends at Arkenthorpe, but I certainly cannot return before my lord Baron comes home. It would be very discourteous of me to go in his absence. He has been very good to me."

"He most certainly has. I cannot think of another servant who has ever been shown such consideration."

"There is also the need to prepare Cecily for my departure."

"Nonsense. The child is now mature enough to accept the need for change. I am sure the Baron did not foresee your being permanently in residence with us. When your departure is imminent, I will tell Cecily myself. I do not wish you to mention anything to her at present."

"I guess you don't", Alice thought, "as you know what a fight you would have on your hands." Aloud, she said, "I will really need to agree this with the Baron before I can do anything."

"Perhaps," Olivia said condescendingly, "but I understand he has always said you are free to go whenever you wish."

"I know that is the case, but it must be done at a time that will least inconvenience him."

"I think you flatter yourself, Alice, that your departure will cause convenience or inconvenience to the Baron. I suggest you make your plans so that you can leave within days of the Baron's return."

"There is one problem, Olivia, which will be difficult for me to solve alone. How am I to get back to my home? We travelled here on horseback and it took four days travelling in mid-Summer. The days are short now, I do not own a horse, and would be unable to carry my belongings on foot. Also, I would have great difficulty in finding my way without a guide."

"I will arrange for two of the staff to accompany you, taking the waggon. I am sure Colum would be able to give instructions to the men and yourself about the route to take."

"Very well. Have you had word as to when the Baron might be back?"

"We have received no message, but his expectations were that he would be away for between a month and six weeks."

"So, sometime in the next three weeks. If that is what you wish, I will plan to leave in early December, if the Baron agrees."

In truth, there was little practical preparation that Alice could make. Her possessions were all in the chest in the bedchamber she shared with Cissy, so if she had started to pack, Cissy would soon have been asking questions. One part of Alice liked to think about being back in the valley, living peacefully and going to visit her friends in Arkenthorpe, and the market. But another part of her said that she was now so used to having people around her, she would probably be more lonely than she had ever been before. Leaving Cissy would be very hard, and the thought of it so painful, that she blocked it from her mind as much as she could.

Alice had never been comfortable with Olivia, but could not understand why she was suddenly so determined that she must leave. She had always intended to return home, but this was not a good time to go. She would have no food stocks in and the weather might make it difficult to get to the market in Skipton for several weeks. Perhaps she should change her mind and insist on staying until March when she would have the prospect of good weather ahead for planting seeds and gathering wool to spin.

Several times over the next two weeks, Cissy asked Alice what was the matter. Was she sick again? Why was she sad? Each time Alice answered that she was fine but just kept thinking of things at Arkenthorpe. Cissy said that perhaps Papa would let them go for a visit in the Spring.

Otherwise, life continued as usual, though Alice rarely managed to go into a lesson with Cissy and Harry, as Olivia expected her to take charge of Edward in the mornings. Eleanor was now a handful for the nursery maid and the boy needed to be outside, using his energy. Alice had the knack of handling him and he responded well to her.

The Baron returned on the fifth day of December. The light had almost gone and the air was damp and clammy. He sent for Cecily to come to see him almost immediately, but he was clearly exhausted from travelling and retired to his chamber straight after supper.

The next day he was closeted for several hours with Stephen, discussing estate business and being disappointed that building of the new solar would now be halted until late Winter or early Spring. True, the shell of the building was almost complete, but the horn panels for the windows, and the delicate stained glass for the chapel would be at risk of damage if transported from York in winter conditions. Not until the window panes were in place could furnishing start.

On the second morning after his return, as soon as the children were in the school room, Alice was somewhat surprised when the Baron sought her out, finding her with Edward.

"Alice, please take Edward to his mother and join me in a walk around the moat—the sun has actually appeared this morning—as I must talk with you."

Alice, wondering what all this could be about—perhaps the rescue at the cliff—took Edward to Olivia, put on her warm cloak and met the Baron by the door to the stable yard.

"Come, Alice, let us walk." He was looking grave and Alice was worried. At last, as they reached the track worn in the grass by the side of the moat, he spoke.

"After you and the children had left the Great Hall at the end of supper last night, Olivia told me that you intend to leave us and return to your home, and she implied that you will go very soon.

"Alice, I must advise you against such a plan. Travelling now will be difficult and dangerous. I know I promised that you can go home whenever you wish, but I beg you to wait until the Spring."

"Oh my lord, please believe me, I had intended consulting you before taking action. I did not realise that Mistress Olivia would tell you. I did explain to her that I would be unable to make the journey on foot, as my travel bags would be too heavy, and that I would need help in finding the way. However, she said that she would send two servants with me and we would travel by waggon. I also assured her that it must be at a time that would cause you least inconvenience."

"Does that mean you will agree to stay until Spring?"

"Yes, my lord, I would prefer that, as I shall have no stores in the cave and the weather might make it difficult to get to Skipton, or even to Arkenthorpe, for several weeks."

"That relieves my mind somewhat," said the Baron, smiling at her. "Now, may I ask if you have been unhappy here? Why have you suddenly come to this decision?"

"No, I have not been unhappy. I have had some wonderful experiences which I shall treasure all my life. I love Cecily deeply and shall miss her very much, but she is now settled in her rightful place and I should return to mine."

"I don't think your 'rightful place' is a lonely valley, living alone. Yes, it is a beautiful spot and you have created a surprisingly comfortable home, but you are an intelligent woman, Alice, and you merit much more. Do you really wish to return to your old life?"

Alice sighed. "Oh, my lord, I don't know. I valued the independence I had and was blessed with good friends. But the day you came to the valley to see Cissy, I was almost in despair at the thought of living there without her."

"So why leave her now?"

"It will be a little easier now, as I know she is safe and loved, and I will be able to picture her here. But, Mistress Olivia is right to say that

Cecily now needs training to fit her for her position in life, and that is something I cannot do."

The Baron gave a sharp intake of breath. "Ah, is it perhaps Olivia's wish that you leave, rather than your own, Alice?"

Alice felt herself suddenly in a difficult position. She did not wish to cause a rift between the Baron and Olivia, but nor did she wish this very kind man to think she was eager to leave his service.

"Mistress Olivia does find my being here difficult, I think. I have tried to be useful to her now that Cecily does not need me so much, but I always put Cecily first."

"According to my brother, you have been making yourself very useful, particularly in relation to that demanding child, Edward. I fail to see why Olivia should not be very pleased to have your here."

"I do not know why, my lord, but my position is difficult for both of us, so it seems best that I return home."

"Olivia gave me to understand that no word of this has reached Cecily."

"Oh no, my lord, I have said nothing. If I do not leave until early Spring, she and I will have time to talk together and get used to the idea of separation."

"I must tell you, Alice, that Cecily will not be the only one who will be sad to have you go. The joy of having Cecily back is still a wonder to me, and having you here as her companion has comforted me greatly. By your presence, you have helped both Cecily and me to learn how to be father and daughter.

"Now, let us say no more about your leaving until the new year at least. If you still feel you must go, you will be escorted and provided with anything you need. I will tell Olivia that you will not be leaving yet."

"Thank you my lord.

"Oh, my lord? Have you been told about Cecily's part in the rescue of the child from the village?"

"Yes, Alice, I have." The Baron smiled. "I must confess that I was concerned at the danger Cecily had put herself in, but it seems that both she and Harry redeemed themselves after disobeying your instructions to them. I am proud of them both, and very glad to find they have concern for others."

This northern area of the country was now quite peaceful and the war almost a thing of the past. Social life among the wealthy folk was starting again and the Baron, Stephen and Olivia had attended two gatherings during the Christmas and New Year season.

It was towards the end of January when the subject of Alice's departure from the castle was mentioned again. The Baron, of course, knew exactly the date of Cissy's birth and so, on the twenty-fourth of January, the family celebrated her ninth birthday. There were party games and dancing and a merry time was had by everyone.

As things were drawing to a close, Alice was surprised when Olivia came to sit next to her at the table on the daïs. They were alone, watching everyone else on the floor of the Great Hall.

"Cecily has had a lovely day," said Alice. "She is so happy."

"Yes," said Olivia, not taking her gaze off the activities below, "I don't think you need concern yourself about her any longer. Have you decided when you will leave us yet?"

Alice felt as though someone had just thrown a bucket of cold water over her. She turned to look at Olivia, but that lady continued to gaze straight ahead.

"No, I have not," said Alice cautiously. "I have to discuss it with the Baron first."

"You must really make a decision very soon. It will be as well for you to go before the rumour reaches the Baron's ears."

"What rumour? I have no idea what you mean."

"No, I don't suppose you do, but some people have apparently seen through your sweet, reasonable demeanour. It was quite embarrassing for me to hear, when we visited Sir James and Lady de Vallon last week, that others have become aware of your attempts to become Baroness Muirhill."

Alice felt as though she would faint, and every vestige of colour drained from her face. Gripping the edge of the table until her knuckles were white, she eventually gasped, "No, that is not possible. I have never even thought of it. Who is saying this terrible thing?"

"I understand that the person who informed me, heard it from someone who had been in the company of Baroness Derwent."

"I have never heard of Baroness Derwent." Then, suddenly out of the swirling mists in her head, Alice remembered Baron Derwent at the inn in York.

"I remember that Baron Derwent stayed one night at our inn when we visited York, but I did not speak to him."

"Whether you spoke or not is beside the point. He obviously watched you."

"But I did nothing improper."

"Don't try to charm me with your 'reasonableness'. I have seen with my own eyes, and heard with my own ears. "Oh, my lord . . .", you say, and you smile up at him. I have seen you and he walking alone, with no servant in attendance, deep in conversation, and laughing together."

At this moment, the musicians stopped playing and a dance ended. Cecily turned to look for Alice, just as Alice stood up to leave the hall, but found herself unable to stand. She crumpled slowly down to the floor.

"Alice," Cecily shrieked, and rushed to the daïs. Kneeling down beside her, she picked up Alice's hand. "Alice, you're ill. What's wrong? Alice! Aunt Olivia, please get Alice some help."

"Don't be concerned my dear. I'm sure she will be fine in a few minutes. Perhaps a little too much wine."

By this time, others had noticed something was wrong, and the general hubbub was dying down. Stephen came striding across.

"What is wrong?"

"I think Alice is ill," Cecily moaned. "She can't speak to me."

Just then, Alice moved and opened her eyes. "Cecily?"

"Oh, Alice, yes, it's me. You stood up, but then you fell to the floor. I was frightened."

"I did feel ill but I think I will be better in a few minutes."

Stephen bent down. "Let me help you on to a chair. Give me your arm."

Suddenly the Baron arrived. "Wait a moment Stephen. I will take Alice's other arm."

Between them they raised her easily, and sat her in the Baron's dining chair.

"You are very white, Alice; perhaps I should fetch a doctor," Stephen offered.

"No, I will soon be well again. I don't know why I fainted. Please return to the party. I will rest for a couple of minutes then go to my bedchamber."

"I will come with you," Cecily said firmly.

"No, Cissy, it is your birthday. You must stay."

"I have had a lovely birthday, but now I must look after my Alice. I will come with you. Papa, will you ask Colum to help Alice up the stairs in case she feels faint again."

"No need to ask Colum," said the Baron, "I will help her myself.

"Stephen, signal to the band to play another dance; the party can continue for a while longer."

So the little group crossed the daïs to the stairwell. With the Baron's arm firmly round her shoulders, Alice felt her cheeks flooding red with embarrassment, as she remembered the rumour that had caused her to faint. This would not help to kill the rumour at all.

Cecily had been very relieved when Alice made a rapid and complete recovery, but she also sensed that all was not right.

Alice now knew that she must leave the castle as soon as possible. She could not bear the thought that the Baron's reputation and good name could be damaged by his kindness to her. She admired him greatly and had certainly developed a deep affection for him, but the idea of becoming his wife had not entered her mind. However, now that someone else had put the idea there, she did imagine it from time to time. Given that she had no family and no dowry, and that she did not even know who her father had been, it was never more than a flight of fancy. The difficulty now was what reason to give for her need to depart. She certainly could not give the real reason to the Baron, or to Cissy.

After days of thought, she decided it would have to be that she must get home and be ready to start planting as soon as the weather allowed. Once she had settled on this, she looked for an opportunity to speak to the Baron.

On the second morning after her decision, she saw the Baron in the Great Hall when he came in for refreshment after riding into the village.

"My lord," Alice said quietly, after he had greeted her, "may we speak?"

"Of course, Alice. Please come to the table with me."

When one of the servants had brought him a flagon of ale, the Baron turned to her. "What is it, Alice?"

"I think the time has come for me to leave, my lord. If I am to be ready to plant my vegetables, I must be at home and have the ground cleared and prepared by the middle of March. I would like to ask your help in providing transport and directions, and also to ask your advice about telling Cecily."

"So, the time has come. Are you sure you are well enough to make the journey? It is only just over a week since you gave us all a fright by fainting. Are you fully recovered?"

"Yes, thank you, my lord."

"Very well then, I will arrange your transport and an escort. You must also list what you will need to get your home comfortable and equipped. You must take a store of food that will last you for at least two months, and you must take well-dried wood for fires. I will also ensure you have money to meet your needs for a year."

"My lord, I cannot accept such generosity."

"You cannot refuse it, Alice. I will not allow you to do so. I would also give you a horse, but that might create problems for you in caring and providing for it. But, I will include some extra money in case you have the opportunity to purchase a donkey, which would be more manageable, or perhaps a young Dales pony like Freya. Freya is too old now to be of use to you for long.

Alice opened her mouth to protest again, but the Baron held up his hand. "Cerdic will drive the waggon and Colum will accompany you on horseback. They are both men I trust. They will care for you and Colum knows the way."

"But my lord, Colum is your personal man-servant. He will not wish to leave you."

"He will do as I ask, and there is a younger boy who will serve me while Colum is away. I shall have my wants taken care of well-enough for a few days.

"Now to the really difficult thing. When and where do we tell Cecily? I truly wish that you would stay, but as you are determined on going, we must face the task."

"She must hear it from me or from you. It would be terrible for her to hear it from anyone else."

"I agree, Alice."

In the end it was decided that the Baron would tell Cissy, and a departure date was agreed two weeks hence, if the weather permitted. Cecily would be told a week before Alice was due to go.

On the Sunday, as the family walked back to the castle after Mass in the village church, the Baron said quietly to Alice, "I shall speak to Cecily this afternoon. I will call her to my room."

Alice was playing a counting game with Edward when Cissy came over to her. "I'm going to see Papa. He wants to talk with me, so don't worry that I have disappeared."

"Thank you for telling me. I will see you later then."

Cecily skipped off up the stairs to the family quarters. Alice continued to play with Edward for a while; then she took him back to the nursery and retired to the chamber to await the storm she knew must come.

When Cissy entered the room, she came in very quietly and her eyes were red from weeping.

"Oh, Alice . . . . Alice." She came over and flung her arms around her. For a little while, Alice just held her tight then, slowly, Cissy pulled back a little.

"Why Alice? Why must you go?"

"I have stayed much longer than I intended. When I came with you, I expected to stay a few months only. The time had to come."

"I know you miss our lovely valley, and you miss Maud and John, but I would really have liked you to stay and perhaps just go to visit sometimes. If you go back to live there, I might never see you again. Won't you miss me?"

"Oh my sweet child, I will miss you very much, and part of me wants to stay here, but it is not really my home."

"Papa would be happy for you to stay for ever. I'm sure he does not want you to go away. Harry and Edward will miss you too, though not so much as I will."

"Your Papa has been very good and kind to me, and I shall be sad to leave, but you have now got to learn all the things that a Baron's daughter needs to know, and I cannot teach you those things." There will soon be nothing for me to do here."

Suddenly, Cecily seemed her usual, determined self again. "When Aunt Olivia talks to me about what I have to do to learn to be a young lady, it is mostly about the things I must NOT do." She proceeded to give a fair imitation of Olivia. "Really Cecily, you must not be so familiar with Tilly. Don't ask her to do things—tell her! Cecily do not lift up your skirts and run. It is so undignified. Carry your head higher. Curtsey more gracefully. In only a few years, a wealthy husband must be found for you. We shall have to start looking for possible young men quite soon. You must learn to be charming. An ability to read, write and catch fish will not impress a wealthy young man's family when they are looking for an obedient wife. And so she continues, on and on and on!"

Alice could not help but laugh. "I fear you do need to know most of these things, but it is good to ASK servants to do things for you, and to treat them kindly. Your Papa and your Uncle Stephen always do and the staff here are loyal, and happy to work for such good men. So, I recommend that you still ask Tilly nicely when you want her to do something for you. It will make you more of a lady, not less of one."

"What will you do Alice? Will you have to spin bits of wool again and gather berries to make drinks to sell?"

"I don't know yet. Your Papa is giving me a generous amount of money so that I won't have to rush to do those things straight away. I may find some other work I can do instead."

There was quiet for a few moments, then Cissy spoke. "Alice, can I ask you something?"

"You could always ask me anything. Why hesitate now?"

"It was something Papa said just now. He said that, perhaps if you had not been looking after me, you would have been able to marry some nice man and have children of your own. Is that true?"

Alice was surprised and showed it.

"I never thought of it like that, Cissy. Looking after you made me happy and I soon came to think of you as my own child. As for finding a husband, well, I might have done, but most girls who marry are married before they are as old as I was when I found you. Please don't worry about that."

They talked about many things over the next few days, and each night Cissy snuggled tightly up to Alice in bed.

As the news spread through the castle, many people were shocked and surprised. Tilly wept; Cook said how much she would miss her friendship; Colum and Cerdic both expressed surprise but assured her, and Cissy, that they would care for her on the journey. Harry was horrified.

"Alice, please don't go," he pleaded. "You let us do such interesting things. Are you going because you don't like having to look after terrible Ted all the time?" (This nick-name for his young brother had pleased

Harry greatly when he had thought it up a few days before.) Edward was there and heard the remark. He immediately burst into tears.

"I'm not terrible Ted. You like me don't you Alice? I like you. I don't want you to go away."

Alice comforted Edward. "Of course I like you. I love all of you and I shall miss you all, but I really do have to go home now."

After two more days of heartfelt dismay and kind comments from the servants and the children, Alice suddenly thought, "Now I know why Olivia has become so hostile! She fears she is losing her authority over the children and servants. She sees me as a threat. The rumour must have been the final straw. Poor Olivia."

The day of parting finally came. Alice had slept little the night before, and soon after first light, the waggon was ready and Colum was steadying Acorn, who was eager to go.

Alice was coming out to the stable yard, with Cissy carrying Alice's last few items in a small bag. Just before they reached the door to the yard, the Baron met them.

"Everyone in the castle is waiting out there to bid you farewell. God be with you, Alice. I am sure we will meet again, and whenever someone in the household is travelling through a place near Skipton, they will leave a message to be passed to you. A letter may be left with Brother Luke, so be sure to see him whenever you visit Skipton."

"I will." Alice's voice trembled. "God bless you, my lord."

Alice and Cecily walked out into the cold, slightly misty morning, with the Baron following several paces behind. Harry rushed forward to shake hands with Alice, then decided he was not too big to hug her instead. (Edward was still asleep in bed.) Even Olivia was there, standing with Stephen.

Alice spoke first. "Farewell, Olivia. I hope all goes well with the baby and that your laying-in will not be difficult."

Olivia inclined her head, "Thank you Alice. I wish you a good journey."

"Farewell Alice," said Stephen, "and thank you for all the help you have given to our children. I hope we will all meet again."

Then it was time to give Cissy a final embrace, as both of them shed a few tears. Cerdic handed Alice into the waggon and Cecily put the bag into it beside her. Colum then raised his arm. Cerdic clicked to the horse in the shafts, and they moved off, through the portcullis, and rumbled across the drawbridge.

From the yard, shouts of blessing and farewells followed them and, as Alice turned for a last look back, she saw Cissy waving and leaning against her Papa, who had his arm tightly around her.

Chapter Fifteen

For the first few weeks after her return to Home Valley, Alice was very lonely. The loneliness assailed her when she went to bed and again when she awoke in the morning. She had had Cissy sleeping near her almost every night for the previous seven years. She prayed for Cissy and the Baron before she went to sleep and thought about Cissy between waking and starting her work for the day.

Her life in the cave and the cot was now much more comfortable than it had been before she went away, thanks to the generosity of the Baron. Her possessions had come back with her in the chest they had been stored in at the castle. She had the comfortable mattress and fur bed cover from her bed there. She also had a store of flour, oatmeal, dried grapes and herbs, cheese and salt-pork. She even had a supply of paper, quills and ink.

The journey home had been difficult on muddy, rutted roads, and at times mist had slowed them even further. When they had arrived, it had been hard work getting all her things from the waggon, which had to be left by the oak tree, down the steep, rocky track into the valley. Colum and Cerdic had worked very hard. Then, once everything had been unloaded, Colum had ridden across to Arkenthorpe to the wheelwright's, to let Alice's friends know that she had returned home. While he was away,

Cerdic had helped to put things where she wanted them, and at one point he lifted up a cloth bag which Alice thought could not be hers.

"Oh, it's definitely for you Miss Alice," he assured her. Inside the bag were assorted, very small bags, each tied tightly with coarse twine.

"They're seeds, Miss. When folk in the village heard you was leaving, some of them asked me if there was anything they could give you. I'd heard you telling someone you had to get here in time to prepare for planting your vegetables, so I said perhaps they could spare a few seeds. So that's what you've got. It might be difficult to know what you're planting. You'll just have to see what comes up."

Alice was deeply touched by everyone's kindness and asked Cerdic to give them her grateful thanks.

By the time the two men left to start their long journey back to the castle, her fire was alight and all her possessions safely under cover in the cave.

Next morning, she had checked the condition of the few possessions she had hidden in Eden, and was reassured to find, apart from some dampness, they were as she had left them almost two years ago. The morning promised to be fair, so she had walked to Arkenthorpe to see her friends.

Maud was delighted to have Alice back and demanded to hear about all her adventures, but having told her of the castle and a few things she had seen on her travels, Alice insisted that Maud tell her what had happened to her family and in Arkenthorpe in her absence.

There was the sad news that Maud had been pregnant again, but the baby came early and was still-born. Maud had been quite unwell and the doctor had said it would not be wise for her to have any more children, so young Jack, now four years old, was likely to be her last. Thomas had accepted this and had been most considerate of her. She told Alice how grateful they felt that the money from the Baron had meant they could afford to have the doctor come to her.

There was good news also. As Alice had immediately noticed, Maud's house now had two extra rooms. Thomas had used a large part of the money from the Baron to pay for the building of the rooms and one was now a workroom for Maud. She had a regular flow or orders for her dressmaking and their eldest girl, Joan, was helping her mother and learning the trade.

Thomas's business was still thriving and he had been able to pay for young Tom to be apprenticed to the blacksmith in the village. The blacksmith was getting old and only had two daughters. It was hoped that eventually Tom would take over the forge and the family business would be able to offer the services of wheelwright and blacksmith. It was also hoped that the next son, Lucas, would follow his father's trade.

John and Mary were still gardener and cook to Squire Harald. They had spent some of the Baron's gift on a new bed and mattress, and a chair, which helped John to rest his wounded leg more comfortably after a day's work. He had also purchased a salve from an apothecary to ease the discomfort. John had continued gardening but was considering buying a pony and cart so that he could go regularly to Skipton, or other local market, and bring back goods to sell in the village. Pedlars came to Arkenthorpe, but each one rarely came more than twice a year, and would have only one or two kinds of goods to offer. John's plan was to have a shop where he would sell many different types of things, so that people did not have to wait for the pedlar. One difficulty could be where he and Mary would live, as their cottage went with the job of gardener.

Squire Harald's wife had borne him a third child, and this time it was a son. The villagers were used to the Squire now and, although he would never be liked as his father had been, he was not disliked.

Gradually therefore, Alice found herself adjusting to her return to Arkenthorpe, but never a day went by when she did not think of Cissy and what she might be doing and feeling.

It took several weeks of work to get her little field strip in the valley prepared and sown with her vegetable seeds, but she also made a small bed for vegetables in her garden of Eden. She was sure that, because it was more sheltered from the winds, the seeds would sprout earlier than those in the valley, and she was right. Also, no rabbits had found their way into Eden, so she did not have to put protection around the new plants. There did seem to be quite a lot more rabbits in Home Valley than before.

When she went into Eden, she took an oil lamp with her, which she could leave, alight, on a ledge just inside the cave, ready to light her way back. However, she also found a way of fixing a piece of rope to the cave wall, so that if at any time her lamp failed, she could hold on to the rope and feel her way back safely in the dark.

The weeks passed, then, on her fourth visit to Skipton, she was thrilled to find a letter waiting for her at the church. Father Luke told her that a messenger, travelling south, had left it.

The first few lines were from the Baron. He asked after her well-being and assured her that anyone from the castle, or from the neighbouring villages, who was passing Skipton on his travels, would call at the church, so that if Alice wished to write to Cecily, her letter would be collected and delivered at the earliest opportunity. He asked that she give his greetings to her friends, and that if she ever had any request he could help her with, he would do his utmost to meet it.

The rest of the letter was from Cissy.

> "Oh my dear, dear Alice. I do miss you and think of you so much, and I miss Home Valley. Of course, I love my Papa,

> who is so kind, but he does get cross with me sometimes, just like you did. Everyone here is well. Aunt Olivia gave birth to another girl who is named Margot. There is a new nursery maid to take care of Eleanor who is now playing with everything and being nearly as naughty as Edward was. He is still naughty but does not get so cross. Harry and I have more lessons now, and in the afternoons he has to learn sword-fighting and how to use his lance when riding. He misses you too. I have to learn more embroidery and plain sewing. I have just had some new boots as my feet have grown again. Oh and Colum has married Edith, a notary's daughter. Please write to me Alice, so that I know what you are doing. Please tell my friends in Arkenthorpe I wish I could see them again, but most of all I miss you my Alice. From your loving Cissy.

Alice wept as she read her letter—the first letter she had ever received in her life. She was so glad she could read and write. She gave a lot of thought to what she could say in a letter to Cissy, then a week before she next would go to Skipton, she started to write one very carefully.

> Dearest Cissy, thank you for writing to me. I miss you very much. I think about you a lot particularly if I am trying to catch fish. All our friends here are well. Maud had another baby while I was away with you. It came early and died at birth, so that was sad. Maud was sick but is better now. She now has a workshop room built on to their cottage where she does her sewing. Young Tom is apprenticed to the blacksmith. I have collected some wool and cleaned it but have not done any spinning yet. My vegetables are planted and growing well. Tell Harry and Edward that I think of them often. Please tell

> you Papa that I am well. I pray for you both every night. Your devoted and loving Alice.

Alice left the letter with Father Luke to await the next traveller from Muirhill. Father Luke had been interested to hear about her experiences, especially her travels to York and the coast. He had visited the Minster and listened eagerly to Alice's description of her visit. He had never seen the sea and was amazed by the things she told him.

As she walked to and from Skipton, Alice would muse on all the things she had been fortunate enough to see and experience: the travelling; the sea; York; learning to ride; the opportunity to improve her own reading and writing and so being able to send and receive letters; harvesting; living in a castle—so many things which, only two years ago, she could not even have imagined. As she passed the place where she had found Cissy so long ago, she would say to herself, "Yes, I was right when I predicted that the baby would change my life."

Her first year back at Home Valley passed very quickly. Her crops grew well. She gathered rose hips, heather flowers and bilberries from the moors around to make her drinks. She bought better storage pots for them and was able to buy honey to sweeten some of the drinks. She gathered and cleaned wool ready to spin during the Winter and she had been able to spend more time in Arkenthorpe village. John was finding the gardening much more difficult by the Autumn and he went to see Squire Harald, who agreed that he could hand over that work to someone else. A cottage, very old and in great need of repair, was empty and the Squire agreed to put it to rights for John and Mary to rent. He also agreed to build a small, extra room for John to turn into a shop, for which he would pay a small additional rent, and be granted a licence to trade.

On her visits to the village, Alice now began to teach John the reading, writing and calculating that he would need to be able to buy and sell goods. He did not find it easy and it was a slow process. In the end, Mary asked Alice if she would be willing to help John with the business for a while, and this was agreed. Alice would sell some of the drinks she made and the wool she spun, in the shop. The Widow Litton had become too old and frail to weave, but one or two other village women were weaving cheap cloth for their own use, and would probably buy Alice's wool, if she would barter it and not insist on payment in coin.

Now that John was not working for the Squire, he spent some of the day at Thomas's workshop, constructing, under his brother-in-law's supervision, a cart suitable to take him to and from the nearest small towns to purchase stock for his shop.

Together, with Alice writing on some of her precious paper, Mary, Maud, John and Thomas tried to decide what items villagers would be likely to buy from John. Very few people left the village more than once or twice a year (some never left) to visit Skipton or other places big enough to have a market or shops. It was agreed that little food would be bought, as the village could meet its own needs, but storage jars, cooking pots and utensils, some rush-lights and candles, salt and oatmeal would be the initial stock. If a person wanted a particular item, they could ask John to purchase it for them and pay a small charge above the price for his services.

The Squire had men working to repair the old cottage whenever weather permitted, and when January ended, John and Mary moved in. A week later John purchased a pony called "Briar" to pull the completed cart. So it was, that at the end of February, John, with Alice accompanying him, set off on his first purchasing trip to Skipton.

It was a successful trip. They found that potters and wood-workers would reduce the price of an item when John was buying perhaps four or five of the same thing. This meant, Alice told him, that he would be able to re-sell each one for more than he had paid, but it still should be affordable for most of their likely customers. It was also a successful trip for Alice, as Father Luke had another letter for her from Cissy. With the cart and the strong little pony, the journey home again was at a good, steady pace. The moon rose early too, so even when the daylight faded, they were able to reach Arkenthorpe safely.

Alice stayed at John and Mary's for the night, and once in her bed, she untied her letter from Cissy.

> My dear, dear Alice, I was so happy to receive your letter and hear about everyone. I was sad that Maud's baby died, but very glad she is well again. Tom must be grown up now that he is learning the trade of blacksmith. The exciting news here is that the King's brother, Richard, Duke of Gloucester and his new wife have come to live at Middleham Castle. Papa says that our family will soon be invited to visit the Duke and that I am old enough to go. Aunt Olivia is making me practise my curtsey again and again and I am to have a dress made in the latest fashion. I wish you were here to come with us. The other good news is that we have moved into the new house at last. It is light inside and the chambers have fine bone windows so the daylight can come in even when it is cold outside. My chamber has a big curtain around the bed and Tilly has a truckle bed outside the curtain, but in my room. There is a hearth with a chimney and we have kept warm all winter. I remember to say my prayers every day and I always ask God to bless my Alice. From your loving Cissy.

Alice blew out her candle and lay thinking about the letter. The family visit to the Duke and Duchess would be a very important occasion. Cissy would have to remember the correct way to speak to royal persons, and she would have to remember her training in good manners. Alice laughed ruefully to herself when she thought of Cissy's "I wish you were here to come with us." Of course, even if she had been there, she would not have been included in the invitation. Olivia would have been mortified by such an idea.

The new house, she guessed, would be much more comfortable than the old castle. It would be similar in size to Arkenthorpe Manor and would be easier to keep warm than the castle and, with a chimney to carry away the smoke, things would keep cleaner.

Next day, she helped John to sort the items purchased for the shop and it was agreed that she would return in two days' time, bringing her own goods to be sold.

Throughout that Spring and Summer, Alice divided her time between Home Valley and Arkenthorpe. She kept telling herself that it would be sensible to find somewhere to live in the village. She could, with the money she still had left from the Baron's gift, afford to rent a small cottage but, if Squire Harald were to rent such a cottage to her, she would be expected to pay at least part of that rent in some form of service to him. She was sure now that he would no longer want her for his bed, but something inside her kept saying, "No Alice, keep your independence a while longer yet." When she needed to stay the night in Arkenthorpe, she now had a truckle bed in the shop.

She decided that her current life suited her well. She had company when she needed it but she also had her beautiful Home Valley. She had no idea who owned the land around the valley—perhaps it belonged to the King. After the horrors of the Black Death many years ago, pieces of land had been unclaimed where many members of the same family had died. Perhaps this was one of them, but it felt like her land. It was peaceful and beautiful. It provided her with food and shelter and now she had some comforts which the Baron's money had enabled her to buy, she had no wish to change. John and Mary, or Maud and Thomas would sometimes come to visit and for them it was a pleasant change. Maud still worried a little that her friend was living there alone, but even she would have been sorry for Alice to leave the valley altogether.

One day, Alice had shown them her "Garden of Eden", which regularly produced its fruit and vegetables a week or more ahead of anywhere else. They were amazed, and also relieved that Alice had a place to retreat to should she ever feel threatened.

Twice during the year, Alice received a letter from Cissy and sent one in return. She heard of the visit to Middleham and how Cissy had pleased her Papa in the way she had conducted herself. In the second letter, Cissy said that they were expecting Olivia's brother, Piers du Bois, his wife and family to join them for Christmas. Alice knew nothing of Olivia's family except that they were of French stock and lived in Derbyshire, but owned land elsewhere too, including some near the border of West Scotland.

It was a good Summer with plenty of warm sunshine and only occasional showers of rain. Autumn continued mild and dry. By Christmas there had been a few frosty days, but no rain or snow. The rivers and streams were low, which made for easy travelling. Alice's stream continued to trickle from the hills, so she had sufficient water for her needs, but where folk were dependent on wells for their water, some of the shallower ones ran dry. For the deeper wells, longer ropes had to be fitted to buckets, and there was a serious shortage of water in some towns.

In January some snow fell on the moors and in the valleys. The ground was dry and very hard. Then, in the last few days of January, the weather changed. The wind came from the West and brought with it solid, black clouds which unleashed torrential rain for day after day. The land, which was so hard, flooded and was impassable in many places. Alice's stream flooded the lowest part of Home Valley where a wall of rock almost closed off the end. She could not reach Arkenthorpe. Most of the way to the village was on higher ground but it dipped steeply in two places and the flood water was knee deep. Surprisingly, Eden did not flood. Its little waterfall poured into its basin, but the water disappeared. Everywhere in the cave, however, Alice could hear the sound of rushing water below ground. At last the hard ground began to soften under the water and the floods slowly subsided, leaving behind thick mud or squelchy bog where the moss grew on the moors.

It was, therefore, a great relief to wake one morning to a sky that was blue and had white clouds instead of the heavy pall of grey. The sun was gaining strength and soon everywhere steam was rising from the ground. On the second day of blue sky, Alice set off for Arkenthorpe. It was not an easy walk, and she had to make one detour where the mud was too deep to cross. To save her boots, she was wearing wooden pattens bound to her feet with rags. She eventually arrived safely, looking rather dirty and bedraggled, to find Arkenthorpe was in a far worse condition than she was. Mud was everywhere down the main street and, from the dark stains on walls, the water had clearly been high enough to flood many of the cottages. The contents of middens had been washed into the street and in the warmth of the sun, an unpleasant smell was now rising into the air.

Maud was shovelling mud out of her cottage, which had its door and shutters wide open. Joan was helping her, while across the yard, Thomas and Lucas were working to clear the workshop floor.

"We were fortunate," Maud told Alice, "the water only reached our ankles. We managed to keep most things dry. Joan, Jack and me slept on the table, while Thomas and Lucas slept in a cart in the workshop. Young Tom stayed at the blacksmith's most of the time."

"What can I do to help?" Alice asked.

"You'd best go and help John with the shop. I'm not sure how they fared. Joan and me'll manage here."

At every cottage she passed, Alice saw people clearing out mud and worse from their homes. Lengths of cord had been strung between trees, and blankets, cloaks and other garments were hung there for the breeze to dry them. Every bush seemed to have something spread on it too.

Sure enough, John was outside the shop, leaning on a shovel, surveying a pile of mud that he had just cleared from inside. He saw Alice approaching.

"Glad to see you've survived, Alice. Everything is such a mess."

"I've survived much better than folk here in Arkenthorpe. The cave stayed dry, although there is a great, rushing torrent raging somewhere in the rocks below."

"How have you and Mary coped?"

"Mary stayed at the Manor one night. Even they had flooding in the scullery. The shop floor was almost knee-deep, but I got almost everything off the floor in time. There's a lot more mud to get out."

"What about your other rooms?"

"Not much damage. They're a bit higher than this 'un and because t'Squire had t'cottage repaired before we moved in, I guess we've done better 'n most."

"Well, now I'm here," said Alice, "I'll help with clearing the mud. Have you another shovel?"

"No, there's only a spade."

John limped across to where his tools hung on the wall and reached down a spade. As he turned to come back, Alice saw a look of severe pain cross his face.

"Oh John, you're in pain. Have you hurt your leg again?"

"No, it's just pain's real bad in wet weather, and I've none of the balm left."

"You must sit in the sun and rest it. I'll use the shovel—no, you really must!"

John handed her the shovel, hung the spade back up and struggled across to a bench against the outside wall of the cottage.

Alice began shovelling. It was hard work, but John had done a lot and she soon cleared the areas where the mud was thickest. At one time, as she gave herself a short break, she said, "I'll go to Skipton the day after the morrow and I'll make sure I get you more of the balm."

When Mary came home in the evening, she was pleased and surprised to see Alice there. She had brought a meat pudding home for supper and some bread, so there was sufficient to share between three. She also brought the news that the Squire had sent someone to find out the condition of the road to Skipton. The man had come back and told him that it was passable on horseback, and that it should be passable for carts in a day or so, so long as there was no more rain.

It was arranged that Alice would return to Home Valley next day and that the day after, John would drive the pony and cart to Skipton, picking Alice up at the oak tree on the way.

Chapter Sixteen

The trip was a hard one, but worthwhile. Because most people had been unable to travel for almost three weeks, many had seized the opportunity to reach market or the shops to sell their wares and buy food. Alice and John bought cheeses, ale, bags of flour, oatmeal and honey which had come in from a near-by abbey. These purchases were mostly to feed Alice, John and Mary, Maud and her family, but there would be a small surplus to sell in the shop. They also bought stocks of general items such as candles and twine, and John found a pot of the precious balm for his leg.

There was no letter awaiting her, so Alice had no idea how the folk at Muirhill had fared, but she was soon to find out. She and John set out on the journey back to Arkenthorpe. They were making surprisingly good time when, on an undulating stretch of track, Alice was sure she could occasionally hear the sound of horses' hooves behind. She and John began to feel uneasy, fearing robbers. After they had descended a long, gentle slope, Alice looked back and saw two horses come over the crest of the hill behind. The late sun caught them and suddenly Alice thought, "That's Acorn!"

She took a second look—there was no rider on the second horse. They were gaining on the cart very quickly.

"Pull to one side, John. We don't have ruffians behind us. I am certain that the rider is Colum, the manservant to the Baron."

John chose a level piece of ground to his left and pulled the cart on to it. In no time, the two horses came near enough for Alice to be sure, and she raised her hand, calling to Colum.

He reigned in his horse and the other responded too. It was Misty, the horse Alice had ridden at Muirhill. The horses looked tired and so did Colum. They were all very mud-bespattered.

"Oh Alice, it is you. God be praised!"

"I'm glad to see you Colum, but I suspect that you are not the bearer of good tidings. This is my good friend, John, who you have heard me speak of. Whatever is wrong to bring you in such haste?"

"Oh Alice, it's Miss Cecily. She is very ill and has been asking for you. The Baron pleads for you to come. I said I would come for you, bringing Misty so that we can ride back together, and travel more swiftly than with a cart. Please Alice, say you will come."

Alice felt cold fear gripping her heart. Cissy must be very ill indeed for Colum to come on such a mission.

"Of course I will come."

"Can you be ready to leave in the morning? The horses must be rested tonight. We cannot carry many bags."

Alice took a deep breath to try to steady her pounding heart. "I need a few moments to think, Colum, but I am sure I can be ready.

"John, I think you must leave me by the oak tree. Can you get the cart the rest of the way to Arkenthorpe alone?"

"I'll be fine, Alice. You must go to Cissy, lass. You'll be mithered to death if you don't. And don't worry about Home Valley. I'll go and put your things away safe and make sure all's well there. Come on, let's get you home."

John clicked to his pony and they set off for the oak tree, with Colum and the horses following behind. At the oak, Alice lifted a few of her purchases for her own use from the cart.

"I don't know how long it will be before I return, John. Please tell the others what has happened. When you visit Skipton market, call at the church and ask Father Luke if he has a message for you. I will send a letter to him when I can, to give you news. He will read it to you."

"I'll be sure and do that, Alice. When you see Cissy, you tell her we all love her and will be saying prayers for her, and for that great man, the Baron. God go with you."

As the cart pulled away, Alice turned to Colum, who was slumped on Acorn's neck, totally exhausted. "You must stay in the valley tonight, Colum. I have food and there is grazing and water for the horses. Can you dismount?"

Colum raised himself with an effort and slid down from his horse. Alice took Misty's rein and led the way down the winding, narrow track to her home.

While Colum attended to the horses, Alice swiftly prepared a meal. The evening had turned chilly and they sat by the fire, near the entrance to the cave, to eat.

"How long has Cecily been ill?" Alice asked.

"About a week when I left the castle. There's been a number of village folk ill. The water got very low, but we all thought things would get better after the rain came. Then Miss Cecily suddenly took ill. She has a fever, Alice, but I'm told in the times when she was in her own mind, she kept asking for you. The fever just won't seem to go away.

"It was lucky I called on Father Luke today," Colum added. "He was able to tell me that you had been in Skipton today and he had spoken to you this morning. He advised me you would be travelling in a cart and had probably already left for Arkenthorpe. When I sighted the cart ahead of me, I was so relieved that I would not have to search for you."

After the meal, Alice made a bed for Colum in one corner of the cave, to which he retired almost immediately. They agreed that they would try to leave as soon after first light as possible.

Alice, mindful that she could only carry a few items in her luggage, packed very carefully. Apart from clothing, she packed a tinderbox and candles, in case they did not find an inn when they stopped for the night, and food for the journey. She had a skin of ale and two skins into which she poured some of her own fruit and heather drinks. She got out her pouch of coins, then assuring herself that she would be able to buy any essential she had forgotten, she damped down the fire and prepared for bed.

The horses were grazing peacefully, perhaps knowing that they had more travels ahead of them. Alice gazed out over her little valley, dimly-lit in the faint moonlight, and wondered when she would see it again. She was reluctant to leave it but the anxiety in her heart was such that she was fretting to leave as soon as possible too.

Colum was in deep slumber but, although she must have slept at times, Alice passed the night in restless worrying. She tried to put the unthinkable out of her mind but the thought that Cissy might die was there all the time. Would she get to Muirhill in time? The Baron would have brought in the doctors; he would have consulted the monks. Why could they not make the fever leave her? The thoughts just would not go away. Alice prayed and prayed again, but her mind still would not rest.

It was a great relief when the first grey light crept into the sky. At almost the same moment that Alice moved, Colum woke. Alice stirred the embers of the fire and put a pot of porage on to heat. While Colum went to check on the horses, she dressed in extra clothes. They ate the porage and drank water. Alice took their bowls and the porage pot to the stream and washed them out. Then, filling the pot with water she carried it back to pour on to the fire, ensuring no spark was left. Colum had the horses harnessed and the luggage strapped on, so before even the edge of the sun had appeared above the horizon, they were leading Acorn and Misty out of the valley and on to the moorland track.

The day was dry, though not as bright as the previous few days, and they generally made good progress. Alice enjoyed riding again, although she knew that her body would ache at the end of the day. Colum advised a steady loping pace wherever possible as the horses would tire more easily if pushed harder. The tracks were difficult in places as churned up mud had started to dry into a hard, uneven surface, and in such places the horses had to pick their way carefully—and even had to be led along. Because they were not encumbered with a cart or pack horses, they travelled more quickly than on Alice's first journey, despite the areas of mud. It also meant they could cross some streams which previously they had had to travel beside until they found a bridge, so, by the time they stopped for the night at a small, shabby wayside inn, they had covered about a third of the journey.

Alice slept from exhaustion, in spite of her nagging worries and the discomfort of the bench on which she rested. Next morning, as she expected, she ached in every limb.

However, they were on their way again soon after dawn. As the morning passed the weather became brighter and, with a fresh breeze coming from behind them, the horses quickened their pace willingly. When they reached Dere Street, road conditions were much improved. Alice watched for the milestones and was relieved to see how swiftly they were passing. On the second night they stayed at the inn where, on Alice's first journey, they had spent the third night, so she knew that next day they should reach the castle. She was desperate to get there but very fearful of what she might find.

A spell of driving rain hit them an hour after they set off next morning, but it soon passed when the wind changed direction a little.

Before midday they reached the hill from where Muirhead Castle could be seen. As before, Colum stopped briefly to light the signal beacon. This time the answering flame appeared very quickly on the castle roof.

"The Baron ordered a dawn-to-dark watch from the tower", said Colum in answer to a comment from Alice.

Colum re-mounted. They had to skirt one area which was too boggy for the horses to cross, but at last the castle and the drawbridge were ahead and their journey was over.

Cerdic appeared to take Misty. Familiar servants rushed out to take Alice's bag. She was led this time to the new house and to a small chamber in the solar where Tilly was waiting.

"What news, Tilly?" Alice asked fearfully.

"She still lives, Miss Alice, but she is so very, very sick."

"Does she still ask for me?"

"She has not spoken clearly for two days, Miss. The Baron spends many hours with her, but she does not seem to know him. Oh Miss, it's awful; worse 'n when Mam died. She went quick, sudden like. Oh I'm glad you're here!"

"I don't know what I can do that you won't all have done already, Tilly. Now as soon as I have washed myself and put on a cleaner dress, I must go to Cissy."

Cecily's room was only a few yards along the passage from Alice's room. Tilly lifted back the heavy door-curtain and quietly ushered Alice into the room. The room was quite light from the window panels, but as Cissy has told Alice in a letter, her bed was surrounded by a curtain which was drawn.

Alice moved the curtain a little to one side. Cissy, her face thin and showing spots of high colour on her cheeks, lay back against the pillows, her eyes closed. At the foot of the bed a servant girl sat on a stool, while near the head of the bed, the Baron sat on a chair, watching his daughter. At the movement of the curtain, he turned.

"Oh Alice, my dear, you have come!"

He rose to his feet and came outside the curtain to greet her.

"Oh," Alice thought to herself, "he looks so old."

"My lord Baron," Alice curtseyed. "How is she?"

"She changes so. Sometimes she seems to show signs of recovery and her mind will be lucid for a while. Then suddenly the fever overtakes her again and she sweats and shakes. The doctor has bled her and we have a potion to give her when she can swallow, but he holds out little hope. It is so long since she has eaten; she is very weak. Come and see for yourself."

Cissy looked so different. She had grown, of course, in the two years since Alice left, but now her face was thin, her cheeks hollow and her hair matted from the sweating of the fever. She seemed half-awake, even though her eyes were closed. At times her lips moved. They were dry and looked sore. Alice's heart sank and she staggered a little with the shock.

She felt the Baron take her gently by the shoulders and lead her to the chair at the bedside.

"Have you eaten since you arrived?" he asked.

"No my lord, but it is not hunger that ails me. It is seeing my beloved child so desperately ill. Colum told me she was very ill but I still was not expecting what I see. May I stay here and watch with you, my lord?"

"Of course you may, but I suggest you leave long enough to have some food; then when you return, I will go to eat. You will need to keep your strength up Alice. She may pull through yet, God willing, but we may have a long vigil ahead.

"You do not know Nan, do you?" The Baron indicated the maid-servant sitting at the foot of the bed.

Alice turned and looked at the girl: probably around thirteen years of age and a fleshier child than Tilly. She had a placid face. Alice guessed she was of limited intelligence.

"No, we have not met before."

"Nan," said the Baron, "this lady is Miss Alice, the one that raised Miss Cecily as a small child. You must do anything Miss Alice asks of you, just as if the instruction came from me. Do you understand?"

Nan looked at Alice. "Yes, lord, I understand. I will do as this lady asks."

Alice smiled a faint smile, "Thank you, Nan."

"Now Alice, go and eat."

"Where will I find the kitchen, my lord?"

"Of course, you have not seen the solar since it was completed. Tilly will show you. I will stay here until you return."

Alice walked with Tilly through the new building to a dining hall, much smaller than the old great hall. It was light and pleasant but currently deserted. In fact, the whole building was very quiet.

"Where is everyone?" Alice asked.

"Master Stephen and Mistress Olivia have moved back into their old rooms in the castle since Miss Cecily became ill. Mistress Olivia wishes to keep the children away in case they catch the fever. Most of the servants are there too. Just a few of us stay here to look after the Baron and Miss Cecily. I will run across to the castle kitchen and tell Cook you are here. She will send you some food."

Tilly ran off. Alice noticed a big change in Tilly too, but this change was an improvement. She was still thin, but not so dreadfully thin as she had been. She had a woman's shape now, and had gained in confidence.

Left alone, Alice looked at her new surroundings—anything to take her mind off Cissy—and she liked what she saw. The light was fading now and the wind was rising, but there was much less draught from the doors and windows. The wall hangings were beautiful and Alice could see that at least two of the large panels were Olivia's work.

At last, footsteps approached and Cook herself came into the hall carrying a large tray.

"Oh Miss Alice, I'm so glad you've come back. Have you seen Cecily yet?"

"Yes, Josse, I have seen her. She is so very ill, and the Baron looks old and weary too."

"He does, the poor man. He has barely left her side. Now you are here he will perhaps allow himself some real sleep. Of course, there is always a servant with her, but he insisted that there must be someone else too, and since the family has moved back to the castle, that has usually been himself."

"Has no-one else been ill?"

"Well, yes. One or two in the village have died of a fever, but we haven't told the Baron that. We don't want to give him more worries."

"What about here, in the house and castle?"

"A few people have had sore throats. Edward did, but although he seemed feverish for a day or two, he soon was better. We can't understand why Miss Cecily's so bad.

"Now, come along Alice, have your food. When you finish, leave the platter here. Someone will collect it."

"Thank you Josse. It is good to talk to you again."

"You can talk to me any time, Alice. I won't tell anyone anything you say to me, so if you need to talk, please come."

Alice felt tears in her eyes. Yes, Josse was someone she could really trust. She might need her very much.

When Alice returned to Cecily's room, Nan had left and Tilly was keeping watch. The Baron and Alice talked briefly, before he went for food and rest. Cecily, who had been lying quietly, suddenly began to mutter and jerk her head from side to side.

Tilly grabbed a cloth and, dipping it in some water, started to bathe Cecily's forehead. Alice lifted one of Cecily's hands, gently stroking it and quietly calling her name.

"Cissy, Cissy my dearest, it's me, Alice. Look at me Cissy. Look at me."

Tilly continued bathing Cecily's forehead and gradually the head-tossing eased.

"If I keep bathing a bit longer, Miss Alice, she might wake enough to take a few drops of the doctor's potion."

"When did she last have some?"

"Early this morning."

"Has she had anything since?"

"Only a little water. We cannot get anything else into her."

A few minutes later, Cissy's eyes suddenly opened in a wide, startled look, but she was not looking in Alice's direction. Tilly immediately reached for a bottle with a very narrow neck and attempted, successfully to administer a few drops into Cecily's mouth. One drop landed on her bottom lip and a second or so later, the parched tongue came out to lick it.

Alice gasped and the tears ran down her cheeks as she remembered the lost baby whose little tongue had popped out to catch a tear-drop and had then been persuaded to eat when a drop of honey had been placed on her lip.

"Oh Cissy, Cissy, come back to Alice," she whispered, taking the hand she was holding to her mouth and kissing it. "Come back to Alice."

Slowly, Cissy's head turned and her eyes looked vaguely at Alice.

"Cissy, it's me. It's your Alice."

The eyes focused and a faint voice came from the sore, dry throat, "Alice? Alice." The hand moved, felt for Alice's hand, grasped and held on. For a few moments more the eyes stared at Alice's face, then closed, but her hand did not let go.

"Oh, Miss," whispered Tilly, "she knows you."

Cecily's hand was hot, but it continued to hold Alice's until sleep came, when its grip relaxed, but Alice continued stroking it and talking to her quietly.

Twice more during the night, Cissy roused, tossing and turning her head. Both times Tilly bathed her forehead, but told Alice she could not administer any more potion before daylight. Instead, she gave Cissy a few drops of water.

Alice remained in the chair at the bedside, but sent Tilly outside the curtain to her own bed, assuring her that she would call her if she needed her.

As Alice kept watch, she tried to think of anything that might help. What would she have done if she was at home? The room was quiet, with that dead atmosphere and unpleasant odour of the sick room.

"I need some fresh air," Alice told herself. Quietly she pulled aside the curtain around the bed, just at one corner. She felt a movement in the air and could breathe a little more easily. The candle in the lantern glowed more brightly. A little later, she was thirsty and, not wanting to disturb Tilly, she helped herself to a small drink from the container brought for Cecily.

Ugh! The water had a strange taste to it. It was not at all like the lovely water of Home Valley; nor was it like the water she had drunk here at the castle before. Why did it taste as it did? Still thirsty, she went to rouse Tilly, who woke instantly.

"What's wrong, Miss?"

"Ssh, nothing's changed, Tilly. I just need to visit the *garde-robe* and to get myself a drink. Please watch Cissy while I do this?"

She left the room and did indeed visit the *garde-robe*, then went into her own room to find the skin of heather drink that had not been touched on the journey, as they had found inns to stay at. She opened it and poured herself a small cup, expecting that it would have been tainted by the skin, but it had not. It was slightly warm but still tasted far better than the water in Cissy's room, so she took the skin with her.

Next time Cissy started to toss and turn, she substituted the heather drink for the water and Tilly was delighted when Cissy swallowed almost twice as much liquid than she had done before. When Cissy was quiet again, Tilly suggested that Alice should try to get some sleep on her truckle bed. Alice gratefully lay down and did sleep for a short time.

The bed curtain was still open at the corner where Alice had pulled it back, and when she awoke she could just see Cissy lying very still, but not looking quite so flushed. Alice rose and returned to the chair; lifting Cissy's hand, she began stroking it again.

"How has she been, Tilly?"

"She shook again a little while ago, and I gave her the drink again, not the water. She took a little more than last time. She's still hot, but perhaps not quite as hot. I think you did a good thing opening the curtain."

The night was nearly over and dawn light appeared, but it was well after sun-rise when the Baron returned to the chamber.

"Alice, I am so sorry. I left you to watch all night. I am afraid I slept very deeply and only woke a short time ago."

"I am glad you slept well, my lord. Tilly and I have managed well enough."

"How is she this morning?"

"Little changed, my lord, although it is possible she is not as hot as she was."

The Baron touched his daughter's brow. "You may be right."

Cecily stirred and turned her head uneasily. Tilly reached for her cloth and squeezed it out in the water, but before she touched Cissy's face, Cissy's eyes opened and gradually focused on her father.

"Papa."

"Yes my dearest, I am here."

"Papa, I saw Alice."

"Yes, yes, you did. Alice is here. She is holding your hand."

Cissy looked at her hand, then her eyes followed Alice's arm upwards to her face. The sore lips tried to form a smile, "My Alice," she croaked.

"If you can watch a short time longer, I will go to the chapel to pray," the Baron said with a tremble in his voice. "Then, I will return to watch while you and Tilly eat and rest."

When the Baron returned from the chapel, Nan was back, but Alice asked Tilly to wait just a few more minutes before going to eat.

"I wish to speak with you, my lord, privately, if I may."

"Of course, Alice. Come, let us step outside." He led her down some steps to an outer door, and into a small courtyard. It promised to be a beautiful Spring day.

"Now, Alice, what is concerning you?"

"Two things, my lord. Last night as I watched Cissy, I tried to think what things could be changed, and then realised that two things were very differed from in Home Valley. The air and the water. There is a miasma in Cecily's room, so I drew the bed-curtain aside a little. The miasma lifted slightly but if a way can be found to admit some of this pleasant Spring air, Cecily's fever may cool a little."

"But will cold air not be harmful?"

"I do not think so, my lord, as long as her body has warm covers over it and no draught blows directly on to her. She has not been used to warm rooms. Even her room in the castle was only a little warmer than our cave."

"We will try it today. I will watch her carefully and ensure there are no ill effects. But, you said the water concerns you too."

"Yes, my lord. I felt thirsty during the night and poured myself a small drink from Cissy's ewer. It tasted most unpleasant. Where does it come from?"

"From a well which was dug specially for the new dwelling. The water has been drawn from it since we took up residence. The well is not as deep as the castle well, but I have not noticed an unpleasantness."

"Do you often drink the water my lord?"

The Baron paused. "No, you are right, I rarely drink water alone."

"I remembered the stream that you took Cecily and Harry to when they had an afternoon fishing. That water was clear like the stream in Home Valley. Could water for Cecily be fetched from the highest of the little waterfalls on that stream, my lord? I think that will be good water."

"Whatever you say, Alice. It will be done immediately."

"Thank you."

"No, I should thank you. These matters had not occurred to me. As I return to Cissy, I will pass my own chamber where I think Colum may still be. I will tell him to pass on my order and ensure that water is collected from where you suggest.

"Now, my dear, you must eat and rest."

"I will, my lord, but please have me called at any time if Cissy needs me."

Alice was not called and woke feeling rested. She made her way to the hall, but finding no-one there, she sought the more familiar territory of the castle kitchen. Cook was resting after the busy midday meal preparations, while other servants were clearing the hall tables. When she saw Alice enter, she got to her feet straight away.

"Ah my dear friend, what news?"

"There is little change, Josse, but Cecily's fever may have reduced a little. I have not seen her for several hours as I have been sleeping. The Baron is with her. I was hoping to have a morsel to eat before I return to the chamber."

"Of course you shall have whatever you want. There is a hearty broth and some roast beef. Will that please you?"

"That will please me well."

"I will fetch it myself."

As Cook busied herself with heating the broth and carving some beef, she asked Alice how she had fared since leaving Muirhill, and Alice told her something of her Arkenthorpe friends and of helping John to start the shop.

The food refreshed Alice as much as the sleep had done and a short time later she was ready to take up her vigil once more. When she entered the chamber, the Baron was standing outside the bed curtains, near to an open casement. The miasma had gone and the air was much sweeter. He turned at the sound of her entry.

"Ah, you have slept well, I hope."

"Yes, my lord, and had some excellent broth and roast beef. How is Cecily?"

"Slightly improved, I am sure. Nan is tending to her personal welfare at the moment.

"I was deeply disturbed by the taste of the water that we were administering to her. I drank a little myself. I do not understand why it is so bad. Fresh water has now been brought from the stream, as you suggested. It is in a clean ewer. Cecily has taken more of the water each time it has been offered to her lips. In the last hours she has not been so restless as she was. Why did it take you to point out these things to us? Why could we not see them for ourselves?"

"Perhaps I saw them, my lord, because I have come recently from a place with pure air and water. My body noticed the changes at once, and that was what made me think about their effects on Cissy."

Nan emerged from the curtained-off bed area, carrying the used linen from Cissy's bed. Alice turned to go in and take her seat again. The Baron stepped in to look at his daughter. Her eyes were open, and her freshly washed face was not gleaming with perspiration.

"For the first time in many days, Alice, I have some hope that my prayers may be answered and she will be spared.

"Now I must go and find my brother. There is an urgent matter I must discuss with him.

That night the Baron and Alice shared the vigil with the Baron taking the first session. Not long after Alice had returned to duty, she was deep in thought when she became aware that Cissy's eyes were open and looking at her.

"I'm thirsty," came a whisper.

Tilly was dozing, so Alice gave Cissy a drink.

"Thank you, Alice."

"Oh my dearest child, I think you are getting better. Let me feel your head and your hands. Yes, they are much cooler."

"Where is Papa?"

"He has gone to have a rest. He and I watch you turn and turn about."

Tilly roused as she heard the quiet voices. "Miss? Miss Cecily, was that you talking?"

"Tilly, are you watching me too?"

Tilly moved over and took Cissy's hand. "Oh Miss, you're truly getting better. Oh I am so pleased I want to cry!"

For a few more minutes Cissy remained awake, looking at Alice and Tilly and weakly squeezing the hand of each of them, then her eyes closed and she drifted off to sleep. Her breathing was quiet, gentle like a baby's.

First light came and Tilly went to her own bed, leaving Alice on watch. Alice heard the Baron enter the outer part of the room; he pulled the curtain quietly aside. Suddenly, all colour left his face as he looked at Cissy.

"My lord," said Alice, startled. "What is it?"

"She . . . . she looks so white and still. She is not . . . . ?"

"No, no my lord. She is sleeping. The fever has gone. Touch her brow."

The Baron took a long, deep breath and moved to the side of the bed. "It is true. Her brow is cool. The fever has gone!"

"It will take many days to build up her strength again, but I think we have her back, my lord."

"Alice, oh Alice, I think we do." The Baron stood by Alice's side and put his arm around her.

As he released her from his gentle embrace, he turned quickly and left the chamber, but not before Alice had seen tears filling his eyes.

A short time later he returned to take over from Alice, just as Cecily awoke."

"Papa, Alice, I'm hungry."

"Then you shall have something to eat. What should she have, Alice?"

"I think a bowl of Cook's finest gruel. I will fetch some at once."

"Can I please have some drops of honey in it?" Cissy asked, looking straight at Alice.

"Perhaps," said Alice with a smile, "perhaps just a few drops," and she ran out of the room to spread the good tidings.

For a week, Cissy kept to her bed, sleeping frequently and eating a little more each day. She soon had the strength to sit propped against her pillows and some of her sparkle was coming back. At the end of the week, she complained about how horrid her hair felt and asked for it to be washed. She had a lot of long hair and Alice was worried that it would take so long to dry that she would be at risk of a chill. Cissy was so insistent, however, that she would not recover more until her hair was clean, that it was agreed that it would be cut much shorter, then washed, and that is what happened. She looked very different with short hair, but it actually complemented her much thinner face.

The Baron allowed himself to return to many of his normal duties, and he was most touched by the concern that was expressed by even the poorest of his peasants, and their pleasure in the news that Cecily was now recovering. He told Alice so when they next met.

"You are well respected by all your people, my lord, and Cecily is loved by them."

"Many have heard of your return to us, Alice, and enquiries were made after your well-being."

"They are mostly good people. Did you know that, when I left to return home, many of them put together little bags of seeds from their own supplies—turnip, carrot, peas and beans—and entrusted them to Cerdic, who gave them to me just before he and Colum started their return journey?"

"No, I didn't know. I would say that that makes you well-loved too, Alice."

This conversation had taken place at the table where a midday meal had been served to them. As they were leaving to return to their different duties, Harry entered the room. When he saw Alice, his face lit up."

"Good day, Alice. I am so pleased you are back again."

"Good day, Harry. It is good to see you again. How is Edward?"

"Oh he is well. Not such trouble as he used to be." Then, remembering his manners, her turned to the Baron.

"Sorry. Good morning, Uncle. May I ask something of you?"

"Of course, Harry. What is it?"

"May I be allowed to visit Cecily?"

"I am sure you may, if your mother now feels it is safe for you to do so. What do you think, Alice?"

"Cecily would be happy to see you Harry. She is actually out of bed for the first time today, and is resting on a couch. I do not think there is any risk to your well-being if you make a short visit.

"If you will excuse us, my lord, I will take Harry to see her."

"Thank you, Uncle. I will be careful not to tire Cecily. Oh, and Papa has discovered the problem with the well and would like to explain it to you when you have the time."

"I will seek him out at once. The matter has been of considerable worry to me. Perhaps, Alice, when you have shown Harry into Cecily's chamber, you will come to find Stephen and I, and hear his explanation."

"Yes, my lord, I will."

As Alice and Harry made their way to Cissy's chamber, Harry asked, "Why would Uncle wish you to see a problem with a well?"

Alice laughed. "Yes, it must seem strange, but I was the one who realised something was wrong with the water."

"What was wrong with it?"

"It tasted most foul and as it was being given to Cissy when she was very, very ill, I did not think it could be good for her. I asked the Baron to get a supply of fresh water from one of the hill streams for her—you know, Harry, the one he took you both to to catch fish."

"So, did the good water make Cecily better?"

"I think it must have helped, because the fever started to leave her soon after."

"Where did the bad water come from?"

"It seems it came from the new well, built to supply this house. I think the Baron asked your Papa to try to find the reason for the new well water being bad."

"I think I would like to know that too, but first I must see Cecily."

"Yes, wait here a moment," said Alice, pausing outside the door. "I'll just speak to her."

Cecily was very pleased to see Harry, and gallantly he raised her hand to his lips and kissed it. Alice smiled to herself. Harry had almost turned into a young man during her absence. Tilly was, as usual, in the room, so telling her to make sure Harry didn't tire Cecily, Alice left the young people together and went to find the Baron and his brother.

The men were standing in the main courtyard area between the old castle and the new house, near to the new well. Alice joined them and Stephen started his explanation.

"It has been a very difficult problem. I took water from the old well in the inner court, and some from the new well and, as you said Alice, the water from the new well tastes foul, but that from the old well is good.

"The long, dry Summer and Autumn had caused the level of water in both wells to drop, and we had had to lengthen the ropes for the buckets on both wells, even though the new well is not so deep as the old one. Neither well ran dry.

"I next thought about the days of heavy rain and flooding. I talked to all the servants and all assured me that even when the flood waters were highest, no water could have washed down into the well from above ground. It had come no higher than the first row of stones in the wall of the new well.

"The next time I took small amounts of water from the wells, I tipped some on to plain, white cloth and saw that the foul water left a faint yellow stain.

"I was really at a loss to think of a cause, brother. Perhaps someone had dropped something into the well. So we lowered an old bucket on a very long rope, to try to see if we could locate any strange objects in the water, but again, we had no success.

"For a few days I altered course, deciding it was more pressing to ensure a supply of good water. The servants were instructed that all water must be drawn from the old well; but Alice's advice to use fresh mountain water for drinking gave me the idea of diverting one of the local streams to pass close to the solar, so bringing clear, running water closer. I walked the moors around and found a small stream which comes quite near. I saw how it can be diverted, and a group of men is now digging out a shallow bed along the line I have marked.

"Today, I gave my mind back to the problem of the well. I was sitting on the wall of the well thinking, when the sun shone on a streak of a yellow-brown colour running down the inside wall of the well. It starts about two feet below the level of the ground, but was out of reach when leaning over the wall. I called Simon the Factor to come and rope me up so that I could be lowered just the short distance needed to examine the streak, but Simon persuaded me of the wisdom of lowering someone of lighter weight, and volunteered his son. The lad is bright and small for his age—he is thirteen, I think—and he agreed to be lowered. We had several ropes attached to him with two men holding each rope, and he had his feet in a well-bucket so that he could support himself on the well rope too. He informed us that there is yellow-coloured water seeping through from the surrounding ground into the well. He used a cloth to soak up a little of the water and brought it back up to us. When I squeezed it into a vessel, it tasted very unpleasant—like the water drawn from the well but worse. It also had a faint, unpleasant smell and, suddenly, I was sure I knew what it was, and where I had seen a similar stain. I hate to tell you, brother, when I think Cecily was drinking it, fortunately not in great amounts, but it is from the *garde-robe* in the castle tower."

"The *garde-robe* in the tower! How can that be, Stephen?"

"When the water level of the moat dropped last Summer, I saw a similar stain from the base of the tower, below where the *garde robe* is situated, which, as you know, falls directly into the moat. Today I went back to that place and found a major crack in the top edge of the moat banking. It must have opened up when the ground was so dry—cracks did open in many areas of land. I followed the crack from the moat. It got narrower and narrower and stopped within four feet of the wall of the new well. My guess is that there is still a thin crack in the ground here"—Stephen indicated a line from the well outwards towards the tower—"but below the surface. When the heavy rains came and the level of the moat rose to the top of the banking, much of the waste from the *garde-robe* was washed straight into the crack and the slight fall of the land on this side allowed it to flow down, then seep into the well."

"How dreadful," said Alice, "but how clever of you to work out what has happened."

"What can be done about it?" asked the Baron.

"First we must dig down here at the side of the well and fill in the crack, however small, to prevent any more getting into the well. Then we must work along the crack, back towards the moat, digging out then filling in. We cannot work on the moat embankment until the water level drops again, but tomorrow we can stop anymore noisome liquid entering the well. It will be many weeks before we can use the well again, but I will check the water every week until I find the water good again."

"Stephen, I cannot praise you enough for your work in solving this mystery. If employing more men will help, employ all you need."

"I will meet with Simon this afternoon, brother. At the present he is over-seeing the work on the stream, but I will bring him on to this job tomorrow. He will know better than I what materials to use to make the land good again."

Alice had found the explanation very interesting, but now she realised how long she had been away from Cissy.

"Thank you for letting me hear the explanation, my lord, Master Stephen, it is an amazing chain of happenings. I must now return to Cecily. I think it best we do not tell her at present what a noisome liquid we were administering to her. The very thought might make her ill again!"

As Alice returned, she wondered that more people had not been affected. Cecily must have developed her fever at the beginning of the rains, so Olivia had thankfully moved her family back into the castle before the flooding had happened. Cecily had never liked the taste of ale (which most folk in the household drank), preferring water, as that was what she and Alice drank in her early childhood. She would most likely have recovered from the fever quite quickly if she had been given ale. Instead, after the moat overflowed its banks, every time she had needed a drink, she had been given foul, tainted water which would have made her even more ill. No, it was definitely best that she was not told yet what had happened!

That Cecily was definitely recovering now was very clear when Alice entered the chamber. Cissy and Harry were laughing at some jest Harry had made, and colour had returned to Cissy's cheeks, but this time it was a touch of healthy pink.

Chapter Seventeen

At the beginning of May, Olivia, Stephen and their children moved back into the house, so more servants were about during the day. Meals were now usually prepared by Cook in the new kitchen, although large roasts were still cooked on the spit in the old kitchen. It was when this move took place that Alice and Olivia crossed paths again.

"So you are back with us again, Alice. How long will you be staying this time?"

"As long as I am needed Mistress Olivia."

"Ah well, with Cissy making such a good recovery, that should not be for long. I'm sure your garden will require your attention."

"Mama! exclaimed Harry, who had overheard this exchange, "if I had said something like that, you would have told me I was rude. We are really pleased to have you back, Alice, and I hope you will stay a long time."

"Thank you, Harry, but I understand your Mama, so I am not deeply offended. The time will come when I must return, but not for a little while yet."

"I'm glad we understand each other," Olivia said, closing the conversation and moving away.

The month of May was beautiful. The weather was mild enough for Cissy to sit outside most days and by the second week she was strong enough to take short walks inside the castle walls. She tired easily and still had regular rests, nor had she re-started her lessons. Her bond with Alice was, if possible, stronger than before.

In spite of her illness, Cissy seemed to have grown again during her long stay in bed and her head was now level with Alice's shoulder. When the dressmaker was called in to make new gowns for Cissy, Alice ordered some too, as her lighter, summer clothing had not been included in the small amount of luggage she had been able to bring with her.

Alice wrote a short letter to Father Luke, when the Baron told her that a messenger would be riding south. In it, she asked the Father to read the letter to John when he next called at the church. To tell him that their prayers had been heard and that Cissy had recovered from her illness and was slowly regaining her strength. That she did not know when she would return to Arkenthorpe but she expected that it would be several weeks yet. Please tell him also that Cissy sends her love to everyone, and that they both hoped all their friends were well.

For about another week, life settled into a pleasant and smooth routine. Harry and Edward attended lessons in the morning and, although Edward's finished an hour before noon, Harry had at least another hour, sometimes two. Cecily did a little reading and embroidery in the morning, so that she could spend some time with Harry in the afternoon. It was one such afternoon when things were to change again.

Harry and Cecily had walked most of the way around the inside of the curtain wall. It was getting quite hot, so Cecily found a shady place near the bottom of the castle mound. Alice spread a blanket on one of the projecting base stones so that Cissy could sit and lean back against the embankment. A few minutes later, Stephen arrived on his way to see progress on the repairs to the crack in the land, and at the same time, Edward came rushing around, pretending he was a knight on horseback, brandishing a wooden sword.

"Come on Harry; come on Cissy, let's have a tournament."

"No, Edward, I'm tired and I'll get too hot," said Cissy.

"Aw! Will you play with me, Harry? I'm bored."

"Oh alright, terrible Ted, I'll play for a short time. We'll have a mock tournament. Cissy can be our fair maid whose hand is to be won. Then she can just sit on her throne and watch us."

"Oh good, yes, but will you let me win Harry, 'cos I'll never beat you fair. You're too big."

"Very well, but only in the first joust. I must win the fair damsel's hand in the second one. Now, we need to pick our names—something funny—and I must find a weapon. I'll be the Duke of Dunghill, and this stick can be my sword."

"I'll be Lady Anne Appletree," said Cissy. "Who will you be, Edward? Shall we choose your name?"

"No, let me think . . . . I'll be . . . . I know, Daniel of Whitby."

"That's not a funny name," said Harry.

"Yes it is. Yes it is."

"No, it is not."

"Well it must be funny, 'cos I heard Mama call Uncle Piers 'Daniel of Whitby', and they both laughed."

Alice caught her breath and looked across at Stephen. His face was rigid, but then he looked across at his youngest son and calmly said, "Why don't you be Sir Hengist Horseface? That's what I used to call myself sometimes when I was a boy."

"Oh yes, Papa, that's a good name, but I think Sir Harry Horseface is better!" Edward shrieked with laughter.

The game started as Edward charged at Harry, trying to hit him with his flat wooden sword, while Harry just stood there, blocking his young brother's attempts with his stick.

Edward's cries of frustration were lost on both Alice and Stephen. Stephen walked across to Alice and said quietly, "I can tell from your face that we both heard Edward say 'Daniel of Whitby'. Can I ask if you have ever talked of that man to Olivia?"

"No, Stephen. As far as I remember, Olivia and I have only made the occasional reference to Cissy and the Baroness's disappearance, and I have never mentioned him."

"It clearly had no significance for Cecily or Harry, but why should Olivia and Piers have mentioned it now, and found it amusing?

"I must go to check the work, but this worries me a little. Please don't say anything about this to anyone, Alice."

She assured him she would not, and he continued on his way.

Edward's cries of "that's not fair, I'm supposed to win," brought Alice's attention back to the children and she intervened to attempt to bring peace.

"It's Harry Horseface's fault. He wouldn't let me win."

"I only said I'd let you win the first joust," retorted Harry, and anyway, **you** are Harry Horseface."

"It was the first joust."

"No it was not!"

"Whether it was the first one or not, no-one will win because it is time your fair maiden was inside resting. Come along, Lady Anne Appletree; come with me boys, we are going inside."

At the evening meal, neither Stephen nor Olivia appeared. When the Baron asked Joseph, Stephen's manservant, where they were, he replied that they had requested food to be taken to their chambers. When it was time for Edward to go to bed, Alice escorted him to the maidservant. There was no sign of Olivia.

Later, after Cecily was in bed, Alice went for a short walk in the mild evening air. She passed the small, private chapel and, to her surprise, she could see Stephen kneeling in prayer. That was not something he usually did in an evening; clearly something was disturbing him, and Alice had the uneasy feeling that 'Daniel of Whitby' was at the root of his troubles.

Next morning, Stephen breakfasted early and alone, then disappeared. Again, Olivia did not appear.

"Where's Mama?" Harry asked Alice.

"I don't know, Harry. Perhaps she is with Eleanor and Margot."

"I saw her, with Papa, going across to the castle last night. Perhaps she is still there. Oh, there's Joseph. He might know."

Harry asked Joseph.

"Yes, Master Harry, she is still over there and must not be disturbed."

"Why not? Is she ill?"

"I do not know why, but she does not appear to be sick."

"Oh well, I'll find out later. I must go to my lessons now."

Cecily had eaten breakfast in her room. When Alice went in to see her, she was dressed for the day, but was looking concerned.

"Alice, do you know what is happening?"

"What do you mean?"

"Papa has not been to see me this morning, and when I tried to see him in his chamber, Colum was outside the room. He said Papa was not to be disturbed; not even by me. Then, when Tilly came in, she said she had seen Uncle Stephen going into Papa's room when she brought my food. I think something serious must have happened."

"Well, if it has, we will be told soon. Now, it is not so warm today, so how would you like to pass the morning?"

"Perhaps I should go and amuse Eleanor for a time. She can be quite sweet sometimes, but she does have a temper when she is crossed. She can shriek like Edward used to do."

"Very well, Cissy. I will tidy my chamber and take some of my linen to the laundry. Later we will try to do something with your hair. Now it has grown longer again, you might think about how you would like it."

"Yes, let's do that; but I will be glad when I may start lessons again. I am feeling stronger now."

About an hour later, Cissy returned, finding Alice in her own chamber..

"There is really something very strange, Alice. As I came out of the nursery, Papa and Uncle Stephen were going out of the house. When I spoke to Papa, he just looked at me and said, 'I'll see you later, Cecily. I have a serious matter to attend to'. But, Alice, both Papa and Uncle Stephen looked dreadfully worried—Uncle Stephen more than Papa. Oh, and Aunt Olivia has not been to see her children this morning. What do you think has happened, Alice?"

"I don't know. I can't tell you anything."

The midday meal came and went, and still Olivia did not appear. The Baron and Stephen came but ate little. The Baron apologised to Cissy for his neglect of her, and when Harry asked his father about his mother, and if the serious matter concerned her, Stephen told him they would talk later, and asked him to be patient. There was generally an air of unease and puzzlement among both family and servants.

At around two hours after noon, Alice was brushing Cecily's hair and trying it in different styles, when Colum came to the door of Alice's chamber. "Please Miss Alice, the Baron requests you to join him in the old castle, in the children's school room. As soon as you can, please."

"I will go at once, Colum. Be careful, Cissy, while I am gone. If you go outside, please stay in the courtyard."

"I will. Don't concern yourself about me. Let us hope you will find out what all this mystery is about."

Alice entered the room to find the Baron and Stephen still together. There was a ewer of ale, bread and some sweetmeats on the table, but both men looked weary as though the ills of the world rested on their heads.

"Please sit down, Alice," said the Baron. "We have a most unpleasant matter on our hands. As result of the innocent remark made by Edward in his childish game yesterday, a most terrible matter has come to light. Stephen has told me that you were there when Edward referred to 'Daniel of Whitby'."

"Yes, my lord, I was."

"Edward's use of that name worried my brother, especially when the child had heard it causing amusement to Olivia and her brother, so he confronted Olivia about the matter. At first she claimed that Edward must have mis-heard, but eventually under Stephen's pressing her, she confessed that her brother, Piers, had been 'Daniel of Whitby'."

Alice gasped. "Why, why should he have done such a thing?"

"Why indeed? That is what Stephen asked Olivia."

"With your permission, Michael, I will continue." Stephen lifted his head and looked at Alice. "I could not understand how such dreadful things could be plotted, or why by my own wife, because there is no doubt that it was she who had the idea for their scheme."

Alice quietly interrupted, "Are you sure that you wish to confide these things in me, Master Stephen?"

"Yes, Alice, I am sure. Your own life has been shaped by these events and we need to discuss with you how, and how much, we should tell Cecily and Harry.

"I pressed Olivia for an explanation, and she eventually unleashed such a bitter tirade that I feel, in all these years, I have never really known her.

"The du Bois family lived not many miles from the Talbots, the family of Belle, Michael's wife, and apparently Olivia and Belle were acquainted as girls. They did not, however, like each other much. At the time of our marriages, our father was the Baron and our marriages were arranged for us. Michael married Belle then, a year or so later, Olivia and I were wed. It seems that when I brought Olivia to the castle as my bride, she was horrified to find that her former acquaintance was already married to the eldest son and, in fullness of time, would become the Baroness. Our mother was already dead, so there was no Baroness at the time.

"In the first year after Michael and Belle married, Belle did not conceive a child, and soon after Olivia and I were married, the war took Michael away from home frequently. So it came about that Olivia conceived a child before Belle did. I was already running the estate for our father, so I only fought in one battle as my role here seemed of greater import.

"Then, our father died, and Belle conceived only a few weeks later. Michael, of course, became the Baron and Belle the Baroness. We were both aware that there was little warmth between our wives, but I had not thought that Olivia was nurturing such a hatred of Belle."

Stephen paused to take a sip of his ale and began idly to pull pieces from the loaf of bread in front of him.

"The war was becoming worse and battles came nearer to us here. Life for everyone was unsettled and social life very limited. That was why, when Michael's duty was taking him south, Belle asked Michael if she and Cecily could travel with him as far as the Talbot family house. The rest of the story you know."

There was quiet for a minute or so. Stephen picked up and ate some of the bits of bread he had torn into small morsels. The Baron placed a hand on his brother's arm then nibbled a sweet-meat for something to do.

Quietly, Alice said, "But why did Olivia's brother need to adopt a false name? Surely the Baroness would have recognised him and easily have believed his story that he had come from you, my lord?"

"It is unlikely that Belle would have recognised him, as they had not met since Piers was a boy. If she had known his true identity, she would have known he could not have come from me, as the du Bois family did not support the Yorkists."

"I see. But why would he have driven the Baroness and Cecily to my part of the country to kill them?"

The Baron answered. "Stephen and I do not get the impression that Belle was deliberately killed. If Olivia is to be believed, the plan, at least at first, was to drive them to the du Bois family's property on the Solway but, at some point, Belle found a chance to try to escape. When 'Daniel' and the driver of the cart were otherwise engaged, she seized the reins and set back along the track. She was a good horsewoman but had no experience of handling a cart. At that spot you know well, the cart left the track and threw her out. She hit her head on a rock and died."

"Perhaps that was what happened," Alice said thoughtfully, "but that does not explain why Cecily was uninjured, or why the bags were opened. And where was the horse?"

"Olivia admitted that Piers caught up with the cart and rescued the horse, taking it away with him. He and the driver tried to make the scene suggest that the travellers had been attacked and robbed."

"But they left a baby to die of hunger and cold, by the body of its dead mother. How could anyone do that?" Physical revulsion rose in her and she felt as if she would choke.

"Well," the Baron said at last, that is the ghastly story. Now we have to decide what to do with Olivia."

"You would be within your rights to have her executed," Stephen said quietly.

"No, I have no reason to have her executed. She is not guilty of murder, and nor is her brother, if what she says is true. They are guilty of plotting, kidnap and other things, but they have not committed murder.

"Nor do I wish to deprive your children of their mother."

"Cecily was deprived of her mother and you of your wife."

"Yes, I certainly lost my wife and had years of anxiety about them both. By God's grace, Cecily found a new mother within hours, and while I'm sure her initial anguish was real, she was too young to be aware of that loss for long. For your oldest children, brother, the wound would be deep."

"Whatever else is decided, you must allow me to renounce my right as your heir. We will go away—live somewhere else."

"Let us not be hasty in that matter. You are guilty of nothing, Stephen."

"Where is Olivia now?" Alice asked.

"In the dungeon of the castle," Stephen answered.

"The dungeon! Why there?" demanded the Baron.

"Because, when we had finished yesterday, I was frightened she would flee or try to send a message to warn Piers that their infamy was discovered. She has a light, water, food and a blanket."

"Go and bring her here," the Baron said gently to his brother. "Now you have told me what occurred, she must answer to me herself. Go. Give her half-an-hour to refresh her person then bring her here. I will take a walk to think again about the best course of action. We will all meet again here in half-an-hour."

Stephen staggered as he got to his feet, before regaining his balance and leaving the room. The Baron rose.

"This is a very bad business, Alice. I have always hated the scheming and plotting that goes on among kings, queens, princes and nobles of all ranks, but for it to have happened here in my own household! . . . . my brother is mortified. He is not to blame and nor are his children. How can I punish Olivia without punishing the innocent too?"

"And what about her brother, my lord? He was the one who actually kidnapped your wife and child, and he was the one who was prepared to leave a baby to die alone on the moors."

"Yes. Once I have found a way of dealing with this more domestic matter, I will ensure that he faces an appropriate court. Now, I must get out into some clean, fresh air. What will you do, Alice?"

"Perhaps I will go to sit in the chapel. If Cissy sees me, she will be pressing me to tell her what is wrong, and as yet I can say nothing."

"I really cannot think what we should tell Cecily and Harry. The younger children will not need to be told."

"Edward will ask a few questions, I think."

"He may, but Stephen will perhaps be able simply to tell him that his mother did something wrong which has upset everyone."

When Olivia entered the school room, followed by Stephen, Alice was shocked. She had expected Olivia to be fearful, or weeping, but she walked in like a queen.

The Baron had risen and indicated to Olivia where he wished her to sit.

"I shall not sit and will certainly not answer any of your questions in front of a common nursemaid."

Stephen drew in his breath sharply; Alice started to get to her feet to leave, when the Baron, with a voice cold and sharp as a sword, said, "Mistress, you are not in a position to make conditions. You will sit, and you will answer my questions in front of Alice, who has never been a servant here, as you well know."

Alice sat down again.

The Baron paced around a while before speaking. Then he began, "When Stephen came to me yesterday, he was in a state of shock and I speedily became so too. You had been living here in the castle, as my brother's wife, plotting to kidnap my wife and child. You involved your brother in your plans, and for reasons I cannot imagine, he agreed to carry out those plans.

"I now understand that you had been acquainted with my wife before either of you married, and that you resented the fact that Belle was the one who became Baroness Muirhill. Your jealousy was such that you plotted to have her removed."

Olivia spoke. "My dislike of Belle was not the only reason. I knew that, although Stephen was the second son, I had married the better man. Oh yes, Michael, you were in line to inherit the title, but you are weak and your piety makes you very boring. Then, more and more, Stephen was doing the work you would not turn your hand to, and I was running the household. It was clear to me that Stephen would be a far stronger Baron than you, and it was my duty to find a means to change things. I almost succeeded. You were on the point of retiring to a monastery and handing all to Stephen, when **she** had to turn up, and Stephen was deprived of his rightful place."

"My rightful place!" Stephen exclaimed. "I was already in my rightful place. I have absolutely no desire to be Baron. Having to attend meetings of barons, knights and squires and provide money when the King demands it to pay for the war. Having to find men to fight. No, that is the last thing I want. Did it never occur to you that I might be happy with things as they were?"

Olivia looked at her husband and shrugged her shoulders. "It is a good thing then, that I have enough ambition for both of us."

Stephen responded angrily. “The only ambition is yours, Olivia. I had not realised you want so much to have the title of Baroness. What kind of a woman are you? You know full well the months and months of agony my brother suffered when Belle and Cecily disappeared. Of course I carried out many of his duties to free him as much as possible for the search. He would have done the same for me if it had been you and Harry who were missing.”

“Tell me,” said the Baron, “how did you communicate with your brother to plan the kidnap? I don’t remember that he visited you here, nor did you go to visit him.”

“No, he did not come here. But I received a messenger who told me that Piers would be a few days at the house of our cousins in Pickering. I went there to introduce our son Harry to my family.”

“Yes, I remember that,” Stephen agreed. “I also remember thinking how well and happy you looked on your return. Little did I know the awful reason for your happiness. But that was a while before we knew that Michael would be travelling south and Belle’s decision to travel with him.”

“Of course. When I knew Belle’s plans, I saw the chance and sent a messenger to Piers.”

“What was the message? You cannot write!”

“Oh, that was easy. I sent a message to be given to my parents and brother, to report that their first grandchild was doing well and growing into a strong boy, and secondly to tell them that Belle had just travelled south to visit her family for a few weeks to introduce them to their granddaughter, so would be in their neighbourhood. I knew that Piers would understand the message and would be able to discover their fuller plans through careful local enquiries.”

“So,” said the Baron, “throughout the time I was seeking for Belle and Cecily, you knew what had happened.”

"Well, I did not get any message, so I thought they would have been taken to Solway and hidden away. I did not know what had really happened until you told me Michael. I did not know HOW it had happened until Piers came to visit at Christmas time."

Throughout this interrogation, Alice had remained silent. She could not imagine how Olivia could stand there and talk of something so dreadful as though she had merely been reporting on some unfortunate mishap. Now the Baron turned to her.

"Alice, do you have any questions you wish to ask Olivia?"

Alice thought of the things that he been coursing through her mind, then asked, "How did you feel when Cecily came home? You did not seem to be hostile to her."

"Cecily does not concern me. Belle was the threat. She would have borne more children, and it was likely one at least would be a boy and become Michael's heir."

Suddenly light illuminated Alice's mind! "Ah, now I see;" she said quietly, "that explains much, Olivia."

Olivia gave Alice a haughty look. "I knew you would understand."

The men looked puzzled by this exchange, but neither woman offered to explain. For a few moments there was silence, then the Baron spoke to Olivia.

"Your wicked scheme now presents me with a dilemma. I would dearly like to punish you for what you have caused to happen. You were the cause of my wife's death, even though you did not actually kill her. My daughter's life was saved by Alice when she was guided to the baby your brother had abandoned in a lonely valley. Alice's life changed when she took the baby home and raised her at her own expense, even though she herself had barely enough to keep her body and soul together.

"You deprived me of my wife and Cecily of her mother. Much as I might wish to do so, I cannot deprive my brother and his children in the same way. For the present you will resume your place in the household, supervising the care of your own children and organising the work of the servants.

"You will not, however, have any contact with your brother and you will send no communication, in any form, from this place without Stephen or myself approving it and being present when any such message is given to a messenger.

"All orders to trades-people or merchants will be given by Cook or the Chief Steward. Whenever you have visits from dressmakers, shoe makers or others who bring their trade or goods here, you will always be under someone's watchful eye. All members of the household will have strict orders that they must not carry messages for you to anyone without particular permission from Stephen or me. Do you understand?"

Olivia inclined her head, but did not speak.

"The servants will not be given the reason for their orders. If Stephen or you see fit to give an explanation to a particular servant, you may do so.

"However, the children are another matter. Cecily and Harry must be told. Stephen will tell Harry what he needs to know, while I will tell Cecily. Edward will doubtless pester us with questions, but until he is older will need to know little. Stephen will answer him, but with Harry and Cecily a fuller version of events must be told. If, at any time, they need to talk about the matter, which I am sure they will, they will be allowed to talk to each other, or to Stephen, Alice or me.

"Now, Mistress, you may go. For the next two days you will keep to your chamber, except that you will join us at table for meals. After two days, all the servants will have been given their orders and the children will have been told. Then you may go about your normal duties again, unless your husband thinks differently."

Stephen stood up. "Before we leave this room, I wish to state that I now renounce my right to be heir to my brother's title. If, Michael, you do not have a son of your own, you may wish to make Harry your heir, but I will never hold your title, so my wife will never, never become baroness."

For the first time since she had entered the room, Olivia showed a genuine reaction. She paled and held on to the edge of the table, her knuckles white. Stunned by shock, her face registering bitterness and fury, she slowly released her grip on the table, turned and preceded Stephen from the room.

The Baron sat with his head in his hands and for several minutes neither he nor Alice spoke. Then he rose, and smiling faintly at Alice he said, "Thank God that is over, and may he give me strength and wisdom as I talk to Cecily.

"Will you ensure that she is suitably dressed for outside, then ask her to join me in a walk around the moat?"

"Of course, my lord. I will then go to my chamber where she can come to me if she so wishes."

Eventually, Cecily returned from walking with her father and sought out Alice in her chamber. Without preliminaries, as she removed her shawl, she said, "Oh Alice, what a dreadful thing this was. No wonder Uncle Stephen looked so terrible. Papa is very deeply upset."

"He is. He is angry and sorrowful and yet does not wish to punish the innocent by inflicting a severe punishment on your Aunt."

"I can now clearly understand why Aunt Olivia dislikes you so much, Alice."

"Ah, you had seen that?"

"Yes, I've known it for a long time and so has Harry. We could not understand it.

"Papa said that Harry is being told what his mother has done."

"Yes. It will be terrible news for him. I don't think he will remember your Mama, but it will not be nice to learn of such a wicked deed, even if it happened a long time ago."

"I think Harry will need you, Alice. He will need someone to comfort him."

"He can come to talk to me whenever he wishes, but he will need you too, Cissy. He will need to know that you are still his friend. You are one of the people his mother plotted against and her deed changed your life."

"Of course I will still be his friend. My Mama dying changed my life, but while I know I would have loved my Mama, you found me. I love you so much, Alice, and I loved the life I had with you in Home Valley and Arkenthorpe. One thing I have learned is that being poor does not make people bad and being rich does not make them good."

Olivia appeared at the meal that evening and to most around her she seemed little changed. However, there was no flow of conversation at the high table. Stephen and the Baron talked of the well and the repairs to the cracks in the ground. Cissy and Alice talked about hair-styles and about Cissy starting lessons again. Harry sat silently and showed very little appetite. Only Edward chattered as usual and, as usual, was reprimanded by Olivia for his table manners.

When they finished eating, Stephen called Edward to him, then taking his hand, he ushered Olivia up to their rooms ahead of him. The Baron retired to the chapel, while Cecily went to Harry and they left the hall together. It was a beautiful evening, so Alice collected a light shawl and went outside.

Wandering in the new garden that was being made around the house, the gentle warm air and the breeze carrying the sweet scent of May blossom, began to soothe her. She strolled to the postern gate and, greeting the sentry, let herself out on to the moorland. A curlew was calling and those birds of Summer, the swallows, were darting through the air catching insects. Gradually, the nastiness of the last few days receded in her mind.

Her thoughts turned again to Home Valley. She had left it two months ago, but she had been so worried about Cissy, that she had given it little thought. How were her vegetables growing? Would frost have damaged her young fruit trees? Was John able to run the shop? There were so many things to take her back there.

Cissy would need her for a few weeks more yet. She was almost fully recovered from her illness, although she tired easily and was still too thin. That was partly because she had grown taller. She would also need to recover from the news of the last few days, although, strangely, Alice could see that Cecily would perhaps be less affected than others.

The Baron, Stephen and Harry would find it difficult to come to terms with Olivia's wickedness, and as for Olivia herself, Alice could not imagine what would become of her.

The sun was lower in the sky now and the breeze felt cooler, so Alice returned to the postern and knocked to be admitted. Before going to her chamber, she entered the little chapel. It was beautiful, with warm colours from the stained glass, glowing in the late evening sun. She knelt on the mat provided at the altar rail and looked at the crucifix. "Christ died for our transgressions," she thought. "If we truly repent, our wrong doings can be forgiven. Perhaps Olivia will seek God's forgiveness."

For her own soul, Alice quietly recited Our Lord's prayer then, turning to the small statue of the Holy Mother, she humbly asked her to pray for all the family members and for herself.

At the midday meal two days later, it became clear that the servants had received their orders regarding Olivia. She was served politely but with a noticeable reserve and caution. The Baron had called the senior staff to him, and they in turn had instructed the staff under them.

Over the next week or two, it was observed that Stephen and Olivia were never in the same bedchamber, and relations between Harry and his mother were cold in the extreme. Edward was also finding life very difficult, and often came to Alice for a while in an afternoon. Alice could not question him and, strangely, he hardly questioned her at all. He was quite withdrawn for such a previously boisterous child. Eventually, Cissy threw some light on the situation.

One afternoon, she and Harry had found Edward in the armoury, trying to get a clear view of himself in a well-polished shield. He looked very sad. Cissy asked him what was troubling him.

"Mama says my ears are much too big. I can't see them properly but they don't feel very big."

For once, Harry had compassion for his young brother. "Your ears are fine, Edward. They are just the right size. Mama was cross because your ears had heard something she didn't want you to hear."

Cissy had also reassured her cousin and they had taken him outside with them.

With Cissy back in her lessons, Alice was frequently able to sit in and was enjoying her opportunity to learn again. Cissy also spent time with Olivia learning to sew and embroider. It was not a comfortable activity, she told Alice, as she and Olivia found little to talk about. But Cissy was becoming more skilled and enjoyed the actual work. She was making a small tapestry strip as a gift for her Papa.

Gradually life in the castle settled down and reports were that throughout the country, the political situation was calmer too, though still precarious between the rival factions. Under normal circumstances, this would have led to the family participating in more social occasions with the local nobility. The Baron accepted one or two invitations, going alone, but Stephen refused all such invitations as he could not risk Olivia having chances to meet with other ladies and using one of them to pass on a message about her situation. Cissy too, although feeling well enough to attend, was restricted by lack of a chaperone, as Alice was not, of course, invited.

Once, in mid-June, it came to light that Olivia was still trying to get a message to her brother. Not being able to read and write herself, Olivia had tried to enlist Edward's help. He was making progress in his lessons, and was quite flattered when, one afternoon, his mother asked him to do some writing for her. She told him the words she wanted him to write, but he soon reached the limit of his abilities, and suggested she get Harry or Cecily to write the message. Olivia turned on him, telling him that he was always such a disappointment to her.

The attempt came to light when Edward went to Harry and asked if he would write a letter for their Mama, as when he had tried he did not know how to spell some of the words. Harry later reported the conversation to his father and to Alice.

"If Mama asks you to write another letter, you must tell me, or Papa. She is not allowed to send messages out of the castle."

"Harry, why is Mama being so cross? She is only nice when she is playing with Eleanor or Margot. She doesn't like me at all."

"You wouldn't really understand, little brother, but a long time ago, before you were born, Mama and Uncle Piers did something very, very wrong and sinful. Papa and Uncle Michael did not know about it until after Uncle Piers had visited us at Christmas. They only found out then because of something you said when we were all playing a game."

"But what did I say, Harry?"

"It was when we started to play the tournament game—you remember, when I said I'd be the Duke of Dunghill, and you said you'd be Daniel of Whitby."

"Yes, but then Papa suggested Harry Horseface, which was much funnier!" Edward giggled.

"When you said 'Daniel of Whitby', I said it wasn't funny and you said Mama and Uncle Piers thought it was. The name wasn't one that Cecily or I had heard before, but Papa and Alice had heard it, and knew it to be the name of someone who had done something very wicked to this family. Uncle Michael had not been able to find the man, although he had searched and searched."

"So," Edward jumped in remarkably quickly, "when I said Mama had called Uncle Piers 'Daniel of Whitby', Papa knew that the bad man was Uncle Piers using a pretend name?"

"Yes, Edward, and Mama had planned the wicked deed with him, so now she is being punished and she must not send messages out of the castle without Papa or Uncle Michael seeing them first."

"I don't suppose Mama will ever like me again," Edward said wistfully.

After hearing about this conversation, Alice wondered what the Baron was doing about punishing Piers du Bois, and one evening she got the chance to ask Stephen.

"I think he is finding it very difficult to know what to do, Alice," Stephen replied. "There has been so much treason and plotting going on in the country that no court could be expected to deal with what they would see as a family matter. They would expect Michael to use his own Baronial powers. His jurisdiction, though, does not cover Piers' lands.

He may decide to ask the Common Court to confiscate some of Piers' land and grant ownership to him.

"This is why it is important that Olivia does not make contact with her brother by any means. If he is warned that their wickedness has been discovered, he may be able to prepare to defend himself. His willingness to go along with Olivia's plot may have been mostly political. He probably saw it as a way of striking a blow against the Yorkists, as well as pleasing his sister.

"Oh Alice, how could Olivia plot so wickedly against this family out of jealousy for a title? She caused dreadful pain to my brother and now her own children are suffering."

"She is suffering herself now," Alice commented. "I saw her face when you renounced your right to the title. That is probably her true punishment, as it was the aim of all her plotting."

"Yes, you are right. It must hurt that all her scheming has come to naught."

Chapter Eighteen

The weather in late June was glorious. The gloom that had pervaded the castle for weeks began to lift. Even Olivia seemed to have accepted her fate and spent time walking outside with her two little girls and their maid, or sitting in the shade working on her embroidery.

There was a good cut from the hay meadows and it dried sweetly in the hot sun. Haycocks were built and Alice admired the skill that went into creating them, and especially thatching the top of each one. She remembered her own poor efforts at re-thatching the cot in Home Valley. It was mostly water-tight, but its appearance was neither neat nor attractive.

Once again she found herself thinking of her home and when she should return. Then, to her great surprise, a messenger, returning to the castle, brought a letter for her. It had been written by Father Luke, and read:

> To Alice Moore, greetings from your friends in Arkenthorpe. John says to tell you all is well. Your possessions are safe and your vegetables growing well. John was able to pay rent for the shop when it was due to the Squire on Quarter Day, and has earned enough money to keep himself and Mary comfortable. Maud, Thomas and the children are well.

> Everyone was glad to have the news that Cissy has recovered from her sickness, and thank God. They trust that you are well too, Alice, and miss you. They ask you to give the Baron their most respectful greetings, and send affectionate greetings to you and Cissy.
>
> (Father Luke had then added): I send my greetings to Baron Michael, to you Alice and to Cecily, and pray for God's blessing on you all.

Having read the letter, Alice sought Cissy at the end of lessons and gave it to her. The Baron was away for a few days, so she could not yet pass on the greetings to him. Cissy read the letter and handed it back to Alice saying, "It is good to hear from our friends, but I am afraid they will make you think about leaving me again, Alice."

"I confess I have been thinking about it."

"You are happy here, aren't you? I would hate to think you were not—oh, I know that it has not been pleasant since we found out what Aunt Olivia and Piers had done, but otherwise you are happy, aren't you?"

"Yes Cissy, I like it here, but I now have the same problem as before, that there is no role for me."

"But I really need you to talk to Alice. Who could I talk to if you weren't here? Harry and Edward need you too."

"I know it seems so but, Cissy, you said yourself that Olivia dislikes me, and I am sure that part of the reason is because her own children began to make me too important in their lives. She felt that I was trying to take her place. I wasn't, but she was not happy. It will be worse for her if that happens again now."

Cissy suddenly looked angry and snapped, "Well I really think my feelings and Harry's and Edward's too, should be more important than

Aunt Olivia's. She didn't care about my Papa's and Mama's when she plotted, did she?"

"Cissy! Of course your feelings count, but I cannot stay here just to sit around like some old wise woman, waiting to be consulted. Harry will soon be a young man and you will be going out socially to meet others of your age among the rich and noble families. I cannot help you there."

"You could come too and be my chaperone. I can't go without one, and I don't think Aunt Olivia will be going visiting much."

"I cannot go on such visits with you Cissy. For one thing, I will not be invited. I am not a noblewoman. If Olivia cannot do it, your Papa will make arrangements for some noble lady with daughters to take you under her wing and give you the guidance you need."

Cissy sighed, "I sometimes wish I wasn't of noble birth. If we were back in Arkenthorpe, I could just meet with everyone and you would be there."

"But that is not your place in life, Cissy. If you had stayed there, you would eventually have married and had a hard life as the wife of a blacksmith, or a tenant farmer. I don't think that would have been right for you."

"Oh, I know I have come to like nice things and pretty clothes and, of course, I love Papa, but I love you too Alice. I don't want you to go away again."

After this conversation with Cissy, Alice spent even more time thinking about what she should do and when she should leave, but was unable to reach a conclusion.

The Baron returned three days later. He had been seeking advice on how he should bring Piers du Bois to account for the kidnapping and succeeding events, but the news he brought made that unnecessary. He had travelled to Derbyshire where the du Bois family's main residence was, and having told his story to the local Justice of the Peace, they had gone together to put the charges to Piers. On their arrival, however, they found a family in mourning, as only the previous day, while out riding, Piers' horse had stumbled at the gallop and thrown its rider over its head. He had suffered a broken neck and died instantly.

Conveying their condolences to the family, the Baron and the Justice had left without explaining the reason for their call.

On his return home, the Baron called Stephen and Olivia to him and gave them the news. Olivia collapsed with the shock and needed Stephen for support as she returned to her chamber. There she remained for two days, seeing no-one but her maid.

It was after the evening meal on his first night home that the Baron summoned Stephen, Alice, Cissy and Harry to him.

"Piers's death brings to an end this whole, unhappy story. He has not had to face justice here but he is now in the highest court of all, facing God, his maker. Olivia is very upset, but when she recovers from the shock, I will lift the restrictions imposed upon her and she may live as freely as she did before.

"I shall do my best to forgive her in due time. Each of you can re-build your relationship with Olivia as you think best.

Stephen rose, and spoke quietly to Michael as he did so. "Thank you, brother. I too will try to forgive her, but my decision on the title still remains."

"As you wish, Stephen. As you wish."

Alice soon realised that with the watch on her activities lifted, Olivia would be able to participate in social life again and be available to chaperone Cecily. It was most unlikely that she would resort to plotting again, as she would have nothing to gain; nor would she have a co-conspirator.

So finally, Alice decided she must ask the Baron to arrange for her transport back to Home Valley. The last few months had been very stressful; first thinking that Cissy might die, and watching the worry etching itself into the Baron's face; then his wonder at Cissy's recovery, before suddenly being plunged back into darkness with the horror of discovering that a member of his own family had hatched such a foul plot against his loved ones. Now, once again, the Baron was looking happier, though his hair was much whiter than it had been two years ago.

"This time when I go home," Alice admitted to herself, "it won't only be Cissy that I miss. I shall miss the opportunities to discuss things with the Baron and with Stephen. I have learned so much from both of them and they have treated me with such consideration.

"I think," she mused, "that I am the one person who has gained much from Olivia's wicked deed. When I found Cissy, the course of my life completely changed. It was very hard at times but I have learned so much and travelled and seen things I would never otherwise have seen. I must find some way of using what I have gained."

Next day, Alice approached the Baron after breakfast and asked, in the hearing of both Olivia and Stephen, "May I have time with you to discuss when it will be convenient for me to be taken to my home?"

The Baron smiled, sighing at the same time. "Oh dear, the time has come has it? I will certainly discuss this with you, but I will be absent from the castle today, returning tomorrow after noon. Perhaps we can talk tomorrow evening after the meal."

"Of course, my lord. As you wish."

As the Baron walked away, Olivia opened her mouth as if to say something to Alice, then clearly thought better of it.

The next day was dull and humid producing heavy showers of rain in late afternoon, but in the early evening, the sky cleared and the sun was shining. At the end of the meal, the Baron stood up, stretching to ease his aching limbs after being on horseback most of the day.

"I think we will have our discussion outside, Alice, to take benefit of this pleasant evening."

"May I come too, Papa?" Cecily asked.

"On this occasion, no," the Baron replied. "Alice and I have important matters to discuss."

"Very well, Papa. I will see if Harry will come out for a while."

A few minutes later, as Alice and the Baron strolled along by the side of the moat, he opened the conversation. "So, once again Alice, you feel you must leave my household and return to Arkenthorpe. You do not seem to be unhappy here, although this time your visit has certainly been full of upsetting happenings. Can I ask if your wish to leave is because you truly prefer your life in your valley, or because you still feel you do not have a rightful place here?"

"I don't really know the answer to that myself, my lord. Since my mother died, many years ago, there has not been a rightful place for me. The valley became my home and when I am there it feels right, but I know the land must belong to someone and, perhaps, I should be paying rent, which I have never done. The rabbits worry me too, as I need them but I am almost certainly guilty of poaching and so could be severely punished if found out.

"Life is not easy, especially in Winter and early Spring, but your generous gift when I returned home last time, enabled me to buy extra stores and better clothing, covers and blankets, which helped me to keep warm and well-fed."

"Home Valley is beautiful," said the Baron, "but what about loneliness, Alice?"

"There have been times when not having other folk around made me feel very lonely. The time when I was ill and Cissy was so young, I dearly wished there was someone else. Cissy was amazing, but we could not have continued much longer. Then, for the first few weeks on my return from here, I missed having people around me, but most of all I missed Cissy."

"What about this time, Alice? What will you miss this time?"

"The same things, I expect. Perhaps a few others too. It has been good to learn again, not only from Brother James's lessons, but from you and from your brother in your discussions about business and about the hostility between the different groups of noble families wishing to rule this country. I do not fully understand the issues, but I know much more than I did before. I have felt very privileged to hear those conversations and be allowed to ask questions, or to pass comment. I shall miss that very much."

"So, if you felt you had a rightful place here with us, would you stay?"

"Perhaps, my lord, although I cannot think of the form such a rightful place could take."

"I think I may have an answer." The Baron stretched out his arm. "Look, we are almost at the new garden. Let us go in to it and I will tell you what I think. Of course, if you are not happy with my suggestion, you must say so, and I will arrange for your journey as promised."

Alice was now intrigued. She followed the Baron into the garden, where he stopped at a stone bench which was still bathed in the rays of the evening sun.

"Sit here beside me, Alice."

Somewhat self-consciously, she did so, hoping they could not be observed from any windows. He half-turned so that he could see her face. "When you left us last time, Cecily was not the only person to wish you had not gone. I missed your presence and being able to consult you about Cecily. When you came back at my request and you entered Cecily's bed chamber, the relief I felt almost unmanned me. I slept so well that night because I knew Cecily was being watched by someone who loves her as much as I do. You had called her 'my beloved child'. I am her father and you have become her mother. This is your rightful place, Alice, and I wish you to consider becoming my wife."

Suddenly, Alice felt as though the world had stopped. She lifted her head and looked directly at the Baron's face, eventually gasping, "You said 'your wife'?"

"Yes, my dearest Alice, I am asking you to marry me."

The silence seemed to last for ever as a confusion of thoughts tumbled over and over in Alice's mind, but eventually she managed, "But my lord, you are a Baron. I don't even know who I am . . . . I have no dowry."

"I know these things. I have known them almost since we first met. Neither of us is young, though you are several years younger than I am. We have no-one to arrange marriage for us. I have no need of more wealth or land that a dowry would bring, nor have I need of an alliance for reason of politics, but I do have need of you.

"From your face and reaction, I do not think you find the idea an unpleasant one?"

"No, no, my lord, it is not unpleasant. It is just a shock."

"Has the idea never crossed your mind?"

Alice hesitated, and looked confused.

"You may tell me, you know. I was hoping you would have warm feelings for me."

"Well, the idea was put into my mind by someone else. I was accused of using female wiles to ensnare you. I was not aware that I had done anything to give others that impression. When I suddenly asked to leave earlier than expected last time, it was because I could not bear the idea that I was causing you to be the subject of gossip among those of high rank."

"I don't think I need to ask who that 'someone else' was, in view of events in the recent past."

"Olivia told me what was being said during Cissy's birthday celebration. I was mortified, my lord, that the wife of another baron should be saying such things about me!"

"And that was why you fainted?"

"Yes, my lord."

"Who was that baron's wife? That is, if Olivia is to be believed that such conversation took place."

"Baroness Derwent."

"Derwent! Do you remember him, Alice? He was at the inn we stayed at on the visit to York. How stories become changed in the telling! At York, Derwent suggested that it was I that was planning to take you to my bed that night. He thought it a subject for merriment, but I did not.

"You must forget about all that. Are your feelings for me warm enough to make the idea of marriage a pleasing one?"

"Oh yes, my lord, it is pleasing. It is a great honour. I hesitate because I worry that I will fail you in my duties, or that in the eyes of others I would cause you to lose esteem."

"If I thought that likely, my dear, I would not have proposed marriage. You have faced challenges in your life and have met them successfully. We are already friends, Alice, which is an advantage few couples have when they marry.

"If you assure me that the idea is not displeasing to you, I will not ask you for your final answer now. Tomorrow is Sunday. You will have time to think and pray about your decision. May we meet on Monday morning when Cecily goes to her lessons? You can give me your answer then."

Alice looked up at him and smiled. "Yes, I will decide by then."

He stood, "Come then, the midges are starting to bite. Let us go in." He bent forward, took Alice's hand and raised her to her feet. She walked from the garden as if in a dream.

She slept little that night. Strangely, it was not fear of the nobility that concerned her most, although she was sure big social gatherings would be an ordeal. It was the reaction of the servants at the castle, especially those she thought of as friends. How would they feel about the change in her position?

And what about the family? Cissy, she guessed, would accept it happily, but Olivia? Would the duties of managing the household become Alice's responsibility? If so, what would Olivia do and say?

Then there was the intimate side of marriage about which she knew little. Would she be able to bear a child? She knew she did not have many child-bearing years left, even if she was not barren.

She went over and over everything the Baron had said to her in the garden. He had missed her! He didn't mind that she had no family. Who, she wondered, had been her father? Also, she knew almost nothing of her mother's family; just vague, early-childhood memories of a grandmother. Why had her mother not told her more? The Old Squire might have known something, but it was unlikely that Miss Ellie would know. Could she . . . . would she dare to take on such responsibility?

Alice must have fallen asleep around dawn and so woke later than usual. She had to hurry to be ready for Mass. As she walked to the church, Cissy came to walk with her.

"You look very thoughtful this morning, Alice, and you seem tired. Are you well?"

"Yes, very well thank you. I am rather tired as I lay awake for a long time last night."

"You must have had **very long**, serious discussions with Papa"

As the Mass progressed, Alice felt that everything in the ritual was telling her to accept. This decision was one she had never expected to have to make. Yes, at one time she had thought a husband might be found for her, but that was a long time ago. Now she had to make the decision herself. Not only marriage, but marriage to such an important man!

After church she made herself think seriously about what her life would be like if she said 'no' to the Baron and returned home. The shop would provide for John and a little for her, but she would have to earn in other ways too—perhaps she could write letters for people? No, few ordinary village folk needed letters writing and merchants or squires would either write for themselves or ask a priest to do it. Perhaps she could teach village children to read and write, but would their parents be able to pay her? No. She would have to return to spinning and making herbal drinks, selling her goods through the shop. Did she really want to do that for the rest of her life?

At the midday meal, the Baron smiled at her and asked if she had passed a peaceful night?

"No Papa, she did not," Cecily responded swiftly. "She was very tired this morning. I think your discussion of serious matters must have disturbed her mind. I hope you won't need more of those discussions today."

The Baron inwardly smiled at his daughter's thinly veiled curiosity. "No Cecily, no more serious discussions today."

"Good. I think you should rest this afternoon, Alice."

Alice did retire to her room, but after an hour or so, she went to find Josse. The cook was herself resting, but was pleased to see Alice.

"I'd like to talk to you about something important, Josse, and seek your advice. Can we go somewhere to talk in private?"

"Yes, my friend. Shall we go into the old castle? There are many quiet corners there."

Eventually the two women sat in a turret room, where the narrow window opening was admitting a gentle breeze and giving them a view of some hills with grey clouds casting moving shadows across them.

"Right my friend, what is it?"

"I have a very, very important decision to make, Josse, and for now anything I tell you has to be a complete secret. I don't know that I should even be talking to you, but I do need to talk to someone."

"Don't fret, Alice. Not a word shall pass my lips to a soul."

"Yesterday I went to speak to the Baron about arranging my travel home, but instead of that, he asked me to consider staying here."

"That does not surprise me. He is a much happier man when you are here."

"But Josse, this will surprise you. He asked me to stay as his wife. He has asked me to marry him!"

Josse gasped! "Oh mercy, mercy me, Alice! That certainly is a surprise."

There was a long pause, then she continued, "Had you had no suspicion that the Baron was thinking in that way?"

"No, I had not. But, do you remember last time I went home, although I was planning to go, it was a very sudden decision and I left earlier than planned?"

"Yes, I remember."

"That was because Mistress Olivia told me that people in society were saying that I was attempting to become Baroness Muirhill. When I protested that the thought had never come into my mind, she said that she herself had watched me and had seen me walking with the Baron alone, and laughing with him. I had to admit that that was true but I had no thought of enticement. I knew then I would have to go home at once, as I could not bear the idea that after all his kindness to me, I was a threat to his good name."

"And now, Alice, he has asked you to marry him."

"Yes. Folk are going to think that the gossip was true."

"I see your dilemma. Perhaps what Mistress Olivia, and others had seen, was the Baron's developing interest in you. If that is your only worry, I am sure time will put it right."

"It is not the only problem, Josse. Another one is perhaps more important, and one on which I would really like your honest advice. How would you, and all the other servants, feel if I accepted and so became the Baroness?"

Josse looked thoughtfully at Alice before replying. "Do you know, I think most of us, probably all of us, would be delighted. I see it this way: everyone who serves the Baron here, respects him as a good man and a considerate master. You, Alice, are also respected in a different way and we have affection for you. He has suffered so much unhappiness, if marrying you makes the Baron happy, most of us would not question his choice. You are not a servant, although I suspect Mistress Olivia would like to think you are. Neither are you in the family. I can see that has been a problem for you, but it has never been a problem for us. No, I can think of no-one who would be unhappy to serve you too."

"Thank you, Josse. I would do my best to keep things that way. I know there will be problems with Olivia, but I cannot allow her feelings to make the decision for me. I must decide by tomorrow whether to say 'yes' or 'no'. It is such a great honour that he has asked me, that I don't feel I can refuse.

"I have nothing to bring him—no family connection; no land; no dowry. I do not even know who fathered me."

"Aye, I remember you telling me that. But then, many other folk don't know, or are not sure. So I say, if you don't know, you can imagine, and why imagine a peasant when it costs no more to imagine a prince."

Alice laughed.

"I have great respect for the Baron and, I have to admit, affection too, because of his kindness to me and his deep love for Cissy. If I were to say 'no' it would be because I feel I am not worthy of the honour and have a fear of failing him."

"Well, only you can make the decision, my friend, but my advice would be to accept. He will have given the matter a great deal of thought before asking you, and it will certainly please Miss Cecily if you say 'yes'.

"Now, it must be time I was back in my kitchen. I'll keep my promise—not a word will I speak—but I will be agog to know your decision . . . . my lady!" Josse laughed and gave a mock curtsey.

By the time she reached her own chamber, Alice realised she was going to say 'yes'. For the rest of the day, whenever she was alone, her mind turned over and over the things that worried her about that decision.

If she herself was sensitive in her dealings with the servants, she hoped Josse's prediction would be true. She hoped her friends in Arkenthorpe would not think she had abandoned them. Perhaps it would be possible to visit them before too long.

She allowed herself to think of the Baron taking her body in their marriage bed. How would she cope with his attentions? How would she react to seeing a man ready for the act of conjoining with a woman? She remembered a brief description from her mother so many years ago, and she had picked up small bits of information from conversations with Maud.

There was the reaction of the wives of other nobles to face when they knew that one among them was not of noble birth. Perhaps Josse was right on that too, and it would gradually cease to be a matter of significance.

With her decision made, she went to the chapel after the evening meal and asked the Blessèd Virgin to guide her through this new way of life. She slept a little better that night.

As usual, she spent time with Cissy next morning before her lessons began. She felt she was being watched and eventually Cissy said, "You look different today, Alice. Better than you did yesterday. Will you tell me what has been worrying you?"

"You will know very soon, but it is nothing bad. At least I hope you will not think so."

"Hmm.." Cissy mused, "this is becoming interesting. Can you not tell me now?"

"No, but I promise you it won't be long."

"Good. Well, I suppose I must go to my lessons or Brother James will not be happy."

With Cissy gone for the morning, Alice tidied her hair, straightened her gown and wimple and made her way to the end of the hall where the Baron conducted the affairs of his demesne when he was at home. Sure enough, he was there in discussion with Stephen and Simon the Factor. She sat down at the other end of the hall, watching three young kittens annoying their mother, fencing with each other and tumbling among the strewn rushes. Soon the men finished their business and walked down the hall towards her. Stephen and Simon both acknowledged her as they left the building. The Baron stopped in front of her.

"Good morning, Alice. Can we have our meeting now?"

"Good morning, my lord. Yes, I am ready."

"Come then, let us walk outside."

They were going to enter the garden but saw that Olivia and the nursery maid were playing on the grassy sward with the two little girls, so they left by the postern and made their way slowly on to a nearby stretch of moorland. It was ablaze with gorse and starred with a riotous carpet of summer flowers. A lark was singing somewhere high above. They stopped in a small hollow where they were out of view from the castle. The Baron turned to face her.

"Alice, my dear Alice, have you decided? Will you become my wife?"

Alice raised her face and looked at him directly. "Yes, my lord. I am deeply honoured and will accept your proposal that I become your wife."

"Oh, Alice." He reached out and took her hands in his. "Your answer has made me very happy. I hope you will never have cause to regret your decision."

At the touch of his hands, Alice felt a thrill run through her body, and she saw his eyes sparkle as he smiled. He looked almost young again.

"Remove your wimple my dear, and let me see you as I did when I came to Home Valley."

Alice did so, and caressing first her hair and then her cheek, he bent forward and kissed her very gently on the brow.

Overcome with emotions she could not explain, Alice felt tears spring into her eyes and she dropped her face and let it rest against the Baron's shoulder, as again he stroked her hair.

Alice knew that this was another life-changing moment. She lifted her head and looked into his eyes and, once more, time was suspended. Then releasing his hold, and in a voice that trembled slightly, the Baron said, "I am finding it difficult to believe that this is happening. I have admired you for a long time and I have felt warm friendship for you, but while ever I thought you might not feel the same toward me, I did not dare to admit love, even to myself. I shall be so proud when I can say, as Cecily does, 'you are my Alice'."

Soon, too soon, with her wimple restored, Alice and the Baron returned slowly to the castle, knocking at the postern to be admitted. As they were about to part, Alice said, "Cecily must be the first person we tell. I think we must wait until after the meal, or by the end of it everyone will have guessed what is happening."

And so it was that as the meal ended, the Baron summoned his daughter and Alice to meet him in the garden, which this time was empty of other people.

The Baron pointed to a stone seat and, addressing Cecily, he said, "Now my dear daughter, I wish you to sit there and listen most carefully to what I say, without interrupting."

Cecily looked suitably serious and sat demurely on the bench.

"A few days ago, Alice came to ask me to arrange for her travel back to Home Valley."

"I guessed she would," Cecily moaned.

"Cecily, I said do not interrupt!"

"Sorry, Papa."

"I talked to her and asked her to consider staying with us, but she felt that she has no rightful place here."

Cecily took in a breath to speak, but remembered just in time.

"But," continued her father, "I had come to realise that Alice's place should be here and I put a proposition to her, asking her to think carefully about it, promising that if she did not like the idea, I would arrange for her travel home.

"The proposition I put to her was that she should become my wife, and I am delighted to say that she has today agreed."

He paused, then to Cecily, "You may now speak."

Cecily's face was a picture of amazement and she sat as if stunned for several seconds before jumping to her feet and flinging her arms around her father.

"Oh Papa, Papa, how wonderful!" Then she turned and clung to Alice.

"Alice, my Alice, I am so happy. Thank you, thank you for saying 'yes'."

"You will have to share Alice with me now," said her father. "She will be my Alice too."

"Of course I will share her with you, Papa. Oh I don't think I have ever been so happy before."

She danced around the garden, as her delighted 'parents' watched, finally returning and hugging each of them in turn again.

"Will you be telling everyone now, Papa? I don't think I could keep it secret for very long."

"There are certain people who must be told this afternoon. I will announce it to everyone else this evening, first in the hall of the solar, then to all the folk who eat in the great hall. You must come with Alice and me when I do so.

"Now I will leave you and Alice to talk, while I go to tell Stephen and Brother James."

"Can I please be the one to tell Harry?" Cissy begged. "I will swear him to secrecy until this evening."

"Very well, but no-one else. Do you promise?"

"Yes Papa. I promise. Oh I am so, so happy!"

When the Baron had left them, Alice tried to calm Cissy down a little.

"I hoped my decision would please you, Cissy, but when your Papa asked me, it was such a shock, I had to have time to think if it would be the right thing."

"How could you think it would not please me? I will have the two people I love most in the world together, with me. It was so hard when you left before and I did notice that Papa seemed to miss you too. Oh, it was worth being ill just to bring you back."

They wandered into the new dwelling with Cissy still hopping around in excitement.

"I am going to rest for a while now," Alice told Cissy. "Walk normally as you go to seek Harry, otherwise people will want to know what all the excitement is about, and try not to encounter Olivia."

"Oh yes," said Cissy in a suddenly serious voice, "I'd forgotten about her. I suspect she will not be very happy."

"I suspect so too. I think she will be the first of a number of problems, but off you go and remember your promise."

That evening, Alice made a special effort with her appearance before they went to the new hall for their meal. The family members, except baby Margot, were all assembling at the table on the daïs. On the floor of the hall senior personal servants of family members were sitting at a table along one wall, a total of perhaps fifteen people in all. As the family assembled, Alice saw the Baron go across to the Steward, who then went to the kitchen. A few moments later, he returned followed by Cook and the staff who would be serving at table. They entered and stood in a group just inside the door from the kitchens. Then the Steward raised a short, wooden baton and banged it ceremoniously on the table, bringing chatter to a stop and all attention was focused on the top table.

The Baron rose.

"I will not delay your meal for long, but I have an announcement to make. It may seem unusual that I should speak to you in this way, but I know how gossip can carry a message which changes in the telling.

"My friends, after many years of sadness and worry, throughout which I have been conscious of support from so many of you, I will soon be marrying again. At my age, there is no-one to arrange a marriage for me, so I took it upon myself to ask the lady in question, and I am happy to say she has agreed. She is known to you all.

"Alice, please stand. Ladies, gentlemen, friends—my future wife, Miss Alice Moore."

A gasp of surprise could be heard throughout the hall.

"You all know that it was Alice who saved Cecily's life when, as a young baby, she survived the accident which killed her mother. Alice found her in remote moorland, took her home and raised her. Later, she heard of my search and eventually re-united me with my child. Alice is the only mother Cecily can remember and she and I have developed a warm friendship. The date for the wedding is not yet settled, but will be in early September. At the end of this meal, we will visit the Great Hall to tell the rest of my people this news."

The Baron and Alice sat down, but before giving the order to serve, the Steward raised his hand, which again stilled the whispers which were starting.

"My lord Baron, I would like to say, on behalf of all your people here, that we wish you and Miss Alice every happiness and also that it will be our duty and pleasure to serve you both in the future."

He bowed to the Baron, then straightening, he gave the signal to bring in the food, and hubbub broke out in the hall.

Alice looked across to her friend, Josse. That lady's face was aglow and she mouthed something to Alice which seemed to be "well done", before turning back into the kitchen.

Fortunately, Alice's position at table made it difficult for her to see Olivia's reaction, but Harry left his seat and, presenting himself at the other side of the table, he bowed to his uncle saying, "My lord, I am most happy with this news, and I am delighted that Miss Alice will not be leaving us again."

Not to be outdone, Edward followed his brother's example, and bowing in an exaggerated manner, he blurted out, "I think it is a very good idea, 'cos I like Alice too, uncle, my lord."

After the meat course, of which both the Baron and Alice had partaken lightly, they left the table and, accompanied by Cecily, walked across to the Great Hall. The Steward there was clearly on the watch for them.

"The Senior Steward advised me that you would be coming, my lord. The daïs is free and I shall get silence as soon as you wish."

When the three of them had mounted the daïs of this much bigger hall, the steward took a muffled stick and banged it against the suspended metal plate. As the assembled diners realised the Baron had arrived, they hastily got to their feet and turned to face him, some still clutching eating daggers with meat speared upon them.

At the Baron's "Good evening everyone," the reponse of "good evening, my lord," echoed down the hall and curious glances turned on Alice and Cecily.

"I shall interrupt your meal only briefly," said the Baron. "I have a piece of news which I have just given to my people in the hall of the solar and, as many of you here in this hall have served me for many years, I thought it right that I should come to tell you the news too.

"As I am sure you all know, my wife Belle and daughter Cecily were lost to me almost ten years ago, and as you also know, it was with great joy that I eventually found my daughter alive and well but, with sadness, found only the bones of my wife.

"I am here today to tell you that, in a few weeks' time, I shall be marrying again. I shall marry the lady who saved the life of my child and became a mother to her; a lady with whom most of you are acquainted, Miss Alice Moore."

The Baron reached for Alice's hand and drew her level with him, then reached out his other hand and drew Cecily forward.

"Thank you all for your attention. Please resume your meal."

As a hum of excited conversation started, a voice from the hall called out, "Raise your cups my friends and let us drink to the happiness of our lord and his betrothed."

There were cries of "His lordship," "Good health my lord", "His lordship and Miss Alice—God bless them", and as they left the Great Hall, acknowledging the well-wishers, cheering followed them.

Chapter Nineteen

As was to be expected, not all was sweetness. Olivia made no attempt to speak to Alice during the next two days, but on the Thursday, the Baron was away from the castle. Alice had spent a short time in lessons with the children, but returned with Edward when he left the others. She walked with him back to the solar and to the room he shared with Harry.

Olivia was waiting for Alice as she turned to walk back toward the staircase down to the hall. "I wish to speak to you. Come in here," she commanded, turning into the room she and Stephen used during the day. Stephen was, of course, out on the estate. Alice followed Olivia with a sinking feeling.

"Close the door."

Alice did so and, with trepidation, turned to face her future sister-in-law.

"So, witch, your spells have worked. You expect to be baroness in only a few weeks' time. You think you have bettered me."

"No, Olivia, I neither set out to better you, nor to become baroness. I cannot make you believe me, but it is the truth. When I sought a meeting with the Baron, it was to discuss my returning to Arkenthorpe. I expected to be going home."

"Then why are you not going?"

"You know why. He said his wish would be for me to stay here and to stay as his wife. It was a surprise and shock to me, so he allowed me to have two days in which to give him my answer."

"I know you have knowledge of many herbs and potions. You must have been administering something to him, or why should he even look at a peasant, and a bastard one at that!"

Alice felt her colour rising and knew she would weep unless she could vent her anger at this unfair, if not unexpected, attack.

"I *may* have been born a bastard but I do not know that, and nor do you. As for giving the Baron a potion, I have not so much as poured a drink for him in weeks. I am not a noblewoman and the Baron knows that. I shall have to learn what is required of me as his wife, but if he believes that I can make him happy, how could I refuse such an honour?"

"If you care for him, you would have refused. He will be laughed at by all in society when they realise he has taken to wife a nobody—no family, no fortune, no land, no dowry—the name of Muirhill will be of no account any more. You should go, GO! GO!"

Olivia's voice had risen almost to a scream and there was a strange look in her face. Alice's own anger suddenly evaporated and was replaced by a mix of pity and fear. This woman was possessed. It was madness speaking. Alice tried to speak calmly, but very firmly.

"No, Olivia, I will not go. The Baron wants me; Cecily wants me to stay, and I will do my utmost to be worthy of the honour being bestowed on me."

"You witch; you evil witch. Since you came here, everything has gone wrong. Michael would have been in a monastery years ago and Stephen would have been Baron and I would be Baroness, but you came. That child would have died if it hadn't been for you. But you had to interfere. You cast a spell and Michael found her. She came back and you came with her. I made you go away; the child became ill and would have died, but you came back; you cast your spell and she didn't die.

"Witch! Witch! You came back and everything went wrong. Piers is dead. Everything went wrong."

As Olivia shouted and hissed, she prowled around looking as though she would fly at Alice at any moment. Alice was frightened, but daren't show it in case she made Olivia worse. Her heart was pounding.

"Piers is dead," Olivia screamed again. "Witch! Witch! We burn witches. You should burn, burn!"

Olivia turned toward the fire grate, but no fire was there in this warm weather. Suddenly, she bent and grasped a fire iron. As she straightened, she got between Alice and the door. Alice backed away but Olivia raised the fire iron and took a step towards her, just as the door was opened from outside. A man rushed in and grabbed Olivia's arm, not quite in time to prevent the strike but in time to deflect it away from Alice's head, so it just struck a glancing blow on her right shoulder before crashing to the floor.

Alice was dazed by the pain and sank down on a couch clutching her shoulder. She was now aware of others entering the room and Olivia being forcibly held against her will.

The first to enter the room had been Joseph, Stephen's man servant, and he was still holding Olivia from behind as she screeched to be released. Olivia's maid, Mary, was trying to sooth her mistress with gentle words, but finding they had no effect, she moved to help Alice. Then suddenly, Stephen was there and the Steward too.

Stephen joined Joseph and between them they carried Olivia, still struggling and screaming "witch, witch, burn witch", out of the day room to her bed chamber. Re-assured that Alice wasn't seriously injured, the maid followed her mistress, then a kitchen boy arrived with Cook, who immediately went to Alice.

"Are you hurt?"

"I received a blow on my shoulder, and my arm feels numb, but I think it will only be a bruise."

"You are shaking all over. Here lad," she called to the kitchen boy, "run and get a drink of warm milk and honey for Miss Alice—quick as you can. Now, you just lay back until you feel better."

Suddenly, there was quiet. The Steward had retrieved the fire iron and returned it to the hearth. Distant sounds could still be heard from Olivia, but she was obviously calming down. Then, as Alice's dizziness began to recede, she thought she heard a whimpering.

"Listen, Josse, can you hear someone crying?"

Cook crossed the room, opening the door a little wider. "Yes, I can. You stay where you are. I'll look."

A minute later she came back into the room, struggling to carry a cowering, sobbing bundle. "Poor little man. I found him curled up behind the chest in his room."

"Edward?" said Alice. "Oh you poor child. Come here."

Cook lowered Edward to lie next to Alice on the couch, on the side away from her injured shoulder. He curled up against her continuing to sob. She stroked his hair. "Hush, Edward, hush."

Gradually the desperate sobbing slowed to fewer deeper, shuddering ones. The child's swollen, red eyes opened and looked at Alice.

"Alice, you're not deaded?"

"No, I'm only a little bit hurt. Just a nasty bruise."

"Oh Alice, I was so frightened."

"Of course you were. It was frightening for everyone."

"Why did Mama be so horrid?"

"We think she must be very sick. Not belly sick, but mind sick because of nasty things in her head. Your Papa and her maid are putting her to bed."

"I'm glad you're not deaded."

Just then feet could be heard running up the stairs and Harry rushed into the room followed by Cissy. Cook met them at the door. "Quiet now. Calm yourselves. It's all over."

"What happened?" demanded Harry.

"Are you alright?" Cissy asked anxiously.

"I have only a nasty bruise. Nothing to worry about."

"What happened?" demanded Harry again.

"Mama tried to dead Alice," whispered Edward. "She said Alice is a witch and should be burned."

"Where is Mama?"

"Your father and Joseph took her to her bedchamber. Mary is putting her to bed. She is ill, Harry. Very ill."

"Perhaps," Harry said doubtfully, "but are you sure you will be alright Alice?"

"Yes, I will. Joseph arrived just in time to save me from serious injury."

"God alone knows what Uncle Michael will say. Oh I'm so sorry Alice. This is terrible."

Alice realised Edward was almost asleep, but she continued to stroke his hair. "You will have to be very gentle with Edward for some time, Harry, and you Cecily. Cook found him sobbing and shaking from fear, curled up behind the chest in your room, Harry. He heard almost everything and was petrified."

"Oh, poor Edward," said Harry. "How terrible for him."

Joseph entered the room, over-hearing the last couple of remarks.

"If I may say so, Miss Alice, Master Edward was the one who caused me to get here just in time. "We had heard the noise of shouting downstairs, and were just wondering if we needed to do something, when Edward appeared at the musicians' gallery shouting, "Come quick, oh Joseph, please come quick." From his face and the fear in his voice I knew it was something serious, and got here as fast as I could, calling for others to follow."

"Thank you, Joseph," said Alice. "At the time I did not know who it was that grabbed Olivia's arm. It was incredible that you managed to hold her until Stephen arrived. I shall be eternally grateful to you, and to Edward."

"I came just now, as Master Stephen thought you might need help to get to your own room, Miss Alice."

"I think I will manage, thank you. If Edward is asleep, I will go and see if my shoulder needs treatment."

"The poor lamb is fast asleep," said Cook. "It will be best if he can stay that way for some time. Can you lift him gently, Joseph, so that I can help Miss Alice to her feet?"

When Alice was on her feet and being supported by Cook, Joseph laid Edward back on the couch. Cecily looked around and saw one of Olivia's shawls and covered him lightly with it.

"He must not be left alone," said Alice. "Someone must be here when he wakes."

"I'll stay," Harry assured her. "I will stay until Father comes back, then he and I will decide what to do."

"I will come with you, Alice," said Cissy. "I must attend to your shoulder."

"I will come along too," said Cook. "I may need to make up some oatmeal to bathe it. I think dinner will have to wait today. I'll send you a platter up, Master Harry. What about you, Miss Cecily?"

"A small platter, please, Cook. I must stay with Alice, and I don't think either of us will be very hungry."

There was no-one at high table at midday. All the servants were subdued, as the word had gone round that Miss Alice had been attacked by Mistress Olivia. Of course, none of them knew the nature of Olivia's previous wrong doings, and as she had been put to bed and given wine with sleep-inducing herbs in it, she was clearly unwell, so they put the matter down to that cause.

Sensation had returned to Alice's arm but now it was painful to move it. However, she could move it and when the physician, who had been summoned by Stephen, looked at the injury, he was fairly sure that no permanent damage had been inflicted. The blow had landed on the flesh at the top of her arm. The bones did not seem damaged.

Cissy stayed with her all afternoon, and Tilly was in constant attendance.

"Papa will have to do something about Aunt Olivia, or you will never be safe, Alice."

"I am afraid she is a very sick woman, Cissy. As she shrieked those vile things at me, I suddenly realised that the look in her eyes was not anger or jealousy but a form of madness.

"I think the person who will suffer most from today will be Edward. I have never seen a child so lost in terror as he was."

For the rest of the afternoon, the house took on an eerie quiet. Occasionally Eleanor's little voice calling to her maid, and Margot's babbling or cries could be heard as they played in the garden. Stephen called in to see Alice and looked even worse than when he had discovered the plot Olivia had hatched with her brother.

"I don't know what to say, Alice, except that I am so relieved your injuries are not more serious. What Olivia has said and done is unforgivable."

"Joseph saved me from the full force of her blow. Apparently Edward had called for help from the musicians' gallery. How is Edward now?"

"Very quiet; sometimes sleeping a little, at others weeping and trembling. I have talked to him and Harry is with him. He, Harry I mean, is truly concerned for his little brother. The last few weeks have seen Harry turning into a man."

"Joseph must have moved very quickly for a man of his age. I wasn't aware it was Joseph at the time, as I was very dazed, but how did you get there so soon, Stephen?"

"I was on my way back from inspecting the well, when I heard Olivia's voice—the windows were open and I was approaching that side of the house. I heard her shrieking 'witch'. 'evil witch', or some such, and I started to run. Once inside I ran to the stairs to find the Steward ahead of me and we reached the room together. I saw Mary bending over someone—I didn't know it was you at the time—and Joseph in urgent need of assistance with Olivia. As we removed her from the room, I realised from her screaming and raving that you had been the object of her vitriol.

"What can I say, Alice? I am so ashamed that you have had to suffer in such a way. She is possessed. There is an evil spirit in her, but it has been there for many years without my knowing it."

"Yes, I saw that evil spirit in her face today. It was not Olivia's face that I saw. You are not to blame, Stephen, we none of us saw it."

"I shall have to meet Michael very soon. He cannot forgive her this. She must be locked away somewhere or no-one will be safe. I am sure neither Harry nor Edward will ever wish to set eyes on her again. Do not fear her attacking you again, Alice. She will not be left unguarded, day or night, until I have found a place of security for her.

"Now I must go and prepare to face my brother yet again. His return is expected presently."

On his return, the Baron's first concern, after hearing the story from Stephen, was Alice. His relief on seeing her was great; he was sorry for the injury she had sustained, which he knew would cause pain and discomfort for some time, but when he saw the fire iron which had been the weapon, he blanched at the thought of what so nearly had happened. He sought out Joseph and expressed his undying gratitude, and also enquired if he himself had been injured—which no-one else had thought to do.

"A few small bruises only, my lord. They are mostly on my shins where Mistress Olivia kicked to try to make me let go of her."

"I fear those bruises may be larger than you claim, Joseph. You must see the physician about them. He will be here again tomorrow to see Miss Alice and Mistress Olivia. I will instruct him to examine your injuries while he is here. You must do whatever he recommends, and if that includes some days of rest, you will be relieved of your duties until you are fit again."

Next day Alice returned to some of her regular routine, and gradually life at Muirhill resumed its normal pattern, apart from those areas in which Olivia had played a part.

The Baron called the house Steward and Cook to him, and they advised him that they could continue to run the household so long as someone told them of any unusual requirements for a particular day. They also agreed that Alice could see what was involved by watching and talking to them, thus learning what she would need to do in the future.

Alice's main concern, however, was Edward. He was her shadow. He tried to follow her everywhere. He remained subdued, talking little and had no wish to play games. At the Baron's suggestion, and with Stephen's full agreement, Brother James spent more time with Edward. The monk set tasks for Harry and Cecily then, leaving them to complete those tasks, he would take Edward by the hand on a short walk outside, or a visit to the chapel. For the first few days Alice went too, but after that Edward had built up sufficient trust in Brother James to leave Alice with Harry and Cecily. His concern for Alice was such that it became part of his routine to say, "Harry, promise you will look after Alice while I am with Brother James," and Harry would solemnly promise.

A week or so after the attack, the thoughts of Alice and those of the Baron began to turn to their wedding once more, and the bans were written out and affixed to the door of the village church. The date was set for the first Tuesday of September. Preparations began.

Alice and Cecily decided that one of the new gowns Alice had had made for the summer, would be very suitable for her. It was a beautiful shade of blue, trimmed with bands of a dark, soft rose colour. However, the seamstress was called back and given an order for a headdress trimmed with tiny pearls, and a light hood. A new shawl was ordered too, in case the day turned chilly.

A jeweller was brought in to measure Alice's finger for a gold wedding ring and to create a delicate chain for her neck.

The Baron was concerned that Alice had no-one to stand for her as her 'family', but it was agreed that it would not be possible for her friends in Arkenthorpe to travel to Muirhill. Instead the Baron proposed that, after their marriage, they would take two or three weeks travelling and include Arkenthorpe in their journey. It was also agreed that Cecily would travel with them. A messenger would be sent ahead so that they would be expected. Brother James was asked to escort Alice to the church and give her to her husband, and the priest of the village church would hear their vows. Cissy would attend Alice and Harry his Uncle.

A feast would be prepared and held in the Great Hall after the wedding. The hall would be garlanded and invitations would be issued to those who held land under the Baron, and to the villagers. If the weather was fine, there would be jugglers and tumblers to entertain outside and musicians in the Great Hall.

The household servants would, of course, be very busy that day, but the Baron promised them a day's holiday after the wedding. Half of them would be free the day after, and the other half the day after that. The bride and groom would not start their travels until the Monday following, so there would still be ample time to make preparations for the journey.

Gradually the preparations changed the mood of the household again. Only Stephen remained desperately unhappy. He had had two adjoining chambers in the castle made into a secure apartment for Olivia. A staircase led from one of the rooms to a level piece of ground which was being made into an enclosed courtyard. He had hired more staff—women to minister to Olivia's needs, and men to guard the door from the apartment into the rest of the castle. One woman and one guard would be on duty at all times.

Stephen himself spent some time with Olivia each day. Most days she seemed her normal self. She dressed with care and did her embroidery and tapestry. On two or three afternoons each week, her two little girls were brought to her, but neither Harry nor Edward could be induced to visit.

Olivia's apparent normality worried Stephen. It made him think that she did not have the excuse of madness for her behaviour. She sometimes complained bitterly to Stephen about her imprisonment, as though she could not understand the reason for it. Several times he tried to remind her of what she had tried to do, and what she had actually done. If he mentioned Alice or Belle by name, he would see the look of unreason returning to her face. She never showed any sign of remorse for what she had done, and would snap out some comment about the need to 'get rid of vermin', or 'fighting off the evils of witchcraft'. Even when he tried to explain the damage she had inflicted on Edward—the boy had terrible nightmares and was terrified of being alone even for a few minutes—she assured Stephen it was not of her doing. It was Alice who had put an evil spell upon him; or sometimes, that the child was a dreadful disappointment to her. He would never be a great man as Harry would. Then she would demand that Harry be allowed to visit. She would not accept that it was Harry's own choice not to come.

Finally, Stephen talked to Harry, begging him to go to his mother for a few minutes and tell her himself that he did not wish to see her, in the hope that she would stop accusing Stephen of preventing him. After that, she stopped blaming Stephen, instead once more blaming Alice's witchcraft.

The priest came, offering to hear her confession, but she refused saying, how could she possibly have anything to confess when she was imprisoned in this way.

She made Stephen feel very guilty about restricting her, but he knew he would never again be able to trust her, however reasonable she seemed.

Chapter Twenty

Throughout the last week of August, wedding preparations got into full swing. The cooking never stopped. Grouse, pheasant and quail hung in stores; buttery shelves and slabs were being loaded with cakes, biscuits, cheeses and pies; barrels of ale and casks of French wine were assembled under the pantry stone. Musicians were booked for the gallery in the Great Hall and another group hired to play outside on the green. Booths were set up where there were to be games such as skittles, throwing horseshoes and trials of strength.

Some crops were still being harvested and everyone was praying that the dry weather would hold to complete the harvest and to celebrate the wedding. Cissy was not allowed to join in the harvest in case she over-taxed her returning strength, but Harry and Edward played their part. Cissy helped in the kitchen, loading the baskets to go out to the fields. Alice carried baskets out and otherwise helped where she could be of most use. She was relieved to find that the hard, outdoor work was having a good effect on Edward. He had colour in his cheeks and was so tired at night that he slept deeply and for several nights in a row he did not have nightmares. From time to time he would glance up from what he was doing to reassure himself that Harry or Alice was close by.

The Baron was organising the wedding journey, and messengers were sent out to the best inn of each town they would visit to ensure that the best rooms would be available on the nights the travellers expected to be there. One messenger's final call before returning to Muirhill was to the wheelwright in Arkenthorpe. His message was that, on the fourth Sunday of September, the Baron, Miss Cecily and Miss Alice would come to see them. They would meet their Arkenthorpe friends in Home Valley, after early Mass, for an outdoor meal. The Baron's party would bring sufficient food for everyone. They hoped all their friends would be able to come.

The day of the wedding arrived. Around the castle and in the village there was great activity from first light. Everyone wanted to be near the church when the bride and groom arrived, so animals were fed, eggs and milk were collected, before folk returned to their homes to clean themselves as best they could and put on their best clothing. Children were forced to wash and dire threats made if they should get dirty again before the feast.

In Muirhill Castle, things were a little calmer in the family rooms, but everywhere else was bustle. Anxious eyes watched the sky as the early morning mist lifted. Plenty of cloud, but nothing threatening. Strings of pennants were hung everywhere, even along the sides of the drawbridge, which had been lowered and would stay down all day. Guards were posted at its entrance but no-one was expecting trouble.

Alice and Cecily had bathed the day before. Their hair had been washed and perfumed, and their hands manicured and creamed. Tilly was to accompany them to the church, as was Emm, a new personal maid just appointed to Alice. Emm had experience of serving the wife of a local knight and so would be able to give appropriate advice to Alice as she ventured into noble society. Emm's previous mistress had died in childbirth and there had been no further post for her in that household. As yet she and Alice were only slightly acquainted, but Alice felt that they would soon be comfortable with each other.

Cissy was ready first and she looked very pretty in pale green, trimmed with gold ribbon. Then Alice was attired in her best dress, new headdress and shoes, and the new gold chain around her neck.

"You look beautiful, Miss Alice," said Tilly in awe.

"You do," confirmed Cissy. "You look like a queen. Now, I will carry your shawl in case the breeze is cool. If you are ready, I will check that Papa is on his way, then we will go to join Brother James below."

They descended the stairs. Josse, dressed in her own best, was waiting at the bottom with Brother James. "Oh, my dear friend, you look beautiful. The Baron will be proud of you.

"Now I must hurry ahead. God bless you, Alice."

"Thank you, Josse. Thank you my friend."

The walk to the church in the village took only a few minutes. Soon after leaving by the postern, the little procession entered the path running across the dene to the church. As the path approached the church, it was lined with excited villagers, the men standing to the right and the women to the left. They called excitedly as the group passed, first Alice and Brother James, followed by Cissy, in turn followed by Tilly and Emm. As they neared the church door, those lining the path were the household servants and finally the family members.

Outside the door, the Baron stood with Harry, both of them looking very handsome. Stephen and Edward stood together to the right, with Colum, Joseph and the Steward, while Stephen's little daughters, looking very sweet, were with the nursery maid and another maid on the left, with Cook keeping an extra eye on them. Tilly and Emm went to stand there too.

The village priest stepped forward and the short ceremony began. There was, of course, no dowry to declare, but where this would normally happen, Brother James added, "the dowry for Alice was paid in full when she returned the Baron's lost daughter—a gift more precious than land or gold."

After the priest had asked each of them if they would have the other to be their lawful husband or wife, in sickness and in health, keeping only to the other as long as they lived, and each had replied, "I will", they took their vows. As she said, "I, Alice Moore, take thee, Michael, Baron Muirhill, to my wedded husband" and the other words of the vow, the whole, wonderful happening suddenly seemed real. This was no dream.

The priest blessed the ring and Michael slipped it on to her finger. They were now man and wife, and as such they entered the church to receive the priest's blessing at the altar.

The family members followed them into the church for a short nuptial Mass. When it ended, they left the church, walking back through the now cheering villagers—the servants having rushed back to be ready to serve the feast. It was cloudy but warm and Alice did not need her shawl. The sun shone between the moving white clouds, blessing them as they made their way home, entering the castle across the be-decked drawbridge.

The rest of the day was filled with food, music, dancing and games. The Great Hall was decked with greenery and flower garlands. A wonderful sugar creation graced the centre of the high table. It was a representation of the Muirhill coat-of-arms with the twining rose linking all the symbols together.

Outside, the villagers were enjoying themselves as never before. Wonderful pies, pasties, cakes and other sweetmeats and fruits had been provided. There was a generous supply of good ale. Pipers and fiddlers and players of tambours made music to dance to or to sing to, and folk who had to leave the feast to attend to sick relatives, young children, or to do an essential chore, knew that there would still be food and drink on their return. The harvest was almost complete and safely in store. There had been no battles near for many months and now their well-respected master had a new wife whom they already knew and liked. Life was good!

The local nobles and gentry, gathered in the Great Hall, also seemed content. As Alice accompanied her husband to mix with their guests, she sensed no disapproval.

At one time they were conversing with a local squire and his wife, when Alice felt herself being watched. Hoping not to make it obvious, she half-turned and saw a very old lady, whose eyes were puckered up tightly, trying to see her clearly. At a suitable point in the conversation, Alice excused herself saying, "I think a lady there seems to wish to speak with me."

The squire's wife looked and said, "My lady Baroness, that is my husband's ancient mother, Mistress Welbeck. Please do her the kindness of speaking to her, but what she says in return may not make much sense to you."

Alice stepped over to her. "Good day to you, Mistress. I hope you have had an enjoyable afternoon."

The old woman gave an almost toothless smile. "Delicious food, my dear. Delicious! Are you the bride?"

"I am, and here comes my new husband."

The Baron joined her. "Good day, Mistress Welbeck. It is a number of years since we last met."

"Good day, Baron. This young woman says she is the bride."

"She is indeed. I am very happy to be able to call her my wife."

"Strange," said the old woman, "she's got the look of someone I used to know. Can't call to mind who, but she's definitely got the same look. It's the eyes, and the mouth. Can't call him to mind."

At this point, Alice turned back to the squire's wife, and the musicians began a new tune.

"That's it," cackled the old lady. "John, it was. He was a lovely dancer." She closed her eyes and moved her gnarled old hands to the time of the music.

"You must excuse her, my lady," said her daughter-in-law. "This John, John Morland, is someone she claims should have married her. Says they were betrothed as young children. If he existed, he was a distant relative of the Neville family, but of course he married someone else. She always regarded her match with my husband's poor father to be a lower one than she deserved. She will be living her dream for the next hour or two."

Alice smiled. "Let her dream. She looks happy."

Soon the daylight began to fade. Lanterns were lit in the Great Hall, and outside the villagers began to wander back to their homes, well-fed to the point of discomfort, but feeling they had had a day to remember for years.

The Baron turned to Alice, "I think, my dear Alice, we must now retire to our bedchamber so that our guests can go home. As I think you know, our relatives and some of those claiming close friendship, will follow us, with possibly ribald remarks. Hopefully it will not be too undignified, and once they have seen us get into the bed together, they will withdraw and leave us in peace."

They returned to the daïs and the Steward signalled to the musicians to cease playing. He then gave a gentle bang on the metal plate, so as not to seriously discommode those whose heads were suffering a surfeit of ale or wine. The noise of voices subsided to a mutter.

The Baron stood at the front of the daïs. "My lords, ladies and gentlefolk, the time has come for my wife and I to retire. We hope you have had a pleasurable day. Goodnight to you all and a safe journey home."

He took Alice by the hand; they descended to the floor and walked through the guests to the accompaniment of jests and comments. On the walk to the solar, they were followed by a small crowd of friends and relations. First Alice went to her own chamber where Emm helped her to remove her wedding attire. She put on her bed-gown and unloosed her hair. She was then led to the bridal chamber where her husband soon joined her, and in front of the merry group of well-wishers at the door, they climbed into the bed. The Baron leaned over and gave Alice a gentle kiss on the cheek, then turned to face their audience.

"And now, goodnight to you all."

Colum, who was standing just outside the door, stepped up and seized the door handle and pulled the door closed. A few more choice comments were heard as the crowd descended the stair, but then peace at last. They were alone!

"I think we have escaped lightly, my dearest. It must be in deference to our advancing years."

Alice smiled. "My lord, how do I address you now? My lord? Husband? Michael?"

"When we are alone together, it must be Michael. At other times, 'husband' or 'my lord', whichever you think fit. And at those less intimate times, I shall call you 'wife' or 'my lady'. But now we are certainly Alice and Michael.

His arms came around her then he began, gently, to caress her.

It was late when Alice awoke next morning, and it was a full minute before she remembered where she was. The other side of the bed was empty and she sat up quickly. Her husband, in every sense of the word now, was standing by the window. He heard her move and turned.

"Good morning, wife. I think you slept well." He stooped to kiss her forehead.

Alice suddenly felt self-conscious about her dishevelled appearance. "Yes thank you, my lord. I think I have over-slept."

"Yes, thank you, Michael, I think I have over-slept," he corrected her.

"Food awaits us in our day chamber, so as soon as you are ready, we can break our fast."

"I will go and dress, my . . . . Michael, and join you there." Putting her shawl around her shoulders, she made her way to her own chamber. There Emm was waiting and had everything laid out ready for her.

"It was a wonderful day, yesterday, my lady," said Emm. "You looked beautiful and the Baron looked happy and handsome."

"Thank you, Emm. Thank you for making me look beautiful."

"I am glad I was useful, but the beauty was really in your person, my lady. I think that there is already a deep affection between you and the Baron. That is something rarely seen in people on their wedding day."

"Well, our relationship has been a most unusual one, as I am sure you must have been told, Emm. I find it hard to believe I am now a baroness. I shall have to learn very quickly how a baroness should behave. I shall be grateful for your help."

"My advice for the moment, my lady, would be to follow your own feelings. I have been here at Muirhill for only a very short time, but I have heard nothing but good things from the people who serve the Baron. He is admired and known as a good master. You are well liked by all the people who know you.

"It may be more difficult when you meet others of the same or higher rank than yourself. In my time of service, I have seen some good people—kind and considerate ladies of rank whom it is an honour to serve, but there are some who think they have to complain or belittle others all the time. You have learning, my lady, which many do not; you have compassion and you know wrong doing when you see it. You will soon be accepted in any rank of society."

"Thank you, Emm. You are right about the Baron. I have known him to be a very worthy man since we first met. I will try to follow his lead.

"And now, with your help, I am fresh and dressed for the day, so I must join my husband before he is faint from hunger."

Having spent the day quietly together, Alice and the Baron went to the hall for the evening meal. Cecily was pleased to see them, kissing them both warmly. She had moved a place further down the high table, leaving the seat next to her father for Alice. Harry now sat next to his father, so Edward had moved up a place too.

Part way through the meal, Stephen suddenly said, "I must tell you brother, we can now use the water in the new well again. I think it best if water for drinking comes from the stream still, but for all other purposes, the well water is acceptable."

"That is a relief, Stephen. It will reduce the distance the water has to be carried to the solar."

"I shall continue to test both wells and the stream at least twice a week," said Stephen. "The work to seal the crack in the land is complete, so hopefully all danger is past."

"I hope everything will go well here while we are travelling. The harvest is gathered in; the water is safe and repairs completed. God willing, you will be able to devote time to the healing of your family."

"Yes Michael, I have much thinking to do in that regard. Harry and I will talk—he has shown himself to be able to think like a man, albeit an inexperienced one. I can see he will be of help to me in many ways."

"Do not rush decisions, brother. Think and pray."

Chapter Twenty-One

The journey was a great pleasure to them all. Each morning the pack ponies, carrying most of the luggage, set off by the most direct route for the inn which the travellers would reach at the end of the day. Cerdic was in charge of the luggage and had two men with him. The Baron and Baroness, with Cecily, were accompanied by Colum, Emm and a squire as armed escort for extra safety. Emm was used to riding and happy to serve Alice and Cecily as required.

Their party was able to take time to leave the main road if things of interest were to be viewed, then at the end of each day, prepared rooms, warmth and food awaited them. This was especially welcome on two days when the weather was unfavourable and they had cloaks heavy with rain to be dried.

After one night in York, the party had moved steadily southwards, the land becoming flatter and the speed of their journey increasing. They stopped at another magnificent building, Selby Abbey, which seemed of amazing size for a place that was only a town. As the land became even flatter, the rivers became wider, deeper and slower flowing, and more and more they came across water-courses dug by men, linking rivers and streams. Here they discovered that boats were used more than carts to carry goods, and they saw some families who appeared to live on their boats. Often a horse or donkey would walk along the bank of a man-made canal, roped to the boat, towing it through the water. This made life easier than a man poling or rowing it along, and the horse could pull a much heavier load than on a cart.

The soil was deeper here too, and the farmers and peasants seemed to have easier work. There were still some crops growing, though many fields were already being ploughed in preparation for next Spring. Sheep were everywhere, fatter than the ones in the hills of Yorkshire, as they had lush pasture and easy grazing.

The southern-most point of their journey was to be the City of Lincoln. The Baron and Colum had visited before, but they had not told the others anything about it. Suddenly, one day, there it was in the distance—in the middle of very flat land—this hill, rising like a plum pudding from a serving platter, and there on the top a vast cathedral in stone, almost the colour of honey. It had magnificent towers but then, on the top of the central tower rose a spire so high it seemed to reach heaven itself.

Having entered through an ancient gate, the city clustered around the cathedral in steep, narrow streets and almost every time the travellers moved, they were going up or down. The speech of the common people sounded strange to Alice's ears and Cecily was just as confused. They passed an interesting but exhausting afternoon exploring this unusual city and trying to understand what they heard.

The next day was one which Alice was sure would be difficult. They were to call on Belle's family. When Michael had told her he would like to do so, in order that Cecily could meet her grandmother, aunt and uncle, Alice had readily agreed, but she knew that for her it would be something of an ordeal.

Belle's father, Sir James Talbot, had died about three years before, and his widow now lived with their other daughter, Margaret, and her husband, a wealthy wool merchant. Cecily too was nervous, but they were all welcomed warmly by Margaret and her husband. Having refreshed themselves, they were led into a day room, beautifully furnished with couches and tables, where an upright, white-haired lady sat in a comfortable chair, but as the Baron walked in, she rose, smiling.

"Michael, this is an unexpected pleasure."

The Baron crossed the room and bent to kiss her gently. "My dear Lady Talbot, thank you for receiving us."

Lady Talbot turned slightly and looked at Alice. "My lady Baroness, please do not be shy. You are most welcome."

Alice was unsure what to do, but decided that to such a venerable lady, she should curtsey and did so.

Then the old lady saw Cecily, now standing slightly behind her papa. "Cecily, that cannot be you child! Come closer; my sight is not what it was."

Cecily came to stand a few feet in front of her and curtseyed. "Grandmother?"

The old lady's eyes filled with tears. "Oh, dearest child, you are so like your mother, and you will soon be a young lady. Come and let me kiss you."

After Cecily kissed her, the old lady, overcome for a moment with emotion, sat down again, and the others sat too. Margaret spoke.

"Mother has longed for this moment for many years. Thank you, my lord, for including us in your journey." Then, turning to Alice, "And thank you, my lady, for agreeing to it. As mother said, you are most welcome. We know there was nothing you could do for my beloved sister, but you saved Cecily from death and eventually re-united her with Michael. You made this happy day today possible and you will always be welcome here."

Alice felt the genuine warmth of her reception and thanking them, she began to relax.

Meanwhile, Cecily had begun, shyly for her, to talk to her Grandmother, mainly about their travels. Then Alice heard the old lady speaking again. "You know, Cecily, you may think old people always say things like 'you so much resemble your mother', but I can assure you it is true. After we have eaten, you must come to my bedchamber where I have a small portrait of your Mama when she was not much older than you are now. We had a painter to come and do a portrait of each of our children. They hang on the wall in my chamber. You will see I am right!

"Thank you Grandmother, I would love to see the portrait of my Mama."

A meal was served and conversation was easy. Margaret asked questions of Alice without them being a cause of awkwardness or embarrassment, and Alice found herself asking about life in this flat area of country.

After the meal, Cecily followed her grandmother to her chamber, Margaret's husband took the Baron out to view the estate, while Alice was taken by Margaret into the garden near the house, passing the stable yard on the way. It became clear that life was lived at a faster pace here. Horses were selected for speed and stamina, rather than strong, sure-footedness as in the hill country. Vegetables and fruit grew much larger in the deep, less stony soil.

The Baron, Alice and Cecily had all agreed that they should say nothing about the troubles thrust upon them all by Olivia and Piers, but the Baron had said he would tell the story to Margaret's husband and leave him to decide what and when to tell other members of his family. They had no wish to cast any shadows over the old lady's day. Alice guessed that now would be the time Michael would be talking to their host.

As Alice and Margaret strolled in the garden, Alice was able to relate little episodes from Cecily's life with her and fill out the story of her childhood a little more. In return she heard more of Belle's family history. It was clear that Belle had been loved and admired, but at one point in the conversation, Margaret must suddenly have realised that this person she was talking to had, to a large degree, taken her late sister's place in the lives of both Cecily and the Baron. She suddenly stopped in her narrative, and her strolling, and said, "Oh, my lady, I hope I am not sounding as though my sister was an angel on earth. I would not wish you to think I in any way regard you as inferior to her. Please believe me, we shall be eternally in your debt for saving Cecily's life and, as for Michael, if you can give him some years of happiness, so be it. Many men would have given up the search, and hope, long before he did. As my mother said to you earlier, you are most welcome here, as Cecily's rescuer and guardian, and as Michael's wife and Baroness, and you always will be."

Before the Baron's party left in early evening to travel two or so miles to their inn, Cecily had met not only her grandmother, aunt and uncle, but a girl cousin two years older than herself and a boy cousin a year or so younger. Also in the house, though no longer a nursery-maid, was Catherine ('Kaffy' as baby Cecily had called her). She, of course, had been told when Cecily had been found, and was delighted to meet the attractive young woman that the lost baby was now becoming.

As they continued their travels next morning, Cecily, the Baron and Alice all agreed that their visit to the Talbots had been a success.

"It will be the day after the morrow that we shall visit Home Valley," Cecily said excitedly one morning. "Oh I do wish we were going to stay for the night in the cave. I am longing to be there again. Do you realise, Alice, it is more than four years since I left with Papa?"

"Yes, I suppose it must be. I only left earlier this year, but so much has happened since, it seems a long time ago."

That night, the party stopped, as planned, at Skipton. It was at an inn where the Baron had stayed a night or two when arranging to meet Alice and to collect Cecily. The innkeeper, welcoming guests of quality for what was to be three nights, had done his utmost to please them.

Next morning, a Saturday, the Baron, Alice and Cecily rose early to attend Mass at the church where Father Luke presided. After the service he came to speak to them and was amazed to learn that Alice and the Baron were now married.

"It is wonderful to see you all at such a happy time, my lord, ... and my lady," he added, smiling at Alice. "The ways of God are full of mystery, but I am glad that he was able to use his humble priest in bringing this about."

As they returned to the inn, the town was coming to life.

"Now," said the Baron, "Alice, Cecily, you must search the town for the food and drink we will require to have a feast with our Arkenthorpe friends tomorrow. Choose what you think will be best. Emm and Cerdic will accompany you. The pack ponies can carry food instead of luggage tomorrow. You will know best what to get, but make sure to get something special.

"Colum will accompany me this morning. There is an item of business which must be done. We will return this afternoon."

The morning passed very pleasantly as they shopped for cheeses, bread, fruit, ale, cooked meats, pies and sweetmeats. Alice had to curb one or two of Cecily's more exotic choices, as dishes containing jelly would have been difficult to transport by pack horse and would certainly not have arrived still set in the beautiful designs that attracted Cecily to them. But, eventually they agreed they had sufficient for a feast. Alice also remembered to purchase some drinking vessels as she had few at the cave.

Emm found it strange that her mistress and Miss Cecily should be so excited about meeting a group of simple country-folk. She said nothing, but Alice sensed it. Cerdic willingly carried many of their purchases back to the inn, where a cool place was found for overnight storage.

The Baron and Colum returned in late afternoon as expected, and after an excellent meal at the inn, they all retired to bed early.

Next morning Cerdic, with the other men, loaded the pack horses early, and set off towards Home Valley. Alice had asked Emm to put out good clothes, but not the best. "Our friends will be wearing their best clothing, but it is important they are not made to feel uncomfortable. As yet they do not know that the Baron and I are wed. I am not sure how they will react to the news. Please try not to address me as "my lady" until after they have been told."

When the early mist had lifted, the moors glowed purple and gold in the morning sunshine, the heather-clothed hillsides, broken by clumps of be-jewelled rowan trees and swathes of bracken. Birds were feasting on brambles, hung with the gossamer of dewy spider webs, sparkling as the sun created rainbow colours in the dewdrops. After a while, the Baron's group overtook Cerdic and the pack horses, but they would not be very far behind.

Cecily's face shone and her eyes sparkled when, suddenly, the oak tree came into view. "Alice, we're there already! It used to seem such a long way before."

"It is much longer when you are walking," said Alice. "Riding is much easier and quicker."

They all dismounted and Colum led the way down the narrow track into Home Valley. The squire was told to stay by the oak tree, ready to guard the pack horses when Cerdic and his men arrived.

Alice looked around her home and all looked well. The cot roof was clear of bramble and wild rose, although a stray branch of rose was waving towards it in the breeze, still with an occasional pink blossom on it.

Cecily came to stand by Alice's side. "It is still so pretty but, Alice, it is so small. I don't remember the valley being so small!"

"The valley hasn't changed in size, Cissy, but you have grown much taller. Remember you were only seven years old when you left. I think you came just above my elbow when you stood at my side then. Also, you have become accustomed to living in a place with large rooms.

"Now, tether Amber to one of the bushes by the stream, then you can explore. I must find all my belongings and see if this place can be made fit for our feast."

Alice had ensured that a good lantern had been in her own small pack this morning and, finding her old tinderbox in its usual place, she lit the lantern and walked across to the Baron, who was standing with Colum.

"My lord Michael, there is one part of my home that you have never yet seen. Please come with me and I will show it to you."

Cecily turned her head towards her Papa, guessing where Alice was going. "I hope it is as lovely as it used to be. Alice, may I follow in a few minutes?"

"Of course, but be careful. I will leave the lantern to light your way in. Remember to keep close to the wall—there is a rope fixed now which I put there in case I ever had to find my way out without a lamp."

"I will be careful."

Alice entered the cave, followed by the Baron. "Keep close to the wall on your left, my lord. It is not far."

The cave was quiet today. No sounds of rushing water from the depths below. It was too early in the day for the shaft of sunlight to be breaking into the cave, but Alice found the crack in the rocks without difficulty.

"Welcome to my little Garden of Eden, Michael." Placing the lantern on the ledge of the cave to light Cissy's way, Alice took her husband by the hand and led him through the crack.

"So," said the Baron, "Eden did exist. Cecily, if I remember, claimed it was 'just a game she played'. What a beautiful little sanctuary!"

Alice looked around. It was looking unexpectedly good. Some of her bushes had berries on them, many of which were now drying up as no-one had been picking them. Her little apple tree had a few ripe fruit on it and John had clearly been in to hoe around her winter vegetables. There were ferns growing in some of the rocky crevices and moss and lichens too, while on the sunnier parts of the rock face were clumps of heather, small yellow flowers, and the occasional late harebell.

"I had lived here a long time before I found this place. I was thrilled when I did. As you know, it was a time of unrest and I realised that this was somewhere we could hide if we ever needed to. That was why, when Cissy found she had said more than she should, she claimed it was just a game."

"I am not surprised you love this place as you do. Your life here was far from easy, but your hard work was rewarded by most of your needs being supplied.

"Do you remember telling me that you sometimes worried that perhaps you owed rent to someone, and that you might be guilty of poaching the rabbits?"

"Of course I remember. But I had no idea whose land it was."

"Well, my dear Alice, I can now tell you who owned it, and who now owns it. That was the nature of my business in Skipton yesterday. I had discovered the valley belongs to one of the small abbeys, but it was separated from its main land holdings and they had not found a use for it. Occasionally in the last century or so, monks had used it for solitary retreat and also a shepherd had used it for shelter on days or nights of inclement weather, which is how the cot came to be built."

"So, I owed rent to an abbey?"

"Truly, yes, but as you did not know of their ownership and they did not know you were living here, they will not worry about the past. And now, the land does not belong to the abbey any more. Yesterday, I purchased it from them and it now belongs to you."

"To me?!"

"Yes, it is my gift to you. As far as the abbey was concerned, it was of little use to them and they were very happy to accept the price I offered. A deed was drawn up by a notary and yesterday, this valley and the right to use the creatures within it, became yours.

"In the weeks before we married, I thought a great deal about your lot in life. I have always had so much—a childhood with both parents and my brother—we had a sister too, but she died when only eight years old—we had wealth and education. The castle was our home and there was land; there were tenants, sheep and crops, and eventually it all came under my control.

"Then I thought of you, Alice. You had a loving mother when you were a child, but no father; no brothers or sisters, aunts or uncles; a room at the side of the kitchen where your mother worked; fortunately, some education with a son of her employer. Then, with your mother's sudden death, you had nothing. You had nothing of which you could say, 'this belongs to me'. I had to find something which would belong to you and your past. This place which you had made your home and which you had shared with Cecily until you returned her to me, seemed the right thing. You will not need to live here now, and you will not visit often, but it is yours—your land."

Throughout this long speech, Alice had felt tears of gratitude welling up from deep inside her. This man she had married had this amazing ability to feel as others might. She had first seen it when he had come here to see Cissy and had been surprised that anyone might think he would exercise his right to remove her immediately to her true home. She had seen it in the way he put her Arkenthorpe friends at their ease; how his gifts to them had been in sincere gratitude and not the actions of a man of power being gracious to those beneath him. Now this gift to her which she appreciated more than she could express!

She reached out and took both his hands in hers, as he had done when she had agreed to become his wife. She spoke quietly, "My lord, my love, thank you, thank you."

For a moment they stood holding hands, but then became aware they were no longer alone.

Cecily smiled as they turned towards her slightly startled. "If I was not aware that you were already an old, married husband and wife, I would think I had just interrupted an assignation."

"Really, Cecily," said her father, "a little more respect for your parents would become you," but the amusement in his voice belied his words.

"This is our garden of Eden, Papa. Isn't it beautiful?"

"Yes, it is very beautiful."

"Oh, Cissy," said Alice, "your Papa has just told me he has purchased Home Valley and has gifted it to me. Home Valley belongs to me!"

"Oh Papa, you do have some lovely ideas. The best one was asking Alice to marry you, but this one is almost as good.

"I came to see Eden, but also to say that Cerdic and the others are coming down the track with bundles from the pack horses and Emm is wondering however it will be possible to have a feast here without a table. We certainly do not seem to have quite enough rocks. We never had so much food or so many people here before."

A few minutes later, Alice had managed to put the latest surprise to the back of her mind and was organising the laying out of the feast. She put most of the food on the rock ledge in the cave where she had usually slept. She had produced a few wooden platters from other ledges and a few knives and a spoon or two from the chest which held most of her goods. With two lanterns lit and the sunshine still reaching a yard or two into the cave, the bountiful spread could easily be seen.

"Maud and everyone should soon be here," Cecily said excitedly when all seemed to be in order. "May I go up to the top to watch for them coming?"

"Yes, you watch and call out when you see them, but Cecily, do remember to let your Papa and I tell them that we are married. We must just meet as friends first."

"I'll remember. Hopefully," she added mischievously, "they'll be so pleased to see me again, they will forget about you for a while." She skipped off up the rocky slope as she had done as a small child.

With everything as prepared as was possible, Alice suggested that Emm, Colum, Cerdic and the man currently with them, could wander around the valley or rest on a rock or the dry ground. She sat on the old bench outside the cot with Michael.

"I cannot help worrying a little about what they will think about my being your wife. I don't want them to feel I am no longer their friend."

There was a sudden excited shout from Cissy. "I can se-e-e-e-e them!"

"You will soon know, now," said the Baron. "I don't think you need fear."

By the time Cissy re-appeared over the edge of the hill, leading a small group of people down the track, the Baron's staff had moved to sit in a quiet spot at the opposite end of the valley, near where the stream flowed out to run down its rocky bed into the next dale.

Alice, carefully concealing her left hand under a cloth which she had ostensibly just removed from a basket of bread, went forward to greet her friends. Maud and Thomas were followed by their children, Joan, Tom, Lucas and Jack.

"What a lovely day," exclaimed Maud as she greeted Alice. "We are very fortunate so late in the year. When I saw Cissy I could barely recognize her, but she knew me."

"Of course I did, Maud," said Cissy, "it was Tom I did not recognise. And Jack. He was such a sticky little baby last time I saw him."

"You look well, Alice. But where is the Baron? We must pay our respects."

"He is over there by the cot. Take our visitors to your Papa, Cissy.

"Oh, but Maud, where are Mary and John?"

"They'll be here afore long. Mary will leave as soon as lunch is served at the Manor. They'll come in the cart and leave it just the other side of the hill. It will be easier for John than walking down from the oak."

Thomas was first to greet the Baron. He bowed, "It is an honour to meet you again, my lord, and we are all very thankful Miss Cissy has recovered from her illness."

"Thank you, Thomas. It is a pleasure to meet you again. You seem well."

"I am, thank you kindly, and business is good."

"We will talk more later, Thomas. I look forward to hearing about it. I hope John is coming too?"

"He is, my lord, when Mary has finished her duties.

"Now, this here, my lord is our eldest son, Tom."

Tom bowed, "My lord Baron."

"Tom, I understand you are to be a blacksmith."

"Yes, my lord. I'm learning the trade. The Arkenthorpe blacksmith is an old man now. He has no son, so I should be able to take on his business in a year or so."

"Good, I am glad to hear it.

"Ah, Maud," said the Baron, "it is a pleasure to see you again."

"My lord," Maud replied, curtseying, "thank you for the message you sent to tell us you was all coming today. Miss Cissy has changed so much since she left us, but I'm so glad she is well again. We were so worried when Alice was sent for like that."

"I assure you, Maud, no-one was more worried than I. I feared losing her, but thank God she has recovered. Alice's presence was a blessing."

"These are our other children, my lord. Joan, Lucas and Jack."

The children bowed or curtseyed and the Baron greeted each of them.

"Now my friends," he said addressing them all, "there is food and drink available for us in the cave. Alice and Cecily are over there. Come and join them."

For the next few minutes, after exclaiming over the good food in front of them, each person was provided with a plate or a thick slice of bread on which to support their food. When all were sitting or standing around comfortably, Alice asked Colum and the others to help themselves to food.

"My lord," said Alice quietly, "I do not think I can keep my left hand concealed much longer. I would have liked to wait for John and Mary to arrive, but it could be some time before they do. Perhaps you should tell them the news soon."

At this moment, young Jack managed to let juices from his piece of pie drip on to his sister's skirt. The ensuing activity involving Jack being spanked and Joan rushing to the stream to rinse the juice from her skirt before it stained, meant that it was sometime before all was settled enough for the Baron to stand to make the announcement, but at last he rose to his feet.

"My good friends, it is a pleasure to be with you today. As you will have heard by now, Cecily, Alice and I have been on a journey and are now on our way back to Muirhill. However, we also wish to share with you some news. Alice, please come and stand with me."

Alice rose and as she walked the few paces to join the Baron, she felt Maud's eyes on her back, but daren't look at her.

"A few days before we set out on our travels," continued the Baron, "there was a very special day at Muirhill. At the parish church there, Alice became my wife."

There was a sudden hush, and a loud gasp from Maud; no-one seemed to know what to say. Then, from behind, a man's voice suddenly said, "What's wrong? You all look thunderstruck! What's up?"

John and Mary had arrived.

"I'll tell you what's up," said Maud, sounding as though she was being throttled, "the Baron and Alice are wed."

John looked startled, then, a huge smile lit up his face. "If someone will be good enough to pass me some ale, I'll give you a toast."

Cecily quickly supplied the ale, giving him an equally broad smile.

"To the Baron and his new wife, Alice. Good health and long life. You've got a good woman there, my lord."

The men all responded to the toast and the awkward moment was over.

"Thank you one and all," said the Baron, "and yes, John, you are right, I have got a good woman. Please John, Mary, come and join our feast."

Cecily greeted John and Mary very happily. John was so pleased to see Cissy again. "It is a relief to see you looking so bonny, Cissy. I was with Alice when Colum came to fetch her 'cos you were ill. He said it was real bad. We all said our prayers lass, I'll tell you."

"Yes, John, I know you did. I can't really remember how it was when I was very ill, because my mind kept getting confused, but it took me a long time to get better. I do remember when I first knew Alice had come back.

"Oh John, I am so happy that she is now Papa's wife. I think you are pleased about it too, but I'm not sure about Maud."

"Oh, I'm happy alright lass. Alice and I have known one another almost sin' we could walk. She's allus been a good friend to me and Maud, but we allus knew she was different, even though her Ma was just a cook, like my Mary is. If your Pa's seen fit to marry her, all I can say is "God bless 'em both.

"I'll talk to Maud if she thinks different. It's probably just the shock. What do you think, Mary, love?"

"I think it is a very good thing. I didn't know Alice really before you came to her, Cissy. She was a good mother to you and she missed you so much when you went back to your father. Of course, today is the first time I have seen your Papa. Maud has always seen Alice as her friend, and for that friend to suddenly change into a Baroness, is a big shock to ordinary folk like us. But I'm very pleased that Alice now has a husband and a home, and I will certainly be happy to curtsey to her any time."

"I think people are either good or bad," Cissy commented. "Alice was good when she was just Alice, and I'm sure she will still be good now she is called Baroness. Papa is good too, but I think some barons are bad, just as some ordinary men are bad.

"Ah, Alice is coming to talk to you. I will go and see if Tom will still talk to me—he is so grown up now!"

"Hello John. Hello Mary. How are things with you? It seems much more than six months since I went away."

"Things are well enough, lass. I guess you won't be coming back to join me in the shop?"

Alice laughed. "I guess not. Is the shop doing well?"

"Pretty good. I miss your quickness with numbers. I've still got to be very careful when I work out prices to buy or sell, but Joan comes to help and she is quick. She wants to work in the shop more often, but she is still working with Maud at the dress-making."

"I must go and talk to Maud. She seems reluctant to talk to me. Will you come with me, Mary? You get something else to eat John, there's plenty of food left."

As Alice and Mary approached, Maud busied herself with Jack again, but Alice saw that Colum was only a few feet away.

"Hello, Jack," Alice said. "You are a big boy now and looking very smart today. I want to talk to your Ma. Can you be good for a while?"

"I am being good," Jack said in an offended way. "I just don't want to sit still all the time."

"Perhaps you would like Colum to take you to look at the horses?"

"Yes, can I go see the horses, Ma? Please?"

Colum, reading Alice's expression, came forward. "I am happy to show the boy the horses. I will take care he comes to no harm."

Maud had to agree.

"Come on, Maud," said Alice. "Let's go into Eden and talk. Just you, me and Mary."

Reluctantly, Maud got to her feet and walked between Alice and her sister-in-law. When they were safely in the sanctuary, Alice turned to her friend, "Now Maud, tell me what is wrong."

"I don't know. Well, I suppose I do. You have been my friend for a long time Alice, and now you won't be any more."

"That's not true, Maud. We'll always be friends."

"If you're a baroness, which you are, you can't have a common dressmaker as a friend. It's not right."

"The only thing that will make it difficult for us to be friends is that we will be living a long way apart."

"It still don't seem right."

"Then how do you think I felt when the Baron asked me to become his wife? I had met with him to ask his help in getting me back here again. I needed him to provide someone to travel with me so that I could find the way; someone who could take the horse back to Muirhill. Then, suddenly he is telling me that he wants me to stay. That he has a place for me, and he wants that to be as his wife.

"I was stunned. He gave me two days in which to decide. You can guess the heart-searching I did. I'm sure there isn't a question you can ask me that I didn't ask myself in those two days. It was a very hard decision, but in the end I thought it would be so rude and ungrateful of me to say 'no' to such an honour.

"It wasn't that I wanted to be a baroness! My decision had to be based on respect and affection, and that was why I said 'yes'. Think, Maud, after all the kindness and consideration he had shown me, how could I say no?"

Mary said quietly—she was always a quiet person—"If Alice hadn't wanted still to be our friend, they wouldn't have planned to bring us this feast and to celebrate with us."

"We would have liked to invite you all to the wedding, but we knew that it would be impossible for you to come to Muirhill, so the Baron suggested we come to you. He knew you would all be happy to see Cissy again too."

Maud sighed. "I fancy you are right—both of you. I'm sorry Alice, but I will find it difficult to think of you as a baroness."

"Well, don't think of me as a baroness; just think of me as Alice, who now has a good husband and a home. You don't know how much I used to envy you with your skilled, hard-working husband and your children.

"I will have to learn to be a baroness and try to understand what is expected of me when we are in the company of people of high rank. I shall have to be a hostess if my lord invites them sometimes to be our guests. I have a lot to learn, but there are people to help and advise me."

"Oh yes," Maud said suddenly, "you have a sister-in-law at the castle, haven't you?"

"I have, and I am afraid she is not enchanted by this marriage. Please don't let us talk about her. It would spoil my day.

"Now, let us go back as friends, and join the others."

The rest of the afternoon passed quickly and pleasantly. Thomas and the Baron were deep in conversation for a while, then John and the Baron. Cecily and Tom renewed their acquaintance and Joan found she liked the new, more grown up Cissy. Gradually, Alice noticed Colum, Emm and the others were mixing with the locals. At one point she saw Emm in conversation with Maud, after which Maud drifted over to Alice and said in an affected voice, "I have just been in converse with a woman who claims to be my lady's personal maid." Then she added in her normal voice, "Is that true?"

"I fear so."

"Oh my, oh my. But she does seem a nice woman, and she thinks well of you, Alice."

The time came all too soon for farewells. Maud, Thomas and their children left first, and Cissy watched them go from the top of the slope.

Alice found a chance to speak to John, thanking him for his care of her crops and possessions.

"I won't be coming back here to live, John, so all the produce must be yours, and, John, use Home Valley as you wish. It now belongs to me. My lord has bought it from the abbey which owned it, and has given it to me as a gift. You must take care of it. If the rabbits start eating your crops, you can have them for the pot!

"I will take a few more of my possessions with me when we go, but anything I leave is yours and Mary's. I will send a document to you soon, by way of Father Luke, so that if anyone challenges your right to be here, you can prove that right."

"Thanks lass. Your Baron is a wonderful man, and Cissy's going to be a beautiful woman. I'm really pleased for you the way things have turned out."

John and Mary made their farewells, Mary insisting on curtseying to Alice as well as the Baron.

Alice was just deciding which of her possessions she could carry with her, back to Muirhill, when Cissy came rushing to her.

"Alice, I have persuaded Papa to let us stay here for tonight. I couldn't bear to leave so soon, and there is going to be a moon tonight."

"Who is going to stay? Everyone?"

"No, just you, me and Papa, and probably Colum. All the others will go back to the inn. We will go back in the morning."

"If you are sure your Papa has agreed, I would like that."

"Papa," Cecily called, "Papa, tell Alice you have agreed."

The Baron walked across to Alice. "Are you happy with that, my dear?"

"Yes, it will be lovely to be here with you, but you might not find it a very comfortable night."

"I'll take my chance. I thought perhaps Colum should stay."

"Yes, that is a good idea. The others can start back straight way, just leaving us a little food and a lantern, though I think we will not be hungry after all we have eaten today."

Emm was quite shocked when she realised what her mistress was intending to do, but she nobly offered to stay too.

"No, Emm, you return to Skipton. You will be quite safe travelling with Cerdic and the others, and as you know, it isn't very far."

"Oh no, my lady, I am not anxious for myself."

"Have no fears for me Emm. This place has been my home for many years, for most of which I was alone here. This is where I raised Cecily until the Baron found her again. She loves it too, although she is now happy at Muirhill. We would both like to share our home with the Baron, just for the one night. I will see you tomorrow around noon."

And so it was that, as the night drew down into Home Valley, Alice lit a fire near the cave entrance. The mattress which she had put away six months ago, was laid in the bed space, now completely cleared of food. Dry bracken and heather had been spread and covered in a blanket to create a mattress for the Baron, as it was clear that it would be easier for Alice and Cecily to squeeze into the bed space then for Alice and the Baron to do so.

The cot had been inspected, the wooden bed frame there checked for unwelcome visitors and, after evicting one field mouse, Colum declared he would sleep there.

Before retiring for the night, the little group sat around the fire, talking quietly and watching a very full moon rise from behind the hills, glowing large and deep yellow as it did so. The stream could be heard coming over the small waterfall and rippling over its rocky bed. Rabbits appeared and were watched undisturbed. An owl was out hunting and some bats too. One of the horses would occasionally whicker quietly, just emphasising the peace of the place.

Cecily sighed with contentment and snuggled against her father; Alice was at his other side. "I could live here again," Cecily said.

"Yes, I know you could," Alice replied, "but we have found it at its best today. You have forgotten all those wet, windy days when we had to collect wood and the fire would only smoke. And then there were times when thick mist descended for days and we couldn't even go to Arkenthorpe."

The Baron looked at his daughter, "This valley is, and always will be special to us; we are all thankful for what it has given to us, but we have to live in the world outside. We have duties and responsibilities. If we find those duties weighing too heavily upon us, we can return here for a short time to live simply and spend time in contemplation."

"Colum stood up. "If you have no further need of me now, I will go to my bed, my lord, my lady. I wish you a good night."

"Good night, Colum. I trust you will manage to sleep well."

"Thank you, my lady. Last time I was here, I slept as deeply as I ever have. I expect to sleep more lightly tonight but that will not concern me. I have much enjoyed today. Goodnight."

"When did Colum sleep here before?" Cecily asked, puzzled.

"When he came to fetch me back to Muirhill, when you were so ill. The poor man had ridden for more than two days with barely any rest. He was so weary he could scarce sit to have some broth before he lay down over there and slept soundly till first light.

"That night I slept little. I was so worried about you. By sunrise we had started on the journey back.

"Now, I think we should all sleep too."

Alice woke as the early light was creeping across the sky. She slipped from the bed without disturbing Cecily, but she realised the baron was already awake. He was standing at the entrance to the cave.

"Good morning, Michael," Alice said softly. "Did you not sleep well?"

"I slept, but woke at intervals. My bed was just comfortable enough, but I am a little stiff this morning."

"I will stir the embers and make you a warm drink."

The baron watched his wife quietly doing her early morning chores and felt a deep affection for her. He looked out of the cave and saw the floor of the valley was shrouded in mist, but the line of hills now showed clear and black against the lightening sky.

A few minutes later, husband and wife sat side by side on a smooth rock just outside the cave, a warm drink in their hands and the warmth of the glowing embers at their backs.

"Thank you, Michael, for coming here on our journey."

"I am very glad we did, my dear. Yesterday was a pleasant and interesting day. I had a long talk with John, and he said something which I found poetic and thoughtful. We were talking about Cecily when she was living here with you, and he was trying to explain her personality. He said, 'You know, my lord, I always likened her to the wild rose, like yon above the cot. It doesn't seem strong when you look at it, but it is and struggles hard to get where it wants to be. It can be a bit prickly and stubborn at times, but at heart is something beautiful and useful.'

"I think that is so true."

"Yes, that is a good way to describe how she was. It is strange, too, that there is a rose winding around the symbols on your family device."

"Of course! That had not occurred to me. Cecily, our Muirhill wild rose. May we never tame her completely."

The End

Epilogue

After three years of marriage, Alice was well-settled in her new rôle in life, though still bemused in quiet moments to think of her remarkable transformation from "no-one" to Baroness Muirhill. She had never regretted accepting the Baron's proposal. They were happy and still good friends as well as husband and wife.

She had not conceived and this made her feel that she had failed Michael, but in truth he did not seem at all concerned. His nephew, Harry, now approaching his seventeenth birthday, was a very likeable young man, with a strong mind, and Michael was well content that Harry was his heir.

Harry was soon to leave the castle for a period of service with the Duke of Gloucester at Middleham. It was an honour to be given such an opportunity and would ensure that he would become acquainted with many of the most influential people in the country.

Cecily was now fifteen years old and it was time for her parents to start seeking a suitable husband for her. Alice, being so recently married herself, found it strange to be looking for a husband for Cissy, while Michael was hoping that her actual marriage could wait until she was eighteen. Cecily herself was in no hurry to marry. She enjoyed her freedom and attended enough social gatherings to satisfy her need for the company of girls of her own age. She did find most of them rather boring, with very limited interests, the main one being the choice of husband their parents were about to make, or already had made. Several were already betrothed. Cecily made it clear to her parents that she had strong views on the qualities she would expect a suitable husband to have.

For a while Alice had been uncomfortable in the company of ladies of title. Fortunately, as yet she had not encountered Baroness Derwent. She had found little to talk with such ladies about, but after attending several gatherings, she had gradually realised that this was because of their narrow outlook on life and not because of her own background.

The Baron had, after a few months of marriage, encouraged Alice to invite small numbers of guests to Muirhill and, with the help of Josse, the Senior Steward and Emm, her first ventures into entertaining nobility had been a modest success. Michael had been pleased and, since then, two other larger gatherings had been successful and passed off with no major embarrassments. The thing she had found most difficult was, when being introduced to someone, knowing whether she was the one to curtsey, or whether the other person should curtsey to her, or even whether they curtseyed to one another.

Alice's appearance on the social scene and Olivia's almost simultaneous disappearance from it had produced some comment and questions, but these had soon past. The nature of Olivia's illness was only known to one or two people outside the family, and her attack on Alice was never spoken of.

Alice had felt very uncomfortable about not being able to include Olivia in the gatherings at Muirhill, but Stephen assured her that Olivia had declared that there was no way in which she could be persuaded to grace any gathering at which Alice was the hostess. In many ways Olivia seemed to have accepted her confinement and could behave quite normally, but then could suddenly become quite irrational. Recently she had insisted that her companions must taste any food before she did, to ensure that Alice was not trying to poison her.

Edward had gradually overcome the terrors that his mother's outbursts and attack on Alice had raised in him. Now twelve years old, he had become a much more serious boy than his behaviour in early childhood would have suggested. He had developed a deep interest in the Christian church and, if he held to his current purpose, he would eventually train for the priesthood. He still had a deep affection for Alice and when, about a year ago, he had been told of the plotting and treachery that had brought Alice into their lives, he had spent many hours discussing with her and other family members, how those events had changed their lives.

It was now early May, and one morning a messenger arrived from the Duke and Duchess at Middleham, with an invitation to the Baron and Baroness to attend a gathering at the end of the month. A letter from the Duke's secretary was also delivered in which it was suggested that they should bring Harry with them so that he could take up his duties in the Duke's household. The invitation was extended to include other members of the Baron's family as desired.

It was decided that Stephen, Harry and Cecily would accompany the Baron and Baroness, attended by Colum, Joseph and Emm.

Harry was excited, but a little nervous, about this, his first major step into manhood. Cecily was just excited at another chance to visit royalty and the magnificent castle which had impressed her greatly. For Alice it would be the final social mountain for her to conquer. After being introduced, it was unlikely that anything more than the briefest of conversations would be required of her. Under Cecily's guidance, she practised the deeper curtsey required of her in front of royal persons, to ensure she would not lose her balance at the time.

When the day arrived, the weather was fair and the journey uneventful. They stopped for one night a few miles short of their destination so as not to arrive at Middleham tired and travel-stained. Although she had heard descriptions of the castle from both Michael and Cecily, Alice was still amazed by its size and luxury. The Duke and Duchess's living quarters were in a specially built wing, linked by a bridge to the Keep, which one entered at the first-floor level. Guests were housed in a similar wing, again linked by bridge. The rooms were quite luxurious and made their own comfortable chambers at Muirhill seem basic in comparison.

On their arrival, Harry was collected by the Duke's Master-at-Arms and taken to the quarters he would inhabit while in the Duke's service, and where he found a number of other young men, also in the Duke's service or novices like himself. Harry would, however, be joining the rest of his family for meals throughout their stay.

An hour or so before the evening meal, the guests who had arrived were summoned to the Great Hall. On this first evening, although many people were assembled, it was not to be a great banquet. That would be on the second day. Before this meal the Duke and Duchess moved among their guests and it was not long before they reached the Muirhill group and Michael introduced the members of his party.

"Your Royal Highness, since we last met, I have married again. May I present my wife, Alice."

Alice curtseyed deeply and was greeted warmly by the Duke. When Stephen, Harry and Cecily had also been presented, Alice was surprised to find that the Duke knew of their situation.

"Ah, Baroness, I am pleased to make your acquaintance. I understand that you saved the life of Cecily here when she was lost as a baby. When we last met, Cecily told us of your care for her and spoke of you with great affection. I congratulate you and the Baron on your marriage."

The Duke, still in the Baron's company, moved on to speak with Stephen and Harry, while the Duchess continued in conversation with

Alice and Cecily. The Duchess was young and had, only a few months before, given birth to her first child, a boy.

"I trust, Your Highness," Alice ventured, "that your son is well."

"Indeed he is, thank you, Baroness. He grows more interesting by the day."

She turned to Cecily. "And you, Cecily, are you betrothed yet?"

"Oh no, Highness, not yet."

"How old are you now?"

"Fifteen."

"Well, no doubt your Father will be considering the young men of the families here to see if one or two might make suitable husbands. I am sure, Baroness, that Cecily will be regarded as an excellent match by many of our guests."

Cecily blushed furiously.

Alice helped her out. "I know my lord Baron is thinking of the matter, Highness. However, Cecily was lost to him for so long that he is a little reluctant to part with her again for a while."

The Duchess smiled. "Of course, that is understandable, but most families would be happy to accept a betrothal of one or two years if it enabled them to make such an alliance. I look forward to hearing who the fortunate young man will be."

The Duchess moved on and Cecily sighed with relief. "Oh, Alice, I shall now feel as though everyone here is looking at me to see if I will make their son a good wife. Aunt Olivia once told me that someone looking for a wife for their son would not be impressed by my ability to read, write and catch fish. If anyone with a particularly horrid son is watching me, I must make sure we enter some learned conversation on fishing! I don't want to marry yet."

"The Duchess is only about five years older than you, Cecily."

"Five years is a long time," Cecily retorted.

By midday next day, more guests had arrived. The Baron was in discussion with the Duke and several other men for most of the morning. After the light midday meal, Cecily was walking in the company of other girls of her age and one or two young men, including Harry, chaperoned by two of their mothers. Alice and the Baron were enjoying the pleasures of the castle gardens. They had admired the herb garden and were strolling to the flowery mead when the Baron suddenly said, "My dear, I met a man this morning who would very much like to renew his acquaintance with you. His name is Edmund Thorpe."

"Edmund! Edmund is here?"

"Yes. He has become well-regarded by one of the Duke's most trusted knights in the north-west, and as that knight is indisposed, he was sent to represent him at our meeting this morning."

"I gather you have spoken with him. How is he?"

"He is well. You will see for yourself in a few minutes. I suggested we meet here around three hours after noon.

"It was strange how he came to my notice. The meeting was almost over. He had spoken once, but had only prefaced his remarks by saying that he was speaking on behalf of Sir George . . . . someone, I forget the name. As we moved from the table, an elderly man dropped his purse and several coins rolled around the floor. I picked two up, while Edmund retrieved others, including one which had lodged in a very difficult place. As we returned the coins to their owner he said, "My thanks Muirhill. And you sir, to whom do I also owe thanks?"

"Thorpe, sir. Edmund Thorpe."

"I recognised the name as that of your childhood friend, so walked over to him as we left the room. 'Are you perhaps Edmund Thorpe formerly of Arkenthorpe?' He looked very surprised and said 'Yes, my lord, I am indeed. I know who you are, Baron, but how do you know something of me?'

"I said 'you and my wife knew each other as children. Her name is Alice.'

'But, my lord,' he said, 'I only knew one Alice—Alice Moore.'

'She has been my wife for several years now,' I told him. 'She is here with me and would, I am sure, wish to meet you again.'

'And I her,' he assured me, so I arranged to meet him here. I hope I did the right thing."

"Oh yes, Michael, I will be very happy to see Edmund again and hear of his family and his sister, Miss Ellen."

A few minutes later, a figure appeared from behind one of the wings of the castle, walking towards the garden. The Baron raised his hand in greeting and the figure approached. He was much shorter than the Baron and of stocky build, smartly dressed in shades of lovat. He stopped in front of them and bowed, first to the Baron, then to Alice. As he raised his head, the formality slipped away and he gazed at Alice.

"Are you really Alice? Alice Moore?"

Alice laughed. "Yes Edmund. It is so long since we met I would not have recognised you either. Please walk with us. I am longing to hear your news."

"And I yours." He turned to the Baron, "My lord, I hope you will not mind if your wife and I reminisce. If I seem disrespectful at times, please forgive me. It will not be intended—matters are so changed I am a little at a loss."

"Please do not concern yourself on my account, Mr. Thorpe."

And so it was that Alice told Edmund, as briefly as she could, of the strange path her life had taken since her disappearance from Arkenthorpe Manor. It seemed it had been several years since Edmund had heard from his brother so, although he knew that Alice had been seen in the village with a child, and had still been in touch with John the gardener and his sister, he had heard no other mention of her until now.

"My sister did tell me that when you left us so soon after your mother's death, you were worried that you would be in trouble if Harald discovered where you were living. Why was that?"

"It does not matter now, Edmund. I think I perhaps mis-interpreted something he said to me, and worried needlessly."

By now Cecily had joined them and she was walking ahead with her Papa.

Quietly, Edmund said, "So it was true. Harald had suggested he had a better use for you than being the cook?"

"Yes, but how do you know?"

"Because, when I first returned home after you had disappeared, and Ellen told me I should not try to find you, I challenged Harald to explain. Eventually, he told me what he had said, and thought perhaps he had scared you. There was quite a bit of bravado, but I think he was actually ashamed. He could be an unthinking idiot, and having recently inherited the title of 'Squire', he had developed an inordinate sense of his own importance.

"Does Harald know that you have married?"

"I don't know. We didn't tell anyone in Arkenthorpe that we were going to be married and our wedding was at Muirhill, but we did visit my friends there soon afterwards. It is quite possible that it has now become generally known in the village.

"I think Harald has actually become a good squire, Edmund. He has improved some of the cottages and given a licence to John, who was the gardener, to open a shop. John was injured in the fighting and found it difficult to continue as gardener. There isn't the affection for Harald that there was for your father, but there are few complaints.

"And, what of you and Miss Ellen?"

"Ellen is well. She and my wife, Margaret, are comfortable with each other. She is a great help with the children and with my wife's widowed mother who lives with us. She will be so pleased when I tell her I have seen you, Alice. She has wondered on many occasions what had happened to you.

"I must leave you soon, Alice, but something you said when you were telling me about the Baron's proposing marriage to you, worries me."

"What was that?"

"You said that you could bring nothing to him, and that you did not even know who you are. Surely, Alice, that cannot be true?"

"Yes, it is true. I have no idea who my father was. Mother had promised to tell me some day, but she died without having done so."

Edmund stopped dead in his tracks and his expression was one of disbelief and embarrassment. "But Alice, I know who your father was; it never occurred to me that you had never been told.

"Do you want to know?"

Alice too was stunned and looked at Edmund in amazement. "Well . . . . yes, but . . . . wait a moment.

"My lord," she called to the Baron, who with Cecily was now many yards ahead. A moment, my lord."

The Baron stopped, turned and waited for Alice and Edmund. He looked at their faces.

"What is it?" he asked.

"My lord, Edmund knows the name of my father and wonders if he should tell me."

Now the Baron looked surprised and so did Cecily.

"Well," said the Baron, "do you want to know, my dear? Whoever he was will make little difference to you now. You are mine and that will not change."

"I suppose I must know now. It would be in my mind constantly if I did not say yes. Yes please, Edmund, tell us what you know."

Edmund took a deep breath. "My father told my brother and me about how your mother, Agnes, came to be with us. He told us in the days we were with him just before his death. Your father's name was John Morland. He was the son of one of my mother's cousins. My mother, my lord, was one Mary Neville, daughter of a member of a minor branch of the great family from which our hostess, the Duchess, comes. My mother's cousin was Eleanor Neville, daughter of a more senior family member.

"My father told us that John Morland met your mother, Agnes, who was a daughter of the factor on the family's estate. He was no more than eighteen and she was perhaps two years younger. He was very attracted to her and wished to marry her, but he knew his father would never approve. He took matters into his own hands and married her secretly in front of witnesses, intending to have their union blessed by a priest the next time one was available in the rather remote area in which they lived.

"When John took his wife back to his family home, his father was furious. His intention had been that John should marry the daughter of a wealthy merchant who possessed many areas of land. That lady was much older than John and not attractive to him, but both families would have benefitted from the match.

"The merchant and his daughter both complained bitterly when they heard of John's marriage to Agnes and his father tried to prove that such a marriage was not legal. He was still trying to find such proof when John was called to join the King's army and was sent to fight in France. Unfortunately, he was killed by a crossbow during a battle and never returned. Sad though this was, the family's problem was solved, except that Agnes was with child.

"John's mother contacted her cousin, my mother, with a request that she and my father take in Agnes and provide a home for her and the child, when it was born. A sum of money was given to recompense them when they agreed to do so. Agnes was required not to use the Morland family name but, instead of returning to her maiden name, she said she would shorten her husband's name to Moore, and this was accepted. The rest of the story you know."

Edmund came to the end of his long speech and looked imploringly at Alice. "I hope I have explained it clearly. I think there may be a document at Arkenthorpe which will testify to what I have said. I will ask Harald to produce it, if you wish me to do so."

Alice herself was struggling to absorb all that Edmund had said. Her father's name had been John Morland. Where, she thought, had she heard that name before? Her father had died before she was born.

Cecily came over to Alice and put her arms around her. "Are you alright, Alice? I can still remember how I felt when you told me about Papa—at least I think I can. I know I felt very strange."

"Yes, thank you, Cissy, I am fine—certainly feeling strange and trying to sort everything out in my mind. My past no longer stops with my mother in the kitchen at Arkenthorpe. I had never considered that I might be related to your family, Edmund, even distantly."

"I have never tried to work out what that relationship is, but I was happy to know we are kinsfolk."

The Baron had remained quiet throughout Edmund's explanation, but now he came and put his arm around Alice's shoulders. "I am so pleased for you my dear, that you now know your own story. I do not think it was by chance alone that you and I were brought together today, Mr. Thorpe. It was God's will."

"Yes, my lord, you may be right.

"Now, I think I should leave you, my lady. I must thank you Baron for allowing me this time with Alice."

"Will you be at the banquet tonight?"

"Yes, I will. The Duke himself extended the invitation to me when I was presented to him before the meeting this morning."

"We may get chance to speak again, but as we may not, I must tell you that you and your family, including your sister, will be welcome to be our guests at Muirhill before the summer has passed, if that can be conveniently arranged for you. I know my wife would wish to renew her acquaintance with Miss Ellen, and meet your wife."

"My lord Baron, I am deeply honoured. I am sure we will all be most happy to make such a visit. I will send a messge to you when our arrangements can be made."

"It is a journey," said the Baron, "which, as I am sure you know, must be made in good weather, but the most difficult part will be that which you have taken to get here from your home. There is more level ground from here to Muirhill and you would perhaps be able to reach the Roman road well north of here, which would give you easier travelling. We will look forward to your visit, Mr. Thorpe."

"My thanks once more, my lord. I must now take my leave. Farewell, my lord," Edmund bowed, "and farewell, my lady and Miss Cecily." He bowed again, while also accepting the hand Alice proffered.

Edmund left them, and as he did so, Alice sank down on a nearby turf seat, where Cecily joined her, while the Baron stood by.

"What a strange thing, Alice, to find you are distantly related to the Duchess!" Cecily remarked.

"It is very strange indeed, and with your agreement, Michael, I would much prefer that my connection to the Nevilles is not made known. It would only recall history they wished to forget."

"You are right, my dear. It is best left as before. We must ask you never to say anything, Cecily."

"Of course Papa, if that is your wish."

"I know," mused Alice, "that I have heard the name John Morland before, but I cannot remember when. I do feel sad for my mother too, that she must have suffered so."

"Your connection to the Thorpe family does explain why the old Squire was happy to let you join Edmund in his lessons and allow you to be friends."

"Yes, but he was a kind man too. I liked him very much."

"Edmund seems a good man too," Cissy commented.

"Yes, he does. He also resembles the old squire in appearance, more than his brother does. Thank you Michael for inviting him to visit us.

"Now, I think it must be time we returned to our rooms to prepare for the grand banquet tonight."

"I guess it will be an even grander occasion than the banquet for your wedding, Papa."

"Oh yes, there will be many, many courses. I advise, Cecily, that you only have a little of each course if you wish to survive to the end."

"Of course!" Alice suddenly exclaimed, as they reached the end of the garden. "That was where I heard the name of John Morland."

"Where?" asked Cecily.

"At our wedding banquet. You remember the old lady, Michael, in the company of a squire and his wife?"

"Ah, yes, Mistress Welbeck."

"Yes, that was her name. According to her daughter-in-law she had always claimed that she should have married a John Morland. However, they were not sure that he had really existed, especially as she also claimed that he was related to the Nevilles. At the banquet, she looked at me and said I reminded her of someone, but couldn't think who. Then the musicians started to play a new tune and she said, "that's it! John. He was a lovely dancer," and she went off into a dream.

"How strange that I should first hear my father's name at my wedding. Mistress Welbeck must have been the merchant's daughter that John's father had intended him to marry."

"So it would appear," said the Baron. "I think, after all these revelations, we need a time of rest before the banquet. It would not be a good thing to put on our finest clothes but have faces which look tired and worn."

The banquet was indeed the grandest affair that Alice and Cecily had ever attended. The finery and jewels of the Duke and Duchess just out-shone that of many of their guests; the food was delicious and abundant; the conversations started out as interesting, but became louder and more difficult to hear or understand as the meal continued and the wine and ale flowed.

Next day, as they journeyed home, Cecily commented that, while the grand banquet had been a lavish occasion, she hoped she would not have to attend many of them. She and Alice both still found the noise generated by many people, especially when eating and drinking, quite distressing after a time. Cecily also expressed her great relief that no-one had paid her the kind of attention that would suggest they were assessing her suitability for marriage.

Alice woke early one morning a few weeks later. She was in her own bed chamber as Michael had yesterday left for a gathering of Barons in York. She stretched out and lying in comfort, gazed at the patch of morning sky visible through the windows. It promised to be a fine day.

Her mind went back over the events of the past five years or so, marvelling how much her life had changed. Cecily was right—five years is a long time.

Edmund and his family would be visiting in less than two weeks now; how amazing it was that he had been at Middleham at the same time as Michael and herself. He, Edmund, must have visited, or sent a message to, Squire Harald as soon as he had returned home, telling him of their meeting. Two days ago a messenger had arrived with a letter for Michael from Harald.

In it, Harald apologised for only recently learning, for certain, whose wife Alice had become and he enclosed a small sum of money which was the dowry Alice should have brought to her husband. When it was disclosed to John Morland's family, that the child Agnes had given birth to, was a girl, this money had apparently been sent to his father, Old Squire Thorpe, with the message that this would be the final payment for, and on behalf of, the child, and was to be the dowry if she married.

The letter also asked the Baron to give the Baroness, Harald's sincere apologies for the misunderstanding that had arisen between them many years ago, which he had long since regretted. The letter had concluded with the usual pleasantries.

However, also enclosed was the document to which Edmund had referred. It was another letter, this time from Eleanor Neville to her cousin Mary, asking her to care for Agnes and the child. It also expressed Eleanor's love for her son John, and said how much she mourned his loss. She said she herself would dearly have liked to give a home to Agnes and her future grandchild, but her husband would not hear of it, and wished the matter closed and done with. She hoped the sum of money which Agnes would bring with her would compensate her cousin for any expense incurred in the matter, and that Agnes should be put to service of the family after the birth of the child.

Alice now lay musing as to the twists of fate, or the guidance of a divine hand, which had brought that unborn child from such unpromising beginnings, through the tribulations of another child many years later, to this honoured place in society.

"Yes," she thought, as she decided to rise and have a stroll in the freshness and beauty of this early morning, "I do now have a rightful place, and what a place it is!"

Lightning Source UK Ltd.
Milton Keynes UK
UKOW031440250512

193297UK00001B/120/P

9 781456 809188